OCEAN WORLDS

OCEANWORLDS

J.P. LANDAU

OCEANWORLDS

This is a work of fiction. All names, places, and characters—including those based on real people, living or dead—as well as characterizations and opinions are products of the author's imagination or are used fictitiously. Any resemblance to real people, places, or events is entirely coincidental.

For Marie,
Always muse. At times patron.

NOTE TO THE READER

This is a science fiction novel, yet the adventure you are about to read requires no major technological breakthroughs, is achievable with today's manufacturing capabilities, complies with orbital mechanics, and, more generally, the laws of physics. Indeed, for the first time in history a spaceship—SpaceX's Starship, currently in development—will allow manned expeditions much farther than the Moon.

As a result, I felt it was the book's duty to provide additional context—both scientific and historical—for those reading this as a call to action. For the majority of you this will be extraneous and intrusive to the story being told, which is why it was exiled to the footnotes. Some of these are even in the form of dialogue between characters. Ignore them. They are nonessential and will slow the story down.

The Appendix has two sections:

a) The technical solution for this particular mission—launch window, traveling time, required propellant, etc.

b) A short history of astronomy and space exploration.

It is the conviction of many,[1] myself included, that if we are willing to return to a higher risk tolerance, such as the mindset we had during the Heroic Age of Antarctic Exploration or the Space Race culminating in the landing on the Moon, a manned mission—to Mars, to the asteroid belt, to Saturn—is upon us. This book is an imagined account of a journey to Saturn, which could become one of the most decisive events in the history of our species. You are about to read why.

J.P. Landau
April 2019

---

[1] Robert Lightfoot, former head of NASA, said it succinctly in his parting speech in April 2018: "Protecting against risk and being safe are not the same thing ... [W]ould we have ever launched Apollo in the environment we're in today? Would Buzz and Neil have been able to go to the Moon in the risk posture we live in today? ... [W]e must move from risk management to risk leadership. From a risk management perspective, the safest place to be is on the ground. From a risk leadership perspective, I believe that's the worst place this nation can be."

Mars, Earth, Saturn, Jupiter, and the Sun, to scale.

orbit of Mercury

orbit of Venus

orbit of Earth

orbit of Mars

orbit of Jupiter

orbit of Saturn

At their closest, Earth and Mars are 34 million miles apart—that's 140 times farther than any of the Apollo missions ever were from Earth. At their farthest, 249 million miles from each other.

At their closest, Earth and Saturn are 746 million miles apart—that's 3,100 times farther than any of the Apollo missions ever were from Earth. At their farthest, 1,040 million miles from each other.

The orbits of the inner planets and the gas giants around the Sun, to scale.

OCEAN WORLDS

CONTENTS

"The sobering reality is this," the paleontologist said, staring at the audience intently, "99% of all species that ever roamed this Earth have gone extinct. Why should we think us humans will fare any better, when we're running the planet to the ground and haven't left its orbit for half a century?"

PART I
MOTIVATIONS

Part 1. Motivations

I | THE DREAM

SAINT LUCIA, CARIBBEAN

Perched a thousand feet above the beach and surrounded by lush, vibrant jungle, the infinity pool mirrored the glorious vista laid out in front of it. The limitless ocean, a few shades darker than a deep blue sky barely smudged by clouds, was framed on each side by the Pitons—the two volcanic spires for which the Caribbean island was famous.

The woman seated on the pool's edge was performing a repertoire of funny faces to the delighted twin girls wearing floaties in the water.

Her husband's assertions to the hotel clerk regarding the interruption of Internet and telephone services, and the rowdy flock of parrots on the canopy of trees above the pool, muddled the groovy reggae playing in the background. Bribed with cold beers one more time, the man stealthily approached the woman from behind, grabbing and lifting her to the too-late, high-pitched warning cries of the twins. The young couple plunged into the pool.

"Not a week ago it was all about the dress, flower arrangements ... I'll never forget this," said the woman moments later, resting her head against her husband's shoulder as they looked out over the ocean.

For a long time, they remained immobile.

Each one was experiencing an unsettling, growing sensation that something in the landscape wasn't right. At first their minds discarded it as dizziness—it's not you, it's me. But when the parrots' tumult turned dead silent, the couple looked at each other. It didn't make sense: the entire horizon seemed to be ... shifting upward?

Behind them a glass broke, guests murmured. Chairs screeched. Somebody screamed. The reggae was being overwhelmed by an enraged, escalating tidal sound.

"We're safe up here," offered someone, which sounded deflated and hollow. Less than a minute later, it proved widely off the mark.

The husband gaped at the bay below. The two yachts previously moored were retreating at an absurd speed into the ocean while the beach was doubling in size every few seconds as a water mass of boiling currents was yanked back.

The ocean hadn't been this furious for tens of millions of years—before the dawn of man, before the rise of apes, before the triumph of mammals.

The wife's eyes instinctively searched for the twins and found them embraced by a terrified mom trying to appear calm. One was more confused than panicky, the other had dug her face against Mommy. The three were the only ones present looking away from the immenseness closing in on the island.

The couple, hands still joined, grew motionless and mesmerized. The yachts had become dots racing skyward on an impossible wave. The wall of water was so tall that the clouds dissolved against it. The Pitons had become puny.

"Maybe it's just a dream …" said the husband, struggling to sound composed, looking one final time at his wife.

Not the slightest attempt to confirm or deny.

Like an eclipse, the midday Sun disappears. All is lost.

2 | JAMES EGGER

YOSEMITE VALLEY, CALIFORNIA

An old Volkswagen Kombi rested in a busy parking lot by Glacier Point, the scenic viewpoint high above the valley looking at the towering granite face of Half Dome in its best profile. Crowds were retreating even though the best time of day in this, the best time of year, was still half an hour away.

There were three people organizing equipment by the camper. One of them was busy working on the rear, sorting gear, backpacks, and helmets, and meticulously folding what looked like a tent.

A boy, around 6, came casually by, his eager eyes betraying curiosity. He was working on an oversized bag of candy. "What are you doing?" he asked. "Do you work in Cirque du Soleil? My mom and I saw a show many days ago. I liked it very much." The person turned. It was James Egger. Tall and lean, with dark brown hair and a three-day growth of stubble. He could have been 1960s Clint Eastwood's fraternal twin, except for the disarming smile. Seeing all the colorful hardware, the kid went into overdrive, "How do you train? What happens if you fall? How far do you fall? Do you want some? Yummy-yummy!"

James kneeled. "Can't turn down that offer. What's your name, boss?" His hand came out of the bag, stained in pasty chocolate.

"My name is Batman and I can fly. Don't you see my cape?" the boy said, as he swirled it dramatically.

"You look more like Superman to me. Check out those biceps." Batman flexed both arms in the pose of a Schwarzenegger.

"Watch out for that suit ripping."

"Can I watch you?" said the boy.

"Only if you sign me an autograph."

The little fellow's mom called him, and after shaking hands he went away.

Some forty minutes later, there was barely a tourist anymore as the three friends walked in line by a narrow trail running a few feet from the precipice.

All three were dressed in colorful wing-suits. They headed toward a ridiculous-ly exposed rock ledge, a sort of granite diving board projected past the chasm: Glacier Point Ledge.

Ø

Dusk may have heightened the other senses. As the gentle butterscotch from the Ponderosa pines soaked the nostrils, the sounds from the valley far below became clean: guitars playing, dogs barking, children shouting. Half Dome Village, countless feet beneath, felt immediate and intimate.

One of them, Randy, dressed in a screaming yellow wing-suit, tried to walk the talk to the tip of the ledge but encountered the Invisible Wall.

"Jimmy. Becca. Not quite there today. I'm dropping."

"Maturing into adolescence! Didn't get the invite to your Quinceañera cel-ebration," said Becca.

Randy looked at Becca, who was puffing on a joint, and James, away in his own separate reality. Right there lay his mistake, exposed. Most skydivers kept BASE jumping as a daydream safely beyond reach, because if separating from an airplane was watching bull riding on a large, high-definition TV, then abandoning a rock would have been riding the bucking beast. The intensity right before jumping was such that it was stoned down, except if you were one James Egger. And Randy just relearned he was not. He inched forward gecko-like to inspect the jump, his head barely past the platform's edge. Mind failing to trust body was the first casualty in the primal fear of falling, a vexing problem in an activity where split-second reac-tion and zero margin of error were compulsory.

The twilight had turned the sky into myriad shades of red and purple. The shadows closing in accentuated the hard lines and angles of Yosemite Valley. Its creator had been too liberal with the chisel while the hammer weighed too much.

"Jimmy, we need to go now. Or else we'll land pitch dark," said Becca.

"A five-pound pouch of nylon supposed to stop you from dropping the height of three Eiffel Towers. This is why the word 'vicarious' was coined. My heart's pounding into cardiac arrest," said Randy. *Jimmy, Jimmy, Jimmy*, he thought. *What a ride, man.* As average high-school students allowing some leniency on grades, community college around Sacramento had been a worthy aspiration for James and Randy. And then a week after starting junior year, September 6 2008 arrived. *And it happened right there in the Dome.* Put simply, a climber named Alex Honnold had done Half Dome solo and unroped.

The New York Times said it best: "Reasonable people consider projects like these idiotic to the point of outrage. That is perfectly defensible … if you count yourself among those inclined to negative judgment, and even if you don't, I hope you'll indulge a mental exercise for fun. Allow your mind to relax into the possibility that Honnold's climb was not reckless at all, and that his years of dedication really did develop those gifts to the point that he could not only make every move without rest, he could do so with a tolerably minuscule chance of falling. Viewed in that light, Honnold's free solo represents a miraculous opportunity for the rest of us to experience what you might call the human sublime—a performance so far beyond our current understanding of our physical and mental potential that it provokes a pleasurable sensation of mystified awe right alongside the inevitable nausea."

For the two of us, life back then was simple: mediocre but dedicated gym climbing, devoted consumption of science fiction, and thinking about Lizzy. I thought Honnold's achievement was awesome, but for Jimmy it was something much bigger. Two months later, Alex Honnold, THE Alex Honnold, showed up in our gym. When it was our turn to salute him, Jimmy's stammer went wild. That proved life-changing. The three of us talked and climbed for a good seven minutes (I timed it). Alex was from Sacramento. Unassuming, almost unremarkable. A legend at 22, barely six years our senior. Studied at a high school twelve blocks from ours. His GPA was 4.7. Got into engineering at UC Berkeley and soon dropped out. Jimmy also thought their similar height was an important element in the analysis. Things weren't gradual after that. It was the epiphany that threw Jimmy above daily life; above his erratic, alcoholic dad; above any fence that life had put between him and his brand-new goals. Determination. Man, what determination! At graduation, the school principal mentioned Jimmy as the rising tide that lifts all boats. Jim Slackin'! I'm sure his dad thought Old Crow Kentucky bourbon was still batting .200 in his bloodstream. It certainly raised me. My mom's still crying out of astonishment and relief for the letter from Princeton. Jimmy didn't get to Stanford but made it into Harvard. During cocktails, our scolding English teacher Miss Miller said "You're my proudest accomplishment," both misty eyeballs fixated on him. Does faith move mountains? Not for Jimmy, but I would suggest the mountain move aside for its own safety.

"Becca, I go first, you follow at least one second later," said James. Pointing down, he continued, "Remember, you clear the 'V' by the left shoulder." The sixty-degree sloping ridge they were about to speed through ended in a narrow rocky 'V' maybe 150 feet wide—the crux—after which the wall turned vertical for 3,000 feet before hitting the valley.

A raven circled above, mildly interested in the action.

James stepped to the end of Glacier Point Ledge until half his shoes were airborne. Becca was two arms away. Their eyes met briefly for final confirmation. He inhaled a long breath, closed his eyes, and as he exhaled his body dropped forward.

They quickly shrank into dots as their bodies accelerated downward and forward.

Wind noise buried everything as James achieved terminal velocity. He prepared to enter the 'V' from the right when …

⌀

The icy rocks passed by an eerily familiar blue gaseous planet, rotating with constancy and calmness gained from billions of years circumnavigating the black seas of cosmic infinity. A Sun lay in front, still small and meek.

Further inward the comets encountered a vast planet. Its vigilant eye, disguised as a centuries-old raging storm, had watched for eons for The Things Coming From Out There. It was Jupiter, the guardian of the inner Solar System, the formidable protector of that most miraculous and delicate of things, life. This time was no different. Almost. It caught and sucked to its interiors most of the astray, enormous explosions scarring its face. But one skipped the giant.

Further still there was something else. Sound waves. Increasing in volume until they became a cacophony. Radio waves fighting for supremacy. A song here, a speech there. Earthlings communicating, unabashedly defying the deafening silence of space.

The Blue Marble was mostly vibrant blue, interrupted by streaks of land.

As in previous times in James' recurring nightmare, a frozen visitor that had traveled unimpeded for unending years crossed in front of his mind's eye, traversing the thin atmosphere in seconds and igniting brightly before smashing into an ocean.

A shock wave moved through the air, evaporating an area the size of Arizona.

Water and seafloor intestines, a moment ago in the far recesses of the planet, now splashed the upper atmosphere.

The wall of sound plummeted into silence.

A wave rippling through water moved silently to every coast. Far from Ground Zero, a tsunami absurdly out of proportion approached a leafy Caribbean island with two prominent volcanic spires.

☽

James snapped out of his vision an instant before crashing. The left side of the 'V'-shaped rock stood before him and salvation. His consciousness only managed to anticipate the splat, but his instinct twitched his right arm, which serving as a rudder veered the body sharply right, flying an arm's length from certain death. The abrupt turn almost resulted in a collision with Becca.

His parachute deployed seconds later, Becca's shortly afterward.

3 | SOPHIA JONG

Four months later, September 2023

JOSHUA TREE NATIONAL PARK, CALIFORNIA

The grandmother of all Honda Accords screeched in the loose dirt road and before it had come to a full stop, Sophia Jong was already out running, striding, sidling, and finally crawling.

"OH my, you are gorgeous! No, no, no, no. Mama only wants to see you up close. Shhhhhhhh. Shhhh. Shhhhhhhhhh." The fury with Fat John, her boss, which had been brewing for the two-hour ride from NASA's Jet Propulsion Laboratory, suddenly vanished.

A long, plump zebra-patterned desert iguana was immobile, squinting at the blinding headlights, only its neck rocking.

When it realized eating dirt wasn't the end of the encounter, it calmed down in Sophia's arms. The first-rate petting probably helped.

Sophia could see the bonfire ahead, but the moonless Friday night was just starting and she wasn't going to get tipsy on cheap beer anyway. Especially with that ukulele dude trying to put his hands where they did not belong. It was an empirical fact that male engineers at JPL couldn't resist pestering she-scientists.

"… but I'm telling you, my dear!" she explained to the lizard. "You're one of the survivors of the Big Stone. And it crashed kind of close, the Yucatán Peninsula in fact. All those condescending, threatening relatives of yours were promptly shown the exit door. Me? What do I do? I … I traded practicing as MD for working in astrobiology. Crazy, right? Umma wasn't psyched. She still can't fathom sacrificing top dollars for—oh, umma means mom in Korean—for alien microbes we haven't seen and for all we know may not even exist … look, it's my dad's fault, all right? We used to do our annual family camping trips not far from here. Falling asleep in our sleeping bags under the stars while Dad showed us the Black Tortoise of the North—anyway, I don't want to bore on. Besides, you have some hunting and I some dancing to do. Such a pleasure meeting you. And sorry for picking on you, but I guess that's the price of beauty!"

The loud music couldn't mask the wails mixed with laughter from the two frontiersmen lost somewhere between Potato Head and Pee Wee rocks after venturing to irrigate the arid land. From the incoherent screams they seemed set on navigating back to camp via the North Star.

Closer to the bonfire, a symmetrical castle of beer cans gave away the professional leanings of the crew. The burned smell of failed sausages competed with that of roasting marshmallows.

The sparse Mojave Desert vegetation, the furry Joshua trees with their bayonet-shaped leaves, witnessed the nerdy debauchery in silence.

During the last minutes, the gawky engineer standing had been losing the favor of the crowd. "All I'm saying is that it took centuries after Copernicus downgraded Earth from the center of the Universe to neighbor in the hood before we began thinking about extraterrestrial life … I mean, science imitates fiction. In the 1890s, H. G. Wells publishes *The War of the Worlds* and only then our curiosity is awakened. Decades later, we start the SETI program—"

"There. Right there, that's where you lost my respect. That is—pardon me, ladies—bull*shit*. Art imitates life. First, an Italian called Schiaparelli identifies canals on the surface of Mars. Others, looking through hazy telescopes, begin picturing irrigation channels made by Martians … *then* comes H.G. Wells with Martians invading Earth."

Sophia's small frame stood up, which the other interpreted as a passing of the baton. She did a couple of goofy but talented tap dance moves, stopped with her back to the crowd, and jump-flipped with a flashlight clamped under her chin. There was wild applause and howls. She leisurely stared at each of the nine for effect.

"It's much more fundamental than who did it first. In fact, it has nothing to do with us. It's about them … it's … the Fermi Paradox,"—her strong personality overshadowed her soft voice—"because there's an eerie feeling when you look up. Just our humble Milky Way has hundreds of billions of stars, with hundreds of billions of exoplanets, many of them habitable, which should have produced countless civilizations, with billions of years to expand … yet there's no sign of anyone or anything out there."

"What about Michael? He sure don't look local. Just check out that fender forehead for hell's sake." Michael's airborne empty beer can landed on target.

"The Great Silence," she continued, shadows flickering over her alluring face, "where's everybody? There seems to be a Great Filter … that should make us feel not great, for there are really only three possibilities. First: intelligent life is extraordinarily rare—this is to say we somehow made it through whereas the rest did not. Maybe the odds against life are so formidable that one occurrence of intelligent life per galaxy is the best that can be hoped for—the immense chasm with other galaxies makes them effectively unreachable even at speeds approaching light. Possibility one is conceivable, but sounds suspiciously like 'we are the chosen ones.'"

The firmament stared down at them, hiding nothing yet brimming with mysteries. Any glittering light could possess another Earth, in solitary wait or swarmed in unimaginable beings.

"Second: we are the trailblazers. Maybe creation still glistens with morning dew and we really are the first ones. But the Universe is ancient, with our galaxy almost as old at 14 billion years. Our Solar System is a new kid on the block at fewer than 5 billion. And complex life on Earth is an infant at around a billion."

After a few seconds, the night critters restarted chirping choral music, including a drunk wrestling against imagined foes, having fallen short of his tent.

"Third ... the Great Filter lies ahead of us. Perhaps thinking beings have been common around the Milky Way, but civilizations acquire technology faster than wisdom and inevitably self-destruct. If so, many of the stars above us may be tattooed with ruins. Maybe the last one standing from a magnificent civilization left a trove, with a few priceless warnings and commandments, right before going extinct ... this unfortunately resonates all around. This, I'm afraid, is where humanity currently stands. Right on the brink of apocalypse."

Someone in the shadows piped up, "Humankind therefore may be precious beyond comprehension. We blow ourselves up and the whole creation of the Universe may be rendered pointless."

Sophia saw another moth head straight into the flames, immolating itself in an ephemeral sizzle.

"Then we really are screwed," said another.

"It's imprinted in our future," said someone else, "A Third World War. Terrorists genetically engineering the ultimate Black Plague. Fill in the blank, pick your culprit."

A heartfelt burp stressed the gravity of the situation.

"But it's worse than that," continued Sophia, "we don't even need intention. Bad luck or simply time will do. And in this respect, we are as competently prepared as your average dinosaur. I was just speaking to a friend about this ... imagine it's 66 million years ago and this place looks not much different from what it does today. A flock of pterodactyls passes in front of the setting

Sun. The sky flashes white for an instant as a rock enters the atmosphere and disappears south, sinking in the Yucatán Peninsula some 2,000 miles away. We see and hear no more but our fate has been sealed. An orange glow develops in the south that in minutes becomes brighter than the Sun. If we were in Japan, the outcome would be the same, just delayed. At Ground Zero, a massive fireball climbs into space, ejecting material as far as halfway to the Moon, which re-enters Earth's atmosphere as a legion of fiery meteors."

"There are two types of civilizations. Those that can protect themselves from an asteroid impact and those that can't," said somebody.

"You ... you ... need my potty ... amen," the conversation was crowned by an otherwise leading light at JPL.

"I think what Gab was trying to convey with his potty analogy is that we must do all we can to improve our chances of surviving. And that forcefully means becoming a multi-planetary civilization," said Sophia.

The crackling fire filled the night until a newfound Jim Morrison, equipped with a ukulele, started delivering, "This is the end, beautiful friend ..." while glancing at Sophia in veneration. She did not reciprocate.

4 | DERYΔ TERZI

ATACAMA DESERT, CHILE

A flat-nose semi-truck went past the motorcycle, but not before smacking Derya Terzi with an insulting mix of hot air and dust for the twenty-seventh time. *Bastard, hope you topple over.* For the twenty-seventh time he attempted blaming his friend, but the Polack was bulletproof. 'A four-hour drive' and 'air-conditioned car' had been decoded as weakness; 'sunscreen against the ruthless Sun' inapplicable to his unblemished Turkish complexion. Instead, he saw himself crossing the iconic Martian-looking landscapes à la *Easy Rider*. The too-long-awaited Glory Ride.

Things soured in flight with a transatlantic middle seat and a neighbor that kept falling asleep on his jittery right shoulder. Then this real-life version of the rented Harley-looking Yamaha from pictures, which could easily blend in on any Southeast Asia street. He rejected the helmet, as his wild, shoulder-length, jet-black hair looked stolen from a *Vogue* cover—"Allah curses men who imitate women," his father used to yell. By the fourth truck he began suspecting an error of judgment.

His face already felt like a pulsating, overstretched balloon and the novelty of the otherworldly, utterly lifeless scenery was no more. Yet each new affront from the vindictive destiny made him more convinced that tonight would end the decade-long race to the bottom.

Ø

Heavy breathing and a balmy breeze were the only sounds as he walked the overheated motorcycle over the last road coil around the mountain. Rainless erosion, volcanic ash, and the weight of time had blunted the reddish coastal range into an endless succession of rolling hills masking their exceptional height. The powdery plains below were peppered with misplaced boulders, abandoned checkerboards from forgotten titans. Far east, the Andes were marked by snow-capped cones, the tallest volcanoes on Earth. Just ten miles west, the shiny domes of the Paranal Observatory were silhouetted against a sea of clouds below extending past the horizon, burying the Pacific Ocean. The Sun had sunk almost half an hour ago; the sky was a starless palette of light grays to dark violets, a grand drape before the show.

After a final curve, he was above it all. The wide mountaintop had been flattened to house the massive futuristic structure. It looked deserted except for a seemingly scale model pickup truck by its base.

"Three decades in the making. Welcome to the just completed Extremely Large Telescope," shouted a dot named Janusz coming from the giant dome. "What—" began to ask the astronomer friend, pointing to the two-wheeler as they hugged.

"Pizza delivery," said Derya.

"You didn't have enough being airborne for twenty-two hours? You really must have descended from nomadic Huns."

"Possibly." *Closer in bloodline I descend from Father, who emigrated to Germany to shovel shit for us Deutschen under the 'plumber' euphemism.* "Quite a location, huh? I keep getting the impression that the highest life form, perhaps subtracting you, are lichens."

"You would be surprised. There are chinchillas, for example."

"Really? What do they eat?"

"What do I know? Lichens maybe?"

"Didn't see any."

"Chinchillas are night creatures. We all are around here."

∅

Under the clearest night[1] you've never seen, below the twenty-six-story telescope, the two friends relieved a vodka bottle of its contents. The sky was filled

---

[1]   Northern Chile is to astronomy what Las Vegas is to gambling. Not the only option, but the only one that no real astronomer can ignore. About half the worldwide telescope capacity resides there.

It has the lowest atmospheric humidity anywhere on Earth, and it is at a high altitude. The very low population density guarantees low light pollution. And not all views of the sky are created equal: the center of our galaxy is at a latitude thirty degrees south of the equator, visible year-round from there.

The ancient civilizations looked up at the river of milk slashing the heavens from end to end for enlightenment and spirituality. We cannot. In today's world, most of us have never

with celestial majesty. It made the Sistine Chapel ceiling look like stick figures drawn by toddlers.

"Belvedere? No wonder it tastes like ginger ale. You proud Pole. Where's the bottle I brought?"

"Night's young ..." Janusz seemed hesitant. "Derya, you understand this is it, right? Tonight. The Japanese team arrives tomorrow morning."

"I love saké."

"NO. No no no. Look at me! My ass is on the line here. Do you know how many endorsements are needed to file an application to even aspire coming here? And if you win the lottery, it's still a nineteen-month wait. Which you are skipping altogether. This is highly illegal."

"Hey, what are friends for?"

"I'm dead serious here. You know how much's an hour? This is hallowed ground, man. That mirror is the—"

"—most powerful ever assembled."

"The mirror is 130 feet across. That's four tennis courts. It's sixteen times more powerful than Hubble—"

"If I didn't know the specs, I wouldn't have hauled my sorry ass from Munich."

"I'm trying to help ... all that controversy with the *Nature* magazine article ..." Derya's cross-breed face, somewhere between a Western and a Middle Eastern Jesus, was suddenly looking tired. "My friend, I just want to help. We have six hours. A very rare luxury."[2]

---

seen the Milky Way firsthand, the galaxy in which we live. In fact, 80 percent of the world and 99 percent of US and European populations live under light-polluted skies. What was once a deluge of stars outcompeting in brightness against a pitch-black background has become a charcoal gray with a handful of timid stars and planets. The more we know, the less we see. On top of this, 88 percent of humanity lives in the northern hemisphere, where the galactic disc and center are only visible all night long during the month of July.

2   The mirror's massive enclosure dome slowly slid open, revealing the tapestry of the Milky Way.

"Allow me a few minutes to show you the cosmic museum above. We are going back in time ... light covers in a second a distance equivalent to eight loops around Earth, yet the fastest speed in the Universe is modest, pitiful really, when dealing with the enormity of space—" said Janusz.

"Come on, Polack."

"Pluto is five light-hours away. Voyager I, the furthest human-made object, which happens to also be the second fastest, launched in 1977 and right now is eighteen light-hours away from Earth. The edge of our Solar System, a light-day. The nearest sun, Alpha Centauri, 4.4 light-years—"

⌀

"You lied to me! You lied to me again! You fucking lied!"

"Keep going and you may turn it into a jingle," said Derya.

"I am risking being fired here! My reputation … and you come with … with …"

"This bullshit. Vodka always made you a sentimental."

"You … you promised so much. We all saw … yet you've spent, what, a decade in a pointless, delusional, pathetic search for a damn Holy Grail—"

"A white dwarf. A white dwarf that could go supernova. If it's there, it's close enough to our Solar System to be an existential threat to our planet. Yet we don't even know if it exists …"

A supernova is one of the most powerful events known in the Universe. It releases in seconds more energy than our Sun has produced in its 4.6-billion-year history. For a brief period, the supernova outshines the galaxy in which it's in.

"Save this for your grandma."

"Galactic bulge. Zoom to target. Pan left to right," Janusz dictated to the control room computer. The 3,000-ton structure began to rotate while the mirror changed pitch. The entire wall became a cloud of light crammed with nebulas and tens of millions of stars in a desperate dance of death orbiting the invisible supermassive black hole at the center of our galaxy. Staring at the incomprehensible vastness unfailingly readjusts human problems to their proper insignificance—except if you were Derya that night, as the extreme high of the last weeks, days, and hours was capsizing and sinking fast. "We are in a rural part of the Milky Way. A nondescript, unglamorous region in the outskirts of one of its spiral arms. A backwater. The bulge is 26,000 light-years away."

"I didn't exactly study art history in university," said Derya. *Or maybe I did.* "Father and us didn't make all these sacrifices so you could become a poet." "Astrophysicist." "Poet."

"Asshole."

"People keep saying that to me. There could be some truth to it."

"I'm not asking. You suck it up. This is how much I charge—UY Scuti." The telescope slowly turned around. "Bear with me, now it gets fascinating. How much do you know about the star UY Scuti?"

"Is this *Jeopardy!* for retards? Will you throw me a bone now?"

"UY Scuti, a red hypergiant, is the largest star known to us and it's 9,500 light-years away. If you ever felt significant, hear this. If Earth were the size of a cherry, Jupiter or Saturn would be a basketball, the Sun a sphere that's as tall as a refrigerator. UY Scuti? Everest-high," Janusz was lost in his own reverie. "And we haven't even left the Milky Way. Let's visit a neighbor galaxy: NGC 5566, 65 million light-years away. The image that will hit our retinas in minutes departed from there 65 million years ago. We are seeing live into the past, right at the extinction of the dinosaurs. A time machine. If you are not in awe, you're simply not human."

"Around Arcturus, Derya. Arcturus! The fourth brightest star in the sky. That appears twice in the Bible. Which has been studied since Ptolemy. And has never, ever been considered a binary star candidate—"

"That's not true. In 1993, the Hipparcos satellite suggested that Arcturus could be a binary—"

"Which was promptly discarded. Couldn't you pick something more arcane? You have become the laughing stock of the entire astronomical community. You have been digging your own grave in academia for years."

"If it's important enough—"

"Derya, listen for a second. Please. What's the probability that you are right? I will be generous—1 percent?"

"It better be 100 percent." *If this doesn't work … no goal in life. No reputation. Few friends. That's when bullets find their way into—*"Everyone, including Karl before we broke up, has wanted me to acknowledge it's a cul-de-sac … but tonight's different. Tonight's the night."

Janusz shook his head dishearteningly. "You said the same in South Africa two years ago."

"This time it's different."

"HOW!?"

"Unless I publish something meaningful soon, I'm losing my tenure."

"Sweet Jesus."

⌀

A cartoon in a 2015's *Scientific American* magazine showed a kid barely reaching the lectern microphone in front of a large audience. Above him was written '225th American Astronomical Society Meeting.' The kid lectured: "It is time for you to come to terms with my Three Commandments. 1. Immediate adoption of my stupendous late-stage star evolution model; 2. I'm awfully disappointed nobody found it for millennia, but Arcturus has a white dwarf companion; 3. Sorry to burst Earth's bubble, but said white dwarf will explode (refer to Commandment 1)."

Those were the good times.

Derya finished undergrad by 21 and completed his PhD by 24, both at Cambridge University's Trinity College—Isaac Newton's alma mater and where he spent the three most productive decades of his life. Derya's PhD thesis was spellbinding, but its deductions too unconventional for the mainstream scientific community. It didn't help that supernovas are fortunately very rare events.

The last observable by the unaided eye was documented by the great Johannes Kepler in 1604. For a few months it outshone every other star and was visible in daylight. And it was about 20,000 light-years away. Arcturus? Around thirty-seven light-years from us.[3]

For the last nine years, Derya had become ostracized as a fringe physicist pursuing something akin to alchemy, all puff and no magic, feeding himself by being an exceptional lecturer at a second-tier German university. The problem stemmed from his inability to validate Commandment 1 without demonstrating Commandment 2. And observing the supposed white dwarf was next to impossible, as it orbited too close to Arcturus the red giant, hidden behind its brilliance. A firefly around a searchlight. The 'next to' attached to 'impossible' was because there is a phenomenon called an occultation, where an object is hidden by another that passes between it and the observer. A solar eclipse is a good example. However, Derya was going for an exceedingly rare event where an object from our Solar System gets in front of Arcturus for a few seconds. The light would be attenuated to a billionth, which may allow observing its improbable companion.

For the last nine years, Derya had spent every minute of supercomputing power he had gotten his hands on—including half the computational budget of his physics department—to calculate the trajectory of every known object in the sky.

That elusive object turned out to be Uranus, and it was about to cross in front of Arcturus in two hours, seven minutes, and twenty-eight seconds.

---

3   What would happen if a white dwarf orbiting Arcturus boomed into a supernova?

     First, the good news: blissful ignorance for thirty-seven long and golden years.

     Second, the omen followed by wrath. One dandy day, from one instant to the next, the sky would develop a blotch much brighter than a full Moon and many times larger. For months it would bathe the Earth with a cocktail of ultraviolet radiation that gives a tan even at nighttime, then drops back into relative obscurity. For the next 333 years nothing much happens as Death gallops at about 10 percent of light-speed in the form of a giant expanding sphere, except that the night sky facing Arcturus becomes an ever brighter swelling nebula. Until it reaches us. What happens next is speculation. Possible side-effects may include the atmosphere facing the nebula blasting off, and a shock wave traversing the globe at the speed of sound through the remainder. In any case, the planet is probably cleansed of that irksome, sticky thing called life.

Two-thirds of the wall-sized screen was occupied by an unremarkable diffuse circle of chalky red light against a dark background sprinkled with tiny stars. The biggest eye in the world stared at Arcturus. There was nothing for Janusz and Derya to do but wait the last two minutes.

"… I've known you since we were roommates in college. Right before our professional lives divided, as you like to say, with me studying stamp collecting while you studied the one and only science there is," said Janusz.

"As a person I mean."

"You are an asshole. You're the smartest person I've ever met—"

"No, Janusz. I mean, what do you think of me … as a friend?"

Janusz was embarrassed at this violation of Deryan etiquette. "I have seen you three times since we graduated, Derya … you didn't show up at my wedding. You still haven't met my wife—if you leave a soup unattended for too long, it goes cold." He interrupted the difficult silence that followed, "Anyway, how are your folks? Azra? Fatma?"

"Family is good. A little estranged—sometimes, you know." *I think the right word is 'disowned.'*

"You've been doubling down for years. You've burned all the ships and all the bridges, no fallback, like Cortés invading Mexico. Why?"

"Things are easy when you have no choice. I have no choice because I am stuck with the conviction that I'm right." *There's a fine line between fishing and standing on the shore like a moron, Father used to say.*

"That's ballsy."

Derya shook his head. "That's desperate."

They remained frozen for the last eighteen seconds, big green numbers flashing on the screen. Nine … eight … seven … six … five … four … three … two … one …

Nothing.

Nichts.

Nada.

Janusz slowly turned to Derya in dread.

Derya was immobile, fixated on the screen. His chest rose and fell irregularly.

Long, terrible, weighty seconds dragged on, big red numbers flashing on the screen.

Gaze long into the abyss, and the abyss also gazes into you. It's over. I'm finished. Derya tried to speak, but only a grunt came out. He raised a heavy finger and pointed at a wall clock.

"It's … an atomic clock." Derya did not react, so Janusz continued, unsure. "The most accurate timekeeper … on Earth." This time he nodded at a funeral pace.

Almost a minute had gone by when the screen darkened for three fathom- less seconds. Derya's gold-winning triumphal screams made Janusz uneasy. It was gratifying that Derya's orbital data crunching was done correctly, but this was an ocean, a world, a galaxy apart from anything related to a white dwarf.

The replay slowed the occultation 7x, showing the precipitous dimming of Arcturus as Uranus passed in front. Nothing looked abnormal. It surely did not look like a binary star.

"Can we go from visible to ultraviolet?" asked a changed, confident Derya.

This time, as Uranus occulted Arcturus' core, a much smaller deep blue sphere appeared left, well within the star's circle, connected with an umbilical cord to the main star. The greedy white dwarf was stealing mass from the red giant, and cosmic gluttony is punishable by death.

If and when it reaches a mass about 1.4 times our Sun, the physical forces inside can no longer support its own gravity and the ensuing collapse skyrock- ets its temperature, creating an out-of-control fusion chain reaction that within seconds triggers a supernova.

Janusz sat down out of necessity.

This was one of the most important and certainly the most worrying astro- nomic discoveries of the century. A new branch of astronomy would soon be born, exclusively dedicated to researching Arcturus.

The two were transfixed.

"The start of your fame may mark the beginning of the end for us humans."

"Nemesis divina. I'm just its messenger."

"Am I … considered in the discovery?" asked Janusz sheepishly.

"I'm all for sharing. Just not today."

5 | THE SPΔRK

Thirty-four major newspapers around the world ran the same full-page paid article. Below is page five of the UK's *Financial Times*. The title occupied the upper third in attention-grabbing, sky-blue Helvetica against the salmon pink background; the rest was plain text.

LETTER TO HUMANKIND

My name is Pete Drake, United States Senator for Virginia and former astronaut. I have Stage IV cancer and these are my farewell thoughts. I want to thank Yuri Milner for the generous funding that made this possible. Please do not think of me as a Republican, or an American, or a white male. I am a person among 8 billion others. A person who cares about the future of our species. Arcturus precipitated this letter, which should have been written decades back.

In 1961, President Kennedy changed history by defying the impossible. Eight years later, on July 20 1969, the entire Earth stopped to gaze with dreamy eyes at the Eagle landing on the Moon. And the impossible was no more.

You knew this. But sometimes it's useful to restate the evident. Triteness trivializes, even this pinnacle of everything that humanity stands for. This was monumental, and let's remember a few reasons why.

How short is eight years? Boeing takes a decade to design a new airplane that shares 90 percent of the DNA of its predecessors. Enter the Space Race: before Gagarin's 1961 flight, the farthest humans had ventured into the heavens was just over eighteen miles, a mere third of the way to the Kármán line, aka the edge of space. Boundless ingenuity, irrepressible boldness.

Stunning complexity. The Apollo program demanded new mathematics, new engineering, new materials, new instruments. A modern commercial jet aircraft has about a million parts, perfected over decades of incremental improvement. Saturn V, the launch rocket for all Apollo missions, had 3 million parts built from scratch. The NASA workforce in charge was, on average, 27 years of age. An engineering kindergarten. Boundless ingenuity.

Safety margin? Armstrong landed within seconds of running out of fuel and crashing. A computer glitch, a broken landing leg, a failure of the single engine, or a problem in the rendezvous would have stranded them. No evacuation plan. No way to rescue the crew. This mission was the most challenging and hazardous enterprise ever undertaken. I say again: irrepressible boldness.

Entering the 70s, the gateway to the Solar System was wide open. A manned mission to Mars slated by the end of the decade. Five decades later it's 2024. Last time humans left Low Earth Orbit was 1972. We traded exhilarating discovery 250,000 miles away from Earth for running in circles 250 miles above it. Millions of kids venture further to attend college than we have traveled from our planet during this time. How would an 8-year-old respond if we asked her to order these two realities chronologically? In some ways, we race backward in space.

And with each new day, the dazzling Apollo program becomes an ever-increasing, towering barrier for space exploration. What did you say? When a smartphone in anybody's pocket has more computational power than all of NASA back in 1969?

Boldness appears to be inversely proportional to progress. In 2004, President Bush unveiled a plan to return humans to the Moon *in sixteen years*. It was scrapped in 2011 in favor of a manned Mars mission somewhere in the late 2030s, far enough in the future to guarantee no material efforts or accountability. The White House swapped the Moon back in 2017, with a return mission planned for late this decade. The magnificent compass set by Kennedy requires a brave presidential directive to accomplish a well-defined mission, within a short period of time. Do not hold your breath while you wait for change. I should know.

The disease has crept into America's former temple of innovation. NASA funding is no longer guaranteed and its budget[i] gamed yearly by political winds and whims. Let's assume we are just about to head back to the Moon. There is an all-important, tacit rule borne out of Apollo's humongous shadow: no casualties allowed. The most spectacular accomplishment of our civilization came without a single death in space. Half a century ago. But space is unforgiving and really very hard. No amount of preparation and resources can eliminate its multiple, cumulative, correlated all-at-stake risks. Yet a fatality could compromise NASA's very existence. Hence the conundrum. The agency whose mandate is space exploration has incentives stacked against manned exploration of space. Yesterday's success is today's roadblock.

Many inside NASA think returning astronauts to the Moon is harder than before. It's the Sword of Damocles dangling over them. The same that explains the flip from irrepressible boldness to unmitigated risk aversion: the visionary NASA aerospace contractors of yore have become bureaucratic fat cows devoted to "outsourcing to sub-contractors, and then the sub-contractors outsource to sub-contractors, and so on. You have to go four or five layers down to find somebody actually doing something useful. Cutting metal, shaping atoms"— Elon Musk. The same that explains the flip from boundless ingenuity to unalloyed conservatism. Using one spacesuit for launch, walking on the Moon, and re-entry as every Apollo mission did is an impossibility with today's requirements: too uncomfortable, lacking too much mobility, too risky. The rocket must be even bigger to allow for exercise equipment, toilet, galley. The laundry list is long and swelling.

Rocket science that no longer lives up to its reputation. Manned space exploration in perennial hibernation. So what? We have more immediate concerns, like hunger in Africa.

No, we don't.

Let's ignore the ticking bomb of climate change, which threatens livability on our planet. Or that every dollar spent in space has historically returned between $7 and $14 back to the economy. Or that satellites are finding aquifers and improving crop yields in drought-struck East Africa. Or that exploration is really the essence of the human spirit.

Let's concentrate instead on a three-story house called Earth. From time to time, a pea crashes against one of its walls. Big deal. Yes. Last time it did, three-quarters of all living things were no more. But a grain of salt is no slacker:

in 1908, a 200-foot-tall asteroid exploding over Siberia[ii] razed 80 million trees over an area the size of 300,000 soccer fields.

Right now, in the asteroid belt between Mars and Jupiter, the faraway Kuiper belt, or the mysterious Oort cloud, there's a twilight-of-civilization asteroid or comet with Earth's name on it. The only question is timing. Hopefully it won't strike today, hopefully not in a decade, because we would be unable to save ourselves. The more we look up, the more worrying it gets. Each week our inventory of asteroids and comets grows. But many reflect little to no light, so we won't see those until the sky is ablaze.

How can a boulder the size of a city obliterate humanity? Weigh it, then calculate the energy required to accelerate that mass to over ten miles per second. It's 700 times the total energy used worldwide in 2020. That's equivalent to a billion Hiroshima nuclear bombs detonated simultaneously.

So, I hope we agree it's urgent and crucial to reignite manned space exploration, so we can learn to divert peas and salt grains, and have a second home (Mars?) for when the pitch-black pea turns up. Robert Heinlein once described Earth as being "too small and fragile a basket for the human race to keep all of its eggs in." There are dangers against which the only defense is being somewhere else when they happen.

What can we do? How do we solve the deadlock we've been in since 1972?

Lucky for us, technological salvation is coming. But don't look to the space agencies. This time, against all odds and conventional business logic, it's the private sector. Specifically, two visionaries and their creations: Elon Musk's SpaceX and Jeff Bezos' Blue Origin.

It's November 2015. Houston, we have a problem. A cynic, smug, cozy, oligopolistic $300 billion industry gapes in horror. Unfortunately, a technical quantum leap has just happened. Oh no! The foul smell of innovation. The decades-long feast is drawing to a close. No more rear mirror and blinders. Compete or die. In a coincidence that feels like destiny, within a month from one another, Blue Origin and SpaceX independently returned rockets from space and self-landed them. This is the Gutenberg printing press of space travel.

The industry finally heard the dreaded battle cry. But let's put things in perspective: SpaceX's most popular video has a few dozen million views; last decade's Latin song Despacito gained 6 billion views *in its first two years.*

To exert real, unrelenting, and lasting change, we need the entire world in a state of frenzy. We need a Kennedy moment, when dreams came with wings. We need to capture the soul of our generation. And for that the appeal can only point to our hearts.

What we need is a private mission, where failure is not a congressional investigation. A private mission of heroes willing to take immense risks for the greater good of humankind. To venture beyond the unknown. Further than any woman or man has ever dreamed. So, when they do, it is July 20 1969 all over again. The distance vanishes as they touch our essence and move every single one of us into a catharsis of transfixing optimism, awe, pride, gratitude, and kinship for all of us that live in this fragile, unique, and irreplaceable village called Earth.

The future is not what it used to be, but some of you dear readers can make it whole again.

Buzz Aldrin said that exploration is wired into our brains. If we can see the horizon, we want to know what's beyond it. But one does not discover new lands without consenting to lose sight of the shore for a very long time. Godspeed. May you start soon.

i. A sense of proportion: for each dollar of US military spending, NASA gets three cents. NASA's budget peaked at 4.5 percent of the federal budget in 1966 and has been in steady decline to today's 0.4 percent.

ii. On April 16 2018, an asteroid larger than the 200-foot-tall Siberia asteroid—designated 2018 GE3—missed Earth by half the distance to the Moon, barely one day after it was discovered.

6 | DΛRE

Four months later, April 2024

SAN FRANCISCO, CALIFORNIA

James woke entwined in sticky sheets with pasty palms and a feral heart rate. A waterbed in all but functionality. The apocalyptic vision was back, welding night with day. Weary eyes sized up the spartan bedroom, still undecided on which reality was more plausible.

Find the telltales. The Reese's chocolate smudge on the tall Lego Apollo Saturn V rocket over his desk looked legit. But it was the slanted framed photograph hanging from an otherwise blank wall—of himself shaking hands with Vladimir Putin as if there was a fence between them—that tipped the scales this way.

His body felt heavier than last night as he walked to the middle of the loft and swung the curtains open. San Francisco Bay in its morning glory, fog almost hiding a cargo ship gliding under the Golden Gate Bridge. He opened and promptly shut the window. Breathing marine swell brought back the wrong memories today.

James turned on the television.

"—of what's been obligatory conversation from bilateral meetings to airport chit-chat to bar brawls. It looks like 4th of July weekend here at Tappan Zee Bridge, as hordes of New Yorkers escape the city that never sleeps to catch some darkness for the best night of the year to see Arcturus—sir, sir, where are you heading?"

"Our buddies meetin' at The Gunks for some astro action. We've all turned into amateur astronomers, you know."

"Any instruments to watch the sky?"

"Got these birdin' binoculars from my old man."

"However, it may all change today when a joint press conference of several international organizations, including NASA and the European Southern Observatory, will announce the results of five months of feverish research around the discovery, made by Janusz Lisowski and Derya Terzi, of Arcturus being a binary star. A leaked document confirms that the white dwarf is near the end of its lifetime, but a potential supernova event has no chance of happening for at least a million years. A concern, but one for far-in-the-future generations."

The crunchy kick from the new cereal box vanished.

⌀

As James walked along, pushing his commuter bike through the crowd to the Powell Street metro station, an old homeless woman grabbed him by the arm. He was going for his wallet when they locked eyes. She pointed up and produced a wrinkled paper from her wool coat and handed it to him.

"What is it, ma'am?"

"Don't waste your time. She's a mad, mad cow; deaf and mute," another homeless person replied. "I could use some of that wallet though."

Confused, he continued walking.

After stepping down into the station, he opened the piece of paper. Stopped cold and then dashed back up the stairs, identifying the off-season coat among the faceless mass. James encountered a pair of lost eyes, clueless to the world.

"Want to join the club? Membership's free. San Francisco even pay us for staying!" shouted the other homeless person when James returned hesitantly to the metro. "We attract tourists to the city don't you know!"

⌀

STANFORD UNIVERSITY

Two hours later, the volatile cloudy temper of San Francisco had been traded for another picture-perfect sunny day around Silicon Valley. James and his mentor Leonard walked through the university's famous inner courtyard toward the Mechanical Engineering building, where the former taught the ultra-popular 'Space Flight 101' class for undergrads.

"You're reacting impulsively. Based on a hunch. What's the plan? Reshuffle our nation's space priorities because of that dream you've been having?" said Leonard in his raspy voice.

"You saw the smoking gun."

"No. There was a discovery of a binary star and with it a hypothesis. Extensively researched with a thoroughness commensurate with something on which our entire civilization may hinge."

"What I'm—"

"Anyone who's anyone in astronomy and astrophysics studied it at length and it was finally discussed and agreed on unanimously among 400 scientists during a three-day symposium. You heard the results and tripped out. That's a tantrum. Maybe you saw 'sometime soon' without reading further: 'astronomically speaking.'"

"I saw the end. Of everything." It elicited no reaction from Leonard. "The Virginia Senator died last night, a day before the announcement."

"And? Excellent man, sign of the cross and all, but what? Should I start reading the horoscope right after brushing my yellow teeth every morning?" Leonard was pulling on his aspiring Gandalf beard, an impatience reflex.

James explained the puzzling encounter from earlier and handed him the paper. Leonard inspected it.

"And she pointed up?"

"Yes!"

"Powell with Market Street?"

"Yes."

"Then she was pointing to that Burger King on the second floor—hey, I should be the one getting annoyed. You see planets in this scrap of paper? Well, I see polka dots. You see Saturn? I see a Mexican sombrero. And you know what? We're both right. Wanna know why? Because we are both falling prey to humans' amazing ability to find patterns, even when there are none."

James re-embraced science. "Arcturus has decreased humanity's life expectancy by a thousandth. Earth was going to be fine for 3 billion years and now we're down to a million."

"We were frolicking and fornicating with Neanderthals 35,000 years ago. A million's thirty times that. Not so modest anymore, huh? But it's more than that, Jimmy. Look at me. I've been smoking since I was 12—cigarettes, the other stuff came later—even though I knew it would probably kill me within decades. And I still smoke. Why? Because we are really bad at giving the future its proper weight and importance. If a single person flounders, try asking a society—which must come to an overarching agreement—to do anything for a threat a thousand times further into the blurry future."

They walked past Rodin's *Les Bourgeois de Calais*. One sculpture held his head between his hands. Another hid his face with a palm. Another looked down, seemingly lost in tribulation.

"Let's do this little experiment: set the end of the world for one hundred years … a third of the population has just been given a reason to smash the place up: defecate over Earth's immaculate face, vomit in her lap, punch her in the stomach, gangbang her dignity and virginity away. Another third reasons: 'We'll figure it out, we always have,' before hastening back to dancing La Cucaracha or watching whatever game is on TV. The final third starts symposiums, new religions, fundraising campaigns. But after a few years of dog work they get pissed with all the moochers and tightwads, including the future versions of themselves. 'Let them figure it out, bunch of ungrateful shits.' Why do I know this? Because contrary to you, I don't pretend to have seen the future. I observe the present and this is what's happening now. Not just runaway greenhouse gases, but risking an ecological collapse that makes it impossible for us to continue as a species."

James shook his head.

"And if this is still insufficient, my dear boy, your rock from the sky strikes me as worrying about spilling hot coffee on your chest right as the airplane you're in is about to crash. If Arcturus goes supernova, I will be more worried watching the wave of fire from Hell about to engulf our entire Solar System than holding my breath for the pebble."

"Then the cause may not be the supernova."

"Ahh! But then you don't have a motive anymore, do you? Where's the trigger for your comet? See? You're trying to unearth a spark, so you can establish causality, so you can rationalize your vision."

✑

They entered the classroom. A few early students greeted the celebrity mechanical engineering professor and the old man with piercing eyes.

"Science, you know better than most, is not in the business of following prophets. Those were the Dark Ages. Jimmy, credibility is earned through sweat and lost in a breath … you're exhausted. It shows. You have leprechauns jumping between your eyes while you try batting imagined comets before they do us in—take time off, see friends, go travel …"

James wished Leonard's grainy tuba voice was quieter. James' students wished it was louder.

"There's no reset. I can't forget. I'm enslaved to what I saw. I will die trying if that's what it takes."

"Trying what? To convince people? You're no Jesus. You may get a few misfits and enroll a few sects, but that's the extent of your sphere of influence. Didn't I just tell you? We have a much more immediate concern, the avalanche of climate change, yet we snail our way out of apocalypse. Your cause doesn't even make it into the Top 100, yet you demand a mobilization of resources amounting to a new Space Race. Want to create a tipping point? A before and after? Read history, goddammit. Don't coerce, enthrall. Don't scare, inspire. Want to awake humanity? Take us beyond our wildest dreams. Prove it can be done."

Just because the idea is crazy doesn't make it wrong, thought James. The two had long fantasized about it.

"Keep your motivations confidential and to yourself. Never threaten by saying: 'We must go to space to dodge death.' Flip the argument. Arouse the child in every one of us by volunteering to go there to find *life*."

James realized that the idea had long escaped its cloister and had metastasized all over his mind without him being conscious of it until now.

"If anybody can do this—and as I've said before, I'm not implying it's feasible—it's someone like you. Test it out. Do one of those, what's the name, Kickstarter things. Maybe people will care. But then again, they may not. And there will lie your answer. Don't ask me, ask the world," said Leonard.

'The Hunt for Extraterrestrial Life' will be the crusade. But—but the Trojan Horse is the mission. You don't need to find a thing to change history; you just need to get there, thought James.

Leonard continued far back in James' consciousness, "If NASA is looking at Mars in fifteen years … your mission should look at Saturn in seven. For if you get there, you will carry us all. For once you conquer the impossible, you smash the gates open forever. Go beyond Odysseus, beyond Columbus, beyond Apollo, further than any man has ever gone!"

waste our time unless thoroughly qualified. M. L. Barker. 1408 Chapman Bldg.

MEN WANTED

for hazardous journey, small wages, bitter cold, long months of complete darkness, constant danger, safe return doubtful, honor and recognition in case of success.

Ernest Shackleton   4 Burlington st.

MEN—Neat-appearing young men of pleasing personality, between ages of 21 and 40 to work

PART 2
PREPARATIONS

Part 2. Preparations

7 | YI MENG

SOMEWHERE IN THE SOUTH CHINA SEA

Yi saw a still, uninterrupted ocean in his entire field of view. Except for the shimmering sea and lack of main subject, it could have been one of those Renaissance paintings from the West, heavenly cumulus clouds pierced through by sabers of daylight.

He forced himself to look at the windsurf sail resting flat on the water, ripped from the longboard on which he was laying facing down. The culprit, a storm darkening a great expanse and criss-crossed by lightning rods, retreated into the horizon. No signs of land or help anywhere.

He opened a small compartment in the front of the board, inside of which two bottles of water, a few nutrition bars, a flare gun, and a phone rested snugly. He slowly removed his right rubber glove. The hand was shaking, but not from cold. With the care of a barber shaving Chairman Xi Jinping, he took the phone out.

For a long time, he did nothing. The blood from his tongue tasted metallic, like licking a battery. Stalling, he dipped his lips in the sea and washed out his mouth. Bad idea. The salt instantly pinpointed the wounds, promptly setting off fireworks through his nerves. *Besides, no sense in arousing the sharks so early. Barring a miracle, there will be plenty of time to make their acquaintance.*

Before, when life was round and whole, planning for the solo sailing trips was a thorough affair. But those days were gone. *And I get it. Fate finally lost its patience. I would have done the same.*

He turned on the phone: no signal and 70 percent battery. He opened the wind and currents app. It hadn't updated for hours but the currents information was still relevant. The wind blew decidedly back to the coast, but without the means to profit from it, all depended on the little current arrows on the screen. And they were pushing keenly away from the coastline.

He carefully stored the phone back in the compartment, covered both temples with his hands, and howled his soul out.

✿

Arguably the most decisive day of his life. The Gaokao, the higher education en-
trance exam of the People's Republic of China. For a son of peasants from inland,
his odds were a lot worse than the 1/1,000 for the 10 million other students. A
swarm of desks were arranged in rows and columns, with hundreds of students
bent over their exam papers. Yi stared at his crooked right index finger, the phys-
ical token of countless hours of study. He took in the moment, checked one last
time, and stood up. He was the only one walking down the aisle. Furtive looks
from the examinees. The exam officer, confused, squinted up at the wall clock.

✿

It was pitch dark and a veil of rain peppered the sea.

Yi longed for the Sun that smoldered his skin earlier. The shivering was building up lactic acid for an unforgettable night. His stomach felt as if a pair of hands were trying to milk his guts. The sea splashing and spraying was sapping the life out of him—*heat transfer in water is damn efficient.* Body and mind were utterly spent but this clearly no longer guaranteed sleep.

The phone's GPS showed his position on the screen slowly, surely drifting away from salvation. A wave of terror lurked ready to assault. His analytical mind tried to compensate: he was in the South China Sea, one of the world's mercantile hubs. The current was drifting him away from the continent but at some point it should trend upward to Taiwan. His paltry shipwreck would soon start crossing commercial trading routes—but these were gigantic Panamax, almost crewless cargo ships with decks 150 feet above water, and not really looking for flotsam.

It was the year of the Dragon, which was supposed to bring him good luck and prosperity. Not for the first time, he wished he wasn't agnostic.

He fell into a restless snooze, jolting with the slightest variation in rocking rhythm. Time elongated. Coldness became numbness. The here and now were adrift.

✿

At the back window of the departing provincial bus, a 10-year-old Yi gazed at
his family in the middle of the snow-covered dirt road. As his mother dragged
her hands to her chest, Yi grabbed the wooden carved Buddha hanging from his

neck. Her knees weakened and she rested against his father who stood frozen like a terracotta statue. The brother's head looked away at the harsh Inner Mongolian winter.

Ø

Having traveled days for his graduation from Tsinghua University—the Everest of higher education in China—mother and father looked like they were from a different era as they moved shyly among the mass of urban parents to take their seat. Their faces were dizzy with pride. She was there by their side, explaining. The two women had finally met. That day he could have touched the stars.

Ø

Yi half broke from his stupor in the middle of the night and for a moment the weight lifted as he came to the conclusion it was all just a bad dream. It was, the nostalgic past knocking on his conscience. He was still lost in a never-ending ocean, his own personal purgatory. Pitying himself, he tried to cry but only managed a nasal groan and a tearless rictus grin. The grin gave way to a long, deranged laugh. This time the phone came swiftly out of the board compartment, a reflection of its decreased importance as it clung to 2 percent battery, the icon red and flashing angrily. It had been twenty-one hours since he left the continent, yet he was almost one hundred nautical miles from it now. The phone slipped or was let go, he wasn't sure which. The bright screen sank into the unfathomable deep, a dying light in the night.

Life has a way of upending when you least expect it. Seven months before, he had made it: the co-founder of a fast-growing robotics company and about to marry The One. Far, far from the cabin in the Mongolia prairie where his widowed mother still lived.

And then the wrenching news. His mother had died—he had meant to visit for the past two years, always encountering a minor obstacle that added a few more weeks of delay. Time was supposed to heal but he found it didn't help. Now was too late to have kissed and thanked her, for her to have spent the last hours with the children she brought into the world. If he could only believe, as she did, that it was just a change in shape, that she may be roaming happy and peaceful as a butterfly in a spring forest.

Misery loves company. Hours later, his fiancée got a hold of him. She couldn't have known about his mother, yet was crying over the phone. "I'm sorry—I'm sorry." It was over. The ring had been returned. Someone else had stolen that heart. He had no indignation, only resignation. It was clear then, the many times when work got in the way. She never complained but they silently drifted apart. The wedding always sliding forward, its date fluid, mercurial.

It was a moonless, cloudless sky. He looked at the twinkling stars. Bei Ji Xing, the North Star, the direction where he needed to drift to have a chance at living. Shen, Orion's Belt, the most recognizable tattoo in the sky, visible from anywhere on Earth. But he needed something closer, more intimate. He scanned the firmament and found Tǔ xīng, Saturn, low in the heavens. It was much closer than the others yet still impossibly far away, a dot competing among countless thousands. *It's all trivia really. The absurd reality is that anyone on Earth can see it, yet nobody can see me.*

∅

He woke to a low-pitch roar and spotted the Maersk cargo ship pushing forward at great speed. The indescribable relief quickly became concern as it seemed to be coming straight at him. The thing was huge and he could easily be sucked into the massive propellers. That would have been a death for the history books—*the thing is, the only ones in the know will be the fish eating my remains.* In survival mode, he took out the flare gun. There were six 12-gauge flares. They worked during daylight, but competing for the attention of the clueless crew with a bright Sun was unfair at best. His nervous, shaking hands grabbed the first cartridge to put it in the barrel, but fumbled and it fell overboard. *Way to cooperate, survival kit.* He became frantic. He closed the gun, pointed it up, and pulled the trigger. The flare climbed to the morning Sun. He could barely see it ignite. Second time. Aim, shoot. He realized this wouldn't be the ticket home.

Just a few hundred feet away, he could clearly see individual containers. In the urgency of the moment, he was surprised to find a detached part of his mind scanning for a jagged geometrical pattern of colors in the stacked wall of containers coming at him. *Once a mathematician, always a mathematician.* Third time—aim, shoot. For a moment, he recovered hope. *Maybe they saw! No. They did not. Thank you very much.*

He wouldn't need to worry about being eaten alive by the propellers though. Maybe sharks would have better luck. The huge structure of metal, thousands of containers on it, went past him a safe distance away, oblivious to his presence. The sound was overwhelming, yet he still stood on top of the longboard, bouncing up and down and screaming his lungs out. He only realized the board had flipped when his throat choked as his body entered the seawater headfirst. The tranquility under the water was seductive and had it been just about closing his eyes and falling asleep, he may have taken it.

If he got rescued—*when, not if.* Once he was rescued, the news wouldn't travel far past the local Shenzhen newspaper. He had read about Poon Lim, the Chinese sailor who in 1942 became the only survivor of a merchant ship when a German U-boat sank it in the middle of the Atlantic Ocean. Lim managed to get into a minuscule raft and for the next 133 days drifted, resorting to ingenuity to make a hook, catch a fish, then use the fish as bait to catch a shark, then lost it all in a storm, only to start again by catching a bird and drinking its blood. And then one day Brazil finally appeared in front of him.

Ø

How could I make such a stupid mistake? If I die, I know who's to blame. Halfwit. I have been behaving like a 12th-century sailor. Earth's curvature! The Earth is round and having ignored this may cost me my life. It was a geometrical problem: he was flat on the longboard, so his face was at sea level. That meant the horizon was just under a mile away. If he sat up, the horizon would instantly retreat to three miles. He had been scanning for a big ship silhouette in the distance, but if there was one six miles away, the only part above the horizon would have been the bridge. He was expecting to spot a standing cow when only the tip of the horns would have been visible.

Ø

Another day gone by. Tomorrow is my two-day solo anniversary. Hooray. The Sun had sunk a few minutes before. With his newfound knowledge, he had counted three certain and two tentative ship sightings that day. One of the latter was crossing in the distance right then, only its upper half visible. *Time to commit.* If they didn't see him, he probably wouldn't survive the days or weeks before he washed up on Taiwan's southern coast.

He had always been tough, so could conceivably survive weeks without eating. But without water, not even Poon Lim could endure more than a few days, and he only had a quarter of a liter left. His tongue was a dry piece of leather and his throat stung terribly on every inhale and exhale. So, as he loaded the gun with the first of the last three flares, he knew this was it. He waited for the ship, now barely identifiable in the remaining light, to be at what he sensed was the minimal distance. Raised the gun. His heart was pounding. He fired. The flare climbed a good few hundred feet before starting its descent, projecting a strong red light until it fell into the water. He counted in silence for the longest twenty seconds of his life before reloading, pointing, and firing again.

☿

A young Filipino exited the deck. He looked down at the countless, perfectly piled containers, lit a cigarette, and made two deep inhales before he puffed out a cloud of smoke, which flew past his face as the ship raced forward.

He was hurrying the second cigarette so he could resume his position in the control room when something caught his attention. For a few seconds, he saw a red light in the distance. *It's probably nothing,* he thought to himself, yet he didn't move or stop gazing. Then a second light climbed up into the darkening sky. He dropped the cigarette and screamed as he opened the heavy metal door.

☿

The crewman was finishing the report before contacting the different port authorities.

"NAME: YI MENG; HEIGHT: 5 FEET, 9 INCHES; WEIGHT: 157 POUNDS; NATIONALITY: CHINESE; AGE: 28; PROFESSION: NOT KNOWN (SOMETHING ABOUT ROBOTS); IMMEDIATE FAMILY: NO; CONTACT INFORMATION ..."

There were just three people on the ship's no-frills bridge, including Yi. Automation had decimated the shipping industry of its human components.

Yi was seated in the background with a thick blanket around his shoulders. His face looked weathered and exhausted, but he was recovering fast. Dozing in and out of consciousness.

Someone changed the big screen attached to the roof from a soccer game to BBC News.

His face underwent a transformation. Suddenly he wasn't tired anymore.

8 | FΔME

The HARDtalk show anchorwoman sat between the two guests facing each other.

"—a masterclass in bogus marketing and shaman science is all this really amounts to."

"But Chris, as former CEO of the space division at Boeing, I'm sure you agree James Egger's credentials are immaculate," said the anchor. "A PhD in electrical engineering from Harvard; the second-youngest astronaut to live on the International Space Station; and after an early retirement from NASA, goes on to work at SpaceX. Right before this mission proposal, he was associate professor of mechanical engineering at Stanford University. And all this at just 32 years old."

"He's extraordinarily accomplished by any yardstick. I personally know him. And he's unwavering. When Stanford said no to his request for a leave of absence, he resigned. Resigned from a cushy career in academia at one of the top three universities in the world," said Chris. "No, the issue here is not about him but about *it*. I have issues on so many levels with this … idea. Where do I start? Space is really hard. In fact, the first rule of space travel is 'everything that can go wrong, will go wrong.' Yet he's proposing a mission to Saturn. *To Saturn!* Remember Mars One in 2014? It was an outlandish plan by a dreamy-eyed Dutchman to take people on a one-way trip to Mars. Went down in history as yet another Ponzi scheme for gullible people. But at face value, that was frankly more reasonable than this. Mars is on average 600 times further from Earth than the Moon. Saturn is 3,000. We haven't gone to the Moon in half a century and now a *private expedition* intends to go to Saturn? It sounds as if they were playing darts at the local Irish bar and happened to hit the ringed planet. Because why would anybody pick Saturn?"

"I have to take issue with that, Chris," said Anna, a former astronaut, "and considering the respect we have for each other, I have to say that's a rather dim question. Saturn's moons are the best candidates in our Solar System to answer the two most central, pressing questions of mankind: are we alone in the Universe—"

"Anna, sorry for interrupting," said the anchor, "but for the benefit of the audience, please allow us to play a short section of his Kickstarter video where he defends himself."

The three turned to a screen where James was speaking to the camera against a black background, wearing a white T-shirt that said "ASTEROIDS are nature's way of asking: 'How's that space program coming along?'" The T-shirt was not exactly subliminal, but it was the sole mention of Death from Above during the video.

"As Carolyn Porco likes to say, if we could demonstrate that genesis has occurred not once but twice, independently, in our humble Solar System, then it means by inference that it has occurred a staggering number of times, that we are suddenly not alone, that it's only a matter of time before we encounter another civilization. This would be the most profound discovery in history … yet we are far from unveiling the truth.

"In today's age, the search for extraterrestrial life is done by robots. For sixty years, we have searched for past or present life on Mars in vain. Dozens of missions have covered a total distance well under fifty miles and haven't brought so much as an atom of Martian soil back to Earth. Apollo 17's astronauts and lunar rover covered a third of that distance in four hours, bringing back a sackful of Moon dust. Our astrobiology learning pace is equivalent to building the Great Wall by arranging stones with a pair of tweezers. Add to this that a robot can only look for what it was sent for, yet most groundbreaking discoveries in history have been serendipitous findings you weren't searching for. Mind you, these missions are multibillion-dollar enterprises, with decades of lag between conception and start—"

The video stops playing and it's back to the studio.

"A little further on, he reminds us about one of the most egregious faults of his concept: its demented schedule. Departure on June 2027. That's less than three years from today. A thousand days!" Chris pointed out.

"You've spent too much time finding cracks and forgot the logic of it all," said Anna. "And while I agree three years is a really tight window, I do think it's doable. He has made all the information public, so let's dissect the problem. The date of departure is anything but arbitrary. June 2027 allows the shortest possible round trip all the way to 2040, at six years and three months. As for time to departure, eight years elapsed between Kennedy's speech and the landing on the Moon. And that was building a space program from scratch! James' mission uses an existing and proven spacecraft—SpaceX's Starship—which has been in development since at least 2015 and has already landed cargo on Mars. And let's also not forget that he was directly involved in its design."

"Exploration should be gradual—"

"No, it's not. Exploration is by necessity daring. Columbus did not incrementally go to America. You either cross the Atlantic or you don't ... those sailors knew that scurvy, dehydration, starvation, mutiny, the plague, or shipwreck lay ahead. Dreading the moment the leviathan would come from the depths and gobble up their ships, or the fleet would fall off the Earth's edge. Compared to that, our visits to the International Space Station are paddles around the marina in a canoe."

"I'm amazed you can be so—so *naïve*, Anna. I'm going to ignore your *Rime of the Ancient Mariner* for something more current. You are a veteran astronaut with almost 200 days in space. If I hear correctly, you are suggesting that the Apollo program is somehow comparable to this. That's absurd. The communication delay between Earth and the Moon was a second; the delay between Earth and Saturn is seventy minutes. The light, traveling at the fastest speed in the Universe, takes over an hour! As opposed to a second! Using your analogies, you're comparing soaking in a bathtub to crossing the Atlantic inside it. The scales are not even related."

"Bad example. Franz Romer crossed the Atlantic in a handmade kayak in 1928—as Apollo 13's Jim Lovell used to say, 'there are people who make things happen, there are people who watch things happen, and there are people who wonder what happened.' Which one are you? The 'this is impossible' tirade has a long and illustrious history of defeat. It's darn unwise to bet against human ingenuity and courage."

"I think we should leave the history lesson and go back to examine this confusion between science fact and science fiction," said Chris. "How does he intend to finance the expedition? Through Kickstarter. Is he laughing at us? This makes Mars One's intention of selling space-reality-show TV rights sound like a sensible idea."

"That's mudslinging and you know it is. It's clearly stated as Phase I. He is asking for $13 million for an accelerated feasibility study to provide a cost estimate in nine months," said Anna.

"Good luck with that. Besides, there's no need for feasibility studies—NASA has done it already. A manned mission to Mars, much simpler than Saturn, requires in the order of $100 billion and twenty years—"

"When you force risk elimination from an inherently risky field, you end up with $100 billion price tags, which is really the only responsible thing NASA can do to imply but not say, 'with that straightjacket, thank you but no thank you.'"

The anchor said, "From rags to riches in under thirty-six hours. The project goal is already overfunded by 400 percent. $70 million in the project's bank account. Whatever you want to call it, this has turned into a global sensation."

Chris must have felt like coming out of a Faraday cage or an Alaskan cabin after the thaw, but he quickly recovered. "You are confusing being in the news with being real news. It's short-lived sensationalism. He obviously touched a nerve. We are fascinated by exploring the unknown. The Final Frontier will always be space, something we hold so sacred and mystical we call it 'the heavens.' And if this wasn't a cartoon of a mission ... it could well have become the most transformative event in human history. But no amount of wishful thinking can get over the hard facts. Read my lips. They'll get a few weeks of glory, then even the tabloids will hang their heads and dismiss them as charlatans."

"What do you think are the chances of something bad happening, Anna?" asked the anchor.

Chris interjected, "Anna, look at me. Can you say with a straight face they aren't committing suicide?"

"You keep missing the point. I won't be speculating on the probability of a human being dying. Do I think it's risky? Very. I should probably say extremely. Space is merciless. Millions of things must go right, yet one going wrong may be all it takes. It's an incredibly unfair game. Being 99.9 percent right can easily get you killed ... but here's where we depart. A third of all climbers that make it to the summit of Annapurna die, but that doesn't deter people from a selfish and dangerous activity. It's the yearning for adventure, for testing yourself, for daring to overcome the impossible. And while these certainly play a part, the most important one is this: military, police, and firefighters put themselves at risk every day, but nobody could possibly accuse them of recklessness or suicidal tendencies. Because they save and protect people ..."

"You seem to have gone off on a tangent, Anna," said Chris.

"No, I haven't. Let me break it down for you. If you think that humanity is in danger from any of a number of self-inflicted wounds and ailments, there is simply nothing as important as that mission to Saturn. If they succeed, a colony on Mars will not only look possible but well within our immediate reach. If they succeed, survival for long periods of time in space will be irrevocably demonstrated. If they succeed, we will be overwhelmingly closer to being able to defend the Earth from comets and asteroids ... and I'm completely ignoring the principal mission objective—the search for life—that could revolutionize chemistry, biology, medicine, religion, philosophy. Then, when you consider the monumental payoff, the immensity of the consequences—potentially the biggest in the history of mankind—even a very low probability of success makes the attempt almost obligatory. One thing is certain: the probability may be low, but if we don't try, it's zero."

"You're talking about human lives as if they were disposable napkins."

"You've hit the bullseye: the paradox today is that by our unwillingness to take risks for a few, we are gambling our entire civilization. James Egger is evidently convinced that the voyage is worth a handful of human lives, including his own ... someone once asked Alan Shepard if he ever got scared on top of the Saturn V rocket. He answered something like, 'I'll be sitting at the top of a huge amount of explosive fuel, in a vehicle that contains over a million parts, all made by the lowest bidder on a government contract. Why should I be scared?' Neil Armstrong was the one that said, 'The rate of progress is proportional to the risk encountered.' You know it well: the White House had a prepared speech honoring the deaths of Armstrong and Aldrin. To many, the combination of human error, mechanical failures, and analog technology made the triumphal outcome something bordering a miracle ... sending humans to space is nothing but the latest expression of an ancient practice called human sacrifice. Thankfully for our species, a few are willing to take these odds. Thankfully for our species, a few are willing to offer themselves for the wellbeing of many. And today you have a supremely impressive individual determined to sacrifice everything ... for you. And me. For us. What the Greeks called a hero, a demigod."

$$\varnothing$$

The two crewmen looked at Yi in disbelief. He was standing naked in front of the screen, the blanket previously covering his manhood lying on the floor.

His soul had been touched. He had found his calling in life.

Over the next few weeks, he quit his own company, sold his shares, gave most of his belongings to charity, and took a plane to the USA, determined to devote himself to helping the mission to Saturn.

9 | STARSHIP

Three months later, October 2024, 961 days before launch

SPACEX PLANT, PORT OF LOS ANGELES

As James waited in the small rental car for security clearance at the gateway of his former workplace, he tried again to focus on the cranes of all sizes, shapes, and colors muscling around the skyline of the largest port in the country: incessantly packing, stacking, and offloading a fourth of all cargo that entered and left America. *The mission has about $600 million too much … we should have capped the crowd funding—nonsense. Nobody could have anticipated this level of interest. Besides, who doesn't want extra money apart from a Jeff Bezos? We don't. Sometimes less is more.* The Kickstarter campaign had been fabulously successful, which had the side-effect of accelerating everything beyond everyone's expectations—certainly his. *This was meant to be gradual— well, now it's not. Man up. And we said no whining on Tuesdays.* He strove once more to distract his exhausted, feverish mind by paying attention to the port hubbub: clangs of metal against metal, gulls' choirs and soloists, the humming of outsized machinery. *It seems everyone everywhere in the world has a reaction. The one thing this mission doesn't elicit is indifference.* The fiery support and raging opposition had been unrelenting. He was grateful to very many, but also hurt and disturbed by the rabid attacks, sometimes from astronauts from his own class. *We need to increase the team size. Urgently—you must do better than that. If everything is urgent, nothing is. Pick another word. Something more hyperbolic—we need to increase the team size. Desperately.* He grabbed and bit into the half-eaten muffin, but it tasted pasty and ashy. Even his taste buds seemed to have unionized against the lack of sleep. His stomach now had a permanent hollow feeling.

James looked up to meet the gaze of the black bushy-mustachioed security guard on the other side of the car window. He seemed to have been knocking for a while. The gate was open.

Not nearly the right state of mind to meet with Elon.

∅

SpaceX still felt like a start-up to James. There were few dividers inside the hangar, all of them made of glass. No cubicles, no offices. It was designed to force a continuous interaction between the scientists and engineers, and the technicians manufacturing and assembling the largest heavy-lift space vehicle in history. It consisted of two parts: the Super Heavy rocket at the bottom and the Starship spaceship on top.[4] *This is where the future of humanity is being built. In my lowly opinion anyway.*

A museum was suspended from the roof. The second rocket ever to go to space, return, and self-land—on an autonomous drone deck barge in the Atlantic Ocean in April 2016—was right above James. Its paintwork partially burned by the extreme heat it encountered upon Earth's re-entry. Hanging next to it was the first private capsule that delivered supplies to the International Space Station in 2012. This made SpaceX the fourth entity in history that sent and brought back a capsule into orbit after Russia, USA, and China.

There was intense movement. Hundreds of people scattered across the extensive floor area—automated forklifts cutting through invisible lanes, large industrial robots beyond security fences bending metal, welding joints, coating surfaces. Everything and everyone working on the colossus. SpaceX had always

---

4   The rocket's function was to hoist the spaceship out of Earth's atmosphere. The vehicle was a visionary industry checkmate and was quickly becoming the company's workhorse. In the economically eye-watering trade of delivering stuff to orbit, the name of the game used to be reliability above all else—hence the eye-watering prices. SpaceX conquered reliability and turned it into cost-per-pound. This wasn't simply good business, it was essential to build a self-sustaining colony on Mars—after all, the company was founded with the goal of making our species multi-planetary.

The cornerstone for low cost was reusability, considered science fiction among industry insiders until the very day it happened: before the company's 2015 coup d'état, each launch was equivalent to flying a commercial airplane a single time and then crashing it on landing. Furthermore, on the low-cost road the vehicle was a jack of all trades: not just a rocket for launching satellites into orbit, but a spaceship capable of transporting and landing a payload on Mars—which it had already done with cargo in 2022, in preparation for a human landing by the end of the decade. Not just that, but preparations were ongoing for point-to-point intercontinental passenger transport on Earth on a similar time frame. *And not just that, but maybe the spaceship for a manned mission to Saturn.* James knew the multi-purpose vehicle was already doing miracles for the economics of space travel, and within a decade it should effectively become the first space airline in history. *Indeed. Before this vehicle, the mission to Saturn was financially inconceivable and technically impossible.*

been vertically integrated. Raw metal and carbon fiber went in at one end of the factory, rockets and spaceships came out the other.

The Super Heavy rocket and Starship spaceship were so large they could only be transported by barge through the Panama Canal to SpaceX's launch-pads in Cape Canaveral, Florida, and Boca Chica, Texas. That was the practical reason for setting up the factory in the Port of Los Angeles in a Navy destroyers' shipyard from World War II.

"Jimmy! *The* Jimmy Egger?" Lana, the redhead engineer extraordinaire, kissed and hugged her friend, former workmate, and one-time lover. "You were always a celebrity here, an engineer astronaut among mere mortals. But now ... now you're John Lennon! Come on, they're waiting for us at the assembly line."

♄

An all too well-known voice approached Lana and James from behind. "I hope you are aware there's nowhere to land on Saturn." Elon Musk, the legendary business maverick, was as tall as James, but broader.

After a few minutes of light talk, they walked by a line-up of Raptor engines. "From here onward," Elon pointed to an imaginary line on the ground, "everything becomes Gulliverian." The people working on the area recognized James and came over to shake his hand. He looked at the engine standing by his side. A thirteen-foot-tall, bell-shaped metal nozzle, crowned by a combustion chamber wreathed in plumbing whose complexity and lightness was only possible through 3D printing. For the first two minutes after launch, the few-dozen Raptors of the Super Heavy rocket produce enough power to satisfy the electricity demand of the entire United States during that time.

"Obviously I've thought about this mission a lot." Elon had publicly supported the project but James was expecting candid feedback from the quintessential risk-taker, especially on the tight schedule. "Are you prepared to die?" he asked after a long pause. Elon surely didn't beat around the bush.

"No, I'm not ... but I feel it's my destiny to go to Saturn and death is a ..." James searched for the right word.

"Likely."

"... possible consequence of that decision," James concluded.

"If you need to keep one idea from this conversation, let it be this: I am certain the spaceship will make it to Saturn ... but it could be a one-way ticket for the crew. As you move to implementation and launch, keep thinking long and hard about your chances of success. Don't communicate them to anyone, but constantly calibrate. And if you get to a crossroad where the odds begin to stack against success, you owe it to the crew and—listen carefully—all of us on Earth to abort. It will come at a great personal loss, but you will preserve what a lot of people, including all of us at SpaceX, are doing. Because unbeknownst to most, this mission is a bet we are *all* making. If it goes even partially well, it will be a quantum leap in space exploration. But if it fails catastrophically, we could kill manned space exploration for decades."

The comment had no bias and James already knew all this, and yet he had a hard time seeing the glass half full. *I am an incurable optimist. What's going on with me?*

They came to the berthed Super Heavy rocket. No wonder it could carry three times more payload than the second-biggest rocket on Earth, SpaceX's own Falcon Heavy. The thing was gargantuan: twenty stories in height by three stories in diameter. James worked on the design and knew the specs by heart, but was still amazed by the sheer size. *And this is just the rocket.* The Starship spaceship was ahead.

They arrived in front of it—sixteen stories, half of them used by the engines and propellant tanks. The remaining, the pressurized area for crew and cargo, was greater than the cabin of the Airbus A380, the world's largest passenger airplane.

Elon patted the fuselage. "Hard to believe it's already been two years." Two summers since one of her twins carrying equipment had landed on Mars. "And still we missed this year's window because of that public-private partnership. This automatically delays the first crewed mission to late 2029, best of cases." Due to the alignment of Earth and Mars, the optimal launch window happens once every twenty-six months. "The good news is that your mission is running solo on the race to set foot on another celestial body … the bad news is there's no sharing of fixed costs for the refueling infrastructure in orbit. Your mission will need to foot the whole bill. Better get creative on the financing." He sounded apologetic even though SpaceX would operate for the mission at cost.

James looked at the immaculate liquid silver hue, the soft round angles, the two grand observation windows of the Starship. The engineering marvel looked like the offspring of an inspired jam session between Elon Musk, Jony Ive, and Peter Pan.

"It's utterly gorgeous," James said.

"You'll live here for six years. You'd better like it."

10 | SPACE AGENCIES

Four months later, February 2025, 854 days before launch

WASHINGTON, D.C.

The commercial airplane flew above the Potomac River, approaching Ronald Reagan National Airport. James' window was filled with the long strip of green between the Washington Monument obelisk in the foreground and the Capitol in the distance. At both sides of the park the bureaucratic machine of the most powerful nation on Earth resided in the many buildings, including NASA.

Ø

James stared at the sleeves of his old gray suit. *Yep, definitely missing an inch. If I'm being kind.* He avoided the sight of the trousers and concentrated instead on the passing streets. Even the schoolchildren looked overdressed. *Way to go, Jimmy. Why bother buying yourself a new suit, really? This'll only be the most important meeting you've ever had.* The heating inside the limousine was blasting in his face but he had decided this was his atonement for being so sartorially rash and stupid.

The black car stopped in front of NASA's nondescript headquarters. *Less glitzy than I remember.* James exited the vehicle, followed by Helen, the mission's head of communications, and Arne, its chief technical officer.

Ø

The room was packed with about twenty people sitting around a long oval table, plus a similar amount either standing, or subtly leaning against the walls. An hour into the meeting, James felt it was increasingly stifling and unnatural, at times almost like an interrogation.

The introductions were brief, so he only knew the people seated at the table by their prominent desk nametags. Both NASA Administrator and Deputy

Administrator, members from the Advisory Council, the Aerospace Safety Advisory Panel, and the directors from the Kennedy Space Center in Florida and Johnson Space Center in Houston. These were scientists, engineers, former astronauts, or a combination of them. Some he knew personally, but there were also high-ranking people from the Air Force, Pentagon, and Congress. To James' right and left sat Helen and Arne.

"As I said, it's the Shackleton crew managing every aspect of the mission preparation. We decide what's essential, what's important, and what's expendable," answered James. One of the fan groups baptized both mission and spaceship with the legendary polar explorer's name, and it had stuck like cement.

"You are thirty months away from your self-imposed launch, but there are a number of mission-critical systems that haven't progressed beyond sketches," said a NASA official.

"With all due respect, I think we have been stuck in euphemisms. You are hinting specifically about artificial gravity, and the insinuation is that the mission is destined to fail. I propose we talk on those terms," said James, while striving for eye contact or telepathy with a restless Arne. *We call you Pit Bull, but deep down I know there's a poodle in there. Keep cool.*

Artificial gravity was on everyone's mind for a reason. It had never been tried before. Floating in space was fun, but accumulating evidence showed the harmful effects of weightlessness over long periods of time. Muscle atrophy could be greatly minimized by exercise, with bone loss up to a point, but the weakening of the immune system and eyesight deterioration could not. This mission would stretch Valery Polyakov's record of 438 consecutive days in space to 2,300, so the elephant in the room was not whether but what would be the artificial gravity solution for Shackleton.

Artificial gravity was conceptually straightforward. Spin a cylinder, and just like clothes in a washing machine, the centrifugal force would push everything against the edge. Increased spin increased the simulated gravity.[5]

"Fair enough," said the NASA official. "Then how are you tackling artificial gravity?"

"Shackleton's radius is less than thirty feet, which means there is no way

---

5   It was believed but not confirmed that gravity around 40 percent of Earth's should cancel out the negative effects. This sounded suspiciously similar to Mars' 38 percent gravity, which really meant "we don't know." There were several complications, the most evident of which would be physiological: a cylinder inside the spaceship meant that a person standing would experience significantly lower gravity in the head than in the toes, which at the very least would produce motion sickness.

of avoiding low tangential velocity coupled with high angular velocity … it's a complicated way of saying that it only works for humans in a horizontal position. Regardless of the technical solution, it will need to be for sleeping hours only. That means intermittent." James saw a few heads raise, which betrayed them as the engineers. There were few things space system engineers abhorred more than moving parts, one of them being mechanical starts and stops. Both created stresses and material fatigue, and what James just mentioned probably included both. "Two possible solutions are being studied: a wheel that rotates the sleeping quarters or spinning the entire ship."

One of the engineers raised his hand. "You're a big boy. No need to put up your hand to go to the toilet," said Arne. James' stomach contracted.

"How do you know that partial gravity during nighttime won't have side-effects on the human body? Maybe the cure could prove worse than the disease," said the engineer, politely ignoring Arne's remarks.

James cut Arne off before he answered. "The Japanese have done extensive microgravity research with mice on board the International Space Station, and by now there's solid evidence that one third of a day inside a centrifuge cancels out the effects of weightlessness. For mice. We still have a few years to confirm that this translates to humans."

Another engineer said, "A gravity wheel would modify the ship, changing its capabilities. That changes the mass. And that changes the structural loads and stresses, and the possible failures. And the interactions between materials and pieces. The prudent thing to do would be to spend a few years re-developing, doing new simulations and tests. Afterward, draft new rules and procedures—"

Arne hit back, "I see you're all about compromises. You could have been a fine politician. Instead, you made it into a half-baked engineer." *Arne the hope slayer, the gravedigger*, thought James. "Engineering is the art of making the impossible possible. But we don't even need to go that far: the mission is using a vehicle that SpaceX began designing in 2012 and which has already landed on Mars! NASA in the 60s went from having a napkin drawing of Marvin the Martian's flying saucer to a man on the Moon in eight years. You, on the other hand …" he looked around, enlarging his sample to just about everyone in the room, "… seem fixated on making the possible seem impossible. Acknowledging that our generation has become lesser people." James glanced at Helen in despair. She seemed ashamed of having been born. *Salvation won't come from that corner.*

"What I was about to say before you interrupted me," said the engineer, "is that *any* space vessel is, by virtue of being surrounded by a vacuum and subject to a brutal temperature range, a house of cards. One failed rivet in a spaceship made of millions of parts may be enough to produce a catastrophic failure … as with most fields of human endeavor, the KISS principle almost inevitably applies."

Keep It Simple, Stupid. James was about to apologize to smooth things out when the NASA Administrator stood up.

"James, Helen—Arne … as a former astronaut and as a human being, I am enthralled by the concept and its boldness. I really wish the mission the very best …" James' soul sank with the presentation of the shit sandwich, "… but as NASA's representative, I am officially communicating to you that we cannot and will not finance or collaborate with the mission … we also cannot endorse it."

James played his ace. "Sir, doesn't this stance put NASA in an awkward position, considering that both the European Space Agency and Japan will put significant technical and financial resources behind the mission?"

"Jimmy, the three agencies had a conversation this morning. None of us can back your mission anymore. There are too many uncertainties, too many risks, and frankly quite vocal opposition. We are spending taxpayer dollars. There are too many eyes watching."

The meeting was over. People began moving out.

A baffled James saw the Administrator coming over to him and starting to speak. Something about NASA having no say, as both the Senate and House Subcommittees on Space had vetoed it. He sounded ashamed or regretful. He kept talking but James was having a hard time making sense of the words. Until he said it: "Jimmy …" looking around to make sure they were alone, "it was the White House's doing. The President of the United States has, for reasons I can't possibly fathom, a personal vendetta against you or the mission." On the parting handshake he said, "I can promise neutrality. We won't speak publicly about Shackleton."

The press will have a field day tomorrow.

Ø

James had been inside the restroom by the building's entrance for a long time. To the dozen missed calls from Helen he finally replied with a message: "Need to reassess, alone. Don't wait for me."

He looked at the outdated aide-mémoire for a meeting that should have gone radically different.

"No spacecraft could hope to carry instruments matching the capabilities available on Earth. This is why a sample-return mission is often viewed as the end goal of planetary exploration."

"Currently, space agencies spend decades and billions on uncertain outcomes of rather humble mission objectives. Shackleton instead proposes a $2 billion check payable only upon sample returned to Earth. This mission will be tens, if not hundreds of times more valuable than any other mission ever attempted, and risk-free for you!"

"So far it's been a lot of theories but little to no data. Shackleton will make a huge dent in the vast area of science known as Don't Know."

We are the confident collector that got fleeced clean—a timeless fable, I'm sure.

James splashed his face one last time. He needed to escape to the anonymity and freedom of the leafy National Mall three blocks away. Maybe the statue of Lincoln would shine a path forward.

Somebody called him as he was exiting. "James? James Egger?"

No respite. *Here we go again.* He turned and found himself in front of an angel. *If there ever was an agreed canon of beauty …* James flushed when he realized she was becoming uncomfortable by his shameless stare.

"I'm sorry, it was just—strange evening. My … I'm … yes, James."

"I'm awfully sorry to disturb you at such an inappropriate time—" She was English.

"Quite an accent you carry … I mean that in the best sense—I love your voice." *Suave, Jimmy. Not just making a fool of yourself but making it super awkward for her too.*

"What I—"

"I'm Be—"

"I … Belinda Addington …" Both stopped, blushing in unison.

James recovered his dignity, and with that part of his composure. "I am that whom you seek." She had an infectious laugh. *Gorgeous laugh, really—what's all this schmaltzy lovey-dovey first sight stuff?*

"I have been looking for you. I work here and—"

"Didn't know you could work in this building and be under 50." That addictive giggle again.

"Here, only in the sense that it's NASA. The Jet Propulsion Laboratory." The legendary research center run by Caltech, in charge of robotic space missions, probes, and rovers. "… where you have quite a following."

"Good, because we didn't get any converts around here today."

"A group of us at JPL want to help. After office hours naturally …" she said.

"Look, I realize this could sound a bit strange … but I could use a walk. Today has been … well … maybe we can talk about your people at JPL."

"Unfortunately, I have to fly back to California in four hours."

"I totally understand." His face must have looked miserable, because she couldn't contain a warm smile. His face lit up with a broad boyish grin.

Ø

It was a chilly winter sunset. Contrails criss-crossed a fading sky while a current of bitter air drawing from the river washed over all. Belinda and James did not seem to mind, seated at the start of the upper steps of the Lincoln Memorial, right where Martin Luther King delivered his "I Have a Dream" speech. She was as petite as he was tall.

"I have a somewhat similar story, borrowed from my half-sis Stevie. Not Arthur C. Clarke but Isaac Asimov—my older sister was the one that got me hooked on sci-fi," said James. "Asimov was signing books at the Sacramento Public Library, but Stevie's mom was late picking her up from school. As Stevie is dashing to the entrance, the doors swing open and the great man comes out swarmed by a mean-looking fandom. She tries pushing through but only gets glares. She was losing him. In despair, she screamed in invented Yiddish 'Isaak! Isaak Ozimov!'—his original Russian name, mauling every 's' and 'z' into a 'sh.' He turned toward the impostor, came smiling, and signed her *I, Robot* copy. Not long after …" he stopped, choking back unannounced tears. "She's the one that's no longer with us. What he wrote is still my most priceless possession: 'To Stephanie, the best of impersonators, may you never forget the sky's not the limit. Yours truly, Isaak Ozimov.'"

She was visibly moved, again.

"Jimmy, I really must go now."

"I know, I know … well," James turned red again, "at the risk of souring this, could you envision—" He stopped cold at the sight of a band around her right ring finger. He stuttered, "I'm so v' v' very sorry. I did-didn't realize you were married …"

Belinda glanced at her right hand. It was her time to turn pink.

"I think you are confusing left with right."

Both looked at her hand again. It was easier than looking at each other.

Belinda recovered control. "But you have been rather unclear on the proposal …"

11 | SERGEI LAZAREV

Seven months later, September 2025, 656 days before launch

LOW EARTH ORBIT

Sergei Lazarev's impenetrable eyes scanned the view through the single window, the glass almost touching his face, as their Soyuz capsule undocked from the International Space Station. The sphere 250 miles below was, save for a few cotton wisps, an unremitting blue blending with that of his eyes, a greedy Pacific Ocean expanding in all directions. The countdown had begun, and in three and a half hours Sergei and two other crew members should be touching down on the Kazakh Steppe.

His large frame was bent in the narrow seat like a bumper car driver while his shoulder almost rubbed against the German astronaut's in the ultra-tight cockpit. Taller and broader than most cosmonauts, he would have been ineligible in Soviet times. Even now, somebody his size was nobody's pick at Roscosmos, the Russian space agency.

Except that he was Sergei Lazarev. Drafted into the air force following off-the-charts recommendations from aerospace mechanical engineering professors, after only six years as a pilot he was awarded the Hero of the Russian Federation medal for his involvement in the Syrian Civil War. Groomed for space, during his first stint in the ISS he shattered the longest untethered spacewalk record, held by an American. Now he was leaving the ISS for a third time after 203 days as its commander, the youngest to date. A celebrity and national hero, the question creeping into his mind was no different from what a multiple Olympic gold medalist needs to ask himself and the world. At 35, what next?

⌀

The Soyuz emitted three thumps before coming to rest on the monotonous late summer plains. The spring pastures had given way to sparse bouquets of *solyanka* brown wild grass and the occasional stunted birch tree. Russian military transport helicopters landed, creating dust clouds swiftly swept out by the unbroken Eastern winds, and a dozen people commenced the ritual of rescuing the crew from the charcoaled capsule. After months in weightlessness and a punishing re-entry roller coaster, the crew could barely move. The assist team took two out like crash test dummies. Not Sergei, who crawled out by himself. His face couldn't conceal the pain and strain, yet no one called him out on the protocol transgression. It was Sergei Lazarev, after all.

People watching him operate in space could have been forgiven for thinking everything in life came unfairly naturally to him, that he was predestined to be a physical wonder and a virtuoso engineer. But that's not how it had worked for him. Born in Vorkuta, a coal-mining town just north of the Arctic Circle, the son of a couple of high-school teachers, nothing was handed to him on a silver plate. Realizing early in life that he wanted to become a cosmonaut, his obsessive personality made that his one goal in life. Gifted with a privileged intellect, yes, but it had all been sweat and toil for him really.

Ø

A few days later

The courtly 19th-century grand room was mostly empty of furniture, with an overly high ceiling from where long windows stretched down looking at the Moskva River eleven stories below. There was a parade of military bigwigs talking casually, who all snapped to attention in an almost perfect *clack* when the double doors opened. In came the Roscosmos Administrator, the Commander of the Russian Space Forces, and the Marshal of the Russian Federation—the highest military rank in Russia; bringing up the rear unexpectedly was the Minister of Defense.

Ø

All the uniforms were seated by rank at the long table. The meeting had been going on longer than anyone had anticipated, the Minister being the possible exception as he delivered a lingering soliloquy. But the last five minutes had replaced tedium with terror as he went ballistic at Roscosmos.

"—that's for Roscosmos to figure out! The annual budget stays the same, but effective today, a third will go into artificial gravity development."

The Roscosmos Administrator took a long pause. He had better tread lightly, as the Minister was not known for his magnanimity. "Minister Artemyev, I respectfully ask you to reconsider this directive. Tens of thousands of direct and indirect jobs could be compromised."

The Minister of Defense glared at him. "You have ten months to provide a full-scale working prototype," he said, cutting in a single swipe two months off the schedule he had given minutes before, "in space."

"Artificial gravity is a nice name for a hamster wheel. Just larger," said the Marshal of the Russian Federation. Massively underestimating challenges was endemic in the Russian armed forces. Very risky, but on occasion, wildly successful.[6] "Call Captain Lazarev."

---

6   In a shrewd reframing of Cold War accomplishments, President Kennedy galvanized the landing on the Moon as the be-all and end-all, sweeping the overwhelming Russian space superiority of the previous decade as a necessary but comparatively minor accomplishment.

       The Russian space program was born handicapped by a declining economic regime and consequently, as the country had done since Prince Alexander Nevsky in the 13th century, it compensated the comparatively shoestring budget with institutional and individual risk-taking that would have been considered deranged in the West.

       In 1961, Yuri Gagarin became the first human to journey into outer space, with a 50 percent chance of not making it back. In Soviet Russia, those odds were acceptable across the board. When US Colonel Paul Tibbets dropped Little Boy from *Enola Gay* over Hiroshima, the chance of the crew dying was negligible. When Mayor Andrei Durnovtsev dropped Tsar Bomba sixteen years later, the most powerful weapon ever detonated—at 3,000 times the destructive power of Little Boy and twenty-five times that of all bombs dropped in every city during World War II—his bomber was treated with reflective paint to limit heat damage, yet the crew were still assigned only a 50 percent chance of surviving.

       In 1967, the Leader of the Soviet Union wanted a spectacular rendezvous in space to celebrate the fiftieth anniversary of the Communist revolution. That meant flying an untested new capsule, the Soyuz. Gagarin himself had inspected the capsule and found 203 structural problems, and called the mission suicidal. But it proceeded anyway. Colonel Vladimir Komarov, family man and revered cosmonaut, would launch first, followed the next day by another cosmonaut to meet in orbit and dock. Komarov knew launching meant death, but in one of the most poignant deeds in memory he did not refuse to fly, because the backup pilot was Soviet hero and friend Yuri Gagarin. On launch day, Gagarin showed up at the launch site demanding to take Komarov's place, but was removed by guards. Once in space, the Soyuz failures began and the next day's launch was canceled. One of the Kremlin's most powerful men, Alexei Kosygin, along with Komarov's wife, called Komarov a few hours before re-entry, reminding him between bouts of tears that he was a hero to the Russian people. Komarov plunged to his death on re-entry, the Soyuz's parachutes failing to deploy. A historical and readily available photo shows a piece of deformed charcoal in an open casket, Komarov's remains being observed by the inscrutable faces of Soviet officials.

       Today's Soyuz would have looked oddly familiar to Gagarin. During the 70s it became, through incremental improvement, a sturdy, proven, and cheap vehicle to go to and return

Sergei entered and stood at attention in front of his superiors.

"Captain Sergei Dmitrievich Lazarev, this committee has chosen you as a crew member for the international mission to Saturn. This is the greatest honor bestowed upon a cosmonaut. We are committing the reputation of the motherland and significant resources to this endeavor, and you will represent all of us and our nation's interests in the conquest of these new worlds."

If anyone expected an emotional reaction, none came. He thanked the committee, finishing with a steely military salute.

"This is a six-year mission into uncharted territory, with a high chance of not coming back. If you have any qualms, this Monday is your last chance to excuse yourself. After that, it becomes official to the world."

---

from space—as long as you use the very narrow definition of Low Earth Orbit, between 100 to 1,200 miles above the Earth's surface. The Moon, 239,000 miles away, which no earthling has visited since 1972, is off-limits. Because in an industry carrying people while operating in the most unforgiving environment known to man, the name of the game is reliability. If it ain't broke, don't fix it.

The US followed an altogether different path, which would involve a revolutionary new vehicle designed to dramatically reduce the cost of taking people and cargo to Low Earth Orbit. It was to become the Space Shuttle. Instead of disposing of an entire spacecraft each time you go up, as Russia still does up to today, why not partially recover the spacecraft? By 1981, after nine years and tens of billions of dollars, the first shuttle, Columbia, climbed into the sky. But lofty promises gave way to abysmal reality: the expected $20 million cost per launch turned out to be laughably off mark. Like an imploding Ponzi Scheme, the official number of $450 million per launch ended up being $1.2 billion once all fixed and hidden costs were considered. The old-fashioned and increasingly outdated Soyuz cost tens of millions per launch. Russia: 1—USA: 0. But this pales compared to the shuttle's worst failure: security. Two of the five shuttles exploded during launch and re-entry, carrying six and seven astronauts respectively.

Following the Space Shuttle's retirement from service in 2011, the Soyuz became the only means to go to the ISS. Applying monopolistic best practices, Russia jacked up the ticket price per astronaut from $22 million in 2007 to $81 million by 2018. Outrageous opportunism it may be, but still a mere fraction of the shuttle cost, while being an order of magnitude safer.

But market forces were coming back at full strength. SpaceX took the noble aspiration of the shuttle, and through a complete shift in the space design and fabrication paradigm achieved the holy grail of space economics: full reusability.

Today, Russia's Roscosmos knows this means checkmate: from indisputable leader in carrying cargo and people to Low Earth Orbit, to destitution. Unless they can develop enduring competitive advantage in some area of the $300 billion space economy, their demise is inevitable.

12 | RUSSIANS AT THE GATE

Two days later, 650 days before launch

SILICON VALLEY, CALIFORNIA

Yi Meng gripped the stiff narrow passenger seat as the light, two-bladed helicopter dipped in the warm summer air well past the trigger of his free-fall reflex. *This is no civilized way to travel.* Perhaps, but the pastoral sight of houses and low-rise buildings lost between patches of tall trees hundreds of feet below—which a year onward still made Silicon Valley look bizarre, almost suspicious to Yi—was deceiving: I-280 and US 101, the two arteries herding traffic throughout, had bad cholesterol and were prone to standstill. *And the one—maybe the only—thing everyone agrees on about the mission is that time is our mightiest foe.*

Yi had landed at San Francisco International Airport twenty minutes earlier and the conference would start in fifteen. The flimsy rotor blades slicing the air sixteen times each second were the only means of guaranteeing his attendance. James, the mission director and future Shackleton commander, had been adamant about having the relevant crew member at every important meeting, and for this particular one experts from all over the world had flown in. The directive meant a disproportionate amount of traveling for Yi as the 3D Printing and Robotics mission specialist.

He looked to the west at the fluffy tentacles of the mass of Pacific Ocean moisture, clinging to the other side of the coastal range carpeted in pinewoods, vainly trying to cross over into the perpetual spring cocoon of Silicon Valley. The tac-tac-tac-tac of the rotor had settled into a metronome for his thoughts.

"The Chinese Dream's poster child," the *People's Daily* newspaper had anointed him. Being the 3D Printing and Robotics mission specialist on the expedition to Saturn seemed inconceivable following a childhood among Inner Mongolian shepherds. Yet Yi knew something they did not: the title was premature. He was going to quit. *I'm not nearly good enough—Derya Terzi, Mission Scientist. Turned down an offer to become the head of the physics department at ETH Zurich, where Einstein studied. Instead, he became an authority on Saturn and its moons before the mission selection process even began. Talk about commitment—James Egger, Mission Commander. Growing ever taller with each meeting we've had—Sophia Jong, Mission Physician and Molecular Biologist. Came indisputably first among tens of millions of resumes. So creative, confident, yet unassuming—meritocracy like there's never been before. They breathe and sweat The Right Stuff … and then there's me, the weekend warrior battling arthritis, thrown by mistake into the Table Tennis World Cup semi-finals.* A new air pocket flipped his stomach again. *This damn roller coaster is really, really getting old—and why do you always need to fly so high?*

"We're approaching Mountain View. Touching down in seven," said the pilot.

Yi scanned the landscape below. To the east was the end of the placid San Francisco Bay, basking under the morning Sun. To the south he could see the townscape of San Jose, the southernmost tip of Silicon Valley and its only spot that felt like a proper city instead of a sleepy rural idyll. He came from Shenzhen, the hi-tech capital of Asia with its barrage of gleaming skyscrapers and vast industrial zone. The high-tech capital of the world instead had, for the most part, gotten rid of the hardware and dealt in transforming neuronal connections into zeros and ones. *Exporting, in other words, the dirty, messy act of physically making stuff to us, keeping just the Utopia for themselves.* Right below him, the greenery had been interrupted by the sprawling 2,200 acres of Moffett Federal Airfield. In 2014, Google had leased it for sixty years and soon rehabilitated the historic Hangar One, Two, and Three between the two large runways ending by the bay to house robotics, aviation, and space exploration projects. A Bay Area microcosm surrounded the airfield: Google headquarters, Amazon's R&D division, and Ames Research Center, one of NASA's major facilities.

The helicopter began a steep descent to Shackleton's center of operations. The long shadow of Hangar One gave away its soaring height in the otherwise two-dimensional bird's-eye view. It sure seemed an odd location pick: on top of the most expensive land in the US while barely being 350 miles from the aerospace hub and much cheaper real estate of Los Angeles.

Yi glimpsed the Googleplex to the left of the hangar, the search giant's headquarters, a set of buildings and structures under huge translucent canopies of geometries both imitating and defying nature, surrounded by profuse amounts of it.

Ø

Yi hurried to the massive east clamshell doors of Hangar One,[7] one of the world's largest free-standing structures. Larry Page and Sergey Brin, Google's co-founders, rented Hangar One from their company for the sole use of the mission. The reputational boon went a long way to save the mission, the large fund they set up for research and development went even further. Over 800 people were working there. Its floor, equivalent to six American football fields, was littered with cranes, improvised workstations, modular roofless offices, and ant-sized people moving around the facility. An empty section in the middle waited for the Shackleton spaceship, due to arrive in two months for an extended, wide-ranging retrofitting.

Ø

Two hours in, Yi had already mapped almost everyone in the packed room. While the conference was solely devoted to the laser communication system on board Shackleton, not only leading optics researchers were present, but major industrial players such as Facebook's fiber-optic communication division. *Of course. Who would miss it? This is cutting-edge applied science pushing the boundaries of laser technology. Everyone on the planet, certainly in this room, stands to benefit.* Even his boss, James, was unexpectedly seated by Yi's side, checking his computer.

Wireless communication comes in two flavors: radio waves via antenna or light via laser. Both are different energy levels of the same particle, the photon. Photons move through space as waves, and their energy level depends on the inverse relation between frequency and wavelength. Radio waves have low energy. Their low frequency means that once on Saturn, Shackleton would only be able to transfer about fifty megabytes, or three minutes of HD video, per hour. Yet it has been the almost exclusive form of outer space communication, and this is because it comes with a silver lining: the high wavelength means that when the wave arrives at Earth, it's already bigger than our planet, so it's relatively easy for it to be picked up by one of the giant antennas from NASA's Deep Space Network.

---

7   The hangar had been constructed in 1933 to lodge the biggest airship ever built in America, the zeppelin USS *Macon*, which rivaled the *Hindenburg* in size—the first destroyed in a sea storm out of Monterey Bay in 1935, the second infamously exploded while still in the air in 1937.

Light has much higher energy. Its high frequency allows data transfer around forty times greater, but the price to pay is a microscopic wavelength. It is thus the equivalent of going from firing a shotgun at point-blank range to firing a sniper rifle at a target on the Moon. The precision required for sending and intercepting lasers in outer space is stupefying.

Yi summarized in his mind what he saw as the two major issues.

The first was that even though outer space laser communication was already deployed, Saturn stood five times further away than the current technological limit. The consensus in the room was that no matter how much progress they made over the next two years, it wouldn't be enough. Shackleton would therefore carry both laser and antenna. The former would be the communication technology for as long as they possibly could, the latter after they couldn't.

The second was the injustice between uplinking data to versus downlinking data from Shackleton. *The Airbus fellow said it neatly, "Compared to the size of Earth's baseball glove, Shackleton's receiver would be tight on a Barbie."* Therefore, even at this meeting with a natural alignment of interests, the unspoken concerns differed. For the crew, the main anxiety was how to prolong the laser feed from Earth for as long as was technically feasible. For some of the rest, it was the other way around. For the former, how to delay the moment when their already thin communication with the rest of humanity would drop to a few voice and word messages per day; the moment they would be forced to encounter the overwhelming sound of silence. For the latter, how to postpone the instant when data recovery from Shackleton would cut to hardly anything, because if something catastrophic were to happen after this, most of the invaluable mission data would be lost forever.

Yi saw a man tap on James' shoulder and heard him whisper, "Jimmy, someone important is trying to reach you from Russia." James and Yi exchanged confused glances. The last time they had spoken to the Russian government had been five months ago and they had never heard back from them.

Ø

James was smiling profusely. "Come," he told Yi. Their walk toward the center of the hangar turned into a sprint.

Yi stopped behind James in the middle, the other inhaled and shouted at the top of his lungs, "Team … team … friends!" The sound reverberated like a male choir around the massive metal structure. Most sounds died down as people and machinery stopped. "I have bad news … for our detractors and slanderers, because against all odds ..." he waited for the echoes to die down, "Roscosmos is in!"

A mellow wave of awe and pride flooded Yi. *The press will trip over themselves on this one. This is incendiary material.* Yi could already read the headlines: "A New Sputnik Moment," "Russians at the Gate," "Russia Looks at the Sky While the West Looks at its Shoes." *Finally, a victory lap. It was about time.*

As he learned an hour later, the fine print made clear this wasn't charity. In exchange, Roscosmos had put forth two conditions.

First, Sergei Lazarev was to become the fifth crew member as Mission Pilot and Mechanical Engineer. Even Yi had heard of him. If he was a good fit with the rest of the crew, he couldn't think of anyone more ideal. "They don't make them like him anymore," James had said. Yi would have preferred for the artificial gravity wheel to have been made by Chinese or Western engineers, but having a Russian on board was a relief. *He'll probably be able to fix an engine with some baling wire, duct tape, and a few solid kicks.*

Second, moving Mission Control to Star City—the Russian space-training center near Moscow. This was unacceptable, yet nobody was overly worried about rejecting condition number two. With so much at stake for Russia, Yi knew they wouldn't kill the deal over that one point. The suspicion of many surfaced over the coming days from *The Wall Street Journal* to *The Times of India*—Russia's true motive was potential territorial rights in space. The Outer Space Treaty of 1967, signed by the Soviet Union, the United States, and most of the world save a few pockets in Africa and South America, specifically stated that "outer space, including the Moon and other celestial bodies, is not subject to national appropriation by claim of sovereignty, by means of use or occupation, or by any other means." But Russia could be unusually right-brained in matters of land, such as in 2007 when a robotic submarine put a flag on the seabed under the North Pole; the United States promptly answered, dismissing whether it planted "a metal flag, a rubber flag, or a bed sheet" as legally meaningless. But Yi had read that the Outer Space Treaty did have a loophole in that it was silent about individuals owning cosmic real estate. Russia's most probable strategy was playing catch-up, as the crew already had Chinese, American, and German members, and if anything changed regarding international law, *we could regress to the dictum of* terra nullius *or 'nobody's land,' where the earliest explorers would have a natural sovereign right. What no one but me knows is that China is about to get disqualified—I can no longer delay this. I'm presenting my resignation to Jimmy as crew member and asking to be reassigned as engineer in the robotics department. I belong to the masses, not to the few.*

Ø

A perplexed Yi scrutinized James' face, searching for hints giving away his anger or defeat. There were none. Instead, James smiled caringly at him.

"Yi, buddy, I understand what you're going through. Not because I'm compassionate but because I'm feeling the same—"

"Don't think I don't appreciate the camaraderie but I'm telling you, Jimmy, my case is different. You just saw me there. Fumbling in broken English, ending up sounding even more idiotic than in my own head. Meanwhile everyone else was precise, articulate … you, the three of you, are so impressive, so confident."

"Hey, stop right there. First, that was a pretty eloquent delivery. Second, we're all—Sophia, Derya, you, me—stretched beyond our abilities. And yes, the three of us are better than you … at acting. You think you're looking at three peaceful ducks floating on a pond, but if you were to look under the water, you would see us all paddling frantically."

"Jimmy, I'm even afraid of heights."

"So what? There's plenty of astronauts with a fear of heights. From the recent crop, from the famous ones, top of my head I can think of Mike 'Mass' Massimino—or, or Chris Hadfield, and Chris was a Canadian military test pilot! So, your excuse is rejected." Yi kept looking down, dispirited. "Okay, let me tell you a story," Jimmy continued. "Someone from the crew had a crisis two weeks ago, saying the same thing you're saying now, thinking he or she was the one mistake in an otherwise flawless recruiting process. 'I'll tell you a secret,' I said. 'Sell an American for what he thinks he's worth and buy him back for what he's actually worth. You'll make a killing.' One moral of the story is that it's easy to be bold on a stage before a crowd speaking your native tongue. Do not confuse appearance with essence."

Is he talking about Derya? Impossible, thought Yi.

"I know what you're thinking," said James. "But maybe it wasn't one of them. Maybe it was me."

13 | MISSION TRAINING

HOUSTON, TEXAS

"Power drill," Sergei commanded. Sophia rotated her face in his direction but only saw the solid inside of her spheroidal helmet. *Alligator head.* She extended her mockup spacesuit arm and grabbed the handrail of the International Space Station replica fuselage. Her sweaty, throbbing fingers could barely feel the contact through the puffed glove. She hauled her body against the water friction to face Sergei. Too late, he had already reached the tool previously hanging from her belt. *Houston, we have a problem. No, it's not Apollo 13. It's Sophia to report we have an asshole underwater.* Her pride was taking a beating after two hours paired with Sergei fixing a simulated leak. *And I thought we Americans were individualistic. Teamwork anybody?*

The two were submerged inside the Neutral Buoyancy Laboratory, a giant diving tank equivalent to ten Olympic swimming pools where astronauts trained for spacewalks. The facility was part of the Johnson Space Center about a mile away.

"Come on, Sweetie!" said Yi over her helmet speaker from the Simulation Control Room hanging above the tank, watching every movement along with James and Derya via nine underwater cameras. His cheerleading wasn't just ill-timed, but yet another lost-in-translation moment. Never mind, she really liked Yi.

"It's Tweety, Yi," said Derya. "Sweetie's a little too intimate at this stage. Don't blush, you'll get there eventually." Tweety, Sophia's nickname, had followed her from JPL, where her high-pitch laugh was renowned. She liked Derya all right, though he was too cynical for her taste.

She looked up at the half-dozen divers looking back at her among their myriad bubbles, silently floating in black wet suits, waiting to facilitate transitions during the exercise. At first, she felt proud of her learning curve, but that was two long hours ago. *I clearly don't have Jimmy's leadership inclination or skills, but man I'm a good sidekick. If you only tried,*

Sergei—someone else should get paired with Mr. Charm so they realize it's not just my mediocrity.

∅

The crane lifted Sophia's ninety-five-pound body cloistered inside 275 pounds of spacesuit and life support system out of the water tank. When two assistants removed the helmet, James saw none of her festive and carefree demeanor. *This says a lot.* James recalled when Sophia was still an Astronaut Candidate for the mission during the final week of physical and psychological tests. The tour-de-force claustrophobia assessment consisted of putting the candidate inside a coffin without telling them for how long they'd be held captive, while simultaneously monitoring their vital signs. Sophia unexpectedly fell asleep inside and when they opened it and she woke up, disoriented, she warbled incoherently, "Mango … I mean tango … I meant Fargo, you know, bodies inside the bags." *Already Tweety was Shack folklore.*

Avoiding the Sergei question for another minute, James thought about the next three weeks: the crew partially isolated, living and working 24/7 with each other. *All nicely wrapped in a tight-as-a-camel's-ass-in-a-sandstorm schedule.* Then back to their busy personas for two weeks before the cycle restarts—in his case this round included arguably the most significant event of his life.

Mission psychologists had settled on a five-week cycle, which they believed maximized team adaptation while minimizing the unavoidable stress and wear of living day-round in close quarters. The White House, James was still clueless as to why, coerced NASA to deny Shackleton's request to rent two of their facilities—the second one being the NASA Extreme Environment Mission Operations (NEEMO), a metallic shoebox sixty feet underwater off the coast of Key Largo, Florida, which the crew was to inhabit for two weeks in September—but then Paul Mercer, the NASA Administrator, secretly called James and they agreed to jack up the rental price to double the ongoing market rate, which made the denial politically impractical.

Okay, let's deal with this. Tomorrow I team up with Sergei. The rest of the crew would be watching and his condition as commander could weaken if he was unable to keep up. He was an astronaut, after all. No pretexts for underperforming. *But Sergei looks like a damn Bolshoi dancer dressed as Michelin Man.* His dexterity today was bordering supernatural. But more importantly, Sergei was playing solo virtuoso instead of ensemble, something James needed to address ASAP. *Just not today.* Infantile and unworthy of his position as it may be, he wouldn't tell the Russian until after their match. Having worked and lived with cosmonauts, James knew their hound's nose for spotting mental or physical weaknesses, an unforgivable sin. Resourcefulness, steely-mindedness, and physical prowess had always been their way to compensate for their technological lag. *I'll show you I'm no Beach Boys' Californian surfer softie.* The feeling of wanting to be respected was dusty from lack of use. Until today.

Ø

Five days later at their first touchy-feely group session, it was clear to Sophia that Yi and Sergei were perfectly out of their element. Even during the introduction by the psychologist moderating the session, Yi's face contorted like she was amputating a piece of him. There was no script: sit down for hours at a time, commit harakiri, and pour your soul out.

Sergei's turn came up. He didn't look intent on reciprocating to everyone else's prior emotional opening the kimono ritual.

"Sergei, do you want to say something?" said the tutor.

"No."

"If you want, maybe the group can ask you a few questions?" No reaction. "You're married. Any children?"

"No."

"What's your wife's name?"

"Iman."

Everyone's so shy all of a sudden. Let's spice this up an itsy-bitsy. "That's not a Russian name, is it?" asked Sophia.

"She's Syrian. We met during the war in 2017." Even rather disliking him, Sophia recognized that the hefty accent was made pleasant by his bass pitch.

"How old was she?" asked Sophia.

"19 … I was 27."

Let's burp this baby. "Come on, give it up. How did you two meet?" she continued, now genuinely interested.

He studied her, she stared back. After a pause, he breathed heavily. "Arriving at Aleppo from our air base, we were attacked by rebels. Two comrades were killed and a third lost his eyes and half his scalp … he grabbed his best friend and begged to be executed, instead our patrol vehicle broke out of the convoy for the nearest hospital. He died on the operating table. Walking back through the rows of beds and stretchers of people agonizing and dying,

I saw this girl sobbing quietly ... I couldn't not stop ... they told me she had lost her family the night before."

"Does she speak Russian?"

"Enough."

Does he mean to stop asking or is he answering? But this was emotional hardball, so Sophia poked again. "How is she going to cope in Russia with you being gone for six years?" Even Derya looked at her disapprovingly. Had she gone too far?

"She will go to live with her parents."

The truth landed hard on Sophia. When Sergei met Iman, she had just lost her husband and children. "I am so very sorry."

♉

Derya's hand unconsciously probed for the long-gone mane around his nape. It was the twenty-fourth parabola and this felt like Disneyland compared to the SEAL-like diving tank training of two days ago. *A roller coaster hanging from the clouds.* As a passenger who invariably woke up when an airplane experienced turbulence, looking through the window in dread of the wing snapping off, this had been illuminating. Turned out any jet commercial aircraft could become a Vomit Comet. Strip out everything from the cabin and cushion the fuselage inside. Ready.

The airplane was climbing the twenty seconds at a forty-five-degree angle—three times steeper than a passenger plane's take-off—so his body was glued by imaginary tape to a wall. *For once, "jeez!" Yi's new buzzword, to be used never less than once per sentence, is spot on.* In a second the 2-g gave way to 0-g and Derya's body was released from any force or pressure. The airplane had stopped climbing and was now languidly cruising for twenty-five seconds before bolting down the forty-five-degree angle of a ten-mile-long invisible hill to start again. *You don't truly understand slavery until you are freed.* The sensation was as fresh as that first time: there was no sense of falling; levitation meant the body, all of it, in and out, stomach, joints, skin, and muscles were instantly in a state of Zen.

Derya looked at a weightless James and Sergei. Hard not to be appreciative, being there purely in the name of team spirit. *If I was one of them, I would have found a way to skip this.* He then stared at Sophia picking her cute little nose. *A catwalk pose for the flashes.* She noticed.

"What? Only men can do it? We'll live together for six years, you better start treating me as an equal."

He smirked. "Go deeper for the full harvest—Uncle Newton one more time?" She nodded, grinning.

With their bodies hovering unattached to any surface, they extended the arms and used their index fingers to push against one another. They flew into opposite walls. Newton's Third Law: for every action, there's an equal and opposite reaction. In the frictionless world of zero gravity, even Sophia's minute body becomes Atlas' close relative.

♄

The group of about forty people were enjoying the summery sunset over drinks. The large clouds patching the sky reflected sunlight in purple tones, like neon lights in a Mediterranean nightclub. With no next-day homework other than to sleep until late, the ambience was chilled and the music loud.

Training's over. We disband tomorrow morning, thought Yi, while watching the rest of the crew. With three locations and seventeen different projects competing for their man-hours, it was unlikely they would see much of each other until they were back in Houston two weeks from now. Except for Sophia and James, who would fly out to London on the same flight. The former to attend her friend's wedding, the latter to marry said friend. Yi had met Belinda only once but it was enough to develop a crush on her. *There's nothing wrong with it. And anyway, it's absolutely one-sided.* Even he had a man-crush on James. *Who wouldn't?* The couple wasn't just Hollywood-looking: Belinda's credentials were also august, with hundreds of citations from her astrobiology papers. He gazed at the physical enormity of Sergei. *My father was big even by Scandinavian standards. I was supposed to have been raised on yak milk, instead I grew on watery rice at a boarding school.* He spotted a drunken Derya making a large group of people laugh. *Very un-German.* Sergei was silent as Derya was extroverted, but Yi felt he understood Sergei and still didn't know what to make of Derya. *He's so ridiculously smart, he may be solving differential equations in his head as he clowns around.* Maybe that was the issue: his deft mouth sometimes seemed to be operating independently from his head.

"Right there!" shouted Yi a few minutes later, pointing to the dying Sun after reconfirming with his phone app. Everyone turned and started squinting. A bright white star separated from the orange circle and climbed the darkening sky. The International Space Station whizzed by at 4.8 miles per second—New York to London in just twelve minutes—the speed needed to avoid falling back to Earth. At barely 350 feet in length while cruising 250 miles above the ground, spotting it using the naked eye was equivalent to making out the Statue of Liberty from Washington, D.C., a feat only possible in the early morning or late evening, when daylight didn't overwhelm the tiny blob glowing in the sunrays.

In two minutes, the ISS had vanished into the east, but its wake stayed with Yi. *The last outpost of humanity, which Shackleton will visit before the longest, most outrageous voyage ever attempted.*

14 | WEDDING

A week later, May 2026, 383 days before launch

LONDON, UK

The round-the-clock hum of Kensington High Street, not 200 feet away, became subdued as the wedding guests walked through the cloistered entrance of St. Mary Abbots church. Centuries permeated the Gothic building: the intricate ribbed vaulting high above the nave, the tall pointed arcade arches, the ornate multicolored Catherine window crowning five stained-glass windows filtering the outside light into a diaphanous palette of oranges, purples, and reds that painted the altar below.

※

"—she then tells me about this American prince and Jimmy, I won't lie, I frowned some more," Belinda's father was giving a speech to the about-to-be-married twosome and the couple of hundred seated guests. "Irish, Scottish, American, all perfectly good mates but—look, I relish wind turbines and what they stand for, just not on my lawn. Then I pondered and pondered some more. See that look on her face? Never saw that. Until she met you … as I am about to give away the most precious thing I have, I'm sure you'll excuse me for attaching a few strings. We Englishmen have ventured through uncharted seas across the ages, but yours is infinitely wider. That's a degree of boldness nobody can possibly relate to. Your price to embark on this crusade in the name of exploration is a pledge: promise me you'll come back. Promise me you two will grow old together."

An exultant Belinda looked at James in surprise. "Better late than never," she whispered. Thomas Addington had been unapologetically against their union, yet here, for the first time, he seemed to be not only approving the marriage but blessing the lengthy wait. Overjoyed as he was, James couldn't forget his conversation over the phone with Thomas a week before: no children until he came back to Earth.

"I promise."

15 | THE SPACESUIT

Four months later, September 2026, 272 days before launch

HANGAR ONE, MOUNTAIN VIEW

The spacesuit meeting had been heating up in the breakout room. With four plywood walls and no roof for dozens and dozens of feet before the hangar ceiling, it looked like a stage set apartment in a college theater play. There were eleven increasingly agitated engineers, three belittled managers from the spacesuit contractor, and Sergei. He was the only crew representative, a measure of how many loose ends the mission still needed to gather.

∅

To understand spacesuit requirements, it is necessary to understand the reality of death for an unprotected human body exposed to the vacuum of space. Reality is less gory than fiction, but equally gloomy. Instead of exploding pufferfish-style, human flesh doubles its size, a Schwarzeneggerization of sorts. Suddenly doubling internal tissues means everything, from muscles to blood vessels, ripping apart. So, death is certain, just unfortunately not instantaneous. Another misconception is blood boiling, which does not happen because our skin is impervious to a vacuum, meaning the blood remains pressurized within the body. Snap freezing by exposure to hundreds of degrees below zero won't happen either, because outer space is devoid of matter so there is no way to rapidly transfer heat out of the body, only crawling thermal radiation. Instead, death will come from unspectacular oxygen deprivation. Any air instantly escapes the lungs and respiratory tract; thirty seconds after that, the person blacks out; five to seven minutes later, there's irreversible brain damage; and complete brain death comes within fifteen minutes. R.I.P.

Therefore, the spacesuit essentials are maintaining the internal pressure, supplying oxygen, carbon dioxide removal, temperature regulation, and mobility. Nice add-ins are the collection of solid and liquid waste, protection against micrometeorites, and shielding against ultraviolet radiation.

Before this mission, the conservative answer was the Michelin Man marsh-mallow principle of inflating a stiff spacesuit to compensate for the vacuum. However, this comes with two fat side-effects: ungainly weight and poor mobility.

There is another approach that was developed by NASA and the US Air Force in the 50s and 60s but which has never before been implemented. This is the skintight suit concept, where the mechanical pressure against the skin prevents the swelling of the human body. A much simpler temperature regulation system is thrown in for free: body perspiration removal via breathing through the spacesuit. Instead of looking like Neil Armstrong on the Moon, you end up looking like Lance Armstrong on Earth.

♄

Two of the engineers buckled from frustration and broke into recriminations, cursing the bravado decision of two years ago when the golden rule of aerospace engineering was ignored: do not innovate unless you must. They didn't need to, yet they chose to.

The spacesuit was operating fine. A descendant from an MIT prototype that had been worked on since 2005, it was a materials science masterpiece. Light, tough, safer than a traditional suit. All thumbs up. But complex engineering has a tendency to progress by way of balloon squeezing. An improvement here may knock off a working part here or there.

The crisis triggered two days before, when an astronaut doing a spacewalk for final spacesuit certification experienced, in his words, "My grandma's final-stage cataracts." The visor fogged up and vision was seriously impaired. The problem was time, or lack thereof.

"I know this is taboo around here but I'm going to say it anyway. What if we procure standard spacesuits as spares?" offered the less mousy of the contractors.

Only one engineer bothered to answer. "The Payload Team has over-optimized to save a tenth of an ounce on each of five spoons, and you want to send them 1,500 pounds … of spares? Good luck knocking on that door."

Sergei, mute until now, said, "Read that?" pointing to a large sign that was disseminated around the hangar.

"No Band-Aids Before Mission Launch."

16 | NO MORE TIME

Two months later, November 2026, 208 days before launch

PACIFIC HEIGHTS, SAN FRANCISCO

The two old friends were on a rooftop with a panoramic view of the hilly San Francisco, a city outlining the future yet architecturally dwelling in a quaint, early-20th-century style. It was sunny but the wind was prickly. *That explains Leonard's goosebumps,* James wanted to think.

"Are you asking me as a friend?" said Leonard.

"I'm asking you as a mentor." *I'm asking you as the father I wish I had.* Their relationship went back a decade. On his third summer in college James had taken an internship at Blue Origin, the famed rocket company. One day at dawn, as Leonard was leaving—the perennial bachelor had always been a workaholic and night owl—he spotted James curled up crying under a desk. In his apartment the previous night, James had found his visiting father among empty bottles, pointing a pistol in his mouth. When he noticed his son he said, "Are you ashamed of me, you little bastard? Am I not good enough?" He aimed his wobbling arm at James, cocking the gun. "Think you're so special, uh? Our genes are corrupted, girly. No matter what, you'll end up a drunkard like me—maybe I can shoot you now and spare you the misery." That morning James moved in with Leonard and did not see his father again for years.

Leonard rested against a wall. The relaxed stance contrasted with his serious demeanor. He finished yet another cigarette, mashing it out against the brickwork—he had given up his pipe a few doctor appointments back.

"An additional year. Maybe nine months if we are willing to take measured risks." Leonard had been appointed as member to the Shackleton's board of directors, giving him an exceptional vantage point over the mission status. "There are still too many unknowns. Interfaces that could go wrong—worse yet, we don't know which ones. You can't cover the Sun with a finger, Jimmy. The mission needs more time."

"We can't."

"No, it's you that can't force the current schedule on an engineering undertaking of this magnitude. The project is inanimate, it doesn't give a damn about aggressive deadlines. We're not ready."

"Are you finished?"

"No, I'm not. That was Leonard the mentor. Now comes Leonard the friend." He picked a folded paper from the pocket of his customary garment, an embroidered olive shirt. *"An ugly fading piece of history" as he calls it*. The 'ugly' was James' addition. Jerry Garcia had thrown the pulpy shirt into the crowd during a Grateful Dead concert sometime in the 70s. Leonard put on a pair of glasses missing an arm. "'For a successful technology, reality must take precedence over public relations, for nature cannot be fooled.' You know who said that?"

"Yes."

"Richard Feynman, one of the greatest physicists of the 20th century. You know when he said it?"

"Yes."

"As his conclusion on the causes of the Challenger disaster. NASA management's estimates were wildly over-optimistic, differing by tens of times from those of the engineers doing the actual work—do you hear that?"

"Hear what?"

"The haunting echo from the past."

"You know the rules, Leonard—you taught them to me. This is orbital mechanics. If we don't launch this June, the window closes until the following year." Every twenty-six months, the orbits of Earth and Mars put the planets at one quarter their average distance—this creates an optimal launch window to the red planet. It illustrates a critical piece of space traveling: timing. Planets are constantly transitioning. Earth and Saturn complete an orbit around the Sun every 365 days and twenty-nine Earth years, respectively. The optimal launch window happens during a month every few decades, and that was June 2027.

James never smoked, but this time he accepted Leonard's new king-size for a couple of puffs. They long remained quiet, watching the glittering bay.

"There's a thousand hawks waiting for a misstep to rip us apart, including the root of many of our evils, America's honcho," said James. "Meanwhile, Saturn doesn't wait, we postpone to the following year and the mission stretches to seven and a half years … there's no runway left. If we delay, it's not just possible but probable that all we have done crumbles into dust. Don't think I'm being gung-ho, I have regular nightmares about the one hundred ways we could die. But there's no backing down now. We launch this June. And whenever the idea of delaying creeps into your mind, I want you to remember this: I am already homesick from an expedition that hasn't yet started. Each day we postpone, my return gets more distant."

∅

James couldn't fall asleep that night, haunted by a different echo from the past, a memory set to the soundtrack of David Bowie's "Starman." It had happened a few weeks prior on a promotional visit to New York with Belinda.

Hordes flooded the Lincoln Center Plaza in front of The Met, symphony hall, and New York City Ballet buildings. The crowds were mostly children, thousands of them.

A few hundred steps from accessing The Met entrance someone screamed, "It's Jimmy and Belinda!" Like a circling crowd in Mecca, they were quickly surrounded by screaming kids trying to shake their hands, get autographs, take pictures.

Later inside, "From the Metropolitan Opera House in New York City, and beaming out across all of space and time, this is StarTalk, where science and pop culture collide."

For the next hour the children's avid, inquisitive minds explored everything from space to religion to family to aspirations to climate change to Pixar movies. "Can we sign the hull of Shackleton?" (yes, but); "You should make a free astronaut university for people that are really really good but can't pay, like my brother" (maybe once I come back); "Why aren't you bringing a pet?" (we are, it's a bonsai tree); "Why aren't more women in the crew?" (ouch); "Is it possible for someone like me to name the moonlets that Shackleton will discover in the Saturn rings?" (let's do it).

"Finally, we talked over the phone," said the host. "They had an urgent request. No, they demanded my help. It wasn't easy. They required special permits. A charter plane. Heck, they even required security clearance at La Guardia to get here on time. Hailing from Washington State to Florida, from El Paso to Detroit, from small towns to metropolises, Jimmy, allow me to introduce … the Shackleton Cadets."

From the center rows a few letters back, a group of about fifty got up and walked to the stage through both middle aisles. They were not older than 10 or 12. They all wore blue flight suits. Most of them were bald from the side-effects of chemotherapy. As they got on stage, the first one, smaller and bony, picked up the mic.

He proudly recited from memory in a raspy voice, "Dear Jimmy, we're neither big enough nor old enough, but because of circumstances we are born warriors. There are a lot of us around the country, some going through tough times. When that started a few years ago in my case, my body sort of betrayed me and it was really hard sometimes. But your mission—I mean you, Belinda, and all the others, gave people like me a reason to continue fighting, so we can one day be explorers like you, going to Saturn and to other places ... so as our aspiration and inspiration, we did a big big and successful campaign in all of the country and got a lot lot of money, which we want to give you to finance the Shackleton mission."

James was unable to speak. He kneeled in front of the boy and after receiving the yellow envelope, hugged a body even thinner than it looked. *I will make you proud*, he kept thinking.

Back to the present, any temptation to postpone had died out in James' mind. They were launching on June 17 2027.

17 | GOING NUKE

Two months later, February 2027, 125 days before launch

CAMP CENTURY, GREENLAND

I t was the third daylight after 101 days of darkness. Frigid -8 Fahrenheit at 1:53 PM made this a mild Arctic winter day, but the timid Sun that arose by 11:30 AM and had rolled atop the horizon would be offstage within minutes.

A dozen people moved between the five big yellow dome tents comprising the base camp. Two others carefully removed ice from the aircraft propellers—the sole way of returning to Thule Air Base in two weeks, maybe ten days if today's digging pace continued—but stopped to peer into the distance.

A lone figure, faded by the whistling white wind and low light, was returning from the drilling site half a mile away. It could have been a polar bear, except there were no animals so far inland. A few hundred feet before reaching the camp, the Russian climbed the metal staircase of a dark cylinder protruding from the ice, opened a hatch, and disappeared inside. Up to the 1980s, the Americans in the group would have been gravely suspicious: the hatch gave access to the remains of the underground city of Camp Century, built at the apex of the Cold War.

∅

After a long ladder down, Sergei landed in a wide, flat area carved into the ice. There was barely enough light coming from cracks and crevasses to sense the broad emptiness. He turned on a flashlight. This had been a 200-man US Army underground base, spread throughout twenty-one tunnels, including a library, hospital, club, theater, chapel, and the reason for coming here, the nuclear reactor room.

Like all of the best stories from the Cold War, reality outclassed fiction. Northern latitudes acquired critical status by being the shortest path for missiles between the Soviet Union and the US. In 1959, when the nuclear chessboard was verging on checkmate, Camp Century was conceived as the key top-secret location, carved under the ice, for the American nuclear retaliation strategy, consisting of the obliteration of the Soviet Union and everyone within. It was intended to be a grid of 2,500 miles of tunnels hiding 600 mobile launching pads for the Iceman, the intercontinental nuclear missile that would climb high into the atmosphere before dropping all over Russia.

Walking forward, he encountered a collapsed roof of ice blocking the path. There was a narrow slit through which his big body struggled to fit. On the other side, the space felt even more spacious. A thunderous cracking of the ice sent echoes that came back trebled. The tunnel must have been enormous. Further on, Sergei tripped on one of the metal beams of a railroad, twisted like Play-Doh and its supporting timber splintered like a toothpick. The icecap was alive, and this was the reason for the demise of Camp Century six decades before. The military base engineers soon realized the glacier was moving much faster than anticipated, solid water in slow motion. In a matter of months, the tunnels deformed and bulged. In a matter of years, the underground city was evacuated permanently.

∅

Schadenfreude, thought Derya, from the relative warmth and comfort of the kitchen dome tent. Someone's misfortune was another one's prosperity: the base's electricity and heating had been supplied by an on-site nuclear reactor fed with enriched uranium-235. When it was abandoned in 1967, the radioactive waste was left untouched under the assumption that it would remain entombed in perpetuity. But climate change had other plans and the rapid melting of the Greenland ice sheet would soon leave the toxic waste exposed to the elements. Additionally, the ice sheet right under Derya was 7,000 feet thick. These two complementing reasons had brought the sixteen-person team led by Sergei to the end of the world to test and train Waltzy Mole.

"Shouldn't we wait for the boss?" asked the glaciologist-turned-night-cook while stirring a big pot of goulash.

Everyone's so infatuated with the Russian—and by the way, I'm also your boss. "You don't know him, he could take another hour," said Derya, besotted with the stew's steamy aroma. The wind-turned-gale drumming the nylon walls amplified the craving. Nobody knew why Sergei invariably arrived late and last, but Derya thought it obvious. *It's the shame.*

Among the multiple mission objectives, exploring Saturn's sixth biggest moon, icy Enceladus, was at the expedition's soul. Sergei and Derya were slated to land there, but miles of ultra-hard ice stood between the surface and its mysterious subsurface global ocean, possibly bigger than Earth's largest, the Pacific. Meet Waltzy Mole, a torpedo-shaped cryobot with a scorching nose that melts the ice in front of it and sinks downward via gravity.

The use of Camp Century for testing was highly debated and politicized because the cryobot's fuel source was nuclear.[8] Greenland and Denmark were

---

8   As a human being, Derya understood society's reticence with nuclear power: a promise of hope that had instead shown a penchant to "become Death, the destroyer of worlds." But as a physicist and crew member, he knew nuclear power was not optional. It was inescapable.

    The Mole could not be solar powered because Saturn stood about ten times further from the Sun than the Earth, which left the ugly bunch: chemical or nuclear energy. But in a mission where weight was the principal restriction, $E=mc^2$ settled the score.

    The most powerful formula in physics is also its biggest Swiss Army knife. This equation explains, with staggering precision confirmed over a century of empirical experiments, many of the fundamental laws of the Universe. For the purposes of the mission, these five characters establish that matter is energy, and an immense amount of it.

    A gallon of gasoline has intrinsic energy equivalent to 2,500 times the energy released by both Little Boy over Hiroshima and Fat Man over Nagasaki.

    A gallon of gasoline, if we were able to extract all its energy, could power every land vehicle and airplane in the United States for forty hours. Yet a gallon of gasoline lasts less than an hour in a single car on a highway.

    That's the problem with chemical energy. It is a miserable, pathetic, puny energy transformation. Nuclear energy is millions of times more efficient, yet it barely uses 0.1 percent of the intrinsic energy of matter. Still, that's the best we have so far.

    The civilians' squeamishness about nuclear power was perfectly ignored by the military: the first nuclear-powered submarine, USS *Nautilus*, was put to sea in 1954. At present, there are over one hundred submarines and aircraft carriers running on nuclear reactors. The safety record of the US nuclear navy is flawless, and nuclear power's advantages are hard to overstate: a +100-crew nuclear submarine runs on a single lump of uranium-235 for two decades, and not just for propulsion but for its electricity, heating, air, and water.

    A few things stopped a parallel nuclear technology progression in space. While society has more or less tolerated nuclear power in land and sea, the sky has always been off-limits. This was sealed with the Outer Space Treaty of 1967, which barred weapons of mass destruction in space—and nuclear power reactors in overdrive become bombs. Additionally, propulsion in space is much harder: attach a propeller to a boat, car, or an airplane and expect forward motion; attach one to a spacecraft and it becomes a cute, ineffective infant mobile—there's nothing to push against in the vacuum of space.

    Not only would the Mole run on uranium-235, Shackleton's electricity supply and heating would come from a tiny ten-kilowatt nuclear reactor: twelve feet long, a two-ton cylinder with a fifty-pound core four inches in diameter. It had been developed and tested by NASA, the US Department of Energy, and the Los Alamos National Lab during the 2010s as the adamantly against it but finally caved, considering no drilling testing meant no mission, and the location was already no man's land—a nuclear waste cemetery. Others were less conceding: while the team was still at Thule Air Base on Greenland's coast, Greenpeace attempted a night raid with a helicopter to seize critical equipment. After the venture failed, an enraged Sergei forced the two pilots out and battered them while activists broadcasted the beating live. That was already awful PR, but it paled with what came next: a picture in newspapers the world over of a woman falling mid-air into the snow, eyes shut and mouth open, after a face smacking from a sky-high Sergei. *In black and white, to make it extra Cold War—what came right before, namely her kicking him in the nuts after minutes of verbally abusing him, went oddly undocumented.* The easy thing, the reasonable thing, would have been for James to condemn Sergei publicly and support him privately, but that seemed to have fallen outside Jimmy's unwavering principles. *Instead, he stupidly backed Sergei, which cost the mission a very great many brownie points—today we celebrate Shackleton's all-time-low public approval, Sergei's gallant courtesy to the mission, and his most important legacy to date.*

∅

"So, it's 1991 and this European satellite spots one of the largest freshwater lakes in the entire world, more than two miles beneath the Vostok Russian station in Antarctica," said Andrew, a geophysicist, to the lively kitchen tent audience. *That's the place with the lowest temperature ever recorded on Earth, -130 degrees Fahrenheit—Enceladus at noon will be -320 degrees, that's awfully close from absolute zero, the lowest temperature in the Universe,* the shivering idea flashed through Derya's mind. "Further study showed that the lake had been sealed off for millions of years, possibly since Antarctica was tropical and connected to Australia. This was a huge deal because it could mean a museum of living things that had evolved independently from the rest of the planet. The Russians started drilling in 1998, while the worldwide scientific community pleaded for, uh, what's the word?"

---

kilopower initiative for the long-duration crewed missions of the future. *We are the future,* thought Derya. *The wonder of open-source, publicly funded research.*

To allay concerns, both the reactor and the Mole would be launched cold—the former would be turned on far away from Earth, the latter once it landed in Enceladus—which guaranteed no fallout even in the case of an accident at launch.

"Moratorium?" someone suggested.

"Yes, a moratorium," Andrew continued, "until technological advances could ensure exploration without contamination. They stopped a few hundred feet above the lake. Then 2005 arrives, and the Cassini probe orbiting Saturn finds out of left field geysers of water coming out of Enceladus, which soon led to the sensational discovery of an enormous ocean beneath its icy surface ..."

The resemblance is uncanny, thought Derya. Both the lake and Enceladus' ocean remained liquid by being isolated from the exterior and by having a geothermal heat source coming from the seafloor. Both were in complete darkness.

"But hubris entered Lake Vostok—" A cloud of snow and a clout of cold entered the dome tent, along with a snorting Sergei, his thick blond beard covered in icicles. He grabbed a large bowl handed to him—*Papa Bear's porridge. Everyone keeps practicing their rimming technique on the Russian yeti's ass.*

"Continue. Being Russian doesn't make me an accomplice of such stupidity," said Sergei while loading up on goulash.

"Yeah. Well," said Andrew coyly, "in 2012 the, um—"

"Russians," said Sergei.

"—continued drilling and pierced the lake, contaminating it with Freon, kerosene, and bacteria present on the drills. No scientists outside Russia were allowed to examine the water collected before the borehole naturally refroze ..."

"There is a silver lining beyond the desecration," said Derya, anxious for some protagonism. "If Lake Vostok could preserve life, Enceladus almost certainly has the necessary conditions as well. It not only has organic molecules, and water, and energy—the stuff of life-as-we-know-it—but it has an equally important fourth dimension: time. The moon's giant ocean has probably remained liquid uninterrupted for billions of years. I bet Lake Vostok's life forms would thrive in Enceladus ... the remaining and crucial question is whether the moon has been able to incubate life to begin with."

18 | CONCLΛVE DΛY

MOUNTAIN VIEW, CALIFORNIA

The managers of all mission areas, along with the crew, were about to spend the day reviewing every aspect of the expedition. The quarterly gathering turned monthly once the launch countdown crossed the one-year threshold. The forty or so people were inside a high-security soundproof pavilion at X, Alphabet's research and development facility, a mile from Hangar One.

A serious-looking man of around 50 headed the session. He hid his considerable waistline under a Hawaiian shirt. His tablet showed a list of twenty-seven areas for the first, summary pass; eight were already crossed out.

"Tom, status on water recycling." Shackleton's onboard system for water re-use. Every drop counts. Breathing, sweating, showering, peeing, and number two go into a filtration process to become potable. Yesterday's sweat is today's coffee. The International Space Station started in 2008 and by now had reached 94 percent efficiency. The mission needed to do much better. 'Much' is always a relative term: climbing to 97 percent meant a 50 percent decrease in losses.

"Yesterday's readout was 96.3 percent," answered Tom.

The emcee looked at Tom through the glasses resting at the end of his hefty nose. "Pretty darn distant from your team's 97 percent commitment."

"We still have a month and a half."

"You have improved 0.2 percent from last time. I don't see how you can close the gap."

"I hate finger-pointing, but it's all interrelated, right. The food is not yet fully optimized. It is still creating too much solid waste. Trust me, it's hard to squeeze drinkable water out of shit."

"Bookmark for Lana's team ... Lana, you're number seventeen ... next, 3D printing. Sadie?" A mission of this complexity was only possible with this technology, and not just because a significant portion of Shackleton was 3D printed. It was about the failures that would inevitably happen and how to correct them.

In a game where payload weight and volume management were invaluable, bringing spares for all essentials was impossible.

"From Shackleton's 239,517 components, 7,981 are Mission Critical," by which Sadie meant indispensable. "As of yesterday, 87 percent of these can be 3D printed." Her team was large, working around the clock to create substitutes for unprintable components that could, without having ideal specifications, work as acceptable replacements. The work meant transforming physical spares into digital blueprints. Every time a bulky spare was cracked into code and thus avoided as cargo, an excited engineer ran to the Payload Team to break the news.

There was a long list of non-necessities ranked by importance waiting to earn a spot on board. Strange things could happen in space, such as a new meaning to the concept of luxury items. The previous day had seen the boarding authorization for seven Little Caesars classic pepperoni pizzas and twelve portions of Yi's newfound obsession, Mac n' Cheetos, especially engineered for the mission by Burger King. These didn't come cheap, for sponsors.

"How much additional weight can we expect to shave?"

"The low- and mid-hanging fruits are gone ... anything from 200 to maybe 500 pounds. I acknowledge this is quite a downgrade. We over-promised, we'll under-deliver."

Jason from Payload was vocally unhappy.

"Jason, save the comments for your turn. You come ... twenty-fifth. Next is my undying nightmare. Sergei?" Roscosmos had been ironclad about doing 100 percent of the design, construction, and testing of artificial gravity in Russia, by Russians. The rotating wheel prototype was delivered to the ISS as an additional module in the Russian segment in a record nine months, and since then had been inhabited during nighttime, finally proving what was hypothesized and debated for decades. Around 40 percent gravity during sleeping hours, in addition to physical training, seemed to be enough to eliminate the harmful effects of weightlessness. Sergei was the point of contact.

"The magnetic bearing is working nominally." This was where the wheel rotated. It took a lot of convincing for Roscosmos to replace a mechanical ball bearing with a magnetic one. The latter was in fact a magnetic levitation that avoided physical contact between moving parts, producing negligible friction and no wear. Leaks revealed expenses having climbed north of $2 billion, a very tall order for something with direct costs of a few million—but that's what space does to budgets. "No maintenance needed, single piece, 7 percent lighter than expected. Disassembling not possible." Sergei preemptively answered the question in everyone's mind—what if it failed? "Simplicity is the ultimate sophistication." That would have to do.

"Very Russian," replied the emcee.

Seven hours later, the room was still crowded but in absolute silence, except for the emcee and Nitha.

Nitha Sharma had become the mission's head in December when James handed over the role. Some had extrapolated her minute frame to her character, but never more than once. She was breaking tradition in more ways than one. She was a she for a start. She was also very young at 36. She was a foreigner who had come to the US for undergrad. She would also become, beginning at launch, the Flight Director 'FLIGHT' and Capsule Communicator 'CAPCOM.' She wasn't an astronaut, the historic requirement for CAPCOM, the individual who does all communication with the crew. The buzz cut, in other words, had been replaced by a bob cut.

"I never endorsed Cape Canaveral for the launch and you know it. I'm no Lone Ranger here—goddammit, Nitha, it will be hurricane season. We are risking everything for a show," said the emcee.

"Eddy, we are both engineers, but I'm also the mission manager. Not everything is about facts and data. Individuals like you and me financed all of this, and you're right, they count on a spectacle at launch. I don't blame them—and if you want facts and data, Cape Canaveral has only flooded twice since the 1950s. Besides, the launch location was finalized over a year ago."

"That's very faulty logic. Yeah, after getting heads for fifty-eight straight years I do see why people should be forgiven for thinking it's destiny and not luck. But Cape Canaveral did finally get flooded in 2021 and then once again just two years ago. Well, you say, the exception proves the rule. A lot of us disagree. It's not that the era of reckoning has come. It's been here all along. There were close calls before, and now climate change makes the odds much higher—I spoke with the SpaceX folks at Boca Chica on Tuesday. We still have time to clear the paperwork and prepare the pad for a Texas launch. The barge carrying Shackleton doesn't leave California for another two months."

"I deeply respect your point of view and I know you're not the only one. I'm happy to discuss this at length, but not here and not now. This has already been a long and stressful day," said Nitha.

"I will never understand people with fancy MBA degrees like you. Putting the mission at risk so you can appease the crowds?"

"First, it's not 'my' solution. My vote counted for 2 percent of the total, so not quite my definition of swaying the polls. Second, what is this patrician 'for the people but without the people' talk? We *are* the people."

19 | THE EGGERS

A month later, April 2027, 61 days before launch

REGENT'S PARK, LONDON

his being London, the perfectly sunny spring day is one rare blessing, thought James. Belinda said it had been a soggy year and it showed: an army of people flocked the parks, restaurants, streets, and pubs. *The joie de vivre is infectious—and sporadic.* A flickering exhilaration that suddenly darkened into a desolate melancholy. Every minute with Belinda boomed with the tick-tock of countdown.

James' awareness of the surroundings was always heightened in London because there were big rewards in doing so. *Like the blue "Isaac Newton Lived Here" plaque at 87 Jermyn Street this morning.* And with launch now imminent, everything hit him. The fresh morning air, the trees' green hues, the perennial city hum, the architecture, the history of it all, but above all else, Belinda and her bulging cargo. *Which I won't meet for six years*—he neutralized the thought by concentrating on his phone's screen. It was already midday. The peace of his last week in London was almost over. They would leave for the US on Monday and he would not return for years.

They stopped by the gentle topography of Primrose Hill, which looked like a tilted Monaco summer beach day, full of people light on clothing lying on towels on top of the grass, talking, drinking, forcing a lobster tan. James admired the postcard in front: the Shard, the BT Tower, the London Eye wheel against a backdrop of clouds hanging from a deep blue sky; a few old church spires mid-plane; and the ageless woods below—the elms, cypresses, beeches, cedars.

"I've always wondered how nature could achieve such perfection with English forests. Look down there, they seem almost fake," said James.

Belinda turned to look. Her eyes were watery. He pretended not to have noticed. "A Londoner knows better, love. The highest form ... of landscaping ... is the art of hiding intention behind natural looks," her words wobbled with repressed sobbing.

Acknowledge the crying! "Those blue eyes are like the wide ocean. I could swim into them and never come back." She started weeping.

That didn't come out right.

Ø

You will leave us and disappear beyond the darkest of oceans, Belinda thought. "It's the hormones, Jimmy, I cry out of nowhere—I'm feeling a bit nauseous, can we find a spot and sit down?" *I need to control myself in front of him. It erodes his will.* During the bad moments over the past year, she had seen him waking up only by a sheer sense of duty, a boxer desperately dodging the knockout after too many rounds. It was a great deal better now that the mission no longer hinged on him. He was a plain astronaut awaiting lift-off.

James rested his palm on Belinda's tummy. "I'll come home to my family. Late, but I'll come back."

Our 4-month-old Peanut will be 6 years old when you do, she thought. But the promise surprisingly calmed her, blurring the future and sharpening the present.

They zigzagged around the hillside, sidestepping towels and people, looking for a spot. Belinda saw that a few had recognized them, pointing subtly behind them. She loved that about her city. There were plenty of celebrities and most could carry on with their lives in relative peace if only by a well-kept illusion of anonymity. There was a tacit respect, an understanding of privacy. New York two weeks before was the polar opposite: people asking for pictures and autographs on every corner, Chinese tourist groups literally following them, reporters jumping out in front, construction workers screaming from across the street. *Absolutely unnerving. We never—*

"I'm awfully sorry to interrupt," a distinguished lady with graying sides was standing behind them, "I'm Laura."

"A pleasure to meet you, Laura," said James, always friendly.

"So very sorry, but I just couldn't let this go. My late husband was a propulsion engineer at Rolls-Royce. In his last year your mission gave him immense joy. Whenever you appeared in an interview, he would turn into the same 26-year-old I met. I wish he was here to tell you …"

Out of the corner of Belinda's eye, people started to look up.

"You are humanity's treasure. You unite people from all walks of life, from all over the world, around the mission. You've already made a change."

Their cover was blown. For the next two hours, from kids to parents using their kids, people came over to greet them.

They later walked along Regent's Park Road, enjoying the beautiful late-19th-century buildings painted in pastel colors on the left-hand side and exposed red bricks on the other. They passed shops with their multicolor awnings, bakeries, red telephone boxes, tall oaks, until they arrived at Lemonia, a family-run Greek restaurant. A thrilled waiter served them tzatziki, tarama, papoutsakia, keftedes, fish shashlik, 3,000 years of Mediterranean culinary tradition. *His next six years will consist mostly of serving variations of tofu-like food. Even airplane meals will be a treat.*

Belinda again caught James with the 1,000-yard stare. "Jimmy," she said. He smiled back, guiltily as charged. *I need to care for and caress him. Prepare him to leave me.* The next two months would be a marathon and he would be under great stress. *The problem is that everyone expects Jimmy to be Jimmy, an Orpheus capable of going to the underworld and back.* But what made James her hero was that, contrary to what most people thought, he always studied harder, trained harder, pushed harder than anyone else. *It's just that after half a lifetime doing that, it starts looking fluid and carefree.*

20 | DERYA TERZI

BAMBERG, GERMANY

Derya checked the wall clock once again. The first occasion—fifteen minutes after the agreed meeting hour—he had glanced subtly at the clock, just in case Karl entered Schlenkerla tavern at that exact moment. He didn't want to seem too eager, but that had been a while back.

Karl had always been very *pünktlich*. It was usually Derya running late. *Maybe something happened at the hospital, and maybe he forgot his phone—that's two maybes too many.* He looked through the ornamented windows. It was already dark outside. The waiter came by a little unsure, half guessing what was happening. Derya asked for another Rauchbier, surely the best smoked beer in the world. *Screw it, this isn't happening anyway,* so he added three bratwurst with onions to his order.

Disrespectful prima donna. He was a weak, bland partner anyway. All dispelled the moment the door opened and he entered ... no, wrong mate. He tried to calm down by looking around. It was a busy Saturday night; everyone seemed to be having a party. The tavern was medieval, with the first documented owner setting up shop in 1405, as it was prominently pointed out on the menu. It showed. The ceiling was low, with dark, thick wooden beams crossing width and lengthwise, allegedly painted with ox blood. The hanging lamps also seemed stolen from an older era. The walls were plastered, but the renovation maintained the aesthetic.

This was supposed to be a fine evening, *maybe the time to forgive and, who knows, even start again.* He asked for the check, drained, disheartened, and sad. He would leave Germany earlier than planned. No point in staying there.

It was drizzling outside. He took Dominikanerstraße, walking over its slick cobblestones. The passageway was empty. It could have been the year 1600 and everything would have looked the same. On the intersection, he stared to his left at Bamberg Cathedral and decided to walk by for old times' sake.

The Twilight Zone sensation persisted. Built and essentially unchanged for

800 years, it predated the Gothic style—the monumental fashion from the high and late medieval period. Yet its four 250-foot-tall towers gave it an imposing, if more subdued, demeanor.

Derya walked back to the hotel via a long roundabout path by the river, where everything was quiet and peaceful. He fought between feelings of indignation and pensive sadness. *I'm going to the end of the Solar System and you didn't have the decency to try to mend things. That's no way to end up after so many years.*

He stopped in his tracks. Out of Kropf, an upscale restaurant, a male couple came out embracing and laughing. He instantly recognized the tall frame, broad shoulders, and blond hair. His legs weakened. And then something inside escalated as he crossed the street. Next thing he knew, there were recriminations, screaming, crying, and he fell to the ground. Somebody helped him stand up. His chin and his right ear felt swollen.

The queer shit had stood him up on purpose. *You're a nobody. To hell with all this. I'm going to Saturn, you'll have your whole life to regret—I'm ready to go, I'm leaving little behind.*

21 | YI MENG

MIAMI, FLORIDA

Yi had been in America for three years but this kind of thing still baffled him. He had stopped for a quick sandwich at the Subway joint right past the Arrivals at Miami International Airport. Out of curiosity he followed the instructions on the receipt and was promptly handed a free cookie by the Latin lady behind the counter, along with another receipt for $0.00 with a new code.

"I'm sorry but I'm very confused," said Yi. "You mean to say I can get one more free cookie if I fill in another survey and enter this code?"

"Yup. You go ahead, sir."

"But—but I could do this forever." She looked at him disinterested, assenting, as if thinking 'why would anybody ever bother to do that?' *It isn't a more culturally advanced society*, Yi thought, *it's just sheer laziness.*

Ø

It was a breezy evening at Cape Canaveral as Yi's car approached the control post to access the sprawling Kennedy Space Center. Three hours back he had been recognized by the car rental clerk, "I didn't place you at first! You guys all look the same—in a good way, you know." After a fairly obnoxious commotion, including bro-hugs and selfies, he upgraded him from an intentionally low-key Compact to a brand-new Corvette convertible. The temptation to floor the pedal ended up cutting the trip by half an hour, which he was thankful for. It meant he might be able to do it after all.

The security guard did not look welcoming as he hauled his big frame to the car, before resting his left arm on the windshield.

"This is off-limits. Kennedy Space Center is that way," he said, pointing past the barrier. "Tourists. That way." He pointed back to where Yi had come from.

Yi started to explain. "What? I don't ... can you repeat? Hey, Bill, there's a tourist from Asia or something that needs help."

Bill looked much nicer. It took him an instant to realize this was Yi Meng. "Jeez! Duncan—oh crap! Well, I never! Duncan—call the Center to tell them Mr. Meng will be there in five minutes. Now!"

"I'm really sorry, sir. I …" Yi told him not to worry about it. *That startled face paid for all your sins. You look like a dog that knows it ate his master's cat.*

Before Yi left, Bill asked him to please wait for ten seconds. He came out of the booth with a faded framed poster of Alan Shepard seated on the hood of his white Corvette. *The first American astronaut to travel into outer space, signed by the hero himself.* Bill looked very tempted to ask for something, but decided not to.

After Yi departed, Bill reminded Duncan, "You're an idiot."

"I'm an idiot," he conceded.

♌

A few hundred feet down the road, the car turned north, facing the Vehicle Assembly Building a mile or so ahead, the tallest single-story building in the world and one of the largest by volume. A huge American flag and NASA logo were painted on its front.

Crossing the city-like Kennedy Space Center buildings, Yi drove the last miles east to the legendary Launch Complex 39A by the Atlantic waterfront. He deliberately avoided raising his eyes, content with looking at the swamps by the sides of the road.

Until he did. Shackleton looked colossal, dominating the landscape. The reddish, cloudless sunset sky, the perfectly sharp horizon line far into the ocean, the flat shrubby vegetation all around. The spaceship on top of the rocket towered over land, sea, and sky.

He stopped the car, goosebumps mixed with chills going down his spine. The pristine liquid silver Shackleton had the proportions of a cigarette, and at this distance looked almost as featureless. It was two-thirds as wide as the Leaning Tower of Pisa, but twice as high. He got out of the car before the concrete octagon ring surrounding the launching area. Two vehicles were parked nearby and the three people that would show him around stepped out.

The four walked hurriedly to the launchpad around half a mile away. Someone tried to start a conversation but Yi asked politely for some quiet time. The three exchanged looks. The protocol was for at least one person to be with him at all times. Two of them went back. Yi didn't even notice.

Yi and one of the liaison officers walked over a gravel path the width of a highway, leading to the launch platform. From 1965 until the end of the shuttle missions in 2011, the enormous caterpillar tracks of crawler-transporter Franz or Hans—two of the largest vehicles ever built—trampled over this path, carrying the Saturn V rocket and later the Space Shuttles from the Vehicle Assembly Building to here, Launchpad 39A.

On the last 300 feet, Yi looked down at the gaping banana-shaped flame trench arcing out from right under the rocket. This is where the fire and cloud mushroom escape after ignition. *You quickly run out of superlatives and adjectives. Everything is enormous.*

Yi's pulse raced as he stood at the side of the rocket by an elevator structure that climbed all the way up, where a bridge would allow the crew to access the spaceship. The liaison officer put in a security code, a voice through the intercom asked for a vocal confirmation, the elevator door unlocked.

"Sir, I'll wait here. Take as much time as you need."

I wish we could tell that to the dying Sun. "Thank you."

He was thirty-five floors up when the elevator stopped. As he stepped onto the bridge, he pinched his cheek again for proof. This was his lone, spiritual rehearsal. In three weeks, he would walk inside a bright blue spacesuit. *I won't feel the wind or taste the ocean.* He stopped in the middle. Going further felt wrong. He rested his hands on the railing, bent forward, and looked down at the looming shadow. Along the Vehicle Assembly Building, he was higher than anything else in his field of view. In fact, he was higher than any geographic feature in the State of Florida. Not even Britton Hill, 400 miles away, was high enough to match him.

Still hunched over, he looked around. *In a few decades, the entire Cape Canaveral will be underwater. Well, technically 95 percent*—he jerked upright as the car keys slid out of his shirt pocket. They fell unimpeded all the way to the ground.

He was stirred. *There is no symbolism in what just happened*, he kept telling himself.

It was from this very spot that the Challenger Space Shuttle launched on January 28 1986, with a fifth of the US population watching Christa McAuliffe live, selected among 11,000 teachers to fly to space. Last time he saw the footage was a few years back and it left him uneasy for days. Some seventy seconds in and nine miles high, "Roger, go at throttle up," confirmed the commander, and three seconds later white smoke flashed in all directions. The crew cabin survived the explosion and continued climbing for another three miles. A few of the seven astronauts were likely alive and conscious during the next two minutes and forty-five seconds, as the cabin came back to Earth and hit the ocean surface at over 200-g. "We will never forget them, nor the last time we saw them this morning, as they prepared for their journey and waved goodbye and slipped the surly bonds of Earth to touch the face of God." Yi got lightheaded. *Rockets are really, really finicky—balance a pencil by the eraser over your index finger, and then push up as hard as you can while keeping it balanced. That's exactly what Shackleton would need to do after launch to avoid a catastrophic failure.*

Dusk gave way to night. He looked up, searching for Saturn, but he couldn't find it.

"We are ready to go," he repeated over and over. He was rationally calm and emotionally terrified.

22 | THE LAZAREVS

May 26 2027, 22 days before launch

STAR CITY, RUSSIA

Under a timid spring boreal Sun, Iman and Sergei strolled the last stretch to their house. To their right were boxy, nondescript apartment buildings, unaltered since the start of the Soviet space program. She got a lump in her throat and a dreadful sense of foreboding, instinctively embracing her tummy. They had lived in one during 2019 before upgrading to their current house in anticipation of their baby.

She read it once as a schoolgirl and never forgot Hemingway's six-word story, "For sale: baby shoes, never worn." The emotional toll had been unsparing, and every new miscarriage kept reinforcing what she intuitively knew all along: there was a poison somewhere inside her. She was trembling. *Better to let go of his hand.* The doctors tried to identify the cause but found none—until eight months ago.

She looked at the attractive features of her husband. Beneath the stony shell laid a caring, loving man. Sensitive too. She was the only one who could spot his almost imperceptible smile, because she was fourteen weeks pregnant, further than she had been in five years. Sergei was convinced this time was different. *Even I'm getting hopeful,* Iman thought. He had visited a fortune-teller in early January—during the Russian Orthodox Epiphany, the best time of year for omens—which accurately predicted Iman's pregnancy. Everything would be okay the seer had assured him, and a healthy boy would be born at the end of the eighth month. There were many times since the cancer diagnosis when she had almost told him, but the pregnancy convinced her that silence was the right and only approach. "There is both good and bad news," the doctor had told her recently, "the positive is that yours seems to have been brewing for a long time. A slow-growth cancer can last a decade before its runaway growth triggers. Also, mother-to-fetus contagion is very unlikely. The unlucky part is that this particular type has, uh, exceedingly low survival rates."

Entering the house, she saw the boxes of vodka lined up for tonight's dinner.

Following tradition, no doubt everybody will get wasted. Even after nine years she still felt no attachment to Star City. It wasn't the language. It was the drabness of it all, the perennial winters, the lack of social life as she knew it. An hour away from Moscow sounded near but the isolation was stifling. There were no foreigners. Except for a few Asian-looking Kazakhs, everyone was ethnically Russian.

She was resentful of Sergei's fellow cosmonauts. They would steal the last few hours with her husband at home. *The end of everyday life.* Midday tomorrow, an escort would pick them up and take them to Sheremetyevo International Airport in the capital for their flight to America, with an official farewell ceremony led by the President of the Russian Federation. Army battalions, hordes of people, TV crews.

23 | SOPHIA JONG

VENICE, LOS ANGELES

A tipsy Sophia entered her newly purchased fifth-floor apartment. She felt around for the light switch with her left hand, while holding her cellphone with her right. She gave up trying to locate it and used that hand instead to slip off her stilettos. She managed to remove only one before tripping forward on a life-size porcelain doll. They landed side by side. A Japanese fan had sent her what seemed like a ridiculously expensive model of herself dressed in an elaborate kimono, with an embroidered Saturn on the chest and all its sixty-two moons displayed around the rest of the robe.

"What was that, Tweety?" uttered the voice on the other end of the floored cellphone.

"The price of fame, Tina—it's complicated. Listen, I'll call you tomorrow, okay? Kisses." Her sight had adapted to the low light and the big manga eyes looked back at her. *Hi, big sis.* In interviews she claimed to be five foot two, which made the mannequin a full inch taller than she really was. *You're splendid—but the perky boobs and the geisha feet are mostly artistic license, all right?*

Back on her feet, she swung the curtains open. *If Hitchcock was alive today, he would have filmed* Rear Window *right down here.* By then she had more money than could be reasonably spent, but the pangs of guilt had made her—at the very last minute—buy the cheapest unit in the Shores complex. Which meant her flat was cornered against a twin building not fifty feet away.

Sophia stood by the window. A family of four was having supper in the apartment right in front of her. The father seemed to be telling a story while one child stealthily stole something under the table from the other. A fine, mischievous actress, the girl's face betrayed nothing. It precipitated her own childhood memories: Sophia's parents had a struggling all-you-can-eat Korean barbecue restaurant and lived right over it. She and her sister Jackie, now in the military, interacted with clients, taking orders and serving food, while the parents worked in the kitchen.

That afternoon, while having lunch with her family, Sophia did what she and Jackie had dreamed of doing since they could remember: securing their parents' retirement by transferring the proceeds from her Rolex contract to them. Their constant financial worries were over. Her dad cried. Her mom, instead, was troubled by the quarantine. In her broken English, she wanted to know why the crew needed to isolate themselves for two weeks before launch if all previous missions did it a week prior. Jackie had answered, "Umma, their immune system will be weakened in space. The only way to eradicate flu and colds is to make sure no one is sick before they board. The more time they are isolated from the rest of us, the better." Umma repeated her mantra, "But why, why you need go? Your family, ah? We stay here." Sophia had restated her prime motive: because finding extraterrestrial life on Enceladus would be the most transcending, Earth-shattering, far-reaching discovery in the history of mankind. "Not make any sense. Any. Why you?" her mother lashed back. Sophia had dismissed the comment as a lost cause, but during the evening Umma's words amplified in her head as she finally grasped their significance. *Dad is not the healthiest and six years can be a really long time.*

The girl in the apartment in front stood up and moved to the window. She cupped the sides of her eyes and pressed against the glass, looking straight in Sophia's direction. *This can't be.* Sophia's apartment was in shadows. Yet … the actress was waving. At her! She immediately reciprocated. The other smiled widely. Sophia looked up and saw the full Moon shining on her.

24 | D-DAY

June 17 2027, Launch Day

1:45 AM, T-minus twelve hours

JOHN F. KENNEDY SPACE CENTER, FLORIDA

A searchlight ignited, slashing the darkness with a diagonal beam that revealed a metallic giant. A second lit up, intersecting at the apex of the crystalline obelisk. A third. A roar escalated from the hundreds of thousands camping and partying at Cocoa Beach, eighteen miles south of the launchpad. In half a minute, Shackleton and its tower were in the limelight of crossing rays rising from the ground and dispersing into the black like a giant folding fan.

This was the salvo for the opening, twelve miles west of Pad 39A, of the NASA Causeway bridge between the mainland and Cape Canaveral. A line of vehicles had sat idle since early the previous day for a chance to cross into the closest public spot. Half a million cars would be allowed entry, with many hopefuls bound to be upset once the barrier was shut.

Among the remaining 2 million that had flocked to the area during the week, the lucky ones were in or around Titusville, a town thirteen miles away right across the Indian River from Cape Canaveral. Swollen to seven times its resident population, it looked like a First World refugee camp. The rooms of apartments and hotels a few floors up had been trading at ludicrous prices on secondary markets.

Those able to afford the ultimate luxury floated in the ocean. Eight of the largest cruise ships in the world were berthed in Port Canaveral. The US Coast Guard had beefed up their fleet for the thousands of boats in the location and the many more coming, safeguarding the wide and long off-limits area east of Pad 39A, a standard procedure in case something went wrong with the launch.

✪

3:08 AM, T-minus ten hours

MISSION CONTROL @ HANGAR ONE, CALIFORNIA

The seven mission specialists stared at their young Flight Director. Nitha looked absently around Mission Control. There was one solid wall covered in a giant screen digitally divided into seven sections, three glass walls, and a glass ceiling fifty feet above, hence the nickname, 'the fishbowl.' She knew the room was soundproof, but the people pacing around outside still distressed her. *This is my worst possible nightmare*, thought Nitha. They were listening over the phone to a group of senior meteorologists from the National Weather Service.

"So, to summarize, what's the probability, Ben?" asked Nitha.

"It is too early to tell. I can't really commit to a—"

"I will." The voice overlaid with static was Dr. Nowak, a weather sage from the National Oceanic and Atmospheric Administration.

He was on board the crown jewel ship of the agency, NOAAS *Ronald H. Brown*, somewhere east of Miami. "Look, right above me we have the fanciest Doppler weather radar in the world. As we speak, Miss Piggy is inside the storm completing—Miss Piggy is my secret love. She's a Lockheed WP-3D Orion. A weather reconnaissance aircraft armed to the teeth with instrumentation. A hurricane hunter ... in any case, we are in the presence of a tropical storm that—and here we leave facts and enter speculation—I think is developing into a hurricane. And hmm ... I'm afraid it's heading straight for the continent."

"How many hours?"

"It's a function of time and distance, right? I would say ..." the static remained solo for seven painful heartbeats, "... 40 percent chance of hitting Florida during the next, hmm, call it eight to sixteen hours. But even if it gets hundreds of miles from Canaveral, the upper atmosphere will be badly altered ... in any case, I think there's no question about it—you need to postpone the launch."

"Thank you very much for your time, Dr. Nowak. We'll be in contact."

"I'm sorr—" She had cut the line already.

Everyone avoided looking at the boss. She was thinking furiously.

The Atlantic hurricane season lasted from May to September. May and June had historically been the least active months but climate change was pulling the apex earlier and earlier. NASA and SpaceX had known for a long time that

Cape Canaveral had an expiration date. Since the 2017 hurricane season it had shown worrying signs of being closer than anyone anywhere had anticipated. The entire Cape was barely a few feet above sea level. If the storm hit Canaveral, the launchpads would be flooded for weeks. But planet alignment between Earth and Saturn doesn't much care about Earthly matters, thus the launch window would close until next year. *A polite way of saying 'forever' as Jimmy likes to remind everyone*, thought Nitha.

"It is absolutely prohibited to share this information with anybody else until I say otherwise. Understood?"

"Aren't we supposed to tell the crew … at least?" said one of the mission specialists.

"No. We cannot." She couldn't dump the news on the crew yet. She knew they would have approved her decision.

⌀

4:27 AM, T-minus nine hours

JOHN F. KENNEDY SPACE CENTER, FLORIDA

James finally gave up on sleep. He could count his heartbeat just by concentrating on his temples. His eyes trailed back to his visual fixation, the countdown clock hanging from a wall in the austere bedroom. He was awash with déjà vu. *Is this real? Is this even likely? Has this already happened?* He took three long breaths. *Be in the moment, just like Yi taught us.* Was he abandoning Belinda and their unborn child for a mission? Not just out of this world but to the edge of the Solar System? *Concentrate. There's nothing else before or after.* The industrial noises came into focus: the humming of machines, engines, vehicles. Some people below, outside the quarantined building, exchanged brief, terse commands. *I'm Stut-t-t-tering Jim, the s-s-s-scrawny 12-year-old with bad acne from 899 L-l-la Paz Way.* He could envision all of his life's road forks, *a course that has implausibly made me a crew member of, and I'm paraphrasing, 'humanity's spearhead.'*

The crew would be awake by 6:00 AM. Breakfast together half an hour later. And then—an irrational part of him wanted the flight delayed a few days. *But what's the point? We're physically isolated from everyone except a handful of personnel in bunny suits.*

Less than a mile away at the Launch Complex 39 Press Site, thousands of

accredited reporters and cameramen prepared for the uninterrupted live trans-
missions starting soon, in a thick hubbub of accents and languages. A long
serpentine line of broadcasting trucks slowly moved to their allotted spots.

Ø

7:01 AM, T-minus six hours

MISSION CONTROL @ HANGAR ONE, CALIFORNIA

Shackleton employees were gathering by the hundreds outside the fishbowl to
watch, and—since broadcasting began a few minutes before—to listen to the
twenty-seven specialists communicating with technicians on the ground at the
opposite coast. The center of the screen showed a daring rocket pointing upward into a pristine sky, but the weather forecast oscillated between bad and
awful.

There was mounting worldwide speculation about an imminent launch
cancelation, yet Nitha ordered all personnel to clear the pad and authorized
the loading of propellant into the rocket tanks.[9] For the veterans working at

---

9   The propellant transfer lines from tower to rocket chilled down to twice the lowest naturally
occurring temperature ever recorded on Earth. The propellant is composed of a fuel and an
oxidizer, which when combined and ignited create a violent, but in this case controlled, chemical reaction that expands the gases and generates the thrust that launches the rocket upward.

There can be no combustion, no fire, without an oxidizer. Ever wondered about the 'No
Smoking' signs in hospitals? It's not just a lung cancer prevention campaign, it also has to do
with those conspicuous 100 percent oxygen cylinders floating around. Fuel plus oxygen plus
spark equals ignition.

On Earth we forget this all the time because oxygen is everywhere. Our cars' internal
combustion engines make the mixture backstage every time we go for a drive. But in space
the policy is BYOB—bring your own bottle. Shackleton needs 3.6 pounds of oxygen for each
pound of methane, so most of the spaceship's precious weight and volume is taken up by a
giant tank full of the stuff that's free and omnipresent back on Earth.

SpaceX engines use liquid methane as fuel and liquid oxygen as oxidizer. At ambient temperature one becomes natural gas and the other plain oxygen. But if kept under cryogenic conditions,
roughly under -240 degrees Fahrenheit, the volume of the former decreases 600 times and the
latter 900 times. And it still takes a thirty-six-story-high rocket to launch the five-person crew and
their cargo into orbit around the Earth. Escaping the planet's gravity is hard.

Isaac Newton, possibly the biggest intellect in history, created calculus four centuries ago
to solve this problem. His drawings show a person on top of a sphere, throwing an object

the launchpad, the slightly accented, soft, and efficient female voice over the intercom was an abrupt departure from the loud tone ingrained in their minds.

ø

8:53 AM, T-minus five hours

JOHN F. KENNEDY SPACE CENTER, FLORIDA

Derya already felt the strain from grinning to the cameras, but James' succinct order "not the time to be an asshole" while wholly unexpectedly looking at him kept him in character. His body was muggy inside the spacesuit and the effort to keep the helmet under his arm in a heroic, Apollo 11 posture was giving him pins and needles, as they were spurred on by the master of ceremonies—James A. Egger III—to the press conference. *Expect retina damage from the flashes.*

Minutes before, the final goodbye to family and friends across a glass wall ended less awkwardly than he had anticipated. Azra and her family were there but his sister's forced, uninterested chat made it clear they had come for the novelty and free air tickets he had sent them, not for him per se. *A technicality*

---

forward. It climbs and then drops in a parabola, coming to rest further down the sphere. But if the throw is energetic enough, two things can happen.

One, the object moves at a rate such that its fall is exactly the same as the sphere's curvature, so it moves around the sphere forever. This is called orbiting the Earth, and requires a speed of five miles per second—ten times faster than a bullet's speed. But for Saturn that's not nearly enough, which takes us to ...

Two, the object is thrown with such force that it conquers the sphere's gravity and escapes. However, that doesn't come cheap. To go from standing on the ground to orbiting the Earth requires about twenty pounds of propellant per pound of payload. To the Moon the ratio worsens to 60:1, equivalent to carrying enough gasoline on a car to travel back and forth between Los Angeles and New York seven times. The problem is exponential: the lion's share of every gallon of propellant is used to transport the yet-to-be-consumed propellant, and each additional gallon makes it worse. On Earth, this is solved by gas stations. In space, by refilling in orbit.

The Shackleton spaceship needs to be topped up in orbit, but that's not good enough. A modified Super Heavy rocket would need to dock to Shackleton, accelerate both until it runs low on juice, undock and slingshot the latter into deep space. Only then the pennies add up to the propellant price of ferrying the crew and its cargo on a round trip from Low Earth Orbit to Saturn.

really. He wasn't the only one, it seemed: "I wish—" and "Don't—" were the last words in a stark little exchange between father and son James. *In other news, Sergei's misty eyes may be the strongest sign yet that he's not an android after all.* And his wife was definitely not, putting in a solidly melodramatic farewell.

∅

10:24 AM, T-minus three hours

Nitha's voice muted any conversation across news channels, cable networks, and billions of screens and smartphones. "Propellant loading complete. Weather briefing confirms a tropical storm making landfall in the coming hours, showing a distinctive hurricane pattern," she pauses, "we are monitoring the situation closely. The launch schedule proceeds ahead unaltered."

Meanwhile, the Coast Guard used radar to monitor and chase seven vessels that had entered the cordoned off area looking for the perfect vantage point.

∅

10:44 AM, T-minus three hours

The astronauts walked out from the Checkout Building, waved to a boisterous press, and climbed into the Astrovan that would take them to Pad 39A.

The pecking order at the Press Site was plain to see. The bigger canopies, proudly displaying their brand logos, were set up at the front. Well-known faces were being interviewed to keep up the oomph in an otherwise action-less launch site.

"Quite a sight here at Cape Canaveral, as millions jam the Florida coast and three-fourths of the world population prepare to watch one of the most awaited moments in history. We have with us Scott Kelly, the American astronaut with the most days spent in space. Reactions?"

"'Nice to be here!' would be a disgraceful understatement. This is hallowed ground. In addition to Apollo 11's cargo of Armstrongs, Aldrins, and Collins, the launching pad where Shackleton sits is where most shuttle missions launched, including Challenger's 1986 and Columbia's 2003 tragedies. Where the first manned SpaceX rocket lifted off in 2019. And now, where humanity's hope is about to blast off into deep space," said Scott Kelly.[10]

☄

11:16 AM, T-minus two hours fourteen minutes

After a team helped each astronaut board and strap in, they closed Shackleton's hatch.

---

10   Minutes later. "We can see the crew being walked to the elevator that will take them to the bridge at the top, and then it's just a few dozen steps before they enter the spaceship," said the reporter.

"Yes, and they're allowed one last pit stop at a restroom up there, we call it The Last Toilet on Earth—this is a momentous day. In 2004, Neil Armstrong diagnosed the problem that has troubled space exploration for five decades by reminding us that society is much more risk-averse than the individuals sitting at the top of a rocket. Today, two decades later, the deadlock is finally about to be bulldozed. This mission is bringing back a 'can do' attitude that has been buried under our unwillingness to take the necessary risks to push the frontier of exploration. None of our leaders has been as bold, concise, or frank as John F. Kennedy when he set a date by which we would land on the Moon. Now, through the efforts of private enterprise, we are back to the era of extreme accountability. Three years ago they said June 17 2027, and here we stand. Let me add that the $6 billion mission price tag, four days of US military spending, for what could end up being the most important expedition in the history of mankind, is like buying the Taj Mahal for the cost of a Snickers," said Scott Kelly.

"Here's the famous quote from President Kennedy's 1962 speech, 'We choose to go to the Moon. We choose to go to the Moon in this decade and do the other things, not because they are easy, but because they are hard.'"

"But the real tally of the challenge comes further into the speech. Let me get my note-pad ... 'But if I were to say, my fellow citizens, that we shall send to the Moon, 240,000 miles away from the control station in Houston, a giant rocket more than 300 feet tall, made of new metal alloys, some of which have not yet been invented, capable of standing heat and stresses several times more than have ever been experienced, fitted together with a precision better than the finest watch, carrying all the equipment needed for propulsion, guidance, control, communications, food, and survival, on an untried mission, to an unknown celestial body, and then return it safely to Earth, re-entering the atmosphere at speeds of over 25,000 miles an hour, causing heat about half that of the temperature of the Sun and do all this, and do it right, and do it first before this decade is out—then we must be bold.' To some it may sound trite, but I think it's fitting and prescient."

Ø

11:41 AM, T-minus one hour forty-nine minutes

"Shackleton pressurization is complete,"[11] said Nitha over the airwaves.

"Isn't it odd that the Flight Director makes no mention of current weather conditions? A number of experts are urging the launch to be called off," said the reporter.

"NASA's Weather Launch Commit Criteria was violated the moment we heard about the cloud wall south off the Florida coast. But here's where Shackleton diverges. NASA protocols are broadly conservative and avoid possibly adverse conditions. If it were a matter—as it is most of the time—of delaying launch by a day or a week, Mission Control would have pulled the plug hours ago. But the stakes here are much higher. If they cancel, the mission could get postponed for a year. And a year can be a really long time. Many things can change. Trust me. I was in space for a whole one," said Scott Kelly.

"Is that sufficient to put the lives of the crew in danger?" asked the reporter.

"Everything in space is a risk-reward calculation. What Mission Control is doing is taking measured risks. How measured? I have no clue, but I do know that in a few minutes they'll release wind measurement balloons that climb to the upper atmosphere. If they show strong wind shear—a speed or direction change in a short vertical distance—the mission should be canceled. Period. Earth's atmosphere is molasses thick for fast-moving objects. It's like sticking your hand out of the window while driving on a highway. Accelerating to great speeds while in the atmosphere creates enormous friction, pressure, and heat, putting materials through major stresses. I've been there, and it feels like being in the jaws of a huge dog with rabies. You really don't want additional strains on the rocket ... but you do not preemptively cancel. You cancel when you have the information."

---

11   All commercial airplanes and manned spacecraft pump air into the cabin to achieve and maintain an environment resembling the atmospheric pressure where most humans live, at or under
7,000 feet above sea level. At Everest's summit, 29,029 feet, the atmospheric weight is a third
of the sea level's, like running up a staircase while holding your breath for two out of three
steps.

Ø

12:43 PM, T-minus forty-seven minutes

The support structure started separating from the rocket. Meanwhile, 180 miles southeast, Hurricane Isaias makes landfall on Freeport, Bahamas, and for a few minutes its residents looked at a clear sky high above while a churning eye wall besieged the city amid towering thunderstorms.

Ø

1:21 PM, T-minus nine minutes twenty-three seconds

As the countdown marched down to zero, the radio channel between Mission Control and Shackleton opened to the world and something unheard of in the history of space flight happened.

"Shackleton, we are receiving data from the upper atmosphere. There are abnormal conditions, and they are about to worsen," said Nitha.

James' voice came back, "Roger that. How bad?"

"It's 13 percent outside the max safety threshold. Mission Control cannot continue countdown without the crew's authorization."

James seemed to have muted the intercom. "FLIGHTO. Under 30 percent we are GO," he said.

"Copy that Shackleton. Mission Control will cast our final vote at T-minus three minutes."

All bets were off. NOAA hurricane hunter Miss Piggy and its twin brother Kermit the Frog were flying through the middle of the storm, sending back data.

Meanwhile, after being ferried from network to network for the past several hours, the science celebrity settled under the YouTube tent for the interview, his final stop.

"Did you hear what I heard? Jeez, this is really happening!" said Bill Nye 'the Science Guy,' bow tie and all.

"With Hurricane Isaias having a small but real chance of landing here in half a day or so, why aren't the crowds dispersing?" asked the correspondent.

"Because this is happening in ten minutes! But no, seriously, the question is relevant ... have you ever been to Paris?" The correspondent nodded. "I bet you went to the Louvre," Nye continued, and again was answered with a nod. "And you headed straight to the Mona Lisa. I know there would have been a giant queue, because I've been in those same shoes, to see the small rectangle beyond a thick bulletproof slab of glass. Yet you can buy a perfect—and I mean perfect—replica done by a computer, layer by layer, just like Da Vinci's one from half a millennium ago. See it every day, hanging from your bathroom door, as you wash your face. But you don't. And we are talking about things past, while today we are here to witness the birth of a new, brighter future."

He continued, "While we are at it, let's think about that future. Philosophy and the religions were born out of our longing to comprehend 'where do we come from' and 'where are we heading.' Every culture has stories about their existence, about their presence in the world, about their relationship with the rest of the Universe. This mission aligns metaphysics and science like never before in an unparalleled opportunity to seek and find the ultimate truth ... because there are two essential questions deep within each of us: where did we come from? And, are we alone in the Universe? These are the questions at the core of our existence. This mission could potentially answer both. In thirty years, when you're old and I am no more, our civilization will look back at this moment in awe. 'I was there,' you will tell your grandchildren. 'I saw with my own eyes the legend being born, as it launched into the boundless sea of space.'

"Finally, and then I promise to say no more, Carl Sagan said it better than anyone: 'For all its material advantages, the sedentary life has left us edgy, unfulfilled. Even after 400 generations in villages and cities, we haven't forgotten. The open road still softly calls, like a nearly forgotten song of childhood. We invest far-off places with a certain romance. This appeal, I suspect, has been meticulously crafted by natural selection as an essential element in our survival. Long summers, mild winters, rich harvests, plentiful game—none of them lasts forever. Your own life, or your band's, or even your species' might be owed to a restless few—drawn, by a craving they can hardly articulate or understand, to undiscovered lands and new worlds. Maybe it's a little early. Maybe the time is not quite yet. But those other worlds—promising untold opportunities—beckon. Silently, they orbit the Sun, waiting.'"

◯

1:24 PM, T-minus six minutes two seconds

Belinda looked at Iman. *I knew what I was getting into the moment Jimmy asked me out on our first date*, she thought. *Iman, on the other hand, could very well say Sergei was taken away from her by decree.*

At that moment, there was no prime real estate like Launch Complex 39 Observation Gantry, half the distance from Press Site to launchpad. Just over a mile shy from the rocket, closer than any bystander and most personnel. The third and highest deck—holding two-dozen people—was strictly assigned to family members. When White House staff contacted Belinda behind the President's back requesting a spot, she immediately said yes. There were only two bodyguards on that deck. Even the First Lady was one below. The only other non-family was Derya's guest, the German Chancellor. *I guess he had a few tickets too many.*

Belinda was startled by an iconic voice, "Thank you for inviting me, Belinda."

She turned to the President of the United States. She had imagined this encounter many times before. "I did not invite you, Mr. President. Your aides did. Frankly, you're persona non grata around here."

Evidently taken aback, it took him a few moments to reply. "May I ask—"

"Shackleton was always going to be an uphill battle, but we never counted on your office blowing up a dam right over us," said Belinda. *And hopefully you never counted on me recording this conversation right now.*

"I wonder why you say that."

"Mr. President, please. Almost every stop sign and roadblock we have encountered had your fingerprints all over it."

He paused, undecided. "I don't—I didn't think society was prepared for the implications of discovering extraterrestrial life. It may be a low probability event, but it's my life's work to do the best I can for this country and for the world—how do you think some religions would cope with the news?" His melodic, masculine voice seemed to be genuinely wanting to know her view.

"This is the search for the ultimate truth, however inconvenient it may be." Belinda's heavy breathing made the words twitchy and garbled. "That's what scientists do."

"I'm a politician, Belinda. Sometimes less is more."

"Who do you think you are to, to personally decide for the future of our species?"

"Rightfully or not, I am the President of the most powerful nation on Earth, invested with immense authority—and even so, the mission couldn't be derailed. You won't believe this, and that's okay, but I only ordered specific steps against it a handful of times. Because it has been the only time in office when I felt invisible hurdles rendering my actions ineffective. Today I learned why. I was engaging the people's minds but could never convince their hearts. Because in fact I never really convinced myself. I now know I was wrong." He sounded sincere and thoughtful. Against her will, she had already forgiven him.

♄

1:26 PM, T-minus three minutes twenty seconds

Nitha lubricated her mouth and throat with coffee as she prepared for what she knew would be the pinnacle of her career.

Nitha said, "Mission Control, give go/no go for launch. FIDO."

"We're go FLIGHT."

"GUIDANCE."

"Go."

"SURGEON."

"We are go. We are go."

"PROP."

"Go."

"ODIN."

"Go!"

"EECOM."

"Go FLIGHT."

"WEATHER." There were a few seconds of silence.

"We are 24 percent outside the max safety threshold. FLIGHT, we are go!"

"INCO."

"Go. Go FLIGHT."

"Ground Control."

"We are go!"

She took a long breath, "Any specialist can cancel to T-minus fifteen seconds," she reminded them. "This is it. Mission is GO for launch."

The countdown auto-sequence began.

Ø

1:29 PM, T-minus twelve seconds

"*Eleven. Ten. Nine. Ignition Sequence Start. Eight. Seven. Six. Five.*"
The valves inside the Raptor engines opened in tandem as turbopumps higher up the rocket began spinning toward 5,000 rpm. Within a second, they were shoving a flood of oxygen and methane down the giant's throat. The two torrents collided in each of the engine combustion chambers, where a spark transmuted them into a barrage of fire. Meanwhile, over 2 million gallons of water—the lifetime water consumption of one hundred people—were being dumped into the flame trench under the rocket to suppress the throbbing vibration and savage heat. From afar, a flash gave way to a smoke plume that almost instantly hid behind bulging just-made water clouds swaddling the launchpad.
"*Four. Three. Two. One—*"
Shackleton arose so ponderously at first that for a moment it seemed to Belinda as if it had aborted lift-off and was attempting touchdown.
"We have lift-off!"
Belinda hadn't noticed the incongruence between the monumental fireworks and the dead silence until she saw the shock wave rippling over the marsh in front, racing for them at 1,100 feet per second. There was no sound build-up. A booming roar slammed her chest, her skull, her knees in drilling staccato bursts. The ground was quaking. Every bolt and rivet in the Observation Gantry rattled. Some 120 decibels of compression waves pummeled her body as she felt the heat of the engines on her face.
The biggest, most powerful rocket in history emerged from the clouds it had just given birth to and cleared the tower at a hundred miles an hour, shaking the Atlantic shoreline. Hardly eight minutes later it would be cruising in orbit at 17,500 miles an hour.
Belinda was too overwhelmed to continue watching the ascent. Turning around, she saw the President's hardened eyes welling with tears.

Ø

Since launch, Sophia had been drifting between euphoria and terror. On two occasions she was certain something had gone horribly wrong. She had underestimated just about everything: the rumbling of the engines muffled her thoughts behind their noise wall; Shackleton's pulsing and throbbing as it fought at once against both gravity and atmosphere made her body feel like it was having an epileptic seizure; and the 3-g felt like a giant had compressed her chest in a Heimlich maneuver and forgot to let go. The sky past the window had gone from blue to dark blue to indigo, and was now almost black as the sunrays bounced around ever fewer air molecules in the thinning atmosphere. Earth's curvature was now patent. With great effort she turned her head and saw the rest of the crew lined up. *My space-ial family: Fry, Bender, Zoidberg, Professor Farnsworth, and yours truly Amy Wong. Forget ethnicity! Leela is way cooler.*

"Approaching MAX Q," said Sergei, one minute and twenty-six seconds after launch. As the rocket climbed, diminishing air friction was compensated by speed increase. Between ten and thirteen miles high the aerodynamic stress reached critical point. "All nominal."

Over the intercom, Mission Control exhaled a communal sigh of relief.

The rocket continued curving into a horizontal position relative to the planet's surface. The colossal energy expenditure was not centered on going up but on going very fast around the Earth. Getting to space was easy, staying there was hard: just one-tenth of the energy was used to reach orbital altitude, and fully nine-tenths to achieve orbital speed.

"All engines cut-off. Prepare for stage separation," said Sergei at two minutes twenty-six seconds in, forty miles high.

She heard a muffled thump as the pyro bolts previously connecting the now almost-empty rocket to the spaceship exploded. The roaring, shaking, and g-force unceremoniously vanished as the giant white shaft separated and would soon fall back to Earth. All she could hear were the fans of some equipment softly whirring in the background. A few seconds later, Shackleton came to life and she experienced a new, much kinder jolt as the spaceship's engines took over to continue accelerating them to achieve orbit.

"Shackleton, your trajectory is nominal!" said an exultant Nitha.

∅

At eight minutes forty-seven seconds after launch, 17,500 miles an hour and 132 miles high, the engines cut off.

A Yoda figurine hanging down in front of Yi an instant prior began somersaulting with an ease and calmness that could only come from being no longer bound by Earthly physics.

Shackleton was in orbit.

Only Derya screamed in celebration and Yi extrapolated why. He was moved beyond the ability to speak.

After freeing himself from the harness, like all the others except Sergei, he floated to the Observation Window's ninety square feet of opulence—by far the largest window of any spaceship ever. His retinas saturated with the blue of the Earth below, and, inevitably, in moisture. "Wow" was the most Yi was able to say, somewhat breathlessly. He remained immobile for a long while, ogling humanity's cradle and home. If anybody spoke during that time, he didn't hear them.

Mankind's presence was all over. The checkered Pythagorean geometry, like a Scottish tartan, of Great Britain's landscape. The nearly perennial haze over Southeast Asia due to forests burning in Indonesia, one of the last great lungs pumping CO_2 out from the atmosphere. The bombastic brilliance of the metropolises at night, tempered by the humble, reverent soft-treading of the nomadic Saharan tribes, their campfires little peppered specs of light under the night. *A reminder from a time not long past when nature and humankind weren't at such great odds.* But the most unforgettable view for Yi was Korea at night-time. The South had sharply outlined contours of light around it, with a series of contiguous blobs of electric glitz inside. North Korea, instead, connecting the peninsula with the continent, was unlit besides the rare fleck. Three years after Kim Jong-un executed his long-awaited decision to blow his brains out against an immaculate white wall—*in a bizarre tribute to Wu Guanzhong, the founder of modern Chinese painting, as per the photos I saw*—it remained indistinguishable from the ocean at each side of it.

Up there somewhere within the crowded night sky,
the anonymous Saturn awaits.

PART 3

THE ROAD
TO SATURN

Part 3. The Road to Saturn

25 | Δ NEW HOME

A levitating Derya looked through the Observation Window at the International Space Station some 400 feet ahead. It had been six hours since launch and Shackleton was already stationed in its four-day orbit around the Earth before launching for its destination, Saturn. Next morning would see the docking with an autonomous tanker ship—five of them in total would take two days to refill the ship—and at night the first activation of the artificial gravity wheel.

The gleaming, metallic, Lego-like structure of the ISS reminded Derya of his sister Fatma as an adolescent with braces: awkward and ugly. *Seems more of an improvised emergency shelter than a spaceship.* The first cylindrical module was put in orbit in 1998 and it presently consisted of seven American modules, five Russian, two Japanese, and one European. *"The most stunning example of multinational cooperation during peacetime," they like to call it.* But to him, the six-people flying tin can contraption was a red beacon of stagnated space ambitions, a playground for grown-ups doing little more than high-school science experiments.

He was pissed. There was no technical reason for converging with the international station. It all began as an innocent fan group proposal to have a stopover while the spaceship was being refueled—never mind that the ISS was crammed and, if anything, its crew would love to sleep in the relatively spacious luxury of Shackleton instead. The combination of a beautiful, artistic, but factually inaccurate video rendering of both vehicles coming together going viral plus the sluggish reaction from the Public Relations Team is all it took. *What could be a more touching, sensible idea of giving back to the hundreds of millions that donated money than spectacular footage of Shackleton in a space catwalk as seen from the ISS.*

The ISS, that nearly forgotten derelict old fart, offered the perfect pretext at a fitting time. The non-Russian closed-loop water filtration system was failing, which put the Russians' under strain. If the latter were to fail, the problem would become an emergency. The Russian water system had it easier, as cosmonauts could never get around the mental block of drinking recycled urine. The non-Russian, instead, mimicked Mother Earth's water cycle in all its splendor, which included pee from non-Russians, Russians, seventeen guinea pigs, two turtles, three bullfrogs, and one male and five female geckos. The entire infrastructure of the soon-to-be-decommissioned ISS was crumbling and it was rapidly becoming yesterday's news, and, as such, severely cash-strapped. *Enter Shackleton, the Good Samaritan, bringing a bladder replacement to the pensioner for free.*

In two more days, a spacewalk by James and Sergei would bring a water filtration system replacement to the ISS.

♄

Like the other four, Derya had committed every corner of Shackleton to memory. But no blueprint or virtual reality video could compete with a real-life inspection in space. Of its sixteen stories in length, half were filled with propellant tanks and engines that were inaccessible to the crew. The remaining eight were divided into five levels, all joined together by a hollow central backbone that served as passageway.

He stuck his head out the passageway into the two-story cargo area, filled with food, water, various supplies, spares, and the two Dragon spacecraft, one of which would land him and Sergei on Enceladus. Here in the cargo area was the hatch that communicated with the outside.

On the next level were the sleeping quarters, which starting the next day would spin during nighttime. The five cabins stemmed from the center like orange wedges and were cavernous compared to anything that had gone to space before. There were two beds in each, one against the hull for sleeping under artificial gravity, the other a sleeping bag anchored to one wall.

He peeked into the following level. Most of it was dedicated to Demeter— named after the Greek goddess of agriculture—a greenhouse where a limited but steady supply of vegetables would complement their packaged diet. It was a Z-shaped maze, with year-round lettuce, spinach, and onion, plus seasonal crops of potatoes, beets, tomatoes, broccoli, peas, and radishes growing from the walls. *Besides that, it will be nature's equivalent to a tranquilizing pill.* According to mission psychologists, the greenery would be the first go-to place in case of panic attacks. The rest of that floor was Hermes, a zero-gravity gym.

But the heart of the crew's new world was Bacchus, the two-story living and kitchen level. Compared to the spartan nature of everywhere else, this was Baroque. Even though it would be permanently under weightlessness, it was conceived and constructed by arbitrarily defining a roof and floor. A third of the curved fuselage wall was covered with a high-definition screen imitating a programmed iconic landscape every twenty-four hours. It behaved exactly like an Earth day, with changing light intensity, direction, and color. At the moment it was nighttime in Florence. The vista from the rooftop balcony at the Four Seasons Firenze had the Piazza del Duomo standing above the rest of the Renaissance city. The hills in the background were hinted at by the silvery light of a quarter Moon. The sounds of the sleeping town were soothing and soporific, and Derya felt suddenly exhausted. *I was still right, but damn, it does look lifelike.* He fiercely opposed wasting weight allowance on a load of screens to mimic mawkish postcards, but as in other opinions and preferences he lost four to one to the rest of the crew. The floor of Bacchus was made of a special Velcro so the astronauts could stick to it during meals or social activities. Table, chairs, and sofas had electromagnets attaching them to the floor that disengaged at the click of a button. At the side opposite to Florence was the lavish latticed main Observation Window, 130 square feet of real-life planetarium. By default, it was fully dimmed to avoid outcompeting Earth's prerecorded visual impressions.

The last level, a two-story dome, was the flight deck—right in front of another, smaller Observation Window—taking about half of the space. The rest was occupied by life support systems and electronics, including the ship's mainframe—an obliging artificial intelligence named TT. The team in charge thought the acronym sounded genderless. *Sophia disagrees. I side with her, but I won't tell anyone.* It was lauded as one of the most advanced computers in the world. *But it's the year 2027, and* 2001: A Space Odyssey *HAL 9000's intelligence is to TT what a human brain is to a fruit fly's.* TT's artificial neural networks made it something of an idiot savant. It was exceptional at performing basic autopilot navigation, managing the ship's power generation, monitoring life support systems, or more generally freeing the crew from the majority of day-to-day operation and maintenance tasks. But in extended speech interactions or when gauging emotions, the illusion of intelligence broke down fast.

∅

It was 8:02 PM Eastern Time, but from then onward they switched to midnight in Coordinated Universal Time (UTC). After the most intense day of their lives, the five retreated to the sleeping quarters.

Derya glided into his cabin, closing the hatch behind him. A widespread complaint from people that have lived in space was the lack of privacy. Not here. His inner sanctum was spacious and soundproof. Having planned his personal space with a designer for over a year, he knew the location of everything by heart, from nail clippers to his Kindle packed with naughty romantic novels.

He got inside his sleeping bag and zipped it up, swallowed the sleeping pills his mission physician prescribed for the first few days in space, and looked at his schedule for tomorrow. 'Tomorrow' was no longer what it used to be. In space, the concept of a twenty-four-hour day becomes a human construct: Shackleton completes a loop around the planet every ninety-two minutes, including a sunrise and a sunset.

He was already loathing the seven back-to-back interviews starting at 8:30 AM, but knew he shouldn't complain. Among apostles there was always a Jesus, and it wasn't James but Yi. China was experiencing an acute case of Beatlemania.

There were no windows in the cabin and the ambient light had dimmed and transitioned into blue-wavelength-depleted to avoid suppressing nocturnal melatonin and to induce sleep. Without external cues like sunrise and sunset, the traditional way to keep a properly regulated twenty-four-hour circadian rhythm during space missions was a systematic daily eating and exercise routine. But the most biologically fundamental mechanism for setting this clock is light.

Life has a timekeeping system at the molecular level. Even bacteria living in darkness exhibit the twenty-four-hour biochemical clock. Disrupting it goes against billions of years of evolution. For the crew, deviations from the twenty-four-hour day as well as sleep deprivation were to be avoided at all costs. It weakened the immune system, blurred awareness, and degraded social skills. Sleep hygiene was not only recommended but also monitored from Earth. There were a lot of rules on board Shackleton, but this one ruled them all.

26 | HURRICANE ISAIAS

Y i woke in his cabin with a sensation similar to doing a handstand, his head puffed up. His heart, used to pumping against gravity, now pushed too much. The inner ear, which regulates balance in addition to sound, was sending garbage signals to his brain—seasickness in space. His body didn't know what was happening, and for an instant his mind didn't know either. He looked at the digital wall in front of him. It was 7:12 AM. The wall showed his schedule, booked with interviews from 9:00 AM all the way to 8:00 PM, with sixty-five minutes allocated for lunch. *I'll be repeating the space exploration mantra I've been preaching for years—but talking from 250 miles up seems to amplify the message like an Earth-size megaphone, somehow imbuing new meaning into the same old words.*

Later, as he tried to sit down for breakfast at the communal table in Bacchus, he managed to elbow James and kick Derya. Sophia smiled, understanding.

♄

When Sergei appeared in the hatch, Derya asked him to do the kuvyrkat'sya, somersault in Russian. *There is no chance his muscle memory is that good—but we shall see,* thought Derya. Sergei launched forward across the roof and when he was flying right above the table, grabbed one of the hundreds of handrails around the ship, pivoted his body, and sent himself downward, landing a little off-center on his chair. "Give yourselves a month," he quipped.

"If you weren't so blond you could have joined the Harlem Globetrotters," said James. For everyone but Sophia it was yet another lost in translation moment. "Anyway," he continued the previous conversation, "picture this one: David Bowman has terminated HAL 9000, but that has also killed artificial gravity, okay? So, he's floating alone and heading to Jupiter. One day he's heading to the bathroom for a number two, flying like Sergei. Closing in, he grabs a rod sticking out to slow down, kills all his momentum but ... the rod breaks.

He is floating there, perfectly still, an arm's length away from the walls. Can he save himself?"

"I don't get it. What's the problem?" asked Yi.

"Newton."

"Mind adding some flavor, Jimmy?" said Sophia.

Derya replied, "First Law: 'An object shall remain at rest unless acted upon by a force,' Bowman is stuck in the middle. He has nothing to push against. He can jerk and shake and scream all he wants, but he won't move a millimeter closer to any of the walls. After a day he'll get thirsty from so many tears of frustration, and a week or two later he'll join Frank Poole and HAL 9000. And salvation will still be an arm's length away. Pretty cool death, huh?"

"You are a bunch of pitiful nerds. I really hope it's not contagious," said Sophia after finishing her last breakfast bite. She left Bacchus.

No one but Yi seemed keen on the mental gymnastics. "Can he have a tube of toothpaste in his pocket?"

"I'll give you that, but only if it's an airline sample," said James.

"That's like a third of an ounce."

"That's what you've got."

"Let me try Newton's Third Law," said Yi. "For every action, there's an equal and opposite reaction. Bowman unscrews the cap, carefully points toward one wall, and squeezes the tube like his life depends on it."

"That's fairly smart," cut in Derya while thinking *that's damn smart*. "But the difference in mass is like one to 10,000, so any thrust generated will be negligible. Maybe days to move inches …"

"Sorry to kill the mood but it doesn't work," said James. "To create thrust, the toothpaste would need to physically separate from the tube, but I don't see—"

Sophia's fired up voice came from the flight deck, "Guys, you must come and see this …"

Ø

Directly below them, Tennessee—the state of Elvis and country music—looked uninterruptedly green, crossed diagonally by ancient seafloor turned into mountains, one of Earth's most visible wrinkles, the Appalachians running from Newfoundland all the way to Alabama. Geological investigations, fossils, or plainly staring at a world map reveal how it used to belong to the mountain range extending from Scotland to Morocco. But the wheel of time keeps spinning, and continental drift seems to imply the formation of a new super-continent in a couple of hundred million years.

But no one was looking down, only sideways where the coastline should have been, hidden under a white rotating canopy with a footprint stretching from Georgia to north Florida. The effect of watching Hurricane Isaias while listening to news networks was hypnotic.

"—turns out Nitha Sharma was right and I was wrong. I'm okay with that. Long live the Queen of Space and all that jazz." The online celebrity continued, "But to say the mission was saved because of her farsightedness pushing ahead for launch is, sorry to be so blunt, utter horseshit."

Sophia got goosebumps. *Yes, the storm below may be momentous, but compared to any of the hundreds happening right now in the gas giants, it's pint-sized and ephemeral.* Some 400 million miles away, Jupiter's largest had spun for centuries and could easily swallow the entire Earth, the Great Red Spot. Doubling the distance, Saturn's largest tempest may have been raging for billions of years, an even more gargantuan maelstrom capable of gulping all inner planets—Mercury, Venus, Earth, and Mars—moored to the North Pole.

Ø

At 10:15 PM, the artificial gravity wheel started up. At first the spinning was imperceptible but half an hour later it achieved cruising speed—seven rotations per minute, simulating 40 percent of Earth's gravity.

27 | SPACEWALK

James and Sergei were donning their spacesuits by themselves. *This is already revolutionary*, thought James. *Getting into my old sumo wrestler costume used to take two people and forty-five minutes.* It fitted as tight as a surgical glove a size too small. Yi helped each one to mount the propulsion unit for untethered spacewalks on top of the spacesuit's life support system backpack.

First Sergei then James entered the airlock and closed the first airtight door behind them. After checking their screen displays one last time for leaks, they nodded at each other and activated the airlock, which depressurized to vacuum. Their lives were now 100 percent dependent on their spacesuits.

James opened the second airtight door, and as he exited, he was struck by the sight of the planet rotating beneath him. *This will never get old.* The contrast with watching Earth from inside the spacecraft reminded him of the difference between watching whale sharks through an acrylic glass in the Okinawa Aquarium two years back, and Belinda and himself diving among them off the coast of Mozambique last August. *Both views of Earth are life-altering, but spacewalks are epiphanies with God.* The peripheral vision through the new helmet was unlimited, and only the subtle glare on the visor betrayed its presence. The Mediterranean below was a stunning deep blue, followed by scattered clouds over the Syrian Desert unfurling into a uniform coating of icing reaching the horizon, cloaking Iran. He was enraptured. Sergei's stern voice reminded him to keep moving.

Looking back, he saw Shackleton's rear coupled to the back of a semi-twin, an autonomous tanker refueling and giving the impression of staring at the former's reflection.

They moved efficiently through the hull heading to the bow using a handrail, and prepared for the untethered spacewalk right outside Bacchus' Observation Window. Inside Shackleton, Sophia pointed a camera at them, beaming live to the world below.

Their helmets' intercom crackled, "James Egger, Sergei Lazarev, this is Satoshi Fukuda, Commander of the ISS. The Joint Airlock is ready and waiting for you two, and the payload." The water filtration system replacement for the ISS hung from Sergei's harness, packed as a bale.

Not one to waste time with preambles, Sergei untethered from the handrail and fired his nozzle thrusters, promptly separating from Shackleton. Much too quick for James' taste or confidence. Forced to follow the cosmonaut closely, he unclipped and got a drowning surge of adrenaline as he fired his thrusters.

Ø

They were about a third of the distance to the ISS when James looked straight down for the first time since separation. The exposure made him lightheaded. It was one thing to stare down while attached to a structure thousands of times more massive. It was something entirely different to be on his own in what was effectively a skintight, one-person spaceship. It was both pure bravery and pure helplessness. *And dangerous in non-obvious ways.* He remembered his second spacewalk, years earlier. James and his partner had been outside for five hours replacing a large plate half an inch thick when it jolted. Upon inspection, they noticed a hole as if someone had pierced the solid steel with an unbreakable toothpick. A grain of orbital debris is all it took. *Very low probability, very high consequences.*

He concentrated on the landscape revolving under him and immediately recognized the magnificent white ruggedness of the Himalayas, with its tens of thousands of ridges dividing each mountain into glare and shadow. Yet even the highest mountain barely protruded six miles above the ocean, on a planet 8,000 miles in diameter. The three dimensionalities below were a fabrication of his brain extrapolating shapes and colors. In fact, if the planet was painted as a billiard ball it would be indistinguishable from one. Everest, or the Mariana Trench, or its slightly oblate shape, were well within the World Pool-Billiard Association error tolerance for balls. *My overly complicated way of saying the Earth is more or less a perfect sphere.*

James had been battling with a nose itch that wouldn't go away. *My pinky, my pinky's all I need.* Unable to control himself anymore, he sneezed, aiming as low as he could, but it still splattered the visor with saliva. *Well, that's that—fortunately it's a short spacewalk.* The trifle was forgotten when, looking ahead, he saw the Sun about to disappear under the horizon, cutting through the fragile and ailing hazy bluish carapace of the Earth's atmosphere. *Using the previous analogy, a billiard ball's coating is 1 percent of its thickness. The atmosphere? 0.1 percent—0.1 percent that makes the difference between the exuberant life on Earth and the barren desert of Mars.* As soon as the Sun hid, the light switch went off and Sergei, twenty feet ahead, vanished into darkness. The only lights were a ceaseless collection of stars and the ISS right ahead. In seconds, the temperature dropped from 200 to -200 degrees Fahrenheit. James was safe inside his space-suit, but he still felt something akin to a draft of cold air on an otherwise warm and windless autumnal evening.

As James converged upon the ISS airlock, instead of slowing down via thrusters, he attempted Sergei's feat of grabbing the handrail and killing the inertia. He thumped against the hatch frame, bounced, and repeated two more times. *Smile to the live camera, you clumsy rookie—that was stupid and hazard-ous. Mental note: do not try imitating Sergei.*

✄

Some twenty minutes later they were inside, honing the art of the awkward weightless hug. This was the moment old spacesuit technology died: at 30 per-cent of sea level atmospheric pressure, it used to take hours of patient waiting in the airlock before an astronaut could safely return inside without getting the bends. Instead, Sergei and James removed their helmets with the nonchalance of delivery boys.

After the formalities, Sergei went to the Russian segment for a call with Roscosmos, while James stayed with his Swedish friend Mika Holmgren.

"I had forgotten how noisy it's here. Sounds like a tin can loaded with pen-nies," said James.

"I call it the Impending Sinking Shit, or ISS for short. Not sure it was ever that glamorous, but nowadays half of our day is spent as plumbers. It is time. Next October, in recognition of its merit and seniority, it gets an official crema-tion by forcing it to enter the atmosphere. No twenty-one-gun salute or playing of 'Taps' unfortunately."[12]

---

12   James thought about it. *There's no temptation to salvage the $150-billion investment by leav-ing it in orbit.* Doing so would be hugely irresponsible. In 2007, the Chinese military conducted an anti-satellite missile test by blowing up a 0.75-ton weather satellite that disintegrated into 2,000 pieces each larger than a golf ball, scattered in every direction at speeds many times that of a bullet. At that velocity, small things become huge threats. And with almost complete absence of atmosphere to slow things down and force a re-entry, they can remain a threat for centuries. *There are more than half a million pieces of space junk bigger than one centi-meter already destroying one satellite per year.* If the ISS were to be left unattended—thus unable to dodge orbital debris—and something collided with it, the consequences would

Ø

Hours later, after heartfelt farewells, Sergei and James entered the airlock. In minutes they separated from the ISS, their past Bed & Breakfast, one final

---

be apocalyptic: it was around 600 times heavier than the murdered weather satellite, so by extrapolation it may fragment into more than a million pieces, instantly tripling the amount of space junk in orbit. That could trigger the Kessler Syndrome, a recurrent nightmare among space personnel, where shrapnel creates a domino effect of collisions that could destroy the entire satellite network around our planet and make launching into space impossible, leaving us trapped on Earth for hundreds of years. The destruction of communication satellites would severely cripple television, telephone communication, and the Internet. No weather satellites would destroy the ability to predict and track weather events. No navigation satellites would mean a glorious return of the paper map. *As with many things in life, cluttering and dirtying are the easy part*, he reasoned.

To kill time while James waited for Sergei, Mika doubled as tour guide to the experiments being performed aboard.

They floated inside Kibo, the Japanese science module. Mika pointed to a semi-transparent container with a microscope on top. "You look like the sort of person who would be interested in the findings of this one. This is a yeast colony. We're studying how cells divide in the absence of gravity."

"What sort of yeast?"

"*Trichophyton rubrum*, also known as athlete's foot. Now check this one out. It's the coolest place in the Universe."

"Are you positive it's in the Japanese section?"

"You're gonna love this one. This metallic box is the famous Cold Atom Laboratory, one of the most sensitive instruments ever built. The size of an ice chest, it cost $90 million to build. By laser cooling and magnetic fields, the atoms inside the vacuum chamber are cooled to 1 pico Kelvin above absolute zero. Do you know what that means?" James shook his head. "Well, me neither if I'm being perfectly honest. But I've heard a few things here and there. For example, if we are—unless you guys prove otherwise—the only intelligent ones out there, this box is likely to be the coldest place in the entire Universe."

James tried hard to show interest, but each new blink remained shut longer. *I'm genuinely interested but I'm also dead tired.* "Look, here's a plate with some info: 'The Universe has been cooling since the Big Bang for 13.8 billion years, and its current average temperature is 2.73 degrees Kelvin, or -455 degrees Fahrenheit. The coldest natural place known to us is the Boomerang Nebula, 5,000 light-years away, at 1 Kelvin. The Cold Atom Laboratory operates at a temperature less than a billionth of a degree above absolute zero.' Meaning, if you shrank and were put inside it, you wouldn't be just dead: every atom in your body would be inert. Even a small rock floating beyond Pluto would be livelier, as rays from the faint Sun manage to excite a few atoms—Jimmy?" James had fallen asleep in his attentive floating position, snoring softly with a slight hiss.

time. Inside the ISS, the crew stayed immobile, watching the two men return to their ship.

Long after they were back inside Shackleton, Satoshi and Mika continued gazing at the other spaceship in silence. Mika felt disquieted and downcast, and he wondered what was going through Satoshi's mind.

"What are you thinking, Commander?" asked Mika.

"Take a good look at them …" Satoshi's voice was altered and gloomy. He turned and left.

28 | FAREWELL

June 20 2027. Day 4; 3.2 Years to Saturn

A
t 2:23 AM, the crew received confirmation that the modified Super Heavy rocket docked to Shackleton had been approved for ignition. For the next hour, the paired rocket and spaceship steered into a higher orbit. Now they were seconds away from reaching the exact point of departure from Earth's orbit, the true start of their journey. The rocket's engines would burn through over 3,000 tons of propellant in under ten minutes, before disengaging from Shackleton and catapulting it toward the edge of the Solar System. The highest speed ever attained by humans would be shattered. A minute later, the crew would experience a new jolt as Shackleton fired its own engines at full thrust for three minutes. After the cut-off, there wouldn't be more engines blasting until they arrived at Saturn. That's the counterintuitive result of orbital mechanics, the application of ballistics—the science of throwing objects—and celestial mechanics—the science dealing with the motion of heavenly bodies—to the motion of rockets and spacecrafts. Shackleton was about to break free from Earth's gravity, and for the next three years it would decelerate because of the Sun's massive gravitational pull, until Saturn's gravity claimed the spaceship for itself.

Nitha's voice was crystal clear, as if she was seated among the crew. "Ten seconds, nine, eight, seven, six, five, four, three, two, one. Rocket ignition."[13]

13　"Let's talk about bananas," said Derya a few hours later, after corralling the other four into the cargo area. Sophia and Yi remained instinctively near the ship's central backbone, a few feet further than the rest from Waltzy Mole and the nuclear reactor. "I know this is bloody painful to some of you, like writing a high-school paper on Shakespeare on your birthday. But, alas, we will abandon the cocoon of Earth's magnetic field shortly, plus we'll be turning on our small nuclear electric generator. So, our bodies will be exposed to and absorbing three types of ionizing radiation: solar, cosmic, and nuclear. On Earth, a person receives around one millisievert of radiation per year, but of course it all depends, right? If you go to the dentist a lot and get a bunch of X-rays, or are too keen on tanning at the beach, you may end up with one and a half—"

"You're losing me here, Derya," James interrupted.

"Precisely," said Derya. "Hence the humble banana, which has a trace amount of the radioactive isotope potassium-40. So we can forget about millisieverts and rems and rads and talk bananas. One millisievert is equal to 10,000 bananas, so we absorb twenty-seven bananas per day on Earth. In space we'll get about 700 millisievert per year, which equals to 19,200 bananas per day."

"Derya ..."

"Don't know about you, but in this precise moment I have nothing better to do, besides practicing my left-hand grip—I'm a lefty, by the way."

"Bravo. Real highbrow, Derya," said Sophia, more bored than bothered.

Derya saw Yi surreptitiously checking his tablet. *I thought space would cure us from short attention span disorder.* He decided to wrap it up. "Anyway, that digital display sensor on the wall behind Sergei is the daily and cumulative radiation gauge inside Shackleton. I changed the screen units to bananas and attached a sheet for your reference."

The sheet of paper, taped to the wall under the sensor and titled "Single-Event Banana Count," had the following handwritten information:

"Dental X-ray: fifty bananas."

"Flight from London to New York: 400 bananas."

"Day in outer space: 20k bananas."

"Chest CT Scan: 70k bananas."

"One session of radiotherapy: 20 million bananas."

"Fatal Dose (death within two weeks): 40–100 million bananas."

"Solar Flare hitting Shackleton near Mars' orbit: 100–1,000 million bananas."

After gliding to inspect the sheet, Sophia said, "Thank you, Derya, that was both confusing and spooky. But as your loving and devoted Mission Physician, it is my duty to allay some of these concerns. First—and I'm sorry D—I would completely ignore the radiation gauge and its scarecrow sheet, as there is nothing you or I can do about it beyond biting our nails until they bleed. Second, let's dispel the myth about ionizing radiation. 'Ionizing' means the radiation has enough energy to damage the DNA inside the cells if it slams into it. Non-ionizing radiation is the kind emitted by cellphones, televisions, light bulbs, or microwave ovens. That's all it is. Therefore, the health consequences stem from either a very high dose of radiation in a short amount of time or low accumulated doses over the long term. The former is what people at Hiroshima got or what we would get if a solar flare hit Shackleton. This kind is usually referred to as acute radiation sickness, and it kills the person in months to even minutes, depending on the dose. The latter—which is the one we should care about—is basically a story about cancer.

"When a cell's DNA gets damaged, the cell attempts repair. If the damage is too great and the cell dies, that's okay. Cells die all the time. The problem stems from the few instances in which the repair is done imperfectly and it corrupts the DNA code, turning the cell into a zombie instead of a healthy specimen. In rare cases, the zombie cell begins dividing much faster than the other cells, expanding uncontrollably throughout the organs and the body. And this, my dear gentlemen, is called cancer." She looked around. No one looked at ease anymore.

"Which takes us to the good news! I'll paraphrase Robert Zubrin here, the President of the Mars Society—he presides over it from Earth in case you thought I'm already going gaga from

Ø

MOON FLYBY

"—being 9:53 PM UTC, Sophia Jong, Derya Terzi, Yi Meng, Sergei Lazarev, and Jimmy Egger have just broken the distance record made by the ill-fated yet ultimately successful Apollo 13 mission on April 14 1970 as they crossed over the dark side of the Moon. To put this in perspective, if Earth was a soccer ball, Shackleton would now be twenty-four feet away. Saturn? Europe as seen from the English coast—"

Sophia turned off the radio coming out of her headphones and looked at her tablet. Even after her secretaries' patient screening, there were almost one hundred new messages in her inbox. But there was something profoundly impersonal about fame. *There is no real personal connection, just hype*, she thought. After three years of madness, the sound of silence was overwhelming. *And the receding Earth, terrifying—I can sense the existential loneliness creeping in.* She knew how to fight back: aural music replaced oral noise. She closed her eyes to the soothing, famous electric organ chords and remained in a meditative state.

When she took her headphones off, the seventh repetition of Pink Floyd's "Comfortably Numb" trailed away. She scanned around. The Moon stood in the Sun's way and the lights were off, yet it was twilight in Bacchus; an ivory luster stood in for the tangerine orange. Yi floated mid-air between her and the Observation Window—the other three had left for their cabins. He was reading the Quran, a splendid copy with engraved brass plate cover lit by the cosmos. Freed from atmospheric distortion and filtering, the stars did not twinkle and their true colors blossomed into an assortment of yellows, blues, reds, purples, and greens. Sophia shivered as her soul poured out in the form of goosebumps

---

banana overdose. The increase in the risk of getting cancer will be about 2 percent per year, or around 15 percent by the time we return to Earth. Meanwhile, there's a 20 percent increase in the risk for the average American smoker. Meaning, if you sent smokers to space without tobacco, they could actually decrease their chance of getting cancer. Last but not least, all this cancer stuff is probabilistic, random, stochastic. You could travel around the Solar System all your life and die at 110 years from boredom and old age. Or you could be watching the LA Lakers getting pounded while eating steaming popcorn with just-poured hot clarified butter when this one infinitesimal cosmic ray pierces through the atmosphere and slams into a few letters of the DNA code in one single cell of yours among forty trillion others, yet five years later you kick the bucket from terminal cancer. Such is life."

as she witnessed a mesmerizing Milky Way, the greatest display of Christmas lights ever assembled.

"It's so …" Sophia's throat clenched the words. She did not follow through. Silence seemed the most eloquent tribute to the immensity before her.

After some time, Yi said, "'And among His Signs is the creation of the heavens and the Earth, and the living creatures that He has scattered through them.' Are you hearing the same I'm hearing? To me, Muhammad was acknowledging the existence of extraterrestrial life. In the year 632 AD! Such wisdom and humility. Today's Earth would have been unrecognizable to him, yet the night sky he looked at hasn't changed one bit—space defies our intuition and our intellect. On Earth, your eyes may be able to discern a tall mountain one hundred miles away. Get into a car and you can go past it in under two hours. But here … here, instead, we see everything yet we can reach nothing. Think about it. The closest star to our Solar System among hundreds of billions just in our Milky Way is that pinpoint of yellow light over there on the right, Alpha Centauri, 4.4 light-years away. At our current speed, the fastest ever achieved by humans, it would take us 80,000 years to get there.[14] All the mysteries of the Universe are right here before us, naked, uncovered, exposed. But this clairvoyance comes with a terrible curse: they are only reachable by our eyes and imagination."

For an instant during Yi's musings Sophia felt elated, and at every moment she was in awe, hearing the recitation while looking at its inspiration. The sadness from before had pulled back. *That marvelous, childlike curiosity you have— it's not just admirable, but addictive, contagious.* She understood him and felt understood. A kinship. *I really like you, Yi.*

He continued in that same dreamlike cadence that gave Sophia enough time to reflect on his words: "A thousand civilizations may be in front of us right now, staring back, as clueless as we are. Right in front of us there are black holes, orbiting around which we could slow time to a crawl and become effectively immortal. Or wormholes tunneling into other galaxies or maybe even other Universes—now think back to us and assimilate the scale of our insignificance. The number of stars in the Universe is far higher than the number of

---

14   "Or look there, center-left. That blob of light is the closest neighbor and much bigger galaxy to ours, Andromeda. It is so distant as to be laughable. Einstein showed that traveling at the speed of light is an impossibility for any type of matter, but light is already ridiculously slow relative to the scale of galaxies. You and I can see it, despite that it's 2.5 million light-years away. If we ever venture into intergalactic space, it will be a one-way street tens of millions of years long, even in the most optimistic cases of space travel technology. For some perspective, we, Homo sapiens, are barely 300,000 years old."

grains of sand in all the beaches of the Earth, yet our biggest achievement so far has been to walk on the Moon, a satellite orbiting another satellite orbiting a grain of sand known as the Sun. Even when this mission succeeds, we'll still be hopelessly marooned on our lush microscopic island orbiting our star. The chasm to the next, closest grain of sand, Alpha Centauri, remains unbridgeable. We are pinned to a single grain of sand in the limitless cosmic beach of the cosmos. I certainly can't possibly think Muhammad knew this, but I guess he may have sensed the bottomless vastness around us."

"Shiver my timbers! That was mystical, friend. How far into the book are you?"

"A third," Yi said shyly.

"Jumping Yisus, Jesus! And you haven't even started the Vedas or the Bible or the Torah!" Yi had spent part of his personal payload in carrying physical copies of the main religions' holy books on board. "At this rate we'll have an onboard prophet soon. But soon is not yet now, so I'll baptize you 'Profe' meanwhile."

"Why 'Profe'?"

"It's prof in Spanish—as in professor, you know. Not a bad step in your stairway to attain enlightenment ..."

The bottom of the Observation Window steadily turned into the darkest dark Sophia had ever seen, as the rotisserie-like spin initiated hours before, and lasting for the next few months to evenly grill the spaceship's hull with the Sun's heating power, rotated toward the dark side of the Moon. The only thing betraying its presence was its anti-self: a sliding circle of unqualified darkness occupying most of the Observation Window, as if the heavens' Maker had cut away a disk from a canvas swamped with motes of light.

⌀

James had just finished their extended daily chat. Belinda enumerated the preparations for the baby—the gender was a surprise, which complicated logistics. *I could gobble up a political party broadcast if it was told by that never-tiring voice of yours.* The time lag was still a little over a second, making for a delightful conversation. But going forward, each day would increase the lag by four seconds. *We'll soon need to speak in turns, and in two weeks the minute lag will murder the concept of a conversation. After that, it'll be recorded messages only.*

He put his earphones on and jumped through the stations until he landed on one of his favorite programs.

"—yet no one has ever lost visual contact with the Earth, the so-called 'Earth-out-of-view' phenomenon, when our home planet turns into so miniscule a dot that it becomes indistinguishable from the stars. Mark my words, Daniel: their isolation will become intolerable."

Another voice answered back, "You're a full-time professional defeatist, selling pessimism to fuel controversy. But facts are worth 1,000 experts. Arthur C. Clarke saw three stages of reactions to revolutionary ideas: 'It's completely impossible' you used to say just a few months back. Now, you're camouflaging and toning down by resorting to the long-term mental health risks of space traveling, which to me sounds awfully like the second, 'it's possible but not worth doing.' In a couple of months, you'll be preaching 'I said it was a good idea all along.' Problem is, you're live, pal."

James smiled, turned it off, and went to bed.

29 | EVERYDAY LIFE

August 23 2027. Day 68; 3 Years to Saturn

OUTER SPACE

At 7:00 AM, the speakers in each cabin burst into Mission Control's wake-up call, "Fleeing Earthlings, the theme for today is one of the greatest movie openings of all time …" This one required no guessing. Yi instantly pictured a menacing organ, followed by trumpets, full strings, and marching kettle drums to the image of the Sun coming out from behind the Earth as seen from the Moon. Instead, he got the swaggering walk of a pair of leather boots and brilliant flared white pants accompanied by the funky guitar and bass rhythm of "Stayin' Alive."

As an unrepentant space nerd he knew it all had started in 1965, when Wally Schirra and Tom Stafford—crammed inside their Gemini 6A capsule orbiting the Earth—awoke to the crooner Jack Jones' parody of the Broadway hit tune "Hello, Dolly!" *And the tradition stuck until today.* It was a nice spin on the essential need to keep astronauts on a rigid sleeping schedule. Shackleton made it even less discretionary by turning off the gravity wheel, which comes to a full stop fifteen minutes later. *So, it's a choice of willpower or physics, but you are getting out of bed.*

The wake-up call was one of the most coveted platforms for artists and celebrities to jack up their popularity or amplify their message. The mix of line-up secrecy and one-upmanship had turned it into favorite listening for hundreds of millions. The previous day had been the Berliner Philharmoniker, the full orchestra opening with the explosive bull-fighting theme of the opera *Carmen*. A week prior was the Dalai Lama, whose youth was no impediment for dazzling depth and wisdom.

Whenever Yi felt unsure whether he was dreaming up this far-fetched life as an astronaut, his hand instinctively reached for the carved Buddha against his chest. *My totem, like Dominick Cobb's in* Inception. This time was no different. It also grounded and kept him humble as the palpable memory of his mother. *Made with those aged, callused hands of hers.* He remembered their shepherds' small log house in the Inner Mongolian steppes. *Yi Meng, predestined to follow my family's ancestral trade in a world confined between the mountains surrounding the hamlet, is instead heading to Saturn.* There was no arrogance, only pure wonderment and bafflement.

Ø

Next door, James' return to consciousness needed a much longer runway. Belinda's water broke late the previous night and it was only after B's pleading that he went for the pill and pillow a few hours before.

Ø

James entered Bacchus, running late with today's meals from the pantry in the cargo area. His cheerfulness tempered upon seeing Sergei. As a father, he could probably relate to him better than anyone else. The official news they received three weeks ago was cryptic: Iman had had complications and the baby was no more. He had tried giving Sergei his condolences but it didn't land well. The crew knew, yet there was no public acknowledgment. Whatever his misery, Sergei dealt with it alone. *The only perceivable difference is his quietness*, thought James. But a private message he received two days prior from the Russian's mission psychologist hinted at deeper layers: Sergei blamed Iman for the loss and had not talked to her since before the tragedy. James was torn: he still wasn't close enough to Sergei to talk about something this personal; however, he was certain that not talking to your better half was never a good idea.

"Banana bar, Sergei. BBQ nut bar, Tweety and Jimmy. Ginger vanilla bar, Derya. Braised pork … with seaweed salad bar? Profe?" said Derya, distributing rations among his fellow diners at the communal table while James stored lunch and dinner in a cabinet. Their diet was fine-tuned weekly in calorific count and nutritional value for each crew member. Sophia's daily target stood at 2,100 calories whereas Sergei aimed for 3,600, with James north of the middle. A far cry from Columbus and Magellan sea voyages, but not everything has improved. *Bars are at the bottom of the totem pole for a reason. Sure, great nutrition-to-weight ratio, but you pay back in presentation, pasty texture, and that clingy leather shoe aftertaste—about the only thing all-natural in them.*

"Pass the pepper please," asked Sophia. Yi threw her a container with pepper in a liquid form to season the dehydrated eggs she had recovered from the food warmer box, reconstituted with hot water. There was no sprinkling of salt or pepper in space, as it would float away, eventually clogging air vents or landing in somebody's eyes or nose. In space, the inoffensive sometimes becomes threatening. A spilled saltshaker could become an emergency, even requiring the crew to don their helmets. James saw Sophia shaking the chili sauce over her eggs like a maraca. Weightlessness swells the head, which impairs the sense of smell, which dulls the taste, which causes Sophia to fight back by spicing things up.

Spotting the lunch—freeze-dried, thermostabilized shrimp cocktail followed by precooked irradiated spaghetti and meatballs—Derya invoked a sudden return to his claimed vegan adolescence.

"You? A German bratwurst of Turkish descent?" said James.

"How come you're American and know the difference between Austria and Australia? I would have assumed the US border constituted the edge of the known Universe for you too. No preconceptions mate," said Derya.

James saved Derya's day by revealing an unexpected bag tagged, "Candy Coated Chocolates," also known as M&M's. And besides, tonight's dinner would include the Olympus of the food pyramid in space, the earthy-type grown on board Shackleton, fresh produce. *Or more specifically, two tomatoes, three potatoes (sour cream please), lettuce, and seven radishes.*

∅

After dinner everyone had trickled out of Bacchus except for James and Sergei. As the latter was leaving, he patted James on the shoulder, "Everything will turn out all right."

And it did. At 11:06 PM, Emma Egger was born into the world.

30 | THE ΛSTEROID BELT

t was past midnight as James continued clearing an outsized inbox of messages. Even with people curating and pruning his emails, he spotted an intruder that passed the filter by way of impersonation. Billy Martinez was a close college friend; Billie Martinez—whose mail he was staring at—was not. *Billie seems to have graduated from one of those flat Earth societies, but only very recently*, thought James. *I barely missed his diploma ceremony.* By powerful inference, James was able to deduct that junior appeared to be a fervent believer in the Great Flood, with an ark riding high, "All my investigations point to a Universe no older than 6,944 years before our Lord." But Billie had bigger fish to fry. He was a visionary, even if single-eyed and partially blind. "Jimmy, if I can call you that, let's change history together." *You should have started by saying that. Now I'm really engaged.* "The Earth is hollow." *I knew something big was coming.* "But all those conspiracy theories are plainly absurd, not to be believed, and easily disproven by Christian Science or even regular scientists." But when Billie linked Dante's Eighth Circle of Hell with a secret passage that opened in Machu Picchu on the evening of Holy Friday, he decided to let it go. *For now. We're not done, Billie.* Too high an intellectual dare for a tired body about to go to sleep.

Let's deal with the blushing. He had been finding pretexts to postpone the inescapable. He heard about it at dinner, laughs and mockery included. He abhorred the news-lite, scandal-thick, soft-porn, sensationalist tabloids, but he had been force-fed on regurgitated and distorted articles about Belinda and himself. The contempt was not reciprocal, they adored them. And when they couldn't get material, they simply made it up. Somehow, they got hold of yesterday's private correspondence with Belinda. Nothing racy, but no lack of intimate. The UK's *Daily Mail* front page announced, "LOVESICK JIMMY SERENADES FAVORITE EARTHLING. NAKED!" *Not true. Not naked.* But yes, he was proving to be a blossoming, unapologetic romantic. *I'm in love with one and a half women.*

He was dozing off when a foreign sound lifted above his alert threshold.

Adrenaline rushed thoughts in his confused, half-asleep mind. *It sounds—it sounds like ... radio white noise?* He racked his brain trying to make sense of the unusual sound. *It's ... a sandstorm against the hull.* James jumped to his feet and ran for the ladder. At 40 percent gravity, his moves were feline. As he climbed toward the ship's center, the artificial gravity broke down. He did a quick pull-up and the inertia lifted his whole body up, flying.

He intersected an airborne Yi as they headed to the flight deck's Observation Window. Sergei was already there. Soon after Sophia and Derya joined them as well. There was nothing but the black void in front with a deluge of stars in the fathomless background.

"A micro-asteroid shower," said Sergei.

"A few microns in size at most, otherwise we would be dead ... maybe an interplanetary dust storm ..." said James.

They all stood immobile, floating in silence. Slowly they discerned the change in intensity. It deescalated and then picked up, an erratic wave pattern of infinitesimal stones ricocheting against the spaceship's fuselage.

"It's the Universe courteously knocking on our door," said Sophia.

"I commend the poetry, but what guarantees it doesn't slam a fist-sized asteroid into us?" said Derya.

"We are about an eighth into the asteroid belt. Since 1972's Pioneer 10, fifteen unmanned spacecraft have crossed it unharmed," answered Sergei.

"That's a pretty modest sample for me to fall back asleep to," said Derya.

"James, we should do a hull inspection spacewalk over the next few days," said Sergei, the only one who still didn't address the rest of the crew with nicknames.[15]

---

15   **December 25 2027. Day 192; 2.7 Years to Saturn**

Before launch, every crew member had a strict weight allowance for nonessential personal items. Derya spent almost all of his on a telescope especially designed by Meade, the world's largest manufacturer. With a twenty-two-inch aperture, it allowed 1,500x magnification and light-gathering power 5,000x that of the unaided eye. Back on Earth it would have been the most high-end expert recreational telescope available. Here, with no twinkling or optical distortion from the atmosphere, it became a mini-Hubble. Anchored to the center of the flight deck's Observation Window, anyone mistaking it for public property would promptly see the tag: "Achtung. No touching w/o Derya's supervision. Danke."

Sophia tried drumming up the Christmas spirit at dinnertime, but the most she got was Yi promising to watch *Home Alone*, alone. Instead, she found herself accompanying Derya by his telescope. He had become a regular nighttime fixture around it. She still didn't quite get him and sometimes he seemed insincere, even cunning to her. *He's also vain and even he seems to agree: there's this Caravaggio painting in his cabin of Narcissus gazing at his own water reflection—hey, respect, know thyself.* But, and it was a big but, he had proved rabidly loyal to James and the mission. *And maybe, by transitivity, to us—besides, you don't get to pick friends around here.*

"Want to check out Saturn?" asked Derya.

"Grandma Yoo-bin was wise beyond her years. She once said if you ever came across a crystal ball you should run away as if you saw the boogie man. Saturn's coming in three years. I would rather wait. But I would be honored to be shown asteroid Juju, your major-league discovery."

Derya cleared his throat. "Shackleton is crossing the asteroid belt, the giant ring of debris from the formation of our Solar System between the orbits of Mars and Jupiter. If Jimmy was here, I'm sure he would add something like 'with millions of asteroids over half a mile in diameter—a size sufficient to evaporate a country and disrupt Earth's climate for decades—complex life on Earth may have only arisen thanks to the gravitational shepherding effect of Jupiter, the gas giant that maintains martial order and stable orbits over every denizen belonging to the asteroid belt,' no? But as I've shown—as this mission has shown—instead of harbingers of death, asteroids form the essential building blocks of a Utopian future. Asteroids contain metals of both the standard and precious variety, in ultra high grade and virtually unlimited quantities. Platinum, the most precious metal on Earth, for example—thirty times rarer than gold, yet required in minute quantities in one in four manufactured goods. A single tiny platinum-rich asteroid contains more of it than has been mined in the history of humanity. People such as my friend Jeff Bezos—"

Sophia rolled her eyes, "You saw him twice, D. Hardly a compadre."

"And we really hit it off. I got this email from him about a month ago—"

"Four months ago. You read it to the whole crew. And it was rather businessy, regarding his rocket company. I detected zero bromance. I call that an acquaintance at best."

"It's Jeffrey-goddamn-Bezos. You think his friends get to toast marshmallows with him over weekends? Anyway, the bloke envisions millions of people living and working in space, mining asteroids and doing heavy industries, sending finished products down to Earth, which would be restricted to residential and service industries. Good concept, but abstract, intangible ... meet Juju." After he programmed the telescope, its motor drive burred as it turned to locate and track the asteroid. He pushed himself away and clumsily grabbed a roof handrail. Sophia flew nimbly to the telescope, swiftly resting her right eye against the eyepiece.

"It looks like a badly lit black-and-white picture of a banana," said Sophia.

"With three lentils by the waist in a failed attempt at high art. But what it lacks in craft it compensates for in lavish girth and size. A banana-shaped metallic asteroid seventy miles long, orbited by three moons."

Over the last weeks Derya had been spotting and cataloging new asteroids, the vast majority of which called the belt home. But three days back, the optical and infrared spectroscopy data sent to Earth came back loaded with exclamation marks: Juju. "Juju is extremely dense, containing huge quantities of pure metals, probably covering the entire periodic table. Raw materials needing no smelting, almost ready to use, amounting to a scale far larger than all the metal ever mined on Earth. And the moons are altogether different, made of ice and carbon. Vast amounts of fuel from breaking water into hydrogen and oxygen. For all this I'm pretty sure I'll be seeing some Bezos correspondence come this way—my way." Even mainstream media was daydreaming of a huge city-foundry a century forward, dedicated to churning out anything from computer chips to interstellar spaceships.

"It's a white Christmas back home," said James, Sophia and Derya turning their heads to him as he came in from the ship's central backbone passageway. "Shall we do some snowy comet stuff?" Sophia was delighted to see him and it showed. "The pang of conscience got me out of bed, Tweety—she goes by Belinda."

"I told you," said Derya looking at Sophia. "Here's the man-boy that loves soaring stones and snowballs."

"Hardly, but there's this one particular comet that has stalked my dreams for years. In a way, it's the thing that brought us all here," said James.

"You mentioned it's mostly gone," said Sophia.

"Less of a nighttime regular, yes, but it leaves an extensive vapor trail here," said James, touching his forehead. The other two seemed to be waiting for more, so he continued, "I think comets, not asteroids, are the biggest death-from-above danger to our planet." While asteroids are grouped together in stable, well-behaved, predictable orbits; long-period comets—those taking over two centuries to complete a lap around the Sun—are the ancient lone pilgrims awoken from the outer reaches of our Solar System, either the Kuiper Belt just beyond the orbit of Pluto, or the vast, mysterious, faraway Oort cloud that may extend halfway to the nearest star. "They fall into the Sun at enormous speeds before being catapulted back out. And during that time, they move up to three times faster than asteroids."

"Considering energy is the square of speed, that's nine times as deadly," said Derya.

"Plus they tend to be bigger," James continued, "and they fall so fast the warning may come two years before impact, at most. They're made of ice that evaporates as they approach the inner Solar System, forming those grand tails blowing away from the Sun like wind socks. The flares of gas around the comet forming the tail are random and act as little thrusters, altering the trajectory and making it very hard to estimate its path."

"And yet," said Derya, "water on Earth most likely came by way of comets."

Small ones, several feet in diameter, ring the bell about once a year. The nasty ones, half a mile in size or more, pay us a visit every half a million years or so. They likely seeded the Earth with the ingredients needed for life to emerge, and some day one of them may decide to claim life back.

"Can we look at Halley's Comet?" asked Sophia, detecting a rapid deterioration of her hard-earned Christmas spirit. Derya obliged and the telescope moved and locked into a new position. "Am I doing something wrong?" Sophia asked. "I see nothing."

"Imagine a middle-size city, say Munich—can you picture it?" said Derya.

"Sure," said Sophia.

"Halley is roughly Munich's size. It's a short-period comet that visits Earth every 74-79 years, last time in 1986. Now it's beyond the orbit of Neptune, the furthest planet in the Solar System. It's travelled so far that the Sun can't gas it anymore. It's a Munich immersed in a decades-long blackout, tailless and cloaked in black. This instrument's incredible, but you're asking the equivalent of seeing the atom with a high-school microscope. Now you ask, how can it be we can see galaxies 50 million light-years away yet we can't see a comet five light-hours from here? The answer boils down to size. That's why you can seldom see a fly across your garden yet you easily see the Moon—did you know Halley was observed and recorded hundreds or maybe even thousands of years before Christ by Babylonians and Chinese astronomers, yet the name comes from the one person who recognized them as reappearances of the same object in 1705? This 'juju' naming by the International Astronomical Union is bullshit. This is my discovery, and I get to choose the name. It is henceforth baptized Comet Terzi."

"Isn't it a bit self-aggrandizing?" asked Sophia.

"Losers call it vanity, winners call it rightful pride," said Derya.

31 | THINNING COMMUNICATION

March 4 2028. Day 262; 2.5 Years to Saturn

"Do you know the level of responsibility for providing inspiring content to hundreds of millions of followers?"

"I wouldn't know, Derya, I have 2 billion," said Yi.

"Feed them well, we go dark next week," James reminded them.

The laser communication was overstretched. The connection dropped for minutes at a time now and the latency was becoming disruptive.

When half an hour later they were all having breakfast, James repeated, "The next few days are intentionally light on tasks so everyone has enough time to wrap things up. Videos with loved ones, interviews with the press, now's the time." This milestone had long been dreaded but because the mission was pushing the technology a great deal forward, the exact date when laser communication became unfeasible was just a conservative estimate that reality had prolonged for weeks. Not anymore. "The physics of radio communication is unforgiving. Our data transfer will drop to about 2 percent of today's. Sophia?"

"The allotted data limit for non-work communication will be a group quota. You go over, you steal from everybody else. Don't ever do that, don't be that guy. Daily portion is 10 MB per person each way. Use it wisely—that's twice the complete works of Shakespeare in text, or twenty minutes of audio, or fifteen seconds of HD video."

⌀

It was nighttime. From the cabin wall hung a black-and-white photograph of a log raft barely above the waterline, a bulging sail pushing the final stretch of the 4,300-mile journey, topped by proud Norwegian flags and carrying four mostly shirtless men hypnotized by the shoreline after losing sight of it for 101 days. The fabled 1947 Kon-Tiki expedition that proved Polynesia could have been colonized by people from South America.

Under it, a motionless Yi hung in mid-air. His hands were symmetrically in front, semi-closed and separated in between by the distance of an open book, which levitated a few inches above. Without gravity there was no head falling and jerking, making the droopy-eyes-to-asleep transition imperceptible every time. His body was dormant but the brain was firing, attested by the rapid eye-lid movement.

At 10:15 PM, the cabin started rotating. Circling clockwise, one of the walls inched closer. When the contact happened, he jolted back to consciousness. His mind was disoriented and he felt the caustic taste of terror in his mouth. *It's a dream, it's just a dream.* Right before waking up he had the suspicion of inhabiting a dream. *Now I know I'm not.* Here there was no finger-snapping escapism like back on Earth. *We are trapped inside a fragile tin can in the immensity of space. A thin-walled spaceship surrounded by millions of miles of nothingness.* He tried breathing to calm down, but this time it did not work. *Analyze the dream. Rationalize it—I open my eyes and see nothing. Not darkness, but complete pitch-blackness. My other senses try to compensate: I notice the rubbing of my spacesuit, the panting misting up the visor, my sweaty hands. I perceive I'm floating in space but there's no sense of depth or distance. I'm in the middle of a cosmic void, those vast spaces barren of galaxies, one of the loneliest places in the Universe. The closest atoms past the small atmosphere between my head and the visor reflecting my grimaced, petrified face are in some far away galaxy, tens of millions of light-years from me. The light from the trillion stars inside it too faint for my eyes to detect. In desperation I manage to find the helmet lights and turn them on, but they are instantly swallowed by the empty space, ghost lights robbed of their beams. I'm sightless without being blind. My reflex screaming inside the fishbowl merely rings the brain. I need to die, please let me die!*

The panic began to metastasize. Like on other occasions he tried containment by meditation, but this time it was pervasive and much stronger. He flew to Demeter like a freediver holding on to the last molecules of oxygen. He entered the Z-shaped maze of lush greenery with eyes closed. Breathed in the humidity, the smell of wet soil, of peppermint, and tomatoes. Ran his hands over the stems of vegetables, rubbed his fingers against the leaves. Caught the soft current of air-grazing plants against one another. Moving from memory, he stopped by his gardening plot, the size of a shoebox. He caressed the single flower of Margaret Atwood, his second-generation soybean plant. Then measured the germinating Liu Cixin, a third-generation chickpea, and discovered a new developing leaf. Then his fingers climbed the stem of Douglas Adams, a mature pea plant, dislodged one of its three pods, opened it, and slid the peas into his mouth. He was wholly in the moment and felt surrounded and protected by these other life forms from the plant kingdom. Only then did he open his eyes, and was startled to see Derya a few feet away, unaware of his presence. He was facing away from Yi and had headphones on.

Yi tapped Derya's shoulder and after a jerk and a swarm of German expletives, they asked each other about their mutual impromptu visit to Demeter.

"Similar," said Derya. "We couldn't decelerate in Saturn." Yi knew the chance of missing Saturn's gravity claws was remote, but if it were to happen and Shackleton went past the gas giant, the consequences may justify Derya's night terrors. With no gravity field or enough fuel to turn around, in weeks Saturn would shrink into a dot in the rearview mirror. And with five years of supplies, death would slowly strangle them. They'd continue subsisting under the agonizing burden of knowing their expiration date. There wouldn't be more planetary extravaganza for a very, very long time. At their current speed, Alpha Centauri stood 80,000 years away, but this, the closest star system, was in the opposite direction. The tapestry of stars would appear perfectly static for tens of thousands of years. A spaceship of ghosts moving until the end of time. On this occasion Yi played out the scenario in omniscient point of view instead of getting thrown inside the nightmare. *One thing is clear: the crew consensus is that dreams have become particularly vivid as of late.*

"What are you listening to?" asked Yi. Derya took off his headphones and put them on Yi's head. He immediately became immersed in the deep underwater ambience of the ocean, hearing the mass of water, the bubbling, and the enchanting reverberations of sea giants singing to other whales hundreds of miles away. *Even city-dwellers like Derya have become hooked on—no, make it clinically addicted to—regularly listening to nature. Not songs, not voices, but the unassuming simplicity of an owl meditating at nighttime, of rain and wind gusts over a larch forest, of crickets under a thunderstorm.*

"We haven't even broken Valery Polyakov's record of 438 days aboard Mir space station," said Derya.

Ø

Shackleton had been using the dish antenna for mission critical communication for weeks. The laser barely worked anymore: idle most of the time and busy corrupting data when not. But turning it off carried a significance that weighed on everyone.

The crew floated by Bacchus' Observation Window.

The lasers operated in the near-infrared part of the spectrum, invisible to the human eye. But they could picture them nonetheless. Two beams of light, sender and receiver, disappearing into infinity as they pointed to a bluish dot.

"This is the invisible boundary," said James.

"After which isolation becomes extreme," said Derya.

Yi announced, "Laser communication with Earth going off in three, two, one—laser off."

A feeling of emptiness and sadness began to permeate, unexpectedly put on hold by music coming out of Bacchus' speakers:

I see trees of green, red roses too
I see them bloom, for me and you
And I think to myself, what a wonderful world ...

32 | EVERYDAY LIFE II

September 24 2028. Day 466; 1.9 Years to Saturn

The tongue goes from licking her left ear to her nape, as a large hand grabs her red dress between her breasts and pulls down hard, ripping it open. It then climbs back to the bridge of her bra and takes out a breast with a hard nipple. She feels a second hand raising her skirt and pushing down her panties. Somebody gets right behind her. In darkness, all other senses become hypersensitive. Her mind is racing, dizzy with the feeling of being possessed, aware of her inability to stop it. In seconds she's naked except for her bra, hanging uselessly mid-waist—

A metallic, insistent ringing stole her from the dream. Sophia picked the culprit up in frustrated anger and threw it against the wall. The spongy alarm clock jumped back and, seemingly in pure provocation, hit her in the chest. *Hopefully the purring and moaning was purely mental too,* Sophia thought. The raging lust still overpowering, she attempted half successfully to go back to sleep, but failed to trigger the sensation-drenched space porn.

The imposed celibacy elicited strange sexual, almost animal, impulses. *But with a four to one male ratio, this is the one thing I can't talk about.* Maybe the future of space travel was dependent on, as Apollo 11's Mike Collins once quipped, "a cadre of eunuchs." The thought of her crewmates masturbating was disgusting, but she wondered how the others were faring. She tried to keep the image out of her mind, but it developed anyway. *And Jimmy? He must do it too—is it always Belinda, though? Is it always one-to-one? Has he ever done it with me in mind—ENOUGH!*

♄

At breakfast that morning, Sophia saw the last toilet user fly into Bacchus, clearly enraged.

"I want to crush skulls," Derya said. "What's the matter with you people? I'm fixing my urinal funnel and, goddammit, a foreign body enters my nose. You know what it was? Do you know what it was? A floating turd. Somebody else's doo-doo entered my nostril." Sophia barely contained herself, but a jumbo laugh escaped Yi. "Do not provoke me, Shaolin," said Derya threateningly. James burst out laughing too.

Using a toilet in gravity's absence required a broad palette of skills. Each person had a private urinal funnel, which needed to be attached to a hose inside the toilet each time. Then, the body needed to squat over the toilet seat using the leg restraints. Here's where the proper way—explained step by step on the wall in front—was sometimes betrayed by the temptation to speed the process up. The right way made sure there was good seal between buttocks and seat, as the toilet worked like a vacuum cleaner, sucking liquid and solids through the funnel past the hose into the waste tank for water recycling later on.

"It wasn't a sole survivor," said Derya. "When I looked around, I saw other fecal flies meandering about." All of a sudden nobody found it funny anymore.

"Who was it?" demanded Sergei.

"There's shite orbiting the bloody loo. Whoever did it needs to go grab 'em now," said Derya.

"Whoever did it, or suspects he/she may have done it, or wants to serve the greater good, will clean it up during the next couple of hours. No witnesses, no reputational loss," said James. *Good luck with that*, thought Sophia. *Everyone will spy for the felon.* James probably arrived to the same conclusion, because he sighed and said, "I'll volunteer for morale and harmony—but only this one time."

"I really, really wonder how today's reek is even possible," said Derya. "We're all eating the same food. Chemistry should even out the five assholes' stench—unless …" He propelled himself to the roof and moved like an elderly Spider-Man to one of the cabinets. "Aha! I knew it. Listen all, Sino-kleptomaniac keeps playing mind games. The large bag of Ghirardelli chocolates is missing."

"I hid it. From you," said Yi.

"In your stomach, I presume. Which explains today's Delhi belly, you filthy nitwit," said Derya.

"Guys, come on. Chill out," said James.

"Jimmy, you're officially exempt from the clean-up," said Derya.

"It wasn't me! And I hid it to prevent temptation," said Yi.

"Bloody hell! And who granted you so much seniority?" said Derya.

"Yi, I don't think controlling behavior lands well around here. Please return it today," said James.

"Then I've had enough as well," said Yi. "It's the fourth time in a row I've been 'randomly' selected by Derya's 'blind' algorithm to clean the filters. Yesterday a few balls of many-hued hairs, not all scalp related, were awaiting collection."

"Oh god," said Sophia, pulling a face.

And it ended at that. *A much-improved outcome to the previous month's Nutella incident*, she thought. It started one morning when Derya discovered someone had finished off the group's monthly Nutella ration. When he demanded an explanation from the offender, Yi countered that the next bin was scheduled to be opened in two days, which the other misconstrued as inconsiderate behavior. "Are you fulfilled? Have you replenished your breadbasket with our calories?"

"You can take my ration next time."

"You twonk wanker!" Derya followed by throwing his coffee mug at Yi. A moment later, the two were wrestling in a ridiculous floating embrace, and had it not been for Sergei's fast intervention fists drawn would have each landed in the face of the other.

After a long time living together in close quarters, emotions ran raw and fuses tripped fast. Everyone knew there was a stowaway in Shackleton: a silent, inconspicuous little devil stirring up tempers. *It even has a name: Irrational Antagonism*, thought Sophia. There had been extensive warnings from psychologists and sociologists about increasing emotional volatility and confrontational behavior. *This is tipping point stuff. Once the rules of respect are violated, doing it again becomes ever likelier. A variation of the broken windows theory in criminology.*[16]

---

16   Sophia remembered one of the Thursday night talks a few months back about psychological effects of long-term confinement. Each crew member was responsible for a talk one Thursday every five weeks, in which a subject relevant to living in space was presented for half an hour, followed by a lively debate. It went something like this:

    Isolation is tough on the spirit, and if anybody knows how rough, it's probably late US Admiral Richard E. Byrd, who tested the boundaries of human mental endurance to the point of narrowly escaping suicide.

    Following active duty in World War I, he turned into an overnight national hero after flying over the North Pole in 1926. In 1927, he turned his sights to the biggest challenge of his day, the non-stop crossing of the Atlantic. He landed (crashed) in France a month too late, outcompeted by Charles Lindbergh's historic solo epic.

    Flying over the South Pole followed in 1929, going all in and barely making it. A month later, a special act of Congress made him, to this day, the youngest admiral in the history of the US Navy at 41 years of age.

    Escalating the commitment, in 1934 he disappeared alone into the Antarctic winter "to taste peace and quiet and solitude long enough to find out how good they really are." He journeyed into a white frozen land as foreign to us as the Moon, which at least can be stared at most nights. Alone in a hut for five months through a single unbroken night.

Things quickly turned ugly as the stove, his only heat source, malfunctioned. What followed was a harrowing tale of enduring the horrendous cold while desperately trying to contain a mind slipping ever closer to irretrievable insanity, under the breathtaking beauty and eeriness of the southern auroras. He penned *Alone* in 1938, which became an instant bestseller. A chock-full life for anyone, but not Byrd.

He continued with yet another Antarctic expedition in 1939, his presence there cut short by being recalled to active duty for World War II, in which he fought all the way to September 2 1945, when he witnessed the Japanese surrender in Tokyo Bay. He was awarded the Legion of Merit twice before continuing with two more expeditions to Antarctica, all the way to his death in 1957.

He wrote a great deal about interpersonal dynamics in isolation, commenting on innocuous mannerisms magnified into intolerable flaws, such as when one of his men complained about another's "way of breathing, his belief in dreams, and his frequent use of the phrase 'I'm sorry.'"

33 | THE END OF EVERYDAY LIFE

James woke up spontaneously at 5:40 AM, eager to rewatch the video once more. There was an active data allowance bartering system on board: one crew member may be looking for extra capacity today in exchange for future megabytes, while another may be willing to take the reverse transaction. *Even TiTus, formerly known as TT, plays ball by lending work data transfer capacity when there's no counterparty*, thought James. And after weeks of data saving, he had amassed enough capacity to receive a four-minute video from Belinda.

He put the tablet a few inches from his face for extra immersion, even at the expense of pixelation.

Belinda was resplendent in her role as a new mother. Grandpa could be seen in the background reading his newspaper. It was one of those volatile London days, long gray clouds wrestling with patches of blue sky. The brick walls of the garden were covered in vines, a few neat cone-shaped shrubs, a small glass greenhouse with an assortment of flowers inside. But Belinda aside, it was all preamble, like singers onstage before the lead soprano enters. *And … here comes Emma.* The intelligent gleaming eyes, the long eyelashes, the tiny nose, the round face capped by unruly hair. The camera followed her as she moved decidedly even if her plump legs lacked assurance. She babbled and screamed in delight. Belinda shouted her name, but it was only after a few tries that she turned.

It was the babbling that made it so hard for him. Emma had profound hearing loss and would be deaf within a few years. That was the medical diagnosis. *But then I hear her and wonder.* Toddlers with progressive hearing failure grow increasingly silent as they stop trying to listen to themselves. *Emma keeps trying.* Belinda swore the hearing aid barely helped. The doctors said the time was now. *But what if?* Emma was chirping in the video, tapping her tablet screen with excitement. When the camera went above, he saw his own face from a year earlier, narrating and showing the illustrations from *The Little Prince* with the Milky Way background beyond Bacchus' Observation Window.

The clinical solution was a cochlear implant, which bypassed the damaged part of the ear and delivered electrical impulses directly to the auditory nerve, which the brain interpreted as sound. Whereas a hearing aid was really just an amplifier, this sidestepped the hearing process altogether. *But it's invasive: electrodes under her skin, a wire perforating the inner ear, and an external cable and processor. And once you bypass nature, it's irreversible.* Her sonic world would be bleached in white noise, with discernible but metallic, robot-like speech sounds. She would be able to enjoy Bach on a clavichord, but would never be able to fully grasp Beethoven's Ninth. *Why her? Why not—*

Somebody knocked on his cabin's hatch. He glanced at the wall clock. Six in the morning. *Why would anybody—?*

"What is it?" No answer, but the tapping repeated.

As he stood out of bed and felt his way to the ladder, the hatch opened atop. James turned the lights on. Sophia in pajamas closed it behind her and climbed down.

"What's going on? Sophia?" She seemed about to break down. He made her sit on the bed.

She looked at him with imploring red eyes, but did not speak. The urgency overrode sensibilities and he demanded an answer.

"We have a Code Red ... Sergei ..."

"Sergei ..."

"Without warning ... a few hours ago ... Iman went into a coma ..."

She couldn't speak anymore. He saw the tablet in Sophia's hand and gestured for it. After reading it cursorily, he sat by Sophia's side, speechless and lightheaded.

"I need to tell—"

"Earth recommends we wait ..." interrupted Sophia, sobbing.

"I must tell him now," said James.

"... to decide on the proper course of action ..."

Ø

The news about Iman's death had arrived minutes earlier. Sergei's howls echoed in Sophia's head, a bleak reminder of their fragility and the definitive mark that things had changed permanently for the worst.

Sophia's hands were unsteady as she read a printed copy of the Medical Checklist Manual one last time. She had a hard time swallowing, her throat one big lump. She also couldn't shake off the sense of premonition.

```
BEHAVIORAL—ACUTE PSYCHOSIS—EMERGENCY
1.  Unstow:
    Drug Subpack
    Duct Tape
    Bungees
    Towels
2.  Talk with the patient while you are restraining him.
    Explain what you are doing, and that you are using a
    restraint to ensure that he is safe.
    Restrain patient using duct tape around wrists, ankles,
    and use a bungee around the torso.
    If necessary to secure the head, place a rolled towel
    under the neck and restrain with duct tape.
```

As she got into the intramuscular injection section, it unraveled. Something crashed and broke in Sergei's cabin, the chilling screaming started again, the muffled sound of something big hitting a wall.

"You two, stay put," said James rather needlessly. "Sophia, let's go." Yi and Derya were shell-shocked—one unable to talk, the other unable to reason.

Sophia had been clueless about what to do next and when James asked her to get ready, she refused at first. Now her mind rushed in anticipation. *I'm the wrong person for this—I'm a follower, not a leader—I'm, I'm the youngest by three years—I'm the smallest, the least experienced, the lightest, the only one with long hair and missing a penis—*

Her heart raced as they moved their hovering bodies via handrails to Sergei's cabin. She looked at James. For the first time since she knew him, his expressive face had become emotionless and driven by one sole aim. It made her recover at least part of her composure.

James unlocked the latch that had kept an unaware Sergei confined to his cabin. He opened the hatch. The cabin looked like the guts of a tornado in slow motion, dozens of objects and shattered pieces of flotsam and jetsam floating around, with Sergei's large frame languidly banging a wooden box anchored to his desk ten or fifteen feet away from them.

He sensed their presence and turned with scary agility. The image spoke to Sophia as the scene of a fatally wounded lion. She could feel his enormous power draining away, the dignity of a dying face. She became paralyzed with fear. Sergei was nimbler and much stronger than anyone else. If he felt threatened or was unwilling to cooperate, things could turn ugly fast. She glanced at James.

There was no tranquilizer gun on board Shackleton. All they had was a syringe in Sophia's right hand, which Sergei spotted right away.

James did not move at first. He called Sergei by his diminutive, "Serezha ... nobody can understand the extent of your pain, and nobody can help you now. But there's one way to ... to let your consciousness ... drift." He pointed at the sedative drug in Sophia's hands. "This will put you down."

Sergei didn't answer but everything in him seemed to beg for the pain to subside. James extended his hand toward Sophia but she remained frozen. "Sophia, goddammit," James hissed. But she couldn't move. He cautiously moved around her, never losing sight of Sergei, and pulled the syringe from her fingers.

James inched closer to Sergei and gradually reached for his arm with his free hand. Sergei remained docile. Sophia began sobbing, heartbroken. James grabbed Sergei's arm and gently pulled up the sleeve. He swiftly scanned for a protruding vein in the burly, muscular forearm and pierced the needle through the skin.

He held the passing-out Sergei in his arms. The latter slowly curled into a fetal position before blacking out.

34 | SERGEI

July 14 2029. Day 759; 1.1 Years to Saturn

Five months hence, there were four crew members seated at Bacchus' dinner (and arguing) table. The fuselage high-definition wall was displaying Thailand's Railay Beach. It was midday and low tide, with hundreds of people far inside the turquoise, knee-deep sea. To the left, the fantastically shaped vertical limestone cliffs towered over the thick tropical forest. The sky was deep blue, with a few round clouds moving in the distance.

"Just arrived at our doorstep," Sophia read aloud from a tablet. "Main findings from the Weekly Behavioral, Psychological & Sleep Hygiene Report. Data collection based on: crew rest/activity measured with wrist-worn actigraphs; Beck Depression Inventory questionnaire; Psychomotor Vigilance Task—"

"I wish it came in paper form so I could at least use it to swab my rectum," said Derya.

"Here, you read it then," said Sophia, handing it to him.

"Listen to this poetryfaction: 'the ecological validity depends upon the extent to which it instantiates elements relevant to crew behavior during prolonged confinement in space.' A third of a Twix bar to anyone who can explain what I just read. Then … blah blah, and the report ends with a profiling of Sergei Dmitrievich Lazarev requiring special clearance, again. Or in other words, inaccessible to anyone but our commander. I'm deeply thankful for this fostering—no, this sensitive nurturing—of an environment of trust and safety."

"Do me a favor and shut up for an hour," said James tiredly. "And pass it on in the meanwhile." He had been protective of Sergei, whose recent behavior had been strange at best.

As the rest continued Saturday's brunch—weekends were light on work—he concentrated on the report.

"Crew sleep time averaged seven hours and twenty-three minutes per night, with everyone but Sergei Dmitrievich Lazarev above the minimum seven hours recommended by the American Academy of Sleep Medicine."

One graph was based on the weekly individual question of naming the two crew members with whom you communicated the most. The circle size represented the number of times the person had been mentioned. Arrows pointing to and from a person, the interactions with the rest. Sergei's circle was isolated and by far the smallest. *Connected only to me*, thought James.

"Shackleton is rewriting the scientific literature on the Minimum Acceptable Net Habitable Volume for missions over 500 days. NASA's baseline of 870 cubic feet per person, even considering a weightless environment that allows full use of available volume, is no longer deemed appropriate." This was a non-active restriction, as Shackleton had many times that space.

"This week's report reconfirms an increasing premium on personal space, mainly as a result of Sergei Dmitrievich Lazarev's erratic behavior. There is an active effort by Sophia Jong and Derya Terzi to avoid him."

Further down the document, "Sergei Dmitrievich Lazarev has settled into a twenty-five-hour sleep cycle."

The immediate consequence was an out-of-whack schedule. It was midday and Sergei was in his cabin—James had Sergei's wristwatch sleep and light level real-time data displayed in the screen, showing he was in a nighttime sleep phase.

"This week, after consultation with world-renowned experts, our medical team has escalated to Priority One the need to calibrate his circadian sleep cycle back to twenty-four hours. Failure to do so may have unforeseeable consequences on the overall mission."

He jumped to Sergei's diagnosis and prognosis.

"The patient exhibits acute depression, persistent sleep insomnia, chronic sleep deprivation, performance deficit in behavioral alertness, cognitive impairment, irritability, negative affect, and interpersonal tension and conflict. All the neurobehavioral, psychological, and biochemical markers point to an increasingly unstable person with seriously compromised mental health."

A few paragraphs below, "Due to his alpha trait, indicating a tendency to present himself more ideally, along with his cultural background, this report cannot properly assess the risk of Sergei Dmitrievich Lazarev being suicidal or homicidal. WE MAINTAIN THE TOP PRIORITY INSTRUCTION TO KEEP HIM UNDER SURVEILLANCE 24/7."

Easier said than done, thought James. *Sergei knows everything about the ship down to the smallest rivet, on top of being stronger and faster than anyone else. If he has malevolent intentions, there is little anyone can realistically do to stop him.* With no firearms or electroshock weapons, James wished again they had brought a tranquilizer gun, *if only as deterrent.*

✇

"Then what do you propose? Spacing him?" said Yi.

"Come on, don't be so politically correct, *chino*. I'm verbalizing what everyone, including you, is thinking. He has become a huge liability for this mission. We're at the mercy of a psychiatric inmate roaming free around the ship," said Derya.

"'Spacing' him?" said Sophia.

"You know, the sci-fi equivalent to walking the plank. Open the airlock and eject him into the vacuum of outer space," said Derya. "Before he does us all in."

James, quiet until then, thumped his coffee mug against the table. "I am very disappointed in you, Derya. And you too, Sophia." His jaws and lips remained clenched for a few lengthy seconds. He continued, more controlled, "I really would have expected more compassion. Clearly, you've never truly loved somebody before."

"What do you know?" said Derya meekly.

"Nobody, nobody can understand what he's going through. But you are not even trying. You will read that night's Code Red to feel how it burns inside. That's an order. It should give you much-needed empathy," said James.

"We are five people on a ship in the middle of nowhere. Like it or not, we are in this together," said Yi.

"Profound, Yi, very profound. Let me write it down and copyright it," said Derya.

✇

Derya's guilt was strangling him. He couldn't believe his eyes. *Never in my life I could have thought ...* Now it all clicked, the one key needed to understand the whole affair. A revelation so violent his mind staggered to comprehend its full meaning to make the emotional shock bearable.

They never spoke again after their son's death. *He banished her out of his life—forever, as fate would have it. Who knows how many times he may have been on the verge of lifting the silence? Had he got past the blinding grief and anger ... most of this could have been averted.*

Earth decided the rest of the crew needed to know Iman's last video message, nine days before her death. But such a violation of husband and wife intimacy could only be presented in an abridged transcript form.

"*Hello, my love, it's your Iman ...*"

"... it was on those dark days in Syria, when I had lost everything that mattered, that you took me on a walk holding my hand. With my world shattered, you pointed to the sky and told me ancient stories about a planet right above us called Saturn. It was the first time I could see a future again ..."

"... I felt I had no right to take that away. Trapping you on Earth ... it was written in my husband's destiny all along ... I couldn't but let you go ..."

"... my consolation would be our little miracle, and we got him. But he got sick too. My body poisoned him. He was already terminally ill inside me. 'It is you alone or none of the two,' they kept saying. Now you know why they let him go. I wish he will forgive me—I miss him so much. In hindsight, maybe I should have told you the whole truth right after the abortion, yet I was determined to wait for your return before leaving. But my body is finally giving up, I can sense it ..."

"... please talk to me. I need to see that handsome face again. My love. My life."

But what got Derya, what he would never be able to forget, was what she said at the end, *"And please don't ever feel guilty. We did what was best with the information we had."*

35 | TERROR ON BOARD

November 20 2029. Day 888; 288 Days to Saturn

Sophia kept slipping into slumber over the verbose text as she butted heads with *Moby-Dick*'s first chapter. Yi lent it to her the previous day with the promise of first-class storytelling about explorers venturing into the unknown, but made no warning of the high walls of old English rowdy prose that stood guarding its entrance.

She finally broke into evocative ground, "chief among these motives was the overwhelming idea of the great whale himself. Such a portentous and mysterious monster roused all my curiosity. Then the wild and distant seas where he rolled his island bulk," followed by Ishmael's confession, "I am tormented with an everlasting itch for things remote. I love to sail forbidden seas." She was hooked. "By reason of these things, then, the whaling voyage was welcome; the great flood-gates of the wonder-world swung open."

Inspired, she felt an urge to experience the mission's own deep dark sea. She dressed lightly. The clock said 1:23 AM.

Out of her cabin hatch, save for Shackleton's bowels, the silence was complete. A single push projected her to the flight deck's Observation Window. *This view of the Milky Way will never get old*, she thought. She floated an arm away from the latticed window. Only an inch of glass kept them away from the vacuum of space, which makes the most inhospitable environment on Earth feel like a mother's womb. *And to think those seemingly gregarious dots of light are impossibly far from one another, separated by untold swathes of nothingness.* Her hands kept floating up in front of her. *I wish I had somewhere to put them.*

She took a deep, long breath; exhaled it all. Every fiber of her body was at rest and her mind was solely focused on the here and now. She toured her senses. Her nose caught the smell of clean underwear. Her forearm hairs swayed to the delicate breeze from the air filters. She remembered that evening's pleasant bitter taste out of the leaves she plucked a few weeks prior from her green tea plant in her scaled-down, fun-size gardening plot. Her fingertips rubbed against one another, feeling the texture of their whorls and lines. As she untangled the sounds in Shackleton, her left ear picked on a faint variation from her right one. After a few moments of being unable to decipher the disparity, she turned her head. She instinctively covered her mouth to prevent a scream as fear tensed her whole body.

Sergei was suspended motionless a few feet from her in the shadows. His body was naked, the bulging muscles at rest, like a corpse floating face down on an ocean. His face was in profile, partially illuminated by the cosmos, eyes wide open but immobile. The only hint of life was the slow, brooding breathing.

Sophia knew she was well within his peripheral vision, but he didn't acknowledge her presence. *Say something! Announce yourself!* But a visceral panic constricted her throat. With each passing second, she became more disturbed. Trying to be invisible, she stealthily put her right arm against the window and pushed back. The impulse was minimal, she barely receded a few inches per second.

She was falling back toward the ship's central backbone passageway—her eyes remained fixed on his shadow—when the shape started murmuring words in Russian. She tried to speak, say anything, but was incapable.

Once she felt her back touch the ship's backbone, the urgency to get out overcame her. She turned and pushed hard, flying back while constantly looking over her shoulder. She failed to open James' hatch, but the clack sound resonated across the ship. She scurried to open hers, got in, and locked it from the inside.

She stayed awake in bed, her pulse shaky, waiting for a noise to announce something, anything. The silence was spine-chilling. *Only James has an access key to all rooms. Only James has an access key to all rooms. Only James has an access key to all rooms.* The mantra calmed her enough to crash asleep at some point later that night.

36 | BRUCE LEE ET AL.

May 3 2030. Day 1,052; 124 Days to Saturn

Lunch was over but no one moved. After three years of confinement, the old ways were coming back. Not long before, the refuge from a flickering mood was private space. *Nowadays, sociable is chic again*, thought Sophia. The spirit permeated everywhere but Sergei's hatch. *That's all right, Humans versus Humanoid.* They were well past the uncomfortable silence phase. *It isn't about talking anymore given that even unformed thoughts can be anticipated; it's about communion.*

"Anybody know what happened with the Kiwi astronomer's find? Kind of dropped out of the public eye," said Sophia.

Three weeks earlier an amateur astronomer in New Zealand's Southern Alps was filming Saturn, the sky's prima donna, when a flash came out of its blurry outline for a few tenths of a second. An asteroid or a comet bombardment? That's all it took. Within two hours of the unconfirmed sighting, a family stargazing on the slopes of Hawaii's Mauna Kea volcano claimed to have seen it as well. Within a day, the scheduled observations of major telescopes and radio antennas were tossed aside as the entire astronomical arsenal turned to squint at Saturn. The verification came a few hours later from the Large Synoptic Survey Telescope, which photographs the entire sky, producing data equivalent to two Libraries of Congress per day. Its library from the night prior showed that at 5:47 AM Chile time, a flare deformed Saturn's profile. Its size indicated a massive explosion from one or more large impactors.

But that's when it became bewildering. They caught sight of the stone as it broke the window, so to speak, but later on the window appeared intact: Saturn's atmosphere seemed unblemished. As days went by, astronomers were at a loss to explain what a widely read *New York Times* editorial titled, "Astronomy Farsightedness: Both a Feat of Foresight and a Vision Disorder" succinctly called "… training and stretching science formidable eyesight past 13.8 billion years to a decillionth of a second after the Big Bang, disregarding in the process the ordinary and everyday as second-rate pursuits. Suddenly required to pay for parking, we look at our wallet and cannot tell a quarter from a nickel, a Benjamin from a Hamilton. Examples abound. Besides Saturn's bafflingly scarless cloud tops, we've mapped each square foot of Mars' surface, yet barely know what lays under our oceans."

The inability to solve Saturn's meteor impact enigma was aggravated by a history of prescience. On a March night of 1993, a married couple and a friend discovered comet Shoemaker-Levy 9 around Jupiter. Orbital studies soon reconstructed the story: on July 7 1992 the comet defied the gas giant by flying too close and was ripped apart. The prediction? The fragments would be sucked in by the planet by mid-July 1994. With astonishing precision, the multi-day extravaganza started on July 16 and lasted for a week, twenty-one pieces smashing into Jupiter's atmosphere and dotting it with Earth-size smudges for months.

The perplexing cluelessness about Saturn had been extensively rationalized. The blast deep beneath should have forced masses of gas to surge hundreds of miles into the cloud tops. The main thesis was that while such mixing and stirring exposes darker chemistry in Jupiter's heterogeneous atmosphere, it hardly changes the tonality in Saturn's more uniform one.

"No news is good news," said Yi, while diligently working on his pygmy tree. "Besides, sales of telescopes have skyrocketed. You are more likely to find one on eBay than Amazon. I defer to Earth. Everyone is watching for us."

"Did Bruce Lee get a haircut?" said Derya.

"No, pruning was in November. Problem is he's deciduous and all messed up with the seasons," said Yi.

Bruce Lee was a gnarly miniature elm seemingly a millennium old. A gift from the Beijing Natural History Museum, legend had it that during the Second Opium War a British officer fell in love with a geisha living in Canton. As a symbol of her devotion, she planted an elm seed and trained it through pruning, potting, and wiring. After living together through seven seasons, he deserted her with the promise of coming back. She died of despair waiting for him to return. *Nothing like syrupy stories just close enough to warm you, yet not close enough to burn you—even if it's apocryphal. But the dates match!* Dating trees is as simple as removing an old branch and counting the rings. Sophia looked at Bruce Lee in admiration. It was almost two centuries old.

"What's the latest with the tardigrades? Did they survive?" asked James.

"Not one has come back from the dead this time. Couple more days and they will be certified goners," said Sophia.

The most important ongoing biological experiment outside Shackleton related to tardigrades, also known as water bears. These were Sophia's pets and tending to them was one of her favorite pastimes. For anybody who thinks cockroaches are hardy, these are godlike. Cute-looking, plump, eight-legged micro-animals, they have inhabited the Earth for 500 million years—from Antarctica to jungles, Himalayas to sea trenches. *Vegetarians and vegans beware, we ingest them regularly, as they call fresh produce, such as lettuce and spinach, home—oh, that's quite all right! You didn't know.*

Among their feats was the ability to endure minutes at 1 percent above absolute zero, the lowest temperature in the Universe; resist the crushing pressure at the deepest points of our oceans; go on hunger strike for thirty years; or withstand radiation 1,000 times above levels that are lethal to humans.

That's great, you say. Yet how is this peculiar fellow relevant to humans? In a nutshell, by being the most badass species in history. When you've barely noticed the Big Five mass extinction events, seen rocks taller than airplanes' cruising altitude drop from the sky, watched dinosaurs emerge and disappear, found that well over 99 percent of the species that roamed the Earth along with you have gone extinct, it means serious tricks up the sleeve, refined over hundreds of millions of years of life's formidable trial-and-error technique, evolution.[17]

Now Sophia was in the middle of a critical test where tardigrades were lead characters: planetary protection, or how to kill the water bears. Because even with overwhelming support for the mission, there was still heated debate among astrobiologists. Roughly four-fifths supported the exploration of Enceladus' subsurface ocean, the rest were fanatically against. *And they have a fair point, I guess.*

Horror movies fiddle with 'back contamination,' the introduction of extraterrestrial organisms to Earth that become invasive species hell-bent on wreaking havoc. This was the reason Neil Armstrong, Buzz Aldrin, and Mike Collins

---

17   There are two water bear traits that are probably essential for our species to develop if we are ever to venture beyond our Solar System as fleshy mortals:

First is their mastering of cryptobiosis, an extreme version of both science fiction's favorite plot device—suspended animation—as well as Michael Jackson's search for immortality through cryonics. When water bears enter this state, they lose 99 percent of their water content and slow metabolism and energy consumption to 0.01 percent of normal. And they later resuscitate just by being in contact with water again. The most obvious obstacle to cryogenic preservation is our inability to remove most of the water from the human body, which has the inconvenient habit of expanding upon freezing, ripping tissue and causing irreparable damage at the cellular level. The topic of human hibernation in space has never died out, it simply hibernates as it waits for a breakthrough.

Second are their unique, hyper-specialized proteins protecting the genetic code, DNA, from radiation. Cosmic and solar radiation being one of the major challenges for long-term settlements on Mars or anywhere beyond Earth.

spent twenty-one days in quarantine after returning to Earth. *In other words, wipe your feet before coming back inside the house.*

Astrobiologists, on the other hand, were worried about 'forward contamination.' *From us to you, with love. It won't be cats or dogs but microbial life, which is notoriously resilient to sterilization.* Hence the water bears, the last survivors from Sophia's microbial Noah's Ark, sitting right outside Shackleton's airlock, exposed to the vacuum of space. Monthly checking of colony cultures showed mass decimation over the first months of the mission. After a year, the only survivors were a few anaerobic bacteria, even fewer fungus, and a solid mob of water bears.

But a few days back, Sophia harvested the handful of remaining tardigrades, immersed them in water, and awaited their resurrection. This time their bodies showed rigor mortis. *A couple more days and R.I.P. becomes scientific fact.* Their demise would be applauded by those whose curiosity is tempered by the perceived risk of contamination from Waltzy Mole, the torpedo-shaped cryobot that will pierce into Enceladus' vast underground sea.[18]

18　"Maybe you'll get a couple of astrobiology friends back," said Derya.

"I'm not sure I want them," said Sophia. "These people completely misunderstand the alien contamination problem. In my view, the caution with cross-contamination is not about the altruistic goal of allowing possible alien biology to develop unaltered. If you were a fundamentalist about this, all unmanned missions to Mars have been capital sins. Not only is sterilization never guaranteed, but the very process may have created Hulk bacteria resistant to high temperatures and heavy radiation ... instead, the broader rationale should be that if and when we find extraterrestrial life, we must be absolutely certain it is independent from Earth's life. In most cases there shouldn't be any worries because I think it's extremely improbable that alien existence happens to use DNA as their book for life. If it doesn't, then the discovery guarantees the existence of a second, independent genesis of life just in our Solar System ... the nightmare scenario is that both life forms share a similar genetic makeup, because then we either share a common origin or we have contaminated that ecosystem and are tagging 'alien' to Earthly creatures. And the horrifying part is that we may never know for sure. This case is problematic and very real for unmanned missions to, say, Mars, where years or more likely decades pass between the contamination event by a rover and the new life-hunting mission that does the sampling. But in our case, we are immune to this risk by design: we will sample on the spot and do bioprocessing on board Shack days later."

37 | ΛEROCΛPTURE

Yi saw James check the clock—it was fifteen minutes after the appointed time, and all but one of the crew were in Bacchus for their last town hall meeting.

"Does he know—" Yi nodded to James in confirmation. "Let's start then."

"I can check on him again," said Yi.

"Let's not pressure him," said James.

"Pressure him? The Ruski has the highlife of a panda: sleeps, eats, and farts." Derya got the evil eye from James before continuing, "Let's cut to the chase and talk about the Sergei problem while he's not here."

"That's okay, but facts first ... Sergei is the most suitable—" said James.

"Was," interrupted Derya.

"Sergei continues to be the most suitable pilot and his set of skills make him the best prepared for leading both the Orbit Insertion and the Enceladus expedition. On Earth and in my mind, there's no debate about that," said James.

We are about the most valuable guinea pigs in history, thought Yi. Besides extensive, regular psychological and behavioral testing, each one's vital signs were monitored 24/7 through implants, being physically plugged into equipment for about half an hour each day, as well as weekly blood samples and quarterly DNA testing. Their data would become foundational for the coming exploration, and later for the transition to permanent habitation of Mars. *And Jimmy is right. Against all intuition, in the comparative studies between the two pilots, Sergei scores higher for motor skills and reaction time than James by a fair margin.*

"Sorry, Jimmy, but I strongly disagree," said Sophia. "I think you have a technically biased view of what constitutes the 'right stuff.' The best crew members are those comfortable working alone, at which he excelled, but are also team players who enjoy relating with the rest of the crew during meal and leisure times, at which he has failed repeatedly."

"You're again ignoring the catalyst that sent the man into the pit he's in," said James.

"Then let's talk on those terms," said Derya. "Things as they are, not as you want them to be. We have a suicidal or perhaps even homicidal person on board. That's already really, really bad. But we are also twenty-four days away from Saturn, and our Moses for crossing the Red Sea broke his cane and lost his sanity. We depended on him for the aerocapture. I was paired with him for Enceladus, the core of our entire expedition … but I can't—no, I won't—tarnish my resume by becoming the first victim of space cannibalism. What I'm saying to you is that all this, all of us, cannot depend on a psycho gone haywire."

Yi saw Derya recoil and followed his gaze to Bacchus' entrance. *The panther has stepped out of the dark.* Sergei would be almost unrecognizable to family and friends by now, his weight loss appalling. The blond beard and hair, no longer reined in by military duty, had turned him into a barbarian. His face was angular and the blue eyes protruding, reinforcing the semi-feral stare that made Sophia and Derya so uncomfortable.

"Sergei. We were just speaking about you," said James.

"I heard," said Sergei. There were long seconds of silence. "Aerocapture will save a lot of propellant and leave a healthy fuel buffer for the remainder of the mission."

"There are doubts … the maneuver is unprecedented … the question is whether it's safe to attempt it with a pilot that is … impaired," said James.

Even as mere bystander Yi had given extensive thought—both in daytime reverie and nightmare format—to one of the most difficult and dangerous moments of the mission. Shackleton was approaching Saturn too fast to be gravitationally captured, even by the gas giant. To achieve Orbit Insertion, it would need to shed the excess velocity by either turning the spaceship and igniting the engines, or by aerocapture. The first would cost the mission an onerous 0.6 miles per second in propellant. The second was essentially fuel-free. Yet in the illustrious history of manned and unmanned space exploration, it had never been attempted. Had the Cassini robotic spacecraft done it upon reaching Saturn in 2004, 280 percent more science payload could have been carried. *Hard to assess how many more breakthroughs might have come from what was already one of the most successful scientific missions ever—there's a big catch, naturally: it decelerates via friction by doing a deep atmospheric dive.* This makes it impossible to predict the exact particle density and thus braking rate, so real-time feedback and correction are essential. Decades of work and billions of dollars funneled through a few minutes of terror have kept the maneuver safely inside the theory books. *As for Shack, to the many who think there are already too many risk factors in this mission, aerocapture is a siren song. Failure is not an option. One mistake is death.* So much so that if it happened, the aerocapture would be done by Sergei with TiTus and James as copilots.

"As for Enceladus, there's no expedition without a pilot, and as commander James cannot abandon this ship. I'm going with or without you," said Sergei to Derya, matter-of-factly.

"There's still a few days to decide," said James. "Propellant accounting was done with a standard burn insertion procedure, so we have the luxury of deciding. This won't be a democratic vote. Agreeing is not committing. If anybody at any time has qualms about aerocapture, we abort."

Yi was astounded at James' shrewdness. *An elegant solution from a brilliant leader that may, just may, resolve the soul-searching in each of us—he's betting on small actions dragging through big results, like organ donation campaigns back home. By changing the default choice from engine burn to aerocapture, the burden of convincing now shifts to the conservatives. It swaps the mental question from "Am I willing to sacrifice everything for fuel savings?" to "Am I willing to surrender an emergency fuel buffer for a low probability of something in Orbit Insertion going wrong?"*

If anyone else saw the trick, nothing was said.

38 | THE RINGED GIANT

After twenty-nine years passed on Earth—that miniature sibling far away toward the planets' overlord—the giant logged one more loop around the Sun. Winter had settled in its northern hemisphere for the 150-millionth time, tilting up the most famed wonder of the Solar System, the rings of Saturn, into shadowing the north from sunrays and dyeing it a deep Neptunian blue.

It was as if the pendulum of time had frozen into an immutable forever: this wintertime season would be interchangeable with any of those million others when the dinosaurs reigned supreme back on Earth. And yet, had someone put an ear to the railway tracks of time, she would have felt the hushed reverberations of change. Something insignificant in size and pregnant in consequence was approaching.

♄

Even from 4 million miles away, almost twenty times the distance between the Earth and the Moon, an omnipotent Saturn dominated the Observation Window's field of view from the flight deck. Three-fourths of the orb was under the ethereal rings, shining in golden hues with such luminosity that the Milky Way veiled itself away. The surrounding darkness underlined Saturn's magnificence while the inclined rings projected an upward halo crowned by Delphic blues and pitch-black, as if not even the Sun could reach its apex. On the left side, its own oval shadow cut unsparingly through the rings.

With focused intention James could identify a few specks, sprinkled grains of salt around the gas giant's waist, part of the entourage of sixty-two moons around its court. The time of avoiding Saturn to keep it outside of their awareness was over. Instead, like a bullfighter keeping the menace in between the eyes, both Observation Windows were constantly guarded by the crew.

"I have never felt so unprepared," said Sophia.

"It grows in front of your eyes, like a movie in fast forward," said James. There was no need to answer Sophia. Silence had become nodding.

For three years Shackleton had been a ball rolling uphill as it escaped the Sun's massive gravity well, ever losing momentum. But a month ago it finally went over the hilltop. Since then, it ran faster and faster toward Saturn. *The invisible fight between titans has been won, for now,* thought James. *Returning to Earth will be a breeze. A gentle push to escape Saturn and then continuous acceleration as the Sun claims back its prodigal son. By the time Shackleton encounters the Earth our speed will be almost twenty miles per second, four times higher than when we orbited home the days after launch.*

"I'm terrified, Jimmy … for seven years I daydreamed for this to happen, now I wish we had more time," said Sophia.

"We'll never be readier, Tweety. But I feel you … what gets me is Saturn's indifference to our existence. It has been impassive for eons before life emerged on Earth, and it will be impassive for eons after life withers away," said James.

The moon Tethys transits in front of the
immenseness of Saturn, while the giant's
rings cast shadows over its cloud tops.

Photograph taken by the Cassini probe on
December 7 2011. Image credit: NASA/JPL/
Space Science Institute

PART 4
THE KINGDOM OF SATURN

Part 4. The Kingdom of Saturn

39 | BELINDA

September 4 2030. Shackleton's Orbit Insertion

KENSINGTON, LONDON

This was the day when the Earth stood still. Warwick Gardens, the street right outside the building, should have been channeling dense traffic but was instead deserted.

If I was superstitious, I'd say the signs are everywhere, thought Belinda. *A spotless London night sky, a gracious Moon keeping itself offstage, and a very particular bright dot just high enough above the horizon to be gazed at—and the fox!* Trotting over the old brick wall outside the window as she cleaned the dishes, stopping to check on her, then turning back the way it came. *Which can only mean everything will be all right*, she kept telling herself. Something that kept her distracted was imagining James' address to the world in less than two hours. Compared to the ballet over a razor's edge about to commence, the downside here bottomed out at global but sympathetic embarrassment. A man of lofty goals, he confided to her the aim for something visceral that moved people "to tears, something between Carl Sagan's Pale Blue Dot and Beethoven's 'Ode to Joy.'" *But that first draft had, and I adore you, Jimmy, the oversweetness and literary caliber of a telenovela teaser.* They had worked on it sporadically for months but progress was hampered by his procrastination. By the time they left Earth, James had become adept at public speeches but his old reluctance had crawled back.

Belinda searched for Emma. She had stopped stealing "strawbabies" from Grandpa's kitchen garden and was instead plucking "pedals" from his yellow begonias, somehow aware of the extra leniency tonight. She kept glancing back at the screen, anxious like her mother. Grandpa was glued to his Victorian-era armchair.

The soothing voice of the veteran broadcaster explained, "... which brings us to the question of 'surface.' Here on Earth we step over it, but Saturn is made of gas. To calculate the distance of an object from the planet, we arbitrarily set the 'surface' as the height from the core where the atmospheric pressure is equal to one atmosphere or bar, Earth at sea level. It works nicely for Saturn, because it happens to be around its cloud tops, which is the 'surface' we see when we look at pictures …"

Belinda went outside into the garden. The neighborhood was quiet except for that same voice resounding from buildings all over. Orwell's *1984*. After years of abstinence, she took out a cigarette and lit it.

"… salute our heroes and their families, including our very own Belinda and Emma Egger, looking up from somewhere here in London …"

"Feels like the Blitz. Even Heathrow is at a standstill," said John, her father's upstairs neighbor for decades. He, Jane, and their whole family were on their terrace by a telescope. "Emma, come to check on Daddy."

Belinda would rather not but Emma was already running for the entrance.

♄

Saturn looked slanted, blurred, and impossibly far away through John's telescope. With half the world gazing, it was public and universal yet somehow still wholly personal and intimate. Belinda closed her eyes to restrain the emotional swelling that was buffeting her. James, Sophia, and the others had initiated Orbit Insertion over an hour before. Whatever was meant to happen had already happened, its testimony traveling to Earth at the speed of light and about to reach NASA's giant Deep Space Network dishes anytime now, and the world's ears a few seconds after. *But the speed of thought is instantaneous, I want you to know how much I miss you, Jimmy.*

To mitigate the worry, she focused once more on the measured voice narrating, "… Lord Kelvin, whose First Law of Thermodynamics states that energy cannot be created nor destroyed, it can only be transformed. What Shackleton has done is enter Saturn's upper atmosphere to dissipate the excess energy in the form of speed by transforming it to heat …"

For the many expecting a crackling prelude, including her, the transmission was sudden and clear. The first words stirred Belinda. Jimmy's live, unedited voice was speaking to her in the ear, with just a slight echo, "If you were counting on a Kennedy-esque speech, you've waited three years too many. Images are worth a thousand words, but if you only have words really, four broken poets leave only one bard. Tweety—Sophia, I henceforth pass you the baton." This wouldn't make it into the history records but it still moved Belinda to tears. A minute went by before Sophia took over.

"8:34 PM Coordinated Universal Time. Altitude 1,043 miles above Saturn's

1-bar level. The mass spectrometer is detecting hydrogen and helium, meaning we have just officially entered Saturn's atmosphere. Attitude control thrusters tested and ready to correct Shack's orientation in case of frictional rotation. Velocity 19.2 miles/s ... as we aren't certain about the particle density increase as we skim deeper into the atmosphere, Sergei is doing real-time steering to control the angle of attack."

"8:46 PM. Altitude 820 miles above 1-bar level. Velocity 19.0 miles/s ... I'm at a loss for words." Sophia's emotion-soaked voice trailed off and it took a while before she continued. "Nothing, nothing can ever prepare you for this ... and, and nothing could begin to describe it. We are recording 16K video, but at 40 terabytes per hour it would take all our data transfer capacity years to share this footage. You'll need to wait until it lands with us, one good reason why you may want us back ... we are about 3,000 miles from crossing underneath the rings. That's London to New York in three minutes. Things must be done quickly around here or the giant will swallow us ... what from your telescopes must look like a featureless sepia wrap turns out to be an immense spherical cauldron of aimless labyrinthine tropical rivers and tributaries coexisting with unswerving highways of orderly traffic that ... that become a succession of whirlpools and eddies in the clashing border between eastbound and westbound lanes ... and, and then you realize it's not the most intricate canvas ever painted because ... because everything is kinetic, everything is flowing and spinning and shifting in front of my eyes—and in three dimensions! With Earths of gas cascading inward or Venuses of gas gushing outward, and also shadows the size of planets over some plains below, it makes you understand that everything, all we are seeing, is made from hundreds or thousands of vertical layers of pillowy clouds in a collection of browns and yellows and oranges ..."

"8:58 PM. Altitude 801 miles. The vibrations and shaking are very strong as Shack wrestles with Saturn's atmosphere ..."

"9:01 PM. Altitude 807 miles. Yes, we are climbing back up. This may be the saddest moment of my life ... I won't ever again be so close to the hypnotic cloud tops of Saturn ... Galileo, if you only were alive to witness ... I hope one day within my lifetime some of those that follow will go deeper to unveil mysteries beyond imagination."

"9:11 PM. Altitude 813 miles. The twilight zone separating day from night is coming right at us. Once the Sun disappears behind Saturn, it will be a matter of seconds before we lose communication with Earth until we come out into the light on the other side ..."

"9:16 PM. Altitude 832 miles ... I doubt there can be a more, what's the word, rhapsodic sight anywhere in the Solar System … a softly hued Saturn, embraced by the shadows of its majestic rings. The Sun, a tenth of Earth's, is behind the rings like a flashlight twinkling in the back of a patterned dark veil."

"9:19 PM. Altitude 851 miles … we have crossed into the dark side, but it isn't very dark. The rings reflect and scatter more sunlight into Saturn's night-side than a full Moon does on Earth. The moonlit clouds below extend limitless in all directions, it feels like you could rest a dozen Earths, nested like eggs in the dark gray cotton under us."

"9:21 PM. Altitude———thunderstorm—like X-rays reveali——planet insi——watch—in front——cloud decks much tall——"

Belinda's father put his arm around her shoulders and kissed her.

40 | PARTING WAYS

IN THE SATURN SYSTEM

The forty-four-day Main Mission to explore Saturn's kingdom had hardly started and it was already t-97 minutes before separation. Frantic action flared up right after three years of lingering inaction. The whole crew was in the cargo area by the two SpaceX's Dragon spacecraft, and fifteen feet away was the hatch, wide enough to let one of them out. All the epic symbolism of the first craft, James Caird—the very lifeboat Ernest Shackleton had sailed in to salvation—did not cross over to the second, emergency craft called the Dragon.

James looked at Sergei and Derya, who were both in spacesuits. His old self craved to be in those boots. *But there was never a way*, he thought. *Among Shackleton's tenants, one of the pilots happens to be the commander—well, there used to be one way.* This new breed of spacesuit required a tight fit between body and fabric. Sergei used to look like a Roman deity, the powerful thorax, deltoids, and trapezius chiseled into the suit. During the worst of his nosedive into the abyss it probably fit more like a tunic. Now, even after the intense diet to recover part of the lost fifty-seven pounds, it still didn't look quite snug. This was a serious enough concern for Mission Control to order Sergei into two long spacewalks a few weeks before. The fear was that the potential lack of tension between skin and spacesuit could create swelling. That wasn't only extremely painful but also risky. *It turned out okay, I guess.*

"Derya, your heartbeat's at 135 and you're not even moving," said Sophia. "Are you feeling okay?"

"Damn, people. I am about to depart to Enceladus and you keep giving me shit. Even Odysseus would have asked for two pairs of diapers and a barf bag, no? Some ticking should not only be expected but encouraged."

"Perhaps, but your comrade is embarking on the same sortie and is clocking fifty-five heartbeats per minute," said Sophia.

"Good for him. I'm surprised he even—hmm, yeah," said Derya, censoring himself while taking a glimpse at Sergei.

I'm surprised he even has vitals, James completed the phrase in his mind.

As much as James wanted to stay, he needed to head back to the flight deck. The protocol was inflexible. For the coming forty-four days, someone had to be on the flight deck at all times—although except for an emergency, no human intervention would be required.

He hugged the astronaut and cosmonaut, wishing them good luck one last time.

"The bride has been waiting by the altar for years and you're still running late. We're at t-95 minutes. Clock's ticking," said James.

"Well, you enjoy your dinner in Medellín tonight, okay?" Derya's voice sounded high-pitched over the intercom, betraying his agitation. Bacchus that day mimicked the City of Eternal Spring, with its lush tropical rainforest, colonial architecture, and Botero statues. "Meanwhile, yours truly will be shoulder to shoulder with the Bear orbiting Enceladus, trying to figure out the least suicidal way to land Caird."

♄

Shackleton had been captured in a highly elliptical orbit: it would skim the ringed planet before stretching out multiple times the distance between Earth and the Moon, then fall back towards the giant to start again. The spaceship had become another moon of Saturn and without intervention it would continue doing loops until the end of history. *But if by any chance you thought this carries a whiff of improvisation, you've got the wrong impression, pal*, thought James. Every minute of the mission had been precisely plotted since 2026. *Every second of the mission is a highly choreographed dance.* That was the beauty and power of Newton's child, orbital mechanics. *This is how we know decades in advance the exact minute when an eclipse will happen anywhere on Earth.*

At the planning stage, the Navigation Team and mission managers used celestial mathematics to map out orbital trajectories bordering on art. Six weeks and tens of millions of miles on the spaceship's odometer on a series of tangled loops maximizing the mission's science and exploration return, requiring a grand total of one single engine burn and a dozen attitude thruster burns to nudge the ship. They were puppeteers shrewdly using the gravity of Saturn and its biggest moon, Titan.

Shackleton's stay in the Saturn system would last a few weeks after Caird settled back inside its belly with a priceless payload: Sergei, Derya, and the ocean samples from Enceladus. The Enceladus part of the mission would be either twelve or seventeen days long, depending on how much time it took to land Caird and then for Waltzy Mole to cut through the ice shell and pierce into the ocean. This dual rendezvous timeline was dictated by Newton and was absolutely inflexible. Shackleton was about to intercept Enceladus, flying by 400 miles over its surface, and since the moon and spaceship orbited Saturn at different speeds, they wouldn't cross paths for two more years. However, that's where Titan's gravity would act as a virtual gas station, bending and tweaking Shackleton's trajectory so they run into Enceladus on day twelve and day seventeen. *And if Caird doesn't encounter Shackleton by the first or second date? Better not to think about that.* After Enceladus, Shackleton would navigate around the Saturn neighborhood, flying by a handful of other moons and grazing the rings a dozen times. *Not a bad scientific harvest at all*, thought James, pleased at the proposition.

♄

After checking screens and confirming everything to be in order, the view inevitably drew James to the flight deck's Observation Window. The sight was surreal and alien. Having cleared the rings, the only thing in the blackness of space was a white marble seemingly hanging from a hidden thread. There were no dimensional cues regarding scale. Enceladus could have been the size of a coin. Only the tortured face of the whitest object in the Solar System, criss-crossed by terrible scars etched onto its surface by wrenching gravitational forces and geological activity, betrayed its cosmic timescales.

♄

James had violated the protocol and was back in the cargo area. *Only for a few minutes. Come on, rules are sometimes meant to be broken—this is history in the making,* James tried to convince his conscience. Nobody else seemed to mind or notice. The robotic arm was inserting the ten-foot-long, torpedo-shaped Waltzy Mole inside Caird. Weightlessness allows astronauts to perform Herculean feats with the touch of a finger, but the nuclear payload was deemed too delicate and hazardous for them to manually load inside. *For now. Because severe weight restrictions mean that's exactly what Sergei and Derya will do in reverse after landing, with the additional complication of Enceladus' gravity.* Although a timid 1 percent of Earth's, the punishing 1,700 pounds of Waltzy Mole back home become little more than a ridiculously large inflatable pencil on Enceladus.

Ø

At this point, a movie would go into a poignant orchestral crescendo that stirs the audience and gives them goosebumps, thought Sophia. But there was no music, only the unromantic humming and clacking of Shackleton. *There are plenty of goosebumps though.* Whichever way you spin it, the coming days were the climax of eight years of preparation and the most dangerous part of the entire mission by a wide margin.

It was time. The goodbye was hurried, anxious, all too sudden.

Sergei opened Caird's hatch and unceremoniously got in. *Derya said it well, this dude doesn't spacewalk, he space waltzes.* He moved his suited, weightless body with the ease of a memorized routine, contorted and arched through the narrow opening like a high jumper, and waited to help a clumsier Derya from the inside. A couple of minutes later the hatch closed.

"Don't screw up being me," said Sophia over her hands-free headset. *This is bullshit* flashed through her mind for an instant. She was the astrobiologist, not them. It stood to reason she should have been inside that capsule. *Problem is, I'm also the Mission Physician.* The rules had been known since she joined six years earlier but it still tasted bitter. She had taken solace in the fact that the real sample analysis would happen back in Shackleton, done by her. Derya and Sergei were doing the all-important blue-collar job of digging and sampling. *I get to wear the white coat, yay. Sucks to be me—but think of it this way: how scared stiff and distraught would I be alone with a bear, in a space no bigger than a tent, for what will be, best-case scenario, a week and a half?* One more thing for Derya to fret about. *And there's yet another threat for Mr. Radiation Hypochondriac Extraordinaire: the Mole itself.*

Sophia and Yi donned their helmets, then checked and okayed each other's life support system. Sophia walked to the wall and set the go-ahead command. For the next twelve minutes, the cargo area transitioned from an oxygen-rich environment to vacuum. With the inside and outside equalized, the cargo door opened to space.

The robotic arm locked with Caird and in precise slow motion moved it outside and projected it away from the spaceship.

Almost physically forced by Yi, Sophia pulled her head past the hull into the nothingness beyond like a parachutist about to jump into a battlefield. She felt a rush of adrenaline and an unexpected elation at not being inside Caird. Staring forward, the fast-approaching Enceladus was no longer a toy.

"All Caird systems nominal. Ready to disengage." If Sergei's surgical voice was at odds with the significance of the moment, it more than compensated with its reassuring tone.

The separation was slow. Only half an hour after, when Caird became small and distant, its engines fired, directing it to the icy moon.

Once back on the flight deck, Sophia, Yi, and James remained fixed at the Observation Window long after Caird turned into a dot and then dissolved against the backdrop of the mysterious waterworld, mesmerized by the promise of discovery.

"The most significant attempt yet to answer what may be the most important question ever poised, posed? Posted?" Yi scrambled for the right word. "Anyway, 'Is there intelligent life out there?'"

"After reading the news this morning I wonder whether we should first answer Arthur C. Clarke's favorite question, 'Is there intelligent life on Earth?' A classic if ever there was one," said Sophia.

41 | OCEΔNWORLD

Two days later, September 6 2030. Main Mission day 3

ON BOARD JAMES CAIRD

"Look at its profile. First time George Lucas got any physics right," said Derya.

"Who's Joerg Lucas?" asked Sergei.

"Are you—? Mate, your cultural reference blind spots are the size of the Motherland. Did you even hear of TVs in that Arctic Circle hometown of yours? Was school past the abacus? Did you drive around in a sled drawn by reindeer?"

As usual, Sergei did not answer. Derya began taking pictures of Mimas transitioning in front of the immense orb of Saturn through one of Caird's five windows. Enceladus' darker sibling was scarred by craters, including one a third of its size. *It really looks like the Death Star with a severe case of smallpox*, thought Derya. From here, Mimas appeared about the size of the Moon as seen from Earth. Saturn, five times further, dominated the firmament at fifty times that size.

Tediousness and confinement had made for two endless days. *The longest ones in my admittedly youthful life.* Over that time the spaceship had completed seventeen information-gathering, height-decreasing orbits around Enceladus. Right now, they flew nearly twenty miles above the north pole, a cratered surface that hadn't rejuvenated in eons and was thus of no interest. *The goodies are at the other extreme*, where a young, essentially impact-free, geologically active surface full of troughs, scarps, and belts of grooves and ridges expressed dramatically in four canyons, each one hundred miles long, the Tiger Stripes: Alexandria, Cairo, Baghdad, and Damascus. It was here where hundreds of geysers spewed water vapor out into space from that mysterious warm water ocean sloshing for billions of years somewhere beneath the ice. *And where the key to humanity's biggest riddles may lie within.*

Ø

Derya stared at the spectacle before them. Caird was crossing the plume nine miles above the surface. *It is snowing on Enceladus.* For the first time in three years, the engulfing darkness of space gave way to the glittering of a trillion tiny suns reflecting and refracting from snowy ice crystals. The particle density soon increased to the point where it resembled a blizzard in low light conditions. *This is why it's the whitest, most reflective object in the Solar System.* The geysers shoot water ice out into space, most of which settles back down, spray-painting the moon's surface in freshly fallen, pristine snow.

"We may be hitting microscopic aliens as I speak. I say we sample right now." No answer from Sergei. "These monologues are really getting old, you know," Derya said, more to himself than anyone. He peeked at Sergei, who was trying to narrow down the landing area by reviewing the high-resolution topography they had been collecting and enhancing on each new pass over the south pole. *Abacus man again.* "There must be a better way than a human scouting visually. Ever heard of computers, Sergei?"

Minutes later, three rapid beeps broke Derya's lethargy and he threw out a triumphant guffaw. Caird's ice-penetrating radar antenna, sending radio waves down into the ice sheet and gathering back the echoes, had just encountered water. *That's how you do things, with science! Same principle why an ice cube doesn't melt inside a microwave oven: microwaves and radio waves pass straight through ice without interacting.* He impatiently adjusted a digital knob on his tablet, modifying the radio wave's frequency bouncing off the radar. The vertical ice sheet profile in his screen changed almost in real time. Derya confirmed and reconfirmed he was looking at the subsurface ocean circling the moon and not a large water pocket, part of the web of communicating vessels to the surface. *We crossed half the Solar System to sip from the real thing.*

"We found the ice/water boundary," Derya said. *Now I have your attention? I'll delay the gratification and make you salivate like one of Pavlov's dogs, bitch.* The interior ocean's depth beneath the ice shelf was the critical parameter for the Mole's digging time span and thus the duration of their stay on Enceladus.

After a few seconds, Sergei succumbed. "Can you ..."

Derya obliged with six Mississippis. "The thinnest ice section is roughly the same at the bottom of Baghdad and Alexandria canyons, at 3.3 to 3.5 miles."

Sergei seemed uneasy, "Hardly the onion skin we were counting on. Egg shell at best—that's above the upper boundary ..." The gravity measurements performed by the Cassini probe leading to its 2017 burn up in Saturn's upper atmosphere indicated that Enceladus' global ocean lie beneath 12.4 to 15.5 miles of ice on average, thinning to 0.6 to 3.1 miles at the south pole.

"It's no longer speculation but fact," said Derya. "I think that's worth the extra distance."

$$\emptyset$$

"I triggered the automatic descent." Sergei's low-pitched voice woke Derya from an edgy nap. He felt his heart thumping in his eardrums. Even with a drifting mind the body didn't forget what was coming. "Time to make the landing call," Sergei continued. "Seven hours from now I'll take over for the last few miles of descent. Were you visualizing where to touch down just now?"

Are you being funny? Sergei! "You know what they say," replied Derya, "failing to plan is planning to fail." Sergei stared back at him, unimpressed. "I didn't think you were serious an hour ago … I mean, what do I know? But thanks for asking …"

"You Westerners preach collaboration. I'm playing ball, as you say. Besides, I crash and you die."

"And you die as well," Derya replied, almost as a question.

"Correct. We both die."

"You're the boss, boss. I worry this extra-large dildo is killing us softly. Even you're starting to look a shade too green. So, whatever you decide, just remember that fast is good and faster is better."

The lean, ten-foot-tall Mole rested diagonally from floor to roof between the two seats. For the benefit of the ones handling it back on Earth and to the vexation of Derya, it was illustrated with reminders of its contents: skulls, crossbones, and ionizing radiation symbols. It was loaded with uranium-235. *The fuel of choice for power plants, submarines, and bombs of the nuclear flavor.*[19] *Sweet dreams tonight.*

"Alexandria is too high-risk, which leaves Baghdad. This area at the bottom of the canyon is flat enough for a landing," Sergei pointed his finger at a photograph in the Dragon's big touchscreen hanging from the roof, "and is ideal from an exploratory point of view. Down there we're not only the closest to the ocean beneath us but we may even be able to sample the geysers."

"Brilliant! See? There was never any need for my input. This is good. While

---

19   Little Boy carried 140 pounds of the stuff, yet only two pounds of that became the runaway U-235 that killed over 100,000 and turned Hiroshima into a smoldering radioactive ruin.

we wait for the burrowing Mole, we sample the geysers directly from the tap. Two independent water tests. Perfect. We could be analyzing for signs of life tomorrow instead of waiting a week! Mate, this is real good. I'm informing Mission Control."

"That's not all. See the swarm of gray tongue-like shades in and around the landing area?" said Sergei.

"Yes."

"Anything strike you as odd?"

"Hmm, not really," said Derya, squinting at the photograph. There were countless scattered silhouettes. They reminded him of tombstones in a cemetery. After a while, it dawned on him. *Are—are those alien structures!?* "They all point in the same direction!"

"Correct. This was five orbits ago when the Sun was hitting the canyon at an angle. Shadows. Boulder shadows. School trigonometry and you end up with ice blocks five to ten stories tall."

"You mean … a minefield? Bloody hell, Sergei, shouldn't you have started with that disclaimer?"

"I hadn't finished. Everywhere inside the canyon will be littered with frozen rocks. There are no easy spots. Risk mitigation is about picking the lowest density area, which I just did." Sergei stopped Derya from interjecting. "That's not all. If we encounter slushy, pulpy terrain—which we won't know until touchdown—it may be too late."

Too late for—supper? but Derya knew the answer. "Then the decision seems crystal clear, Sergei. We must land on the plains above the Baghdad gorge."

"Had your measurements shown a shallower ice crust, yes. But they didn't, so no. We don't have the luxury of an extra half a mile of digging. We land inside Baghdad."

"You asked for my opinion!" cried Derya.

"Out of politeness, and you waived your right. Twice."

Ø

"And if we find nothing? I want to make sure you're prepared for that outcome," said Sergei.

He's definitely seeking reconciliation. You don't deserve a thing—But I need to speak with someone, even if it's you. "I don't believe in gods but I believe in justice and fairness. It would have been too much toil, sacrifice, and risk for nothing. It simply wouldn't make sense."

"That's putting a lot of hope on us. Being able to discriminate life from everything else. Or hoping that a miserly straw tapping into an ocean bigger than the Pacific will be representative of what's down there …"

"Come on. Cut yourself some slack. Don't be so damn austere all the time. Allow yourself to dream, to hope a little. Barring a catastrophe, this metal rod will pierce into an alien ocean within days … we may be about to change the course of history, a before and after. In millennia, when a kid opens a book or a hologram or whatever it is, he'll see Sergei Dmitrievich Lazarev and Derya Terzi along with the likes of Christopher Columbus, Ferdinand Magellan, and Marco Polo … the Motherland will no longer be remembered for Ivan the Terrible, or Stalin, or Putin."

A hint of a dimple may have flashed in Sergei's right cheek. *I'll take it. When a paraplegic moves an inch, it's unequivocal progress.*

"On the ice thickness … it all but guarantees missing the first rendezvous. And burrowing down could conceivably take double what we have been estimating, which cuts it tight for the next and final rendezvous," said Sergei.

"That's a problem for tomorrow. Our job right now is to think, what would Sophia do?"

"Our role is making it back to Shackleton with the collected samples. Skipping the first window leaves us no margin of error. We miss the boat five days later …" Sergei's eyes fixed on somewhere far, far away.

"It's likely … we die." Sergei remained mute, seemingly avoiding Derya's eyes, which got him restless. "What am I missing?"

"The cargo will be invaluable with or without alien life. It's our responsibility to do anything in our capacity to deliver the payload to the mother ship at any cost. Shack could spend the saved propellant from the Orbit Insertion to put itself in an intersection course with Enceladus about ten days later. No food for a week is fine … the real survival problem is the water and oxygen balance. I redid the calculations. It may be possible to stretch them for a person being absolutely inactive … the samples are worth more than anyone's life …"

"That doesn't—" The realization left Derya speechless. Seconds ticked by, and with a dry mouth he continued, "You can't really be thinking …"

"The mission is more important than you, or me. For now, it's a low probability event. But if and when the time comes, a decision will be made. One of us gets to survive and make a stab at reuniting with Shackleton."

Derya glanced at the impassive eyes, unable to move. The total absence of human decency petrified him. *Unless this monster is in suicide mode, it's pretty clear who would be saying goodbye to dear life.*

"Would you eat me?" said Derya.

"You are not religious."

Almost whispering, "I'm inside a fucking cage with Hannibal Lecter ... would you eat me?"

"I'm undecided."

42 | COMMUNION

Hours later

ON BOARD SHACKLETON

"You are not yourself today. Is everything all right?" Yi asked over the intercom. He floated outside the spaceship, past the flight deck's Observation Window, by Shackleton's conic bow. James was two arms away, wrestling to bolt a device the size of a suitcase to the hull while Yi tried to hold it in place. Sound didn't exist in vacuum, but the incongruency of James' amplified puffing and the mute running power drill still felt preposterous.

"You want me all smiles. Give me a break, okay?"

"Yes. I'm sorry, Jimmy, it's just that ..."

"And stop playing damn Freud. Piss off."

"Okay." Yi was hurt. Words in space were more incisive, psychological wounds healed slower, emotions ran shallower. *So shallow that I need to stop myself from crying? Come on.* Tears in the vacuum of space had nowhere to fall, so they stayed put. Behind a helmet, no rubbing meant blurred vision to the end of the spacewalk at least an hour away.

He distracted himself by playing with the two umbilicals connecting him to the fuselage, but seeing the narrow tip of the spaceship below gave him vertigo. He concentrated instead on the scenery. He saw nothing but night in front. Turning to his right, he spotted something he would have sworn fake if it wasn't right there: three crescent moons, all three identical in shape but different in size, like scattered Russian dolls on a black cloth. The big one was Titan, which they would fly by the following day. *The second should be Rhea but could well be Dione—the third and smallest may be inhabited by several alien species, but at the very least contains two specimens of the Homo sapiens persuasion.* Turning his head back offered the immensity of Saturn. *What if the giant took our Moon's place?* He got the chills, like a shipwreck survivor, when he envisioned the tides. *Wait, I am a shipwreck survivor.* The rise and fall of sea levels because of the gravitational force of the exchanged moon would surge almost one hundred-fold. He remembered a sea level rise map showing the consequences of an extreme climate change scenario that melted all ice at the poles and mountain-tops. *It was about 230 feet, and both Shanghai and Beijing disappeared under the sea.* Entire countries—the Netherlands, Bangladesh—disappeared underwater as well. *But this would be much, much worse.* Taller, plus ebb and flow. A giant tsunami engulfing the coasts every twelve hours. Maritime transport would become impossible, which in turn would destroy the global econo—

"Goddammit. Sophia, over. My visor is showing the installation instructions. In Italian," said James.

"On it."

"I'll keep you entertained while you leisurely peruse through the files. 'Far slittare il radar sull'apposita guida finché non si blocca in posizione. Connettere il cavo di rete e, successivamente, quello elettrico. Il dispositivo è pronto per essere acceso. Quando inizia a trasmettere, evitare di guardare direttamente l'antenna a distanza ravvicinata: gli occhi sono la parte del corpo più sensibile alle onde elettromagnetiche.' Sounds as scientific as a Puccini libretto."

Titan would be the mission's steering wheel and gas station, achieved by making Shackleton fly by at skimming distance of its atmosphere. This was an irresistible opportunity to obtain high-resolution mapping of the vast methane seas in the north polar region. Shackleton had ferried a Synthetic-Aperture Radar that would capture 3D images in unprecedented detail. Protruding from the hull made it infeasible during launch, plus being a short-lived protagonist justified it being stored as cargo until today.

"Unfortunately, it turns out we don't have them in English. I sent the request to Mission Control," said Sophia.

"What do I do meanwhile? Work on my nails? Nobody bothered to check this in three years!?"

"That includes Your Royal Highness. You've been cranky the whole day. No need to infect everyone with your stinky mood."

Ø

The radio crackled. Enceladus was calling.

"Shackleton, over!" Sophia counted one, two, three, four, five, six—

"You'll never know how much I missed this voice. If you ever thought Shack was claustrophobic and constrained, well, you know nothing Sophia Jong. Over."

The audio was crisp and immediate, never mind the fact the two ships were twice as far from each other than any of the Apollos ever were from Earth.

Every soundbite flew at light-speed for almost three seconds before reaching the receiver.

In the fifty-seven hours since parting ways they had established communication on nine occasions. This was about to change dramatically. Radio waves have proven their worth in transmitting data to and from astronomical distances. Voyager 1 and 2's unassuming twelve-foot-wide dish antennas communicated with Earth from interstellar space until the 2020s, half a century after launch, at a distance fifteen times further than that of Saturn—and their last goodbye wasn't for lack of broadcasting range but electrical power to sing back to us.

But like all superheroes, thought Sophia, *radio waves have a glaring weakness and a formidable arch-enemy. Matter.* They conquer unfathomable distances throughout the void of space, yet a few millimeters of metal are an impassable barrier. Or enough inches of rock and ice, as in this case. *The atmospheric bouncing on Earth makes us forget that electromagnetic waves propagate in straight lines. But in space, block the line of sight with matter and it's game over.* Once Caird landed, the transmission window would shrink dramatically.

"The decision ... Sergei ... and I—it's been decided to land inside Baghdad. Over."

Sophia was elated and yet torn.

As an astrobiologist, landing inside one of the four canyons had been a wishful aspiration. *But they mapped the Tiger Stripes and seem to have found a safe way down!* Having the ability to sample directly from the geysers gushing out possibly not-yet-frozen seawater was tantalizing and made the search for signs of life much more thorough.

As a shipmate, she pitied Derya. *The solitude will be brutal. Maybe the worst isolation ever experienced by a human being—no, make it a terrestrial being.* She wondered how bad the communication breaks would be.

"In case you were wondering, yes, it will be dreadful," Derya said. "The transmission window with Shack will be under 1 percent of the time. With Earth, it will depend on how narrow the basin is and how steep the canyon walls are where we land. Probably one third ... I know, I know. Wanna reach me, call my landline. They'll in turn reach me wireless. So, the Shack–Caird communication window will look somewhat like this: six seconds roundtrip during 1 percent of the time. Two-and-a-half-hour roundtrip via Earth for a third of the time. Incommunicado, two thirds of the day. Over."

The rest of the talk was mostly one-sided. She tried interrupting a few times, but without fail it would develop into exasperating over-talking by Derya, who would not let her get a word in. In summary, inference by indirect means pointed to a global ocean covered by an ice shell fourteen miles thick, thinning to three under the Tiger Stripes. No surprises there. The ocean depth, however, was fantastical. Average ocean depth on Earth was 2.3 miles. Average depth in Enceladus? Roughly nineteen miles. And beneath the south pole? Over thirty. *Earth's Mariana Trench, at just under seven miles deep, now sounds lame.*

TiTus' androgynous voice interrupted to warn that the connection would drop shortly.

James and Yi had been offline, removing their spacesuits in the cargo area.

Last chance to say goodbye before Sergei and Derya are GO for landing and remain out of reach for days. Sophia glided toward the cargo area in a hurry. "If you want to tell me any secrets, now's a fitting time—" was the last she heard from Derya. When she reached the spacewalkers, the connection had dropped. *Bad form at best, bad omen at worst.*

∅

It was a quiet, downcast lunch at Bacchus when Sophia said, "You've been very out of character today. I didn't even know a 'James the asshole' existed."

Yi stared down at his reconstituted mushroom and pesto risotto. He was still uneasy with the disregard for rank and the straight, almost confrontational American style.

"It's been a bad day." James sounded low-spirited. *A mission first*, thought Yi.

"For all three, but it needn't have been that way. You're not just one of us, as if that needed saying. You're our commander, we look up to you … you've let us down—" Yi tried to interrupt Sophia, but she countered, "I'm not talking to you, Profe. Don't wanna listen? Then move out."

Which Yi did, promptly floating toward the hatch.

"It's one of my black dog days. But you're right, as usual," said James. "Yi! Man, brother, please come back. I owe you an apology."

∅

It ended up being one of those long, late conversations. *Usually lubricated with red wine—unless you're marooned, incarcerated, a teetotaler, or one of us*, thought Yi.

"… yet you've been preparing for all this during the past ten years. And we're finally here. This is it, right here, right now," said Sophia.

"And that's the problem, I think," said James. "We've given so much while the rest bask in enjoyment, lapping up the entertainment we and they have turned us into. To many this may be the best show ever: it's fun, it's enlightening, it thrills, it moves ... but the sacrifice. Emma will be 6 when we get back, to be embraced by a stranger claiming to be her dad ... and look at us here: we're stuck in a spaceship, but no less spectators to what will happen in Enceladus than someone sitting in a bar in Madrid. In a strange way, and it may be ennui so bear with me, this is less epic than I once imagined."

"No need for a pep talk, Jimmy. I'm not going anywhere. Go Shack!" said Sophia.

"This mission changed, maybe saved, my life," said Yi. "Don't underestimate its power. It's the five of us, but it's also so much more than that. It belongs to everyone watching us. In the cynical society of today we—that's you, Sophia, Sergei, Derya, maybe me—represent idealism. Unity. Inspiration. Second chances. We defied and conquered the impossible. Just imagine how many kids are becoming scientists and engineers because of you, Jimmy Egger. And all here, all of this, it's your brainchild."

"Brain tumor, Yi. A doomsday vision that cannot be described. Something so terribly tangible and intense that it never felt like a dream. It was its own separate reality." James hesitated. "And after torturing me for so long, it's gone, erased from my unconsciousness. But I'm not at peace. Because I can't see the logic. There was no emotional release. No closure. It's just ... gone. It fled without ever saying goodbye or explaining why—it didn't bother me before because I was single-minded about getting here. The Orbit Insertion long ago became the be-all and end-all. And it's over. It's as if the taut shock cord that pulled me here finally snapped and sprung back to Emma and B. The mission climax may be starting, but I just want us to turn around and go back as soon as we possibly can."

"By the way, how's Emma?" asked Yi, trying to gently bend the conversation.

James' eyes lit up as he grabbed his tablet. "Look at this picture. Anything seem different?"

Yi was clueless. Sophia looked over and said, "She's starting to look a lot like Belinda?" James' face betrayed nothing. "She's dressed very English proper? ... her hair is getting darker? ..."

"I couldn't stop thinking her body was incomplete because of her deafness, that we shortchanged her, that she would always miss out on fully experiencing the world around her. Until this photo." He could hardly manage the excitement. "B had called her a few times and she didn't react ... want to know why?

Because she opted for silence! She just turned off the sound processor of her ear implant! She wanted some quiet time before being drowned in noise again! Then it hit me. We go through life gauging things with our measuring tape, assuming our perception of reality is the only truthful, possible actuality. But that's blinding smugness. It's looking down at a peasant in a Nepalese village, pitying her small world, her ignorance of the thrills of New York ... my 3-year-old daughter, who I haven't even met, taught me she doesn't lack one sense, she has four very enhanced ones."

43 | PREPARE FOR LANDING

Hours later

ON BOARD JAMES CAIRD

The silence was deafening and the moment strangely anticlimactic. *Like crippling* Saving Private Ryan's *D-Day landing slaughter by playing it on mute*, thought Derya. He was unemployed, killing time by looking around or counting up in powers of two, as Sergei maneuvered the tiny Caird down the last mile. Boredom was much stronger than anxiety. *If anyone can land this canister, it's the brute to my right.*

Enceladus' puny force of gravity meant the capsule needed to orbit at 350 miles per hour so as not to fall into the moon, barely 60 percent of the cruising speed of a commercial airplane and a measly 2 percent of the speed needed to orbit around the Earth. Caird was now free-falling at a feathery nine miles per hour, and without atmosphere to buffer against, it would decelerate right before touchdown with a short burn. *Little more than an engine fart will do.*

Derya looked around the cockpit meets kitchen meets latrine meets bunk bed. *Very practical, but multi-functionality isn't free. The French know it well. Mix the right kind of smells and you get Chanel No.5. Mix the wrong ones and you get this sleek cabin, combining disinfectant, garbage, body odor, farts of various provenances, and that most ignoble of gases, the unmistakable reek of human scheisse or doo-doo.*

No magic fairy dust around here. Sergei released a load of Number 2 six hours before and it still lingered as new. *Sensorial abuse and all, not much that can be done.* The life support system doesn't care about feelings, only about constantly sucking the CO_2 that lungs expel out of the cabin, thus keeping air at 100 percent oxygen plus the aforementioned trace scents. *But my elementary schoolteacher told us air is only a fifth oxygen, you say? Others may remember 1967's Apollo 1 fire tragedy on the launchpad, which cost the lives of three astronauts because of a pressurized pure oxygen environment, flammable materials, and one spark.* All true, but risk mitigation in space is about imperfectly minimizing hazards, frequently lowering safety in one area to increase it in another.

Caird's challenge was boringly predictable: extreme weight restriction. A 100 percent oxygen environment achieves the same breathability as regular air with only a third of the cabin pressure. *Over the coming days, each time we exit or enter the capsule, the air mass is vented and lost to the vacuum of space—tomorrow's hatch opening will sanitize, although not eradicate, this foul pestilence, restarting nature's cycle—fire risk is alleviated by low air pressure and having little combustible material, that means leaving behind nude calendars and other memorabilia hanging from the walls. If that makes Caird's inside look like a Jesuit cell, welcome to the faith.*

It pays to be unoriginal in space. James Caird was an unmodified SpaceX Dragon, the same reliable spacecraft that had regularly ferried people and cargo to and from Low Earth Orbit since 2020.[20] 390 cubic feet of internal volume—*that's a small bathroom, Tokyo small,* five comparatively lush windows, a spartan interior exposing structural beams and piping, two Bauhaus-looking ergonomic seats with harnesses, a long rectangular touchscreen hanging from the roof divided into four panels full of data meters and graphs and flashing readouts. *That's all Folks! This house is now our life, both literally and figuratively.*

Attached right under the Dragon was a custom-built trunk, essentially an engine and propellant tank to increase the spacecraft's range many times over, allowing a descent to and launch from Enceladus plus a contingency buffer for the unexpected.

When they were 2,100 feet above the target landing site, Sergei rotated the vehicle ninety degrees. Caird was now sideways, allowing visibility from three windows. *Hopefully to the terra firma below.*

"Inspect landing conditions. This is your one task until I say so," said Sergei.

If the surface was suspected of being mushy or semi-liquid, Sergei must

---

20   *To call it sturdy would be a defamation,* thought Derya. By the time it touches down on Earth, the speed with respect to the ground needs to be pretty close to zero—*otherwise the payload goes extinct.* Yet orbital speed is 17,000 miles per hour, so the interim is bound to be hellish. Moving fast in thick atmosphere generates very serious friction, thus very serious heat. You must shave speed high up, where the atmosphere is thin, so the energy transformation from speed to heat is slower, making the capsule 'only' heat up to 4,000 degrees Fahrenheit, 'just' 40 percent of the Sun's surface temperature. *For this, you need to create a path of more resistance, which in today's culture of lean is beautiful means esthetic concessions.*

The name says it all. The geometrical shape of all re-entry capsules is a frustum, a headless cone. *The Dragon negotiates this ugliness by being taller and thinner than the competition, plus soft angles and a fashionable white color scheme.*

abort before touching down, climb out of the canyon, and attempt landing on the plain above.

"On it."

Derya squinted past the windows, trying to decipher the terrain below. But Baghdad was a canyon and the flanking walls were seemingly vertical in places. With the Sun no longer directly above, the left wall shadowed the entire gorge. The rays reflecting on the opposite wall illuminated the dark, but not enough to make the bottom features discernable. *At least not yet.*

He checked himself. *Thinking about this descent back in Shack invariably sent my balls running for groin cover.* Yet here he was, adrenalized but still cool. It reminded him of Jimmy talking about the difference between looking down at the precipice while climbing and then after when at the top. One elicited almost no reaction, the other churned the stomach. *It's the frame of reference. In the vertical, the brain has accepted and adapted to a risky situation. In the horizontal, the brain instinctually reacts violently against voluntarily putting oneself at risk.*

"Check the horizon!" said Derya. The apparent straight line of Earth here became an aggressive curve. A person would disappear from sight after walking half a mile in any direction. *And yet Yi, that lovely nerd, said the other day that it would take 300 Shanghais, the world's largest city, to cover the entire surface of Enceladus. It's tiny for planets, it's huge for humans. Frame of reference again.*

"Looks like Le Petit Prince's Asteroid 325." Derya was effectively speaking to himself.

Cassini's photograph was prophetic. A 2005 image of Enceladus' south pole taken by Cassini on its closest flyby, at twelve feet per pixel, showed what at a distance appeared to be flat, smooth areas turning into irregular terrain littered with ice boulders tens to hundreds of feet tall. Before his eyes, what seemed featureless from afar had become littered with blocks of ice of all sizes, some as high as buildings, farrowed by the tectonic wrestling of an icy outer shell fully decoupled from the moon's core, floating over the mysterious global ocean. *Caution is in order.*

"1,000 feet," said the computer. Derya looked to the side: the horizon had been replaced by a wall a few hundred feet away. On it, he could see the irregular reflection of a small descending object. *Us!* He shifted himself to inspect the other side. The canyon was about a mile wide, besieged by the two arresting V-shaped walls becoming dead vertical in places. His heart shied and bolted as adrenaline dumped into his bloodstream.

"700 feet." *It's all too sudden.*

"600 feet." The ground features began to resolve.

"Sergei—Sergei, when do you plan to put the ship upright? Sergei!" Nothing but disturbing stillness.

"500 feet."

"400 feet."

"300 feet."

"Speak to me, mate! Please!"

"200 feet."

Caird rotated upright.

"One hundred feet." The landing area was clear from the stories-tall boulders, but Derya saw the dark ground interrupted regularly by deeper shadows.

"Boulders below us! Abort!" Sergei didn't react. "We are going to crash! Hurensohn! Scheißkerl!"

Sergei activated the attitude control thrusters and Caird jittered, interrupting the descent. But instead of climbing, it began moving sideways directly against a fast-approaching, house-size ice boulder. The panic froze Derya like a rabbit caught in headlights. When the end was imminent Caird suddenly propelled itself in an upward diagonal barely conquering the icy rock, shutting down seconds later. It fell unhurriedly until the legs softly touched down and the spacecraft rested on firm ground at last.

"My apologies, Derya. When I focus I shut down external voices."

Derya was stunned and confused. "What just happened?"

"We landed on top of a flat boulder."

44 | SETTING UP CAMP

A day later, September 7 2030. Main Mission day 4

ENCELADUS

It had been a few hours since landing and Sergei and Derya were finishing an unfulfilling dinner. *Whatever remains of the pleasure of eating was left behind on board Shack,* thought Derya. He was having fish and chips. *Except there's no distinguishable fish or chips, only this dark gray greasy rectangle with the texture of semolina—it's not the treat but threat that passes food down the gullet.*

Coordinated Universal Time was obsolete. Like most natural satellites in the Solar System including our Moon, Enceladus is tidally locked to its planet. The same hemisphere faces toward Saturn all the time, and the Tiger Stripes are in the wrong direction. This meant the day was now thirty-three hours long, the time it took to complete an orbit. Daytime lasted half of that, although being inside a canyon shrank direct sunlight to nine hours. *Out of this pit it's still daylight but here it's dusk.*

Derya strained his neck to lay his cheek against the hull under the window, which allowed him to see the top of the canyon. The tip of Baghdad's eastern wall gleamed like myriad lighthouses lined up past the horizon, mirroring light toward the valley below, revealing some of its major features. *When the real night falls an hour from now, the only illumination will be the Milky Way.*

"Suit up." Derya was certain he misheard. "Suit up," Sergei repeated.

"It's dark out. Dawn is in seventeen hours," said Derya.

"We're going out."

"Are you ... are you certifiable? We'll freeze to death." Being the brightest object in the Solar System is only possible by mirroring out every ray of light, making it the coldest object too. "Right now, it's fifty degrees above the lowest temperature in the Universe, you ninny."

"We have tasks pending. Anchor Caird, microphones, antenna—"

"Anchoring you said? As in a tent?"

Sergei moved to a corner, grabbed a handrail, and started swaying. Soon after Derya felt two of the four Dragon legs go airborne. "Stop. Please stop. I get it."

"You knew ultra-low gravity rationally, not intuitively. Remember the American marshmallows jumping around the Moon? Gravity here is a fifteenth of that. Caird is eight tons but weighs 200 pounds here. Do not forget that."

"What about the cold?" said Derya.

"What about it? There's three ways of losing heat, physicist. Living things add a fourth: sweating. Convection and conduction require your atoms to transfer heat to other atoms. Vacuum comes from the Latin 'empty,' meaning of matter. And radiation is much slower than the other three. So, trust me—staying out for an hour won't kill you. Take my word for it."

That commodity never traded too high, but now it's worth zero as far as I'm concerned.

Sergei continued, "It's -360 Fahrenheit outside. During cryotherapy back on Earth, people get half-naked for three minutes inside a chamber that's cooled with liquid nitrogen to -300. You ninny, whatever that means."

"I'm really not ready, Sergei. I need to think, I need to sleep. I need time."

"That's a problem for which I have no solution. We start venting in twenty."

"Maybe I can stay?"

"You know the protocol. Every moonwalk together."

⌀

The hatch opened to a frozen landscape that could have been Antarctica on a moonless night. As Derya descended the ladder, Sergei was already hammering and screwing stakes into the icy ground. His first steps served as an acquaintance with the new rules of gravity. *It isn't walking—nor floating—but an in between sort of bouncing.* The two light beams from Derya's helmet did the reconnaissance of the alien topography close by. The terrain seemed chaotic, fractured.

"We're three stories high. How do you plan to get down?" said Derya.

"We jump."

"You don't say. And how do we get back up?"

Sergei squatted and jumped twice his height. "We jump. Let's go."

Once more this feeling of being as useful as a mountain guide's paying customer.

The Russian grabbed the dish antenna and a box, scouted with headlights for the best drop, and disappeared over the edge of the boulder.

Look at this maniac!

With a heart running its own marathon, Derya followed panic-stricken.

However, with no visual cues to feed his fright, the slow fall and landing ended up feeling almost peaceful.

He became mortified. *I endangered the mission and our lives.* The boulders he screamed about before touchdown turned out to be stones no taller than his knee. Caird's legs could have easily negotiated them. *Thanks, gruff man, for the undeserved decency of not rubbing it in my face.*

In a few minutes, the high-gain antenna was erected. The dish was small, but it was never meant for yakking. Its main function was to send the output from sensors and instruments to Earth, where a legion of scientists would be crunching the data and fine-tuning the long list of activities to maximize the scientific return.

Earth will be in line of sight only a third of the time. Derya looked up. After three years gazing at the rearview mirror, it took him little time to spot the inner planets and Jupiter. He concentrated on the bright dot with a sidekick right above the canyon shoulder. *So distant I'm staring at an eighty-minute-old image of the Earth. Meanwhile, countless pairs of eyes gaze at the here of eighty minutes ago—destined to forever pass each other unnoticed.* He noticed Sergei watching him, patiently waiting.

They got back to the base of the boulder. Derya jumped first but didn't reach half its height. By the third attempt his head glimpsed Caird's landing legs. On the fifth attempt he managed to rest his chest on the horizontal, but with nothing to grab on to he slid back down. He heard the rarest of occurrences, a laugh from Sergei.

"A scientist distrustful of science. Escape velocity is 530 miles per hour. Not there yet." Escape velocity is the minimum speed needed for an object to escape the gravitational influence of a massive body.

Next time Derya shot with ample buffer, justifying to himself that the mental block was more about falling somewhere unsafe than catapulting out of Enceladus. It was an atavistic fear of both.

"Forgot to ask how you did," said Derya from upstairs.

"Drove down two seismometers."

"Enough to characterize Enceladus' interior. Come back up so I can go to sleep."

⌀

Two hours later, the cabin was repressurized and at room temperature, and with a new foul bouquet. Derya's soiled spacesuit diaper stank out the capsule in the transit to the trash bag. *I'll maintain it was diarrhea until I die.* The lights were off and Sergei was dormant, but Derya struggled to fall asleep. It was perfectly silent, except for the occasional creaking of Caird reacting to the outside temperature.

After much trying, he gave up and glanced at the clock. *Still eleven hours before sunrise.*

Moving quietly, he grabbed the flashlight and stuck it against the window to minimize reflection. The light was lost a few feet out in a curtain of white, the silhouette of thousands of snowflakes dancing in between. It was snowing. The geysers were back in business.

He put on the headphones and worked on one of the ship's screens. What he heard gave him goosebumps. The two seismometers, part of a suite of instruments to be deployed tomorrow, were already recording data. Derya was the first human to hear what Enceladus had hidden from prying eyes, the secret sound waves of the enormous ocean beneath, unaware of being wiretapped. If he didn't know the scale the sensitive ears were recording, he could have sworn it was the arcane conversation among inscrutable creatures from the deep.

The creaks and groans were the interaction between the thick ice shell and the formidable tides from the gravitational tug of Saturn, while the sharp pops and cracks were the local system of crevasses, subsurface lakes, and fractures connecting Baghdad with the global ocean miles underneath, currently being pulled open as Enceladus approached its farthest distance from the giant planet.

The geysers were gushing intensifying jets of ocean water and organic particles, some much faster than the escape velocity and thus perpetually lost to the heavens beyond, feeding Saturn's almost invisible E Ring far beyond its much more famous and brighter siblings.

He lay back down again. Realizing they were perched on an ice crust floating on top of the vast ocean was enough to feel the ground rocking like an Indian canoe. Fearing a sleepless night—bad preparation for the demands of the next day—he swallowed a pill that took effect almost immediately.

A beep made him turn to the big screen. The first messages from Earth had arrived. One of them was a historical nugget from late 2017, right before Cassini's suicide plunge into Saturn, "Such mysteries are far too enticing to ignore. Perhaps someday, another robotic explorer will sail toward Saturn and turn up wonders we have yet to imagine."

45 | ALIENSCAPE

A day later, September 8 2030. Main Mission day 5

ENCELADUS

Derya was like a child waiting for Santa. *Still pitch dark*, he thought. *Either the clock is being lethargic or dawn loves the anticipation around here.*

Sergei's snoring was becoming irregular and the wake-up alarm would trigger in less than an hour. *Daybreak is imminent.*

But it never arrived.

"Sergei! Sergei!" Derya cried, shaking a slumbering Sergei. "We're in deep shit. We're buried alive," he said while pointing to an unlit window. The snow coat was hiding the daylight.

The adrenaline bypassed all of Sergei's morning rituals. Derya was already suiting up.

After donning the spacesuits, they hastily checked each other twice.

"Okay'd for emergency depressurization," said Derya right before banging the code into the screen.

Both knew that if depressurization didn't work, they were in serious trouble. Opening the hatch without depressurization was impossible: like commercial airplanes the hatch opened inward, which here meant overcoming 5 psi of fierce internal pressure. But unlike them, the vacuum of space also sealed it shut from the outside as if it was welded closed.

Sergei tried opening the hatch. It was jammed. Swearing loudly in Russian he tried again. The attempts became frantic. Never mind breaking the latch, that would be a worry for later.

He stopped, panting over the intercom.

They looked at each other. No words were needed.

There will be no depressurization if the ice shell around Caird doesn't allow some cabin air to be vented.

Sergei placed the soles of his boots on each side of the hatch, grabbed the handle, and thrust his full body weight against it. One. Two. Three. On the fourth attempt it swung open.

Ø

First Sergei, followed by Derya, emerged into a frozen world lit by a dwarfed Sun.

The view is indescribable. Not even video footage could communicate its beauty, thought Derya.

What from orbital altitude looked like one of many elephant skin wrinkles had become a deep canyon with menacing half-a-mile-tall walls over the basin. While further north the cliffs loosened into wide V-shaped slopes, here they overhung inward in a disregard for gravity that would have been impossible even for rock formations back on Earth. The moon's curvature was extreme, any feature beyond a few miles fell behind the horizon. They could count many geysers in each direction, a procession of spurting whales, semi-transparent cones reaching impossible heights. Not all pointed and shot vertical, one was so slanted that it spewed below the rim, producing the effect of a giant waterfall pouring down. The surface surrounding Caird was a jagged terrain of outcrops and fissures, a chaotic mess of jumbled ridges, cracks, and plains, complete with hordes of icy boulders, some as high and wide as ten-story buildings. Everything aside from them appeared to be a black-and-white picture, occasionally stained by oily amber reflections from the Sun.

Using a knife and fork as spatulas, they managed to break the crust around the capsule, which came off in big chunks like the shells of a boiled egg. The heat being radiated from inside created a fluid slush between ship and ice.

Could have been this mission's end, or a lot worse. It appears luck extends to the outer Solar System.

The solution to prevent a similar trap in the future was a flimsy tepee door flap made from that wondrous space material used in you-were-supposed-to-die-but-you-made-it Apollo 13, duct tape.

"Clearing twice a day should do," said Sergei.

"I'm starving. Dinner was twelve hours ago."

"That's repressurizing and then venting to come out. Venting twice a day is too onerous."

Hard to believe, but more pleading broke Sergei's resolution. They went back inside for breakfast.

⌀

The working day started by boring microphones carrying small explosive charges around a predefined perimeter. When they were all in place, Derya detonated them. The bouncing of propagating sound waves at different depths was picked up by the microphone, allowing a precise determination of the height and stratification of the ice mass.

The results were being beamed to Earth, where Mission Control needed to send back a surface spot and digging path for the Mole at some point later that day. This was now the critical path for the mission. The clock was definitely ticking. Each hour waiting was an hour wasted. *The first opportunity to reunite with Shack is almost certainly gone*, thought Derya.

Sergei was fixated on one of the long, bluish gaping crevasses from where the geysers originated, encircled by seracs with vertical walls vanishing into the deep darkness. The geysers were waning and in a few hours would shut down until the next orbit.

"And if you gaze long into an abyss, the abyss also gazes into you," said Derya.

They went to Caird to retrieve the Mole. The coordinates hadn't arrived, but every minute counted.

After a while sitting idle outside, resting his back against the capsule, Sergei said, "The only real measure of progress is the cryobot a foot further from the surface. I'm starting the reactor."

Derya postponed its activation. *By applying advanced psychological techniques—mostly threatening mutiny.*[21]

---

21   Unoccupied and waiting, Derya focused on the Mole a dozen feet out, chock-full of U-235.

He began an unsolicited soliloquy. Sergei seemed accustomed enough to ignore him altogether. "Uranium is one of the heaviest atoms in the Universe, packing ninety-two protons in its nucleus. And like every element above iron, it's only born in that most titanic of explosions." *Just like the gold from our wedding bands. Derya & Karl. Originally forged not by jewelers but inside a supernova. A marriage made in heaven—until you said no, cunt.* "See, uranium comes in different flavors, U-235 being one of the most prevalent, having 143 neutrons for a total nucleus count of 235. It's unstable and decays into stability by breaking into smaller atoms, radiating heat in the process. But without intervention, the splitting rate is excruciatingly slow, with a half-life of 704 million years. No wonder it has been used for dating the Earth. Any questions so far?"

"Hmm," said Sergei absently.

"But here's the thing: being born slow doesn't sentence you to a dull life, as nuclear physics has discovered—I mean, look at Yi. Anyhow, by 1934 the work of the great Enrico Fermi

Within half an hour the triple ding of the incoming message resonated in both helmets. "Let's go," said Sergei.

⌀

Three hours later, Waltzy Mole was upright, held in position by a tripod anchored to the frozen ground. An ultra-thin reinforced wire would be the link between Mole and surface, sending live data from the multi-sensored cryobot up to Caird as it burrowed down. The reactor had been activated and the bottom third of the robot was a scorching hot rod about to touch the surface and begin melting ice.

The two explorers were back inside the capsule. Derya was triple-layered, looking through a window. Sergei was in underwear with Volume 4 of Gibbon's 1789 behemoth *The History of the Decline and Fall of the Roman Empire* on his tablet. He interrupted his reading to shout, "This is the last time. Cut the bullshit and press the damn button."

"We've waited four years ..." said Derya.

"Right. We've waited four years."

"Five minutes is all I'm asking. Let me savor the significance of the moment."

From Derya's vantage point he saw the Mole some 200 feet away. The Sun was about to hide behind the western wall. Back on Earth dusk followed sunset by about half an hour, as the atmosphere kept bouncing sunlight around until our star was deep down over the horizon. Here sunset was nightfall. The last rays gave an otherworldly honey glow to the infinite candles of light at the top of the wall convincingly imitating a twilight.

Derya eventually pressed the button. In went the Mole to explore a sea of mysteries and, perhaps, answers.

---

led physicists to bombard heavy atoms with neutrons, earning him the Nobel Prize barely four years later. Nuclear fission is born. A nuclear fission reactor like the one inside the Mole accelerates the natural atom-splitting rate by millions of times for controlled chain reactions."

"And billions of times in the case of uncontrolled ones, known as nuclear bombs—at least in Russia," said Sergei.

"Correct, and it all begins with one single neutron striking into the nucleus of a uranium atom. Ignoring the human horror unleashed a millionth of a second later, it's hard to be a physicist and not be mesmerized by it. So, this neutron slams against the atom's center, splintering it. Some of those 143 neutrons will slam against other atoms. Repeat this eighty times and you have a nuclear explosion."

Ø

Later that night, with the Mole already over 300 feet deep, there was a strange blue glow coming out of the borehole. Cherenkov radiation, high-energy electrons passing through the liquefied ice around the cryobot. The column of frozen ice functioned as optical fiber, and the high reflectivity of the walls mirrored and bounced the light, whose only escape became the mouth aperture.

Much closer, on top of the boulder outside Caird, a collecting box was gathering falling snowflakes from the geysers. Right there, in that collector, may be a microbe about to change the course of history. With that accumulating sample, tomorrow they would test for signs of alien life.

Sergei stopped reading and put the tablet down. Derya was a goner, snoring just below the decibel threshold that earned a slap. This was the most dangerous part of the sleeping ritual, when Sergei's mind was unoccupied in the transition between reading and falling numb. He closed his eyes and hoped for the best. Everything was running smoothly, ramping down for slumber. He had almost made it when a grunting coming from his neighbor threw him off. A date flashed in his mind—*twenty months next month*. The demons in the recesses of his mind—*eating something, hopefully memories*—had been provoked. The sadness washed over and threatened to drown him. He gulped down a sleeping pill. *I just need to keep busy for fifteen more minutes to push the unbearable over to another day.*[22]

---

22   In his mind he entered Saint Petersburg's Hermitage Winter Palace and teleported himself to the Library of Nicholas II. He committed the palace to memory many years before for mnemonics when he was at university. A few months back he started using it as refuge, safe recollections that kept him away from Iman. The library was a two-level room made of dark wood in the English Gothic style, with bookcases placed along the walls. He imagined himself walking in and climbing the narrow staircase leading to the upper gallery. Now his mind was not only detached from his body, but the place itself gave the impression of being inside an Anglo-Saxon castle during the Middle Ages. With the protection of two deep layers of separation from reality, he picked out a book for tonight, about life.

What is life? There's no more fundamental a question for what happens tomorrow.

The scientific community struggled long with this one and only in 1992 did NASA arrive at a consensual answer: "a self-sustaining chemical system capable of Darwinian evolution."

That's pretentious and confusing. The straightforward answer is I know life when I see it. A bird for instance.

But that's mistaking life with being alive. If a bird reproduces and the offspring is a duplicate of the parent, it doesn't qualify as life. Replace 'bird' with 'virus;' it doesn't cut it. You can see the subtlety more clearly with an inanimate object that imitates life: a fire. It grows, consumes food, and creates imperfect descendants. What's missing?

That Darwinian evolution thing.

In 1861, two years after he had published one of the most influential books of all times, *On the Origins of Species*, Darwin speculated that all organisms that have ever lived on Earth may have descended from one primordial form. Time proved him right. The fact that you—Sergei Dmitrievich Lazarev—are reading this book while your gut has been colonized by thousands of different species of bacteria, all of you descendants from the same ancestor, testifies to the ultimate requirement for life: evolution.

Define 'evolution.'

When a cell divides, it attempts a flawless duplication. This is achieved in the immense majority of cases. However, in exceedingly rare circumstances the high fidelity copying of the ancestor's DNA is imperfect, creating a mutation. This mutation is usually detrimental to the offspring. Nevertheless, it occasionally increases the ability of the new cell to compete, survive, and reproduce. This is Darwinian evolution. A variation arising from an unintentional mutation, which is then filtered by natural selection: the survival of the fittest. Back to the definition of life, it requires those mutations to happen sporadically and to be heritable.

Elaborate.

The concept of 'heritable' entails information. Information being modified and carried over with each new biological iteration. This information, the book of life describing every structure and process that happens inside a living organism, is stored for all life on Earth in the genetic code. DNA is the largest molecule known to man, at 200 billion atoms, comprising an amount of information comparable to 175 Bibles in the case of humans. Its alphabet comprises four letters, each letter itself a molecule called nucleotide. Yet this huge amount of data resides in every living cell, and in the case of complex life—including all animals and plants—inside its nucleus. There is no objective measure of big or small, everything needs frames of reference. The human body is composed of around 40 trillion cells. That makes cells huge compared to viruses. About 100 trillion atoms against 200,000.

However many trillions and complications, all this is just me.

But you can't be so arrogant as to think of 'you' as one monolithic being. You're nothing but an ensemble of cells, each self-sustaining and independent. Each second, millions of cells in your body are dying, while hopefully millions are being born. You need cells, cells don't need you. Need a demonstration? Blood donation. Red blood cells can remain refrigerated outside the body, perfectly blithe, for forty days. And so the requirements of the human body are the aggregation of the requirements of its cells. Complex life forms are masterpieces of cell cooperation, dictated by the specific instructions encoded in DNA.

Blessed to have 175 Bibles packed inside each of my cells, but how do those instructions get implemented?

The arms and legs of those genetic instructions are proteins, which act as structural elements of the cell and perform a vast array of functions. The fundamental building blocks for proteins are amino-acids, twenty of which are arranged in different configurations like Lego pieces to compose any of the millions of different protein types in the human body.

Metabolism is the process beginning by eating other animals and plants, then broken down to the level of amino-acids and sugars by our digestive system, which are then used to fuel cells and make more cells for reproduction, growth, or repair.

Let's cut to the chase here, it's getting late. Is life an extremely rare occurrence or something fairly ordinary?

Because we only have direct knowledge of life on Earth, all of which descends from a single ancestor, our sample consists of exactly one data point to extrapolate its prevalence and chemistry across the Universe. We still have no answer for what are purportedly the two most transcendental enigmas of the human race: Are we the only ones in the Universe? And how did life on Earth originate?

We may never solve them. After all, Carl Sagan said extraordinary claims require extraordinary evidence—yes, he was American, but his father was born in the Russian Empire.

Yet one lone microbe invisible to the eye, which may be freezing its ass off waiting for tomorrow's interrogation in that collecting box right outside the hatch, would be enough to clear up the first one. So far, the evidence for alien life is a paradox. On'one hand, the fact that life took root on Earth 4 billion years ago, while the bombardment from the early Solar System hadn't stopped, looks like a strong indication that, given the right conditions, life takes hold quickly. On the other, there's not one sign of life anywhere we've cared to look. Mars has been unable to provide even a pointer of a molecule made by life, presently or at any point in its long and once wet past. Same with the exploration of the rest of the Solar System.

And then there's Enceladus.

Yes. And then there's Enceladus. Life on Earth requires three primary ingredients: liquid water, the right chemical ingredients, and a source of energy for metabolism. Over 99 percent of the mass of living things comprises four chemical elements: hydrogen, oxygen, carbon, and nitrogen. All of them detected by the Cassini probe in Enceladus' plumes.

Doing well.

Yes, but prerequisite number three is stringent. On the whole, life-as-we-know-it depends on the Sun, directly or indirectly. Yet the giant ocean of Enceladus is completely devoid of sunlight. Impossible roadblock? We don't know, but it could have been. Then in 2017, during the months leading to the probe's immolation, Cassini sniffed silicate crystals as well as molecular hydrogen, H_2. The former all but guarantees hydrothermal vents in a rocky seafloor. The latter is a source of food that sustains microbes in deep, dark undersea environments on Earth. The two combined are the very conditions found in that most famous of white smokers, Lost City. It is increasingly accepted that a jet-black oasis on the bottom of Earth's oceans was the cradle of life. It's hard not to feel these are almost sci-fi times, with a previously inconsequential moon having, on closer inspection, a big sign saying "Free Life Samples."

I say we should feel optimistic.

Conditions suitable for life are not the same as life in suitable conditions. Enceladus has all the ingredients, but life needs building blocks for its infrastructure—such as nucleotides and amino acids. In 1952, seeking to test Darwin's conception on the origin of life, student Miller and professor Urey at Chicago University performed a famous experiment inside a couple of laboratory flasks joined by glass tubes. In one they put water, representing Earth's early ocean, topped with a mix of gases similar to those found in Earth's nascent atmosphere. They heated the flask, and the resulting steam and gases naturally flew to the second flask where an electrical discharge simulated lightning. This closed cycle was repeated time and again for a single week instead of millions of years. When they analyzed the contents of the liquid pool, they found a rich gunk containing many complex molecules, including amino acids, nucleotides, and sugars. This was extraordinary. In a highly simplified primordial soup and ridiculously modest time frame, several organic compounds had formed spontaneously. This foundational experiment, along with considerable biological and geological evidence, lends support to the theory that life arose spontaneously through naturally occurring chemical reactions.

Good. Good.

That said, having yeast, flour, water, and heat does not guarantee a loaf of bread. One skeptic put it neatly: "the chance that higher life forms might have emerged in this way is comparable to the chance that a tornado sweeping through a junkyard might assemble a Boeing 747 from the materials therein." One formidable and potentially sobering fact is our ancestry. Genetics has conclusively shown that all living humans descend in an unbroken line from one woman (un)known as Mitochondrial Eve, who lived hundreds of thousands of years ago in Africa.

For those like mama making the sign of the cross in gratitude, our lineage doesn't stop there.

Right. You may not like it, but we are distant cousins with the fruit fly.

Troublesome indeed.

Around 60 percent of our and their genes are identical. If that's not shocking enough, when scientists inserted a human gene associated with Parkinson's disease into fruit flies, they displayed the same symptoms as those seen in humans with the disorder. Not only is their book of life written in the exact same language, but more than half of the chapters are exactly the same. Chimpanzees 98 percent—although I've heard that for Creationists the percentage could be far higher. Bananas 60 percent. This is simultaneously staggering and humbling. All life coming from a single primordial ancestor could be a warning that life happened because of an exceedingly improbable event and set of circumstances.

I know who mama and babushka would have blamed for the miracle of life. You've been rambling enough. One last sweeping statement as I'm sinking fast into Morpheus.

Is life an extremely rare occurrence or something fairly ordinary? Evidence points both ways, which means we don't have the slightest idea. The probability could be 100 percent or 0 percent. This is worse than random, I'm afraid. Throwing ... a coin in the air has a 50 percent ... chance of landing heads ... but the ... tables may ... turn ... tomorrow.

46 | Δ GLIMPSE

A day later, September 9 2030. Main Mission day 6

ABOVE TITAN

Sophia, James, and Yi floated a few feet above the flight deck's Observation Window, six miles above the autonomous vehicle called Grasshopper and 590 miles above Titan's surface.

The giant moon was bigger than Mercury. A greedy behemoth that gulped down 96 percent of the orbiting mass around the ringed planet during the Solar System's formation, leaving 4 percent to distribute among all the other sixty-one moons. If it orbited the Sun instead of Saturn, we would rightfully call it a planet.

Shackleton's low path meant the spacecraft was dipping its toes in the gaseous tides of Titan's tall, dense atmosphere. The slight, controlled deceleration would provide a critical orbital change for the rest of the mission. *Space traveling is all about butterfly effects*, thought Yi. *A subtle nudge today amplified into a sweeping effect millions of miles later.*

A day ago, still at a distance, Titan looked to Yi like a yellowish billiard ball behind foggy glasses. Now, the embarrassment of riches below was entirely clouded to the three inquisitive pair of eyes by the thick, orange smog of its atmosphere. But it couldn't conceal its shrouded surface from the bionic eyes of radar and infrared cameras. The opaque clouds became transparent to the radio waves and the infrared bands mapping the north polar region below them. Not even rivers or shallow parts of lakes and sea bottoms could hide from the radar.

The cockpit's main display was occupied with the live radar data feed. Sophia and James' avid eyes flicked between the haze beyond the window and the display making it see-through. Yi's avowed obsession with Titan mandated having virtual reality goggles on.

When he donned the goggles, Yi flashed back to a bony 12-year-old barely clinging to his class' average height in boarding school, lying down in his bunk bed during mid-morning recess, a worn *Superman* comic resting on his chest while surrendering to a new foreign sensation, by imagining all those uniformed girls with skinny legs marching in front of his X-ray vision. He also remembered what happened soon after, the dormitory door flinging open and the four bullies coming in for him. Yi was now drenched in another type of longing, the craving to have known Titan better. *I'm like that prophet in the Christians' Old Testament, Moses. The tragedy of only being allowed to watch the Promised Land from a distance—it was never possible though,* he reminded himself. *It was always in my dreams but never in our plans. This may be one of the main psychological costs of exploration—incurable longing.*

The synthetic aperture radar was simultaneously sending radio waves down and picking up the previous ones that had bounced back from Titan's surface, using their slight difference in time of arrival to build a three-dimensional representation of the landscape below. The infrared images being generated were mounted on top of the rugged surface rendering.[23]

The landscape below was both extraordinarily familiar and extraordinarily alien. Steep canyons plowing through jagged, snowy mountain ranges. Restless rivers discharging their volatile contents onto distant shorelines. Sahara-looking wind-sculpted swaths of dunes girding the equatorial region. Sprawling seas similar to the Aegean, invaded by archipelagos and convoluted peninsulas. Titan's skin shaped by eons of chiseling by wind and rain. But for all its Earth-like meteorology and geology, this Mother Nature seemed infertile. Yi could see none of the conspicuousness of flora back on our planet. It felt like a time machine jumping past billions of years into the primitive Earth. *Before or after it evolved into a life-bearing planet? How many decades will pass before we know?*

In our Solar System, Titan is the only world beyond Earth with stable surface liquid bodies—excluding the scorching lava lakes of Jupiter's moon Io. The weather below Yi sloshed in all three states: solid, liquid, and gaseous. Not water, but methane and ethane and other hydrocarbons. Water did abound but in the form of rock-hard pebbles and boulders scattered around its surface. *That's shamefully inaccurate! There is liquid water. Not on Titan but in it.* The moon was a world of two ocean decks: the exterior hydrocarbon seas and an interior water global ocean as salty as the Dead Sea. *But bigger. Much, much bigger: in quantities many times larger than all of Earth's oceans combined, hidden dozens*

---

23   Fully immersed through the goggles, Yi saw Cassini's topographic map in all directions, and right below him the new data being processed in real time, replacing a 200-mile-wide strip with newly 3D textured mapping. The resolution was astonishing. Each pixel within the strip represented ninety square feet on the ground, almost one hundred times better than Cassini's radar, which repeatedly scanned Titan's surface from 2004 to 2017 during its 127 flybys.

of miles under Titan's surface. The Cassini probe, that shrewd sleuth, confirmed its existence in 2012 by inference: the way Titan flexed under Saturn's gravity was only possible by a shell decoupled from the moon's core.

Kraken Mare, Titan's largest exterior sea, glittered beneath.

Hours before, Shackleton had released a heat shield designed to brake against Titan's atmosphere and parachute its payload to the moon's surface. This was the Grasshopper, an autonomous explorer that—all going well—would touch down near Kraken Mare the next day.

The Grasshopper was a direct descendant of the iPhone. Components miniaturization and rechargeable battery improvements allowed a revolution in unmanned aerial vehicles. This three-foot-long quadcopter drone, however, was an exercise in superlatives. It carried both a laboratory and a meteorological station on board to study Titan's atmosphere and to search for organic molecules and chemical signs of life. It would communicate directly with Earth through a dish antenna the size of a platter. At each landing site it would recharge its batteries from a shoebox-size nuclear thermoelectric generator. It would fly once a day. *If this seems hurried, bear in mind that a Titan day is sixteen Earth days long.* And in a few days, it would have covered the distance the long-lasting Opportunity rover covered in its fifteen years roaming around Mars. *I suppose it sounds less impressive when you consider it was a little under thirty miles.* Its cameras would image the terrain and scout for the next scientifically interesting site. And after Mission Control picked the exact route, it would fly and land autonomously.

Grasshopper would achieve all this by fully utilizing Titan's thick atmosphere—four times denser than Earth's—and lower gravity—one-seventh that of Earth's—which make it the easiest location to fly in the Solar System. *In fact, thirty-eight times easier than back on our planet, to be precise—here, the Wright Brothers wouldn't have stood a chance against their countless predecessors strapping wings to their arms.*

Minutes later Yi screamed, "The Magic Islands are back!" The Cassini team had so dubbed the mysterious features that appeared and vanished on observations taken years apart. The phenomenon could be vast patches of bubbles or subsurface ice rising to the sea surface or even waves. At that time the hunting was with sling and stones. *Now we brought the bazooka.* He zoomed in and suddenly got the chills. "They—they're giant waves! I—I'm watching the sunlight reflect off them—" His voice broke down. *This is one of the happiest moments of my life.* They moved in front of his eyes, glinting in gold, 590 miles below. Through the virtual reality goggles, science had healed his blindness and fixed his sight to within a few miles of the fantasy world below. Yet it wasn't that. It was the exhilaration of discovery. It was internalizing that those waves below and indeed himself were partly made of hydrogen, all of which was created by the Big Bang at the beginning of time. It was about no longer sensing the cosmos around him but becoming a part of it. He felt the dopamine rushing in his body. *But that's the drug fix, and this is much deeper than bodily sensations.* The sense of time dissolved, he abandoned the future and the past, delighting instead in the simplicity of the now. *I could die this moment and it would be fine.*

And then it was over. Yi saw the mammoth Titan recede. Distant, indifferent, almost aloof.

But the memories would stay with him for good.

47 | THE SEARCH FOR LIFE

ENCELADUS

Never mind the food, this was Derya's most invigorating breakfast ever. He looked through the window one more time at the collecting box sitting outside Caird. The snow already reached half its height. *More than an adequate sample to begin testing!*

"Today we answer whether Enceladus is inhabited rather than merely habitable," said Derya. The words rolled out of his mouth with the pace and rhythm of a carol.

"I've already told you, temper down. This isn't Germany playing in the World Cup Final. We're not bystanders here. We're referees. The instrumentation will do the work, but then human interpretation follows. We're the only two pairs of eyes on the frontline. You owe it to the world to be less fizzy and more impartial."

"You're starting to sound like C-3PO." Derya got a blank stare from Sergei. "*Star Wars*? Sorry, forgot you skipped childhood."

"Even if alien life is teeming down under, there's no certainty we'll be able to find biosignatures in the geysers' ejecta," said Sergei.

"Ejecta? Bloody hell! Call it snow at least. Find some poetry in life, mate—and given you got all technical, sure, there's no certainty but there's a framework supported by ninety years of empirical evidence in oceans, rivers, lakes, ponds. What's incontrovertible is that Cassini discovered silicate crystals in the jets, which means two things—well, make it three. First, there's hydrothermal activity coming from seafloor vents. Second, the observation of silicon-bearing compounds is in itself a demonstration that seafloor material is rising the tens of miles of ocean depth and traversing through the ice shell to then be expelled in the plume at high enough concentrations to be detected. Third, back home hydrothermal vents are thriving concentrated ecosystems ... now the speculation: bubbles are the ones ferrying the detected particles up, and on Earth they tend to collect organic matter and microbes along the way as they climb the water column, which can increase biological concentrations up to a thousand-fold compared to those in the bulk ocean. So yes, I'm convinced that whatever shows up here will be representative of what's down there."

"Moderate the bullishness. Don't underestimate the capacity of evolution to innovate. Bubbles rise because they're lighter than water. Predators could have evolved to have nets passively waiting for bubbles to pass through to scrub them of microbes."

"Sounds far-fetched," said Derya.

Later, the hatch slid open and Derya went over to the collector box and sealed it before re-entering the microbes' infested capsule. Humans are giant worlds inhabited by microorganisms in mostly symbiotic relationships. Touching or simply breathing instantly colonizes any sterilized environment.

Afterward, the spacesuits were out and they waited for the thawing. The laundry list for that day was long and yet both were focused on the transparent box cover. Derya's head raged with the realization that history may be about to change with whatever was inside that container no bigger than a shoebox, sitting a foot away from his face. *I get whiffs of hospital smell—which is good. Aseptic and all.*

Sergei brought the digital holographic microscope and Derya positioned it over the collector box. Specifically designed to detect the hardest of samples—a semi-transparent, micron-sized, single-celled, featureless, motionless organism—information was fed into a computer algorithm that reconstructed the image as a 4D hologram, 3D plus time. It thus sidestepped one of the primary criticisms of the use of microscopy for life detection: the difficulty of discriminating cells from mineral grains or organic material.

Derya turned it on. At 97x magnification the screen showed a cluster of perfectly symmetrical hexagonal ice crystals. The tree-like dendrites at the end were beginning to show deformation due to melting. Zoomed to 347x it showed never-ending complexity as new wild structures were revealed. Zooming to 1,920x showed thawing was now evident, but there was still geometrical perfection, a long, flat surface engraved with pyramids, cones, cylinders. He turned it off.

"When hunting, you only view through the crosshairs when ready to shoot, otherwise you lose perspective," he said.

They waited until the melting dissolved the ice crystals. Alien liquid water. Bubbles formed at the top and around the sides, like beer foam.

"Looks like tap water," said Derya with an enthusiasm that could only mean it wasn't.

"Holy water does too, yet it protects against evil spirits and cures cancer. Do not judge a book by its cover."

"Are we ready?" asked Derya. Sergei nodded. "And what if we find nothing?"

"Then it's either a sample problem or the absence of life, isn't it?" said Sergei.

Scanning for signs of life began. The first test was for an alien organism in motion, an unambiguous, 100 percent confident detection of life. A quick pass started at 100x zoom for sixty seconds. Nothing. 200x. Nothing. 400x. Nothing. 800x. Nothing. Derya glanced at Sergei, who remained absorbed at the screen. 1,600x. Nothing. 3,200x. Computer detected thirteen corpuscles to which it superposed blue circles for motion tracking on Caird's screen. Derya's reaction was more relief than excitement.

And then nothing happened for five motionless minutes. It could well have been a photograph, both the water sample and Caird's cabin.

"Calm down," said Sergei to an increasingly restless Derya. "The water temperature is 35.6 degrees Fahrenheit. The training samples barely moved during the first hour."

A year before launch, a team including Sophia, Yi, and Sergei flew to northern Canada, well within the Arctic Circle, to an uninhabited piece of land called Axel Heiberg Island. Some 50 million years before it had been covered in wetland forests, now mummified under hundreds of feet of permafrost. Over a week, they calibrated the digital holographic microscope and trained on bacterial samples obtained from englacial ice and an under-ice lagoon, simulating Enceladian conditions. They learned to resolve subcellular features, spot microorganisms by recognizing shapes and swimming patterns, and deal with ambiguous cell-like objects.

After almost an hour had passed, movement was detected by the software, not appreciable to either for a while. It was no impediment for Derya to hum "We Are the Champions." He was temporarily immune to Sergei's glare, instead doubling down by turning it into a chant while stirring his arms theatrically.

As time and temperature went up, the movement accelerated and became progressively erratic.

And Derya lost all composure.

⌀

The computer had been tracking the path of every particle by drawing a line behind it. Within minutes most lines had gone from blue to red. All seemed to follow a random walk: forward, left, retracing, right, the scribble of a toddler—all but three.

Sergei tried to remain calm, but the effort was increasingly futile. The engrossment was such that he no longer heard or saw Derya turn into a chimp. He was focused on one particle, bigger than the rest and with a non-circular form, moving in an almost straight line to the right. He saw himself falling into the anthropomorphizing trap. *But I'll be damned if that thing is not heading with an attitude toward the other particle,* he thought.

He could feel his increased breathing and heartbeat, and then the goosebumps arrived as he was taken into a stupefying crescendo.

"I think—" but he didn't utter the next words.

And then in an instant Sergei's particle blue path turned red. Seconds later they had all been disqualified. 'Brownian Motion' flickered on the top right corner of the screen. Using Einstein's equations,[24] the software had ruled the corpuscles' movement was perfectly consistent with inanimate matter.

They looked at each other, floored.

"What now?" asked Derya, his voice suddenly vulnerable.

"We move on to the next experiment: chemical detection. And we retry tomorrow after overnight incubation. Remember Axel Heiberg Island. We had a similar situation and the following morning the broth showed an increase in cell mobility, which made separating them from the background a much easier task."

"In God We Trust."

"Leave him out of it. You're behaving like a televangelist. I don't think God gave you reason just so that you would abandon it when we need it most. Trust in the experiments and the science behind them, physicist."

---

24   Einstein earned the Nobel Prize of Physics in 1922, but not for his 1916 theory of general relativity—which most physicists did not understand at the time. It was instead for one of the four papers published in his 'annus mirabilis' of 1905, the year in which he reshaped our conception of time, space, mass, and energy. The paper was on Brownian motion, the random movement of particles in a fluid resulting from the collision with other atoms or molecules. Temperature is not a fundamental quality of matter, but a human construct. What we call temperature is really the jiggling of atoms. 'Hotter' temperature is higher energy, which in turn means faster wiggling. Einstein derived the probabilistic equations, which established that the average distance traveled by a particle from a set origin is random, but depends on both time and energy level, aka temperature.

✷

Short of a microscope, the fallback tool in the detection of life's arsenal are long, organic molecules. Organic molecules are chains of atoms that have carbon as their backbone. As far as life on Earth is concerned, this is an essential requirement. But not a guarantee. Methane, CH_4, is a simple five-atom molecule spontaneously occurring across the Universe, which has been detected by telescopes all over our as well as distant solar systems. The name of the game requires 'long' attached to 'organic molecule.'[25]

As the size of an organic molecule escalates, the probability of atoms spontaneously self-arranging decreases exponentially. In the case of a single protein, a mere pawn in those marvel city-states known as cells, the probability falls to zero. A protein is made by hundreds of amino acids—each amino acid itself composed by tens of atoms—forming bewildering geometrical shapes. That sophistication betrays the intervening hand of biosynthesis. But for smaller molecules, say a DNA fragment less than one hundred nucleotides long, the analysis is inconclusive.

In lieu of size there are still two solid tools.

One is chirality. Our hands look identical but are in fact mirrors of each other. The difference becomes obvious by superimposing one over the other. The molecule that gives spearmint its distinctive smell is an exact mirror of the one that gives caraway seeds their pungent aroma. Nature is ambidextrous, life is not. Non-living chemistry creates left- and right-handed molecules in equal amounts. But all of us are left-handed—nineteen out of the twenty amino acids forming every protein in our body are left-handed. Detection of prevalently left- or right-handed molecules all but seals the case for the existence of alien life.

The other is the ratio between carbon-12 and carbon-13. All chemical

---

25   The cosmos is ruled by the laws of thermodynamics. The second law states that anytime and everywhere, everything is either moving swiftly or crawlingly from order to disorder. It's an irreversible process. An uncooked, unbroken egg can be scrambled or boiled, but neither can be reversed into the whole egg. Electricity can be transformed into heat, but that heat cannot be made back into electricity. It's a one-way arrow. Except that life seems to fly in the face of the second law. Take some atoms, sprinkle them with life, and they self-arrange into a staggeringly complex collection called human beings. Only when you die does the second law claim possession of the body and eventually breaks it down—order to disorder. Life cunningly achieves this the way an illusionist turns a jack into an ace. Locally, magic irrefutably just materialized. More broadly, metabolism does the trick by degrading chemical energy into heat, thus the global balance still complies with the second law.

elements have variants that differ in the number of neutrons, which are called isotopes. Carbon has fifteen known isotopes, but only two are stable. Carbon-12, with six neutrons and six protons in the nucleus, is ninety-nine times more naturally abundant than carbon-13. Finding an anomalous deviation from this 99/1 ratio would be a powerful signature of extraterrestrial life.

∅

The first day of sample testing concluded by running the two other instruments aboard Caird. The Enceladus Organic Analyzer, able to detect a wide range of organic molecules using lab-on-a-chip technology that had miniaturized into a palm-sized device that two decades prior would have taken a full laboratory—people included; and the Isotopic Mass Spectrometer.

Derya had been making an active effort to work through the results without processing them in his head. After so many years waiting, the prospect of staring at them was intimidating. He was drained, the mental effort had permeated his body and he felt limp and lethargic.

There was a cloud of unease hanging over Caird. They barely spoke during dinner.

A double beep put them on the alert. The sample analysis had concluded and the summary of the chemical inventory sat on the screen, waiting for their attention.

Derya was surprised to note Sergei wasn't raising his head either. If he was by himself, he would have gone to bed without checking. But having another person in front turned it into a prisoner's dilemma and the outcome unraveled within seconds. Both stared at the screen in silence, long enough to hear each other's breathing.

Derya finally said it. "It's habitable ... it's lifeless."

Quantitatively, it was undeniably promising. All biochemical elements were present. Check. A significant portion of the building blocks of life: two of the four DNA letters, adenine and thymine; three-fourths of RNA's letters; twelve out of the twenty amino acids required for protein assembly; various fatty acids; an assortment of other complex organic molecules, although none larger than fifty or so atoms. Molecular biologists would rejoice in the finding of long-speculated molecules potentially conducive to a parallel chemistry of life: compounds using silicon instead of carbon; and a modified adenine joined with thymine by an additional hydrogen atom, making a stronger bond. Inconclusive evidence, yes. But clearly positive.

It was the last three lines that brought down the celebration. The cosmos' remorseless indifference was once again manifest.

Chirality: No Statistical Preference. All twelve left-hand amino acids had their right-hand siblings in the sample.

Carbon Isotope Ratio: No Statistical Difference. Not only that, it was equal to nature's abundance all the way to the first decimal place.

And the final note of pessimism: Total Concentration of Organic Molecules in water was four full orders of magnitude lower than in Earth's oceans.

"The whole machinery of life is operational, but nothing here is actually alive … all the jigsaw pieces fit snugly, but nobody ever took the time to assemble them," said Derya in a voice as bleak as his words.

Sergei answered after an excessively long time, "Your logic is the same as dropping into Central Park on a winter night during a blizzard, and, not seeing anyone or anything, claiming sovereignty over America as the first human being to ever set foot there … you can't extrapolate from a single sample." But any persuasiveness was defeated by his delivery.

"Utter tosh. You sound like a schoolboy trying to recite from memory a year after the exam. We came here because there was a big sign on Enceladus saying 'FREE SAMPLES.' Well, it was all a big fucking booby trap. Turns out there's nothing. Nothing at all."

"You can't be so stupid and self-important to assume we know better. Perhaps life is so alien that its biosignatures are unrecognizable to us, hidden in plain view. Right here," said Sergei, pointing at the collector box. "Or it's so slow we can't perceive it in such a short amount of time."

"Want some science? Occam's razor. Among competing hypotheses, the one with the fewest assumptions is usually right. Aristotle said: 'nature operates in the shortest way possible.' Sometimes a banana is just a banana. If biology ever began here, it's long gone. Maybe all that organic goo is the last remaining bones from the skeleton of life."

"I didn't travel half a Solar System for bananas," said Sergei.

"You're bloody right we didn't. But we have."

"Even if we find nothing, no sign of life whatsoever, it's still a big discovery."

"Tell that to your wife!" The moment his lips shut, Derya knew he was dead. Yet instead of anticipating the coming slaughter, *please forgive me* was the one thing crossing his mind. He closed his eyes and waited for the mauling. And waited. And waited some more. If there was an axe on board, he knew where it would have landed the moment his eyes opened.

Sergei was in front of him, staring at a point on the floor. Derya looked at the spot, guessing the only possibility for what did not happen was an extra-terrestrial cockroach. His mouth was a desert. Even breathing burned. He was incapable of saying anything, it simply didn't come out.

The lights went off.

Derya was crushed, defeated. The shame and existential sadness were like barbed wire, gashing around wherever his mind turned. Such promise and hope, now dead.

Sergei was shell-shocked. The lid that kept Iman's memories at bay had blown up in his head. Insomnia was back with a vengeance. There wouldn't be any sleep tonight, but that was the least of his troubles. The brooding wouldn't stop. The suicidal tendencies would reappear. The bleakness. Everything became black and white again. They came for nothing, yet he had still paid the ultimate personal price.

⌀

The awkwardness of the next morning was short-lived.

Sergei initiated conversation, skipping any mention of last night, sounding and looking paradoxically calm, almost upbeat.

Something has happened, thought Derya. But the remorse in Derya was too present to ask him. *Whatever it is, the lad seems somehow, absurdly and unlikely, content.*

"There's three 'URGENT' messages from Earth asking, well, demanding information. We just need to authorize Caird to start telegraphing data back. I'm doing it now." Derya's tone was a question, not an assertion.

"And say what? We have good news and bad news. The good news is that there's all kinds of carbon molecules here. The bad news is that there's no life, but we almost found it. Nobody cares we were close. You either have it or you don't."

"Right …" said Derya, confused. "So, should I send the info to Earth?"

"The evidence is inconclusive. It's noise. Serves no purpose and will just confuse people. We don't send information until we have high confidence in the results."

"Right …"

48 | CHΔOS ON EΔRTH

Two days later, September 11 2030. Main Mission day 8

PARIS, FRANCE

I t was a sight to remember. Hundreds of thousands of people were blanketing the twelve streets that feed into the grand roundabout under the Arc de Triomphe, slowly moving onto the Avenue des Champs-Élysées, heading to the president's palace where they would continue to the 7th arrondissement and Palais Bourbon, which housed the French National Assembly.

The march had virtually stopped all traffic inside the Périphérique, Paris' administrative limit ring road, on that Wednesday afternoon.

The multitude was a microcosm of French society. A student sporting a Sorbonne T-shirt. One stylish octogenarian lady caked in make-up. Two Muslim women in purple hijabs. A class of impeccably uniformed 10-year-olds. Dozens of buses hidden right under the rectangular-trimmed sycamore trees at both sides of Europe's grandest boulevard, hauling people in from the provinces for the protest, such as a group of pilgrim-tourists just arriving from Lourdes.

Reporters were scattered around the crowd. One English-speaking news channel was interviewing a 30-something showing off a pair of waist-slung megaphones. The accent made him unmistakably French, but his English was fluent and his delivery eloquent.

"—it's outrage and consternation. Whatever Sergei Lazarev and Derya Terzi have found does not belong to the American government, it belongs to *us*, humanity at large. *We* financed the mission! Those are *our* people out there! So, as we continue marching, the cocotte—the pressure cooker keeps building up. We demand the immediate release of all the information—"

Similar non-violent protests were being staged in cities around the world.

⌀

MISSION CONTROL @ HANGAR ONE, CALIFORNIA

"This dwarfs any interview I've done, so we are both rookies tonight," said the news presenter. Nitha was surprised by how genuine and caring the anchorwoman seemed.

Mission Control was dressed once again for television, but the seventy-minute delay between them and the Saturn system had rendered most of the room's functionality useless. *Its moment of glory is three years behind and three years ahead*, thought Nitha. Of the twenty-seven specialists' seats, only six remained staffed twenty-four hours a day, seven days a week—something the television director found unacceptable. He also found inadmissible that the giant screen occupying the one solid wall inside the 'fishbowl' was filled with numbers, coordinates, and diagrams, but no videos. Nitha went on to explain that using the precious bandwidth from Shackleton to Earth to send anything above low-resolution pictures would be a crime, but he was having none of it. He had even brought a chintzy pastiche of old videos that reminded her of a wedding slideshow. They settled instead on a Saturn photograph using the center half of the screen. One of the mission specialists even superimposed Shackleton's current orbital position. And half the seats were now taken by new faces recruited from Hangar One's floor to boost the numbers.

The anchorwoman looked at Nitha one final time for confirmation. "And Nitha," she said, "remember the message you want to get across. Prove to the world you guys are in no way conspiring with the US government, or anyone for that matter."

Nitha nodded in response, firmly grabbing the seat under her legs to hide the tremble.

One of the four camera operators counted down. "Going live in three, two, one …"

"Nitha Sharma, Shackleton's Mission Director, thank you for having us here."

"My pleasure, Deborah." Her usually thin voice was now full. That dispelled part of the insecurity.

"Straight to the point. Can you explain to the world what is going on?"

"Yes, but I first want to restate what we all know: the Shackleton mission is absolutely, entirely, and completely independent from any government or organization. It began and it has always been a private initiative. And not just private, but multinational: not only is the crew multinational but we have been financed by people from all over the world ... now look at me. Listen to my voice. You guessed correctly. I am a foreigner. And an alien! At least according to the Department of Homeland Security. I've never worked for the US government. I owe them nothing. If anything, I have little sympathy for them. Exactly eighteen years ago my visa application to come to America was rejected, despite a full scholarship from MIT. Guess what. It was rejected again seventeen years ago, apparently because the first rejection cast doubts on the second application. Isn't it Kafkaesque? For those wondering, I did get in on the third try ... I'm from India for God's sake. So, I'm afraid the answer will disappoint a lot of conspiracy theorists." She drank from a plastic water bottle before continuing, "The fact of the matter is that Derya and Sergei have been deliberately holding back information and communication with Earth for over a day. We don't know why. As for Caird and Shack, because of their relative positions in the Saturn system, they have been incommunicado for days and that will continue to be the case for a couple more, so let's hold Sophia, Yi, and Jimmy blameless. That leaves my team, Mission Control, in the hot seat ... except it doesn't. I want everyone hearing me tonight to understand this: I am the mission's Flight Director, but I only have access to the exact same information than anyone else on Earth has access to. At the same time. This is an ironclad rule imbued in the very essence of the mission. It has never been and will never be violated."

"How so?" said the anchorwoman.

"We hired NASA's Deep Space Network, the worldwide complex of antennas, to hear and reach Shack during the entire mission. In that agreement, Article II Section 4 clearly stipulates that all information received is instantaneously made public, protected under International Law, and immediately belongs to the human race ... this means, in practical terms, that a person with mobile Internet connection in a mountain village in Bolivia has access to the same information at the same time as Mission Control. The main assets are the three huge 200-foot parabolic antennas, one each in the US, Spain, and Australia. So, data doesn't even originate on US soil two-thirds of the time. Furthermore, the moment the signal arrives, it is beamed out via the Internet, and that interface is managed by a grassroots organization that anyone can join. And, while we decode it, there are tens of other independent organizations doing the exact same with the same results ... we've thought this through and through."

"Why so many precautions? This may even sound suspicious to some people."

"Because inside those data bits coming from Saturn may lie the most important answer in the history of our species. And if and when that happens, everyone needs to know not only from here," she touched her temple, "but from here," touching her chest, "that there was no meddling, just honest, transparent, undebatable truth."

"Then, what's your guess for Sergei and Derya's actions?" asked the anchorwoman.

"I don't have the faintest idea. Maybe the sampling is not conclusive? But why keep it to themselves? Whatever the cause, I really hope this ends soon." *Great plan, guys, you've caused quite the carnival here on Earth,* thought Nitha. "Now, if people knew Derya and Sergei like I do, well, what's happening would appear less outlandish. Those two are quite something."

"Aren't you worried? Some pretty big names have gone as far as to speculate they have been abducted by ETs."

Nitha chuckled. "Big names in show business, maybe. Not scientists—or at least I hope not! We get their heartbeat and other vital data every five minutes. It's right there, center left on the screen," she turned and pointed to the giant screen behind her. "If I was in front of an alien—another one I mean—I think my heartbeat would reflect that. Instead, Derya is averaging," she turned her face back again, "67, while Sergei is at 48."

"Don't you think the explanation may have to do with them having found something truly big?"

"I certainly hope so," said Nitha, her expressive black eyes sparkling in anticipation.

Ø

MINISTRY OF DEFENSE OF THE RUSSIAN FEDERATION, MOSCOW

The phone started ringing. The dreadful call. Oleg Artemyev, the Russian Minister of Defense, unstuck the previously immaculate button-down shirt now glued to his body by cold sweat.

Lazarev, Sergei Dmitrievich. Decorated national hero. At a different point in history that wouldn't have saved him from a court martial and, possibly, the firing squad.

After Lazarev's wife died, the Russian state seized his personal bandwidth. It amounted to a big pile of shit. Not one word back from him in over a year. During the last twenty-four hours requests had turned into pleas, at least by military standards. "Captain Lazarev, immediately report the Enceladus testing results in encrypted form." This was met by the insulting silence of a traitor. The Foreign Intelligence Service found no leads, but Oleg knew it could only be a defection.

He waited until the fourth ring and raised the handset with his left hand while crossing himself with the right.

The call with the President did not go well.

49 | THE TRIUMPH OF REΔSON?

A day later, September 12 2030. Main Mission day 9

CASABLANCA, MOROCCO

Neil deGrasse Tyson walked down the boarding stairs onto the tarmac of Mohammed V International Airport. Considered the most influential science communicator since his own mentor, Carl Sagan, this was one of the rare occasions where no one among his fellow passengers seemed to have recognized him. The anonymity was blown, however, by the escort awaiting him, which included armed Moroccan military personnel. A hurried stride took them to a transport helicopter with its rotor already powering up, which flew them over Casablanca to the stylish Al Noor Tower, the tallest skyscraper in Africa, a curiously pleasing incongruity between Sauron's tower in *The Lord of the Rings* and Dubai's glitzy skyline. The helicopter approached the 114-story building from the side and landed on a hanging helipad almost half a mile above the city.

This was possibly the weirdest, most surreal moment of his life. The events of the last two days had implausibly turned the round table debate he was about to join into what one commentator called "a papal conclave, US presidential election, and *Titanic 2* premiere, multiplied."

The perfect storm was triggered by Enceladus' bizarre retained data situation and made incendiary by the release, within hours of each other, of alleged Shackleton video footage showing a massive alien spacecraft partially blocking Saturn's view, and WikiLeaks' top-secret US Air Force files reportedly documenting seven decades of covert UFO investigation. The sudden level of worldwide uncertainty and distrust pushed for a last-minute location change of the debate, from New York, seven subway stops from his home, to a so-called neutral country, settling on the Muslim nation of Morocco. Even CNN, the network leading the broadcasting of the show, was replaced by Al Jazeera in the principal role.

Tabloids the world over running headline variations of "they were there all along, examining us" was one thing, but Neil had learned of a high-profile, highbrow German news magazine printing their weekly edition with a similar nail-biting cover just hours before, only convinced to see reason after a call from the Chancellor to its editor-in-chief.

The world was a very small, volatile tribe that evening. The exhilarating prospect of finding alien life in our own backyard turned instantly to terror by just one word: sentient.

Ø

The conference room had been turned into a television studio with a circular stage crowned with lighting rigs and surrounded by video cameras on dollies and pedestals, all of that enclosed by a seated audience of 300 people. All five panelists—a philosopher, a Hindu swami, a Catholic cardinal, a Muslim mullah, and a scientist—were not so much practitioners as they were communicators with massive followings, yet they struggled to proceed with their discussion between shouts from seven hecklers strategically spread throughout the crowd.

"Sir, sir," said the ineffective moderator to one interloper, "I don't think that language is appropriate or conducive to a civilized conversation. I ask you again to please refrain from disrupting—"

"The truth will not be silenced, you swine!" he shouted back amid booing from the rest of the crowd. "I have with me—" he tried to continue while scuffling with someone to his side, "photographs—that prove they are coming—coming for all—for all of us!"

The mullah's voice prevailed momentarily over the general cacophony, "I propose one of you come onstage to present your views, on the condition that afterward you remain—"

"No!" yelled the philosopher panelist. "You degrade this discussion and turn it into a circus whenever you validate them."

Ø

A new chair had been added to the round table. The self-proclaimed conspiracy theorist "you can call me Jason" looked very much at ease, even while listening to the philosopher's tirade.

"So not only was JFK killed by the CIA, the Apollo Moon landings fake, but Russia, Germany, and the USA have been conspiring for decades to cover the UFOs ubiquitous footprints? I don't expect somebody with your IQ to have figured this out so rapidly, but your collection of 'theories' are not even internally consistent. Not that you would know this, but the Second World War was decided on the Russian Front. Just in Stalingrad over a million casualties on each side. A perfect hoax to deviate attention from that flying saucer you keep in the basement. The Cold War? Just prolonging the smoke and mirrors. Are you able to even decipher what your lips are uttering? If I was a taxonomist, my conspiracy theory would be that you were intentionally grouped with humans instead of leeches."

"I would have presumed more thoughtfulness from a philosopher, but I guess all the good ones are long gone," said Jason, enjoying his high ground. "I won't stoop to your level. There's really no need to be condescending. I think the evidence is beyond question and speaks for itself. But if people want to go beyond, and really *understand* 'why' UFOs are being drawn to Earth, there are just two words to remember: water and reproduction. You see, Earth has wonderful wet oceans and seas, rivers and lakes, in prodigious quantities. And if chemistry has taught us anything, it's that water is not just essential for living beings, but hydrogen and oxygen make for an excellent fuel, possibly the best there is. So, it's naturally a commodity that is always in high demand, whether in human or intergalactic circles."

"I would like to tackle that one," said Neil.

"Okay, sure. Go ahead," said Jason.

"Thanks," said Neil. "Let me start by saying that the detection of a sentient alien being, an extraterrestrial microbe, or even so much as pond slime would rank as perhaps the greatest discovery in the history of science. I revel at the mere thought of it … the problem with UFOs is that they are as extraterrestrial as you or me. Why would any advanced alien civilization bother with Earth? There are huge amounts of watery real estate just about everywhere in the galaxy. There are billions, maybe trillions of comets—you know, balls of frozen water, just in our humble Solar System—"

"I meant water in liquid form," said Jason, unfazed.

"Wrong answer, my dear Jason," said Neil. "The laws of physics strongly constrain journeys across the vast gulfs between stars. The speed of light is simply too slow. Therefore, unless we are talking about very patient Methuselahs, aged a millennia and beyond, their spaceships need to accelerate to a fair fraction of the speed of light. And if they built such technological marvels, I would surely hope they mastered the art of fire a few generations back, don't you?"

"You just don't get it, that's the problem," said Jason, but failed to follow this with an argument. After a pause, he continued, "The second point I wanted to make is regarding reproduction. There is ample proof, now publicly available by the disclosed US Air Force top-secret files, that there have been regular UFO excursions to our planet to abduct humans for breeding purposes—"

"I'm sorry, Jason, but I can't let this one go either," said Neil. "I'll only take a minute."

"Okay, I guess."

"Hollywood and people like you are horrendously unimaginative when it comes to alien life. It's shameful really. Aliens, whether in movies or those blurry photographs that ufologists have been waving at us for decades, always look to me like an actor in a bad costume: two legs, two arms, two eyes, head, ears, teeth, a cup-and-ball reproductive system, and, of course, big on mucus. Compared to a jellyfish, extraterrestrials and humans look like identical twins. Yet they are supposed to live on other planets, the product of completely independent lines of evolution. Let me show you something a bit more original. There is an exotic life form that senses its prey by detecting infrared rays; doesn't have arms and legs, yet can slide faster than you can run; it swallows whole live creatures five times bigger than its head. And that, my friend, is called a snake. Anthropomorphic thinking restricts our imagination. I am of the opinion that if there's biology beyond Earth, the vast majority will be microbial—single-celled life forms that tolerate a much greater range of conditions than more complex organisms can. But if complex life exists, I know one thing for certain: its strangeness will be well beyond our imaginative powers ... having gotten that off my chest, let's deal briefly with the issue of sexual reproduction between aliens and humans. And for that, let's consider the definition of 'species:' two individuals that can have fertile offspring. Say, a Chihuahua and a Great Dane. You may not like what comes out, but it's definitely fertile. You go another degree of separation and you encounter the mule, the offspring between a horse and a donkey. But it's no longer fertile. In the case of humans, we long ago branched off from every other living thing. In fact, considering we can't even interbreed with our closest relative, the bonobo, I applaud your fantastic optimism. It's almost contagious—"

He was interrupted by the audience, erupting with applause.

⌀

The age of reason had settled back and Swami Kumbhar, one of the two last panelists, was about to give his opening remarks.

"These are paradoxical times. Barely a week and a half ago the world was one, united by Shackleton. Yet today we have broken ranks into tribalism. So instead of speaking to my billion Hindus, my moral obligation is to try to reach whoever is willing to hear. Let's learn from each other, let's be humble and listen. The Christian, Muslim, and Jewish faiths have the story of the Golden Calf in their scriptures. It says the prophet Moses went up Mount Sinai for guidance from the God of Israel, staying there for many days. The Israelites grew restless. When he finally came down the mountain with the Ten Commandments, the people had already forgotten their true god and turned to idolatry of a Golden Calf. It's a rich tale of many lessons, but I would like to bring out how easily we seem to have forgotten our calling.

"We went to Saturn looking for the truth, whatever it may be. Yet a few missteps and mishaps have sent all of us into a panic, resorting to explanations of profound absurdity, betraying our beliefs in search of quick gratification, distrusting those that don't look or think like us. But we already know from our heroes aboard Shackleton that all those wrinkles and divisions, the seemingly insurmountable chasm between countries and religions, suddenly smooth out to nothingness when we take sufficient perspective to identify our world not as the land of 1,000 languages but as a single mote of dust in the immensity of the cosmos."

After heartfelt clapping, Neil followed.

"I will try my best to follow Swami Kumbhar's insight and wisdom. I'm not one to promise miracles though! As the scientist here, I will speak on behalf of science and technology to the 2 billion Christians, the 2 billion Muslims, the billion Hindus, every other religion, as well as the agnostics and atheists. That phone in everyone's pocket has a processor that requires quantum mechanics; it has a GPS that needs to account for special relativity and thermodynamics; its communication capabilities require electromagnetism, and optics, and acoustics, and satellites orbiting the Earth. It is a nutshell of 10,000 years of technological progress, summarizing most of what we've learned from nature. Technology has improved our lives enormously. That was a question, by the way. And I have no answer. The answer, in fact, may well be 'no.' Although we live in an era of technological wonders, we humans in many ways behave no differently to those during the Crusades. It troubles me to see that in a society absolutely dependent on technology, not only does almost no one understand the science behind it, but many flatly refuse to believe in it! How can we be so irrational to reject as false the underpinnings behind the technologies we use on a daily basis? Categorically rejecting reason because of dogma! That's a recipe for disaster, because we must never forget that technology is amoral. Science and its creations cut both ways: they can be used for good or evil. And that's why Swami Kumbhar's vision resonated strongly with me, and I mean that literally.

"Did you know that when troops marching in unison are about to cross a bridge, they're always ordered to break stride and go out of step? Objects vibrate at a certain frequency when they absorb energy. If a regiment marches over a bridge and the bridge's vibrations are different from the troops', they fight and cancel each other out. But if they coincide, they amplify with potentially disastrous consequences, such as in 1850 when over 200 French soldiers plunged to their deaths when a suspension bridge collapsed. I rejoiced on seeing all of us becoming one nine days ago, but deeply worry when a silly misunderstanding can so quickly break down society into polarized factions. That can spiral out of control by amplifying fears and prejudices of some against others. And all that is made possible by a device that's in every person's pocket, which allows everyone to be permanently connected with everyone else. Technology is not essentially virtuous or evil. Remember nuclear energy: it is the use we give it that can create enormous benefits or untold devastation. We the people, and especially those seated here tonight, have an immense responsibility ... to be responsible. The Nazi Party went from fringe political outsiders to engulfing Germany in one decade. The German people of course weren't intrinsically bad, yet a country marching in tandem did unspeakable things."

✦

Further down, the conversation paused on the origin of life.

"Yes, in the Bible, Genesis 1:26, God says, 'Let us make mankind in our image, in our likeness, so that they may rule over the fish in the sea and the birds in the sky, over the livestock and all the wild animals, and over all the creatures that move along the ground.' This, however, is symbolic writing. Our catechism now discourages literalism," the priest paused and looked at Neil benevolently. "Pope John Paul II sanctioned the acceptance of evolution in 1996, although he reminded us that spiritual questions like the nature of the soul and a person's relationship with God are beyond the realm of science. Religion and science are each a distinct tool for the discovery of truth. The realm of science is concerned with data that can be empirically proven. The realm of religion has to do with the meaning of life and existence in a way that surpasses the physical world. Both the religious believer and scientist make the same mistake when they wrongly attempt to use their own tools to judge the other. Theology and science each have their own methodologies, their own instruments, for the discovery of their particular areas of truth. However, and for the sake of argument, there is one instance in which science still needs an act of God: the beginning of life. Science has been great at explaining its evolution, but has so far failed in explaining its origin. Its inception. As someone once said, science is based on the principle, 'give us one free miracle and we'll explain the rest.' Until science aces that litmus test, the essence of life continues to be a miracle beyond its reach."

Neil followed, "Although it's not my preferred candidate, the 'miracle' hypothesis for the beginning of life is indeed valid. Plus, a lot of scientists agree with you. Let me offer an alternative for what you called life's inception. This view is based in organic chemistry and says that increasingly complex molecules are certain to arise in sufficiently rich chemical soups, at some point satisfying the criteria of 'life.' I haven't explained how it happened, but I offered a path for it to occur. And let's see what the geological records tell us: we have evidence of life on Earth in rocks 4 billion years old. This is remarkable, not only because it's barely a few hundred million years after the formation of our planet but because that's right in the middle of the Heavy Bombardment Era, where a disproportionately large number of asteroids were smashing against the planets of the inner Solar System. Want to see evidence? Look at the Moon, which can't hide its scars through plate tectonics like Earth does. Our planet is eighty times more massive, so its gravity attracted tens of times more blows. Yet here we are—"

The philosopher countered, "But all life on Earth comes from a single ancestor. If life is set to arise so spontaneously, we would surely expect more grandmothers. Your proposition sounds to me as if life on Earth results from an almost intentional winnowing, which sounds so perverse as to be inconceivable. And this intervention is analogous to an invisible hand, known by the gentlemen around us as God."

"Fair point," said Neil. "But the Heavy Bombardment Era does provide a thesis. With the regular visit of falling objects, many of them possibly much bigger than the one that doomed dinosaurs to extinction, life was probably born and died repeatedly. That means life seems to require little time to emerge, maybe millions or even thousands of years to occur. On the question of why we all come from one single ancestor, one interpretation ventures that before life existed, oceans were chemically rich soups. Chemicals everywhere interacted with one another, mixing, breaking apart, reassembling, etc. But after life started, it expanded exponentially and pretty quickly sucked up those freely moving chemicals, using them as nutrients. It's like life drained the soup of its flavor, leaving just the salty brine ... and a staggering collection of complex molecules.

We see this even today in hydrothermal vents. These are pockets of chemically and energy rich environments, but they are surrounded by all kinds of complex life, capturing every nutrient they can get their slimy tentacles on. If this is true, life has no chance of happening again because all the atoms needed have been used in building complex molecules devoted to the biological marketplace of life-as-we-know-it. But at the end, the honest humble reality is that trying to answer an extremely complex question with seriously limited knowledge is a Herculean task, maybe an impossible one. This is where Shackleton promises so much with the potential to change everything."

50 | QUANTUM LEAP

Hours later

Abruptly, the Caird data began to trickle down to Earth. During the next hours, press conferences and official announcements from all major space agencies, as well as reactions from governments, scientists, and the media, mushroomed the world over:

"The answer to the most existential question of all time—are we alone in the Universe?—continues to be both a reassuring and yet disheartening 'Yes.'"

Another, "As a spiritual person, I always thought my religion needed extra-terrestrial life in order to justify the unfathomable size of the Universe, the lar-gesse with which God sized a cosmic arena we can never ever begin to explore. In the time of Isaac Newton, the clockwork Universe he helped make sense of clearly had a Maker behind the mathematical perfection of the five planets revolving around the Sun. Nowadays we know our Milky Way galaxy is so ex-ceedingly big we won't ever colonize it. And there are a trillion other galaxies. Today we have learned that all the exhilarating maybes and could-bes were the deceitful resonances of our own existence, which not only leaves us desperate-ly alone but also bearing a terrible truth: Why? Why such incomprehensible wastefulness for a meager civilization inhabiting a humble planet at the periph-ery of all the major galactic action in a single, modest, no-name galaxy?"

Another, "Among the general public few really understood what a mass spectrometer was, yet everyone knew what could come out because it was so straightforward it required just one word: life. You can forget about all that now."

Another, "This confirms our solitary confinement in this corner of the cos-mos; a chance to feel special, or a chance to be crushed by the weight and beau-ty of our own loneliness."

⌀

CENTRAL VALLEY, CALIFORNIA

"Mummy, it smells stinky around here," said Emma from the back seat of the sedan.

"That would be the famously hard-working Californian cows, pumpkin," said Belinda. "They make more milk and cheese and yogurt than anywhere else in America."

"But it's so dry here. You think they're happy?"

"I'm sure they love the nice weather."

"Where are they?"

"Well ... see those big barns over there in the distance?"

"That looks sad. British cows are happier, I think. What about the funny smell, Mummy?"

"They have lots of gas."

"Eww. So, I'm smelling their farts?"

She's a quick one, thought Belinda proudly. "Hmm. I prefer to call it l'odeur de la merde de vache, which is French for perfume of the countryside."

The car climbed the State Route 152 by the San Luis Reservoir. Two decades of drought made it an ugly tattoo too low down the arm to hide. The road got windy as it traveled along the narrow canyon cutting through wilted needlegrass hills patched with grimy olive stretches of bushy trees, between the central valley and the south Bay Area.

As soon as they cleared into the valley, Belinda's phone dinged like a pinball machine going on a multi-ball rampage. The screen showed fifty-seven missed calls and a flood of messages. Belinda slammed the brakes and swiftly pulled over. A sense of foreboding paralyzed her.

"What happened? Mummy?"

Belinda was unable to answer.

The phone rang. It was her good friend Alex from NASA's Jet Propulsion Laboratory. She couldn't command her hand to answer. Only Emma getting afraid of her made Belinda act. She accepted the call but remained mute.

"B, are you there? B? Everyone on our team has tried to reach you. Belinda?" After a second, she followed, "Hey, gorgeous, it has nothing to do with Shack."

Belinda exhaled the captive air. "Alex, don't ever ever ever do that again. I died ten times."

Emma vocally demanded an explanation, so Belinda put the call on speaker.

"Emma, my dear, I need to speak urgently with Mom, okay?" said Alex. "You get to listen, but you won't understand much—B, where have you been? Half of JPL has been trying to reach you for the past two and a half hours. Worst moment in history to be unreachable. Take my word for it."

"The results ... are here!?"

"I'm reaching out to you not only as a friend, but as one astrobiologist paying professional courtesy to another. This is the most important moment in our careers. Correction. This is *the* most important moment in our young profession's history. The marathon started about two hours ago, the last bits of data reached Earth about thirty minutes ago. You're the laggard playing catch-up. Mind-boggling what's going on. Go to Wikipedia to get the summary. The entry's being edited in real time."

"But what about the results?" Belinda asked.

"Make your own opinion ... but they aren't promising. Talk to you soon!"

Right away new calls started coming in. She silenced the phone and got to work.

"Mummy, I need to go to the loo."

"My love, look at me. How badly do you need to go on a scale of one to ten?"

"Hmm ... one, two, three, four, five, six, seven, eight. An eight, Mummy."

"I want you to promise Mummy one big favor. Try to keep it at eight for as long as you possibly can, okay?"

After wolfing down the Wikipedia entry on her laptop's screen, she got to the thick data log.

High-school chemistry students would be startled to see those old, intimidating bullies they swore never to encounter again strutting around the screen, starting with that worst of tyrants, carbon. $C_3H_7NO_2Se$. $C_4H_5N_3O$. $C_{12}O_9$. Belinda went line by line across the tabulated compounds inventory. Everything looked all right. Everything looked inert. All signs of life were null. The ecstasy tempered down. *It is possible we have gone through such outrageous risks, such outlandish lengths of space and time ... for nothing?* Maybe there's a pattern here somewhere, so blatantly clear it camouflages in its explicitness. *In a few hours we should know—this is a 21st-century marathon after all. We humans are leg amputees compared with the artificial intelligence currently sifting through the data.* Breaking down complexity, trying thousands of variations each second, attempting to decipher the riddles within.

She left the Kingdom of Carbon, the realm of organic molecules responsible for all life on Earth. Skipped over reams of data until she entered the rarefied Kingdom of Silicon. Everything in molecular biology enshrines carbon, which merits an explanation. We say Terran life is carbon-based, even though it depends on other atoms as much as on carbon. Carbon looks unassuming, one proton above boron's five and one less than nitrogen's seven. It composes a relevant 19 percent of our body, but it's no oxygen at 65 percent. The key to its absolute dominance is scaffolding. Most atoms can bond to another single atom. Carbon can bond with up to four others, which makes it the backbone of almost all complex molecules on Earth. Science fiction loves silicon because it's the only other element capable of ménage à quatre. But for all its promise, it comes with a stigma. Life barely uses it even though it is eighty-four times more abundant than carbon on Earth. $CaAl_2Si_2O_8$. SiH_3NMe_2. Belinda mentally discarded one formulation after another. She then transitioned to an exotic family of molecules called organosilicon, sharing both carbon and silicon bonds. Another slap in the face. Nothing.

A decade ago a young biochemist out of university became infatuated with the sweeping promise of astrobiology, that young and resourceful scientific branch full of urgency. The low probability of anything happening during her lifetime was more than offset by the fabulous implications of a future potential success. She certainly wasn't the first or the only one with such hopes and dreams. Some of the most brilliant scientists in the world have dedicated their lives to building the most sensitive instruments ever made to have a chance at addressing whether life exists beyond Earth. Telescopes able to deduce the existence of exoplanets by the extremely faint dimming of a star when they cross in front of them. Parabolic antenna clusters able to listen simultaneously to a million of our nearest stars over countless different frequencies. *And humanity played ball, financing the expensive moonshots, because the promise is so extraordinary—or was.* The answer in front of Belinda, from the most promising test over seven decades of searching, seemed blunt, brutal, and bleak. Failures should push to persevere even further, but this was an early attack and capture that had the strong insinuation of a checkmate. *We have been defeated repeatedly and consistently in the search for life on Mars for decades. That not only didn't dent our motivation, it provoked an ever-stronger push. But this ... this is different.* Enceladus was the gold standard, acing every requirement for life-as-we-know-it. Every requirement was here in front of Belinda. Yet the one thing that really mattered, the consummation of chemistry into biology, looked entirely absent.

"Mummy, I'm at nine and a half."

"Let's go. Sorry for the wait, Em." Belinda tried to sound and feel nonchalant, but the beautiful colors of the sunset were now tinted in sepia. "Do you have any bush in mind?"

"Yes! That one with the unhappy face over there."

I let Jimmy go—Emma—our family shouldered the brunt of the mission. Was the sacrifice worth it? The irony is that while I confront the stark reality, across the vastness of space, a shoulder away from Enceladus, Jimmy, Sophia, and Yi are probably still blissfully ignorant. Jimmy and Yi will be okay, I think. They had other reasons for heading there. But Sophia, she will be devastated.

Emma squatted down behind a small bush near the side of the road. The nostalgia overcame Belinda. She flew back to that postcard spring day in London, looking down at the city from Primrose Hill. The three of them to-gether, Emma kicking Dad's hand from inside her. *Was all this worth it? Jimmy and Emma share so much, yet are perfect strangers. When he comes back, she'll be 6. Those six years of waiting, of longing, of a life on pause, they cannot be claimed back. They are lost forever—and hardly half that time has passed.* She could remember the gentle breeze, the smell of grass, the deep blue sky. James' presence was a halo enveloping her. *His handsome face, his infectious smile.* His promise to come back sounded less weighty that day, less consequential under the shining sun, the bonhomie around them, the ageless woodland below, the church spires, cranes, and skyscrapers in the background. *The elms, cypresses, beeches, cedars.* Something flashed through her mind. She paused. That time Jimmy mentioned how orderly forests appeared in Britain. *I think he said "man-icured."* A casual happy coincidence for the unknowing eye. A Londoner knows better, she had told him. The highest form of landscaping is the art of hiding intention behind natural looks—

"Muuuuummy! I'm done here!"

They went back to the car. Something was brewing inside Belinda, an im-pression of being on the edge of something. Emma took her pill organizer out of her pink unicorn school bag and presented it to her mother. Seven rows, one for each day of the week; one moon symbol, one sun, and one sunset per day. 7×3. $3 + 3 + 3 + 3 + 3 + 3 + 3$. $3n$, *where n goes from 1 to 7.* Belinda's heart pounded faster. She opened her laptop and went back to the organosilicon mol-ecules. Gently, slowly, as if removing Mikados from jumbled pick-up sticks. There were seventeen molecules, all with long backbones of silicon and carbon. She focused on counting the silicon atoms.

$$Si\text{-}Si\text{-}Si\text{-}Si\text{-}Si\text{-}Si\text{-}Si\text{-}Si\text{-}Si\text{-}Si\text{-}Si\text{-}Si = 12$$
$$Si\text{-}Si\text{-}Si\text{-}Si\text{-}Si\text{-}Si\text{-}Si\text{-}Si\text{-}Si\text{-}Si\text{-}Si\text{-}Si\text{-}Si = 14$$

Si-Si-Si-Si = 4
Si-Si-Si-Si-Si-Si-Si-Si = 8
Si-Si-Si-Si = 4
Si-Si-Si-Si-Si-Si-Si-Si-Si-Si = 10
Si-Si = 2
Si-Si-Si-Si-Si-Si = 6

Uncanny. She now felt her heart beating in her temples.

Si-Si-Si-Si-Si-Si = 6
Si-Si-Si-Si = 4
Si-Si-Si-Si-Si-Si-Si-Si-Si-Si-Si-Si-Si-Si-Si-Si-Si-Si = 18
Si-Si-Si-Si-Si-Si-Si-Si-Si-Si = 10
Si-Si-Si-Si-Si-Si-Si-Si-Si-Si-Si-Si = 12

Please, please, please.

Si-Si-Si-Si-Si-Si-Si-Si-Si-Si-Si-Si-Si-Si-Si-Si = 16
Si-Si-Si-Si-Si-Si = 6
Si-Si-Si-Si-Si-Si-Si-Si-Si-Si = 10
Si-Si-Si-Si = 4

She stared at the screen, dazed. Her head felt like it had had too many glasses of pinot grigio. *Am I dreaming?* She tried testing it. "What are you doing my love?" she asked. No answer. She turned back. Emma had zoned out playing a game on her tablet. *This is real. This is happening. This is now!*

She inhaled a few times, trying to clear her mind, and then she stared at the screen again.

12, 14, 4, 8, 4, 10, 2, 6, 6, 4, 18, 10, 12, 16, 6, 10, 4 or as multiples: 2×6, 2×7, 2×2, 2×4, 2×2, 2×5, 2×1, 2×3, 2×3, 2×2, 2×9, 2×5, 2×6, 2×8, 2×3, 2×5, 2×2. Or as notation: Si_{2n}. *Everything is in pairs.*

She tried to be skeptical, but the weight of the evidence made it futile. The tables had turned. In a world of probabilistic randomness, there was suddenly a mathematical pattern. *Nature has no business preferring even instead of odd numbers. Something else is selectively picking chemicals on Enceladus. On Earth, that something else is called*—but she wouldn't form the word in her mind.

She was trembling, her thoughts hazy and bewildered. She called Alex back. "Hey B. What's up?" Belinda couldn't force the words out. "B? Anyone there?"

"I'm here," Emma said a little indignantly.

Slowly, barely audible, "Alex … there are … biosignatures in the data."

There was silence at first, followed by, "OH MY GOD."

51 | MESSIΔH

MOUNTAIN VIEW, CALIFORNIA

Emma and Belinda walked hand in hand, seemingly shrinking in size as they approached Hangar One. This was Emma's first venture to the cavernous free-standing structure, and it showed.

"Mummy, look! It's higher than the Moon!" Emma rejoiced at Belinda raising her eyes almost vertically toward a Moon resting perfectly to the side of the hangar's apex.

Nitha Sharma intercepted the two and introduced herself to Emma.

"I thought you were bigger," said Emma, seeing Shackleton's famous mission head for the first time.

"I thought you were smaller," said Nitha, smiling at the little one.

Emma ran ahead toward a crew unloading concert loudspeakers from a semi-trailer truck.

"She's very articulate. And speaks so well—you could hardly tell ..." said Nitha.

"My Emma's precious. And precocious too. Jimmy, Grandpa, and I are all terribly proud ... there's plenty of work ahead, though. Today I had her call out our order at a Starbucks Drive-Thru and it was all wrong at pick up. I felt for the first time as if she could sense there was something wrong with her voice—" Belinda halted after noticing the cranes, technicians laying cables, loudspeaker arrays, and staff assembling scaffolds. "Nitha ..."

"Tomorrow will be big, B. Really big." Nitha's phone began ringing.

"But, but why me?" said Belinda, upset. "Look at all this. It's turning into, what, a Rolling Stones concert?"

"You made the discovery. But more importantly, you carry the kind of goodwill that few people on Earth have right now."

"Nitha, you know me. I don't do well speaking in public." They walked past the sharp line of the giant clamshell doors, cutting the sunshine under the looming hangar shadow.

"Mainstream media was talking about Area 51 just yesterday. Area 51! Green men and flying saucers. You are sanity's messiah. You, Belinda Egger, are the one who can cut the rampant speculation and make us return to reason." Nitha took the call.

"No."

"No. No and no. We won't accept any bullshit government helicopters landing here. None."

She listened for a while and Belinda could hear a faint urgent voice on the other end of the line. After a few seconds, Nitha cut the caller off with, "Well, get used to it, you have no jurisdiction here. Google leased the Federal Airfield for another five decad—"

"Shackleton was funded by the people, not a dollar from Uncle S—"

"Listen to me very carefully, George. If you try that—"

"I—"

"I will personally announce the press conference cancelation *at* the press conference and we'll move it to another country. That's going to cost you your cushy job, best-case scenario."

Finally, she snapped, "Well, fly economy for once in your life, dammit!"

Nitha hung up and apologized to Belinda. She was irritated by the call. "This is why ... people are confused. They—all of us—we're scared. Those two on Enceladus have inadvertently exposed how thin the fabric of society becomes when everything we held as immutable and hallowed shifts ... humanity needs to see honesty and transparency. You need to tell everyone what has happened in your own words ... the tantalizing dream of alien life is suddenly upon us and we are realizing it's a planet-sized hot potato we don't know how to deal with. An alien microbe is terrific. An alien civilization is terrifying."

52 | BLΔST OFF

ENCELADUS

Derya was tired and craving to be back inside Caird to eat and especially sleep, but Sergei still had an hour and a half of fieldwork and the cabin wouldn't be pressurized until they were both back. *Meanwhile, Yi probably muses about the immortality of the soul as understood by each of the three main Abrahamic religions while—and this is the important part—helping himself to my rations. If you so much as touched one of them, I'll have you on a white rice diet until we land back on Earth*, he thought.

He worked on the Mole's rig, preparing for the piercing. The cryobot was 17,000 feet beneath him—*and not even on a straight line*—yet he could still see the faint blue fluorescence emanating from the borehole. The rig was far more than the support tripod that kept the Mole standing before it burrowed down. Once the latter punctured the ocean, its back section would detach and affix to the ice. Then, as the Mole sank using its propeller toward the long-dreamed of hydrothermal vents at the bottom of the ocean, a thin transmission cable would keep it tethered to the rig by Derya's side, which would relay the sensor data and video feed back to Caird. *Why? Because while radio waves regularly travel billions and lasers millions of miles across space, both are useless after just a few dozen feet of salt water—ahh, the poetic elegance of physics.*

The rig was anchored to the ice by three long bolts. His final outside task that day was stress testing them for the big moment. *More of a shrinking raisin moment.* He gathered his strength and jumped, promptly yanked back by the rope connecting his waist harness to the rig. He did it two more times, hardly with any conviction by the last. *Check. Good enough for my coveted stamp of approval.*

The software on board Caird had been throttling the Mole down—currently ninety-seven feet above the ocean—to penetrate right when Enceladus was furthest from Saturn, in another eleven hours. Right now, the pendulum was at the opposite end and Saturn's gravity squeeze had switched on the jets in all their glory. He extended his gloved palm to catch snowflakes falling at a funeral pace. *That's right. Our stop-and-frisk showed you are all dead. We could have sent a string of expletives instead of data to Earth and it would have amounted to the same—well, except for astrobiologists. You put ten atoms holding hands some-where other than Earth in front of them and they start screaming hysterically. We quadrupled that, so they're probably dreaming up a new branch of science.* Still, Derya was mildly curious about resuming communication with Earth in three hours to read about the world's reaction to the no-life results they had sent the previous day.

∅

Meanwhile, screens inside Caird had been flashing. The radar in the Mole's nose was getting ambiguous readings: sensing an ice mass one hundred feet thick in front and, simultaneously, the ocean almost in contact with the probe. The artificial intelligence was guessing long stalactites and its 3D rendering showed a dense population of icicles as tall as grown conifers, with the Mole about to pierce right in between three of them.

∅

A while later, after his bashing of Yi had gone off the boil, after listening for old times' sake to the Beatles' "Yesterday," and after another chapter of *How to Win Friends and Influence People*—polls back home, the last by *Der Spiegel* magazine a week before, made him the most likely person to get elected to the Bundestag, the German federal parliament, once he came back—Derya changed his killing time strategy to sightseeing. He noticed a few pins lying on the floor around the rig. His eyes followed the path to Caird and registered more litter. *The wake of progress. But we should clean up before we leave. Nothing better than to have the rapture of untrodden nature desecrated by stumbling across a squirted-out McDonald's ketchup packet—or worse, what happened to Father in Greece.*

As soon as Derya made some money after his PhD, he had bought his fa-ther, an amateur historian, a tour package to visit the site of his favorite battle, Marathon. *Father was probably savoring the watershed moment in history, see-ing in his mind's eye the 100,000 Persians charging against the 10,000 Athenians, when he got out of the bus onto the battlefield, stepping right over a used condom surrounded by vomit and empty bottles, scarring his epic visions for life. Needless to say he hated the trip, all of it. And me for coming up with the idea.* "What's

245

wrong with you!? Everything you touch becomes shit," he had later said in a low, threatening voice that could only really mean, "My only son, my firstborn: I love you, I love you, I love you."

Expecting a pitch-dark Christmas-esque Eve, he realized the surroundings were lit up as if it were a full Moon back on Earth. He arched his body backward and was perplexed to see Earth's natural satellite in front of him: a ghostly white disk covered in its characteristic pockmarks. *What—how's that …?* Like an April Fools' prank, reality eventually clicked. He was looking at Dione,[26] Enceladus' big sister. A third of the diameter of Earth's Moon and a third of the distance made them identical in the sky at a casual glance. Staring at it, he identified the Janiculum Dorsa, a long ridge that looked like the scarring in Derya's left forearm after that deep cut nine years before. *An accident to all but me.* Images of this ridge and its surrounding depression taken in 2013 by Cassini gave evidence of tectonic activity and unmasked yet another deep-water ocean underneath.

He scanned to his right for Sergei. He was a few hundred steps away, collecting more samples. *The bloke never gives up. He could probably use a helping hand.* Derya looked down at the rope still strapping him to the rig. *Nah, he's doing great. Me too.*

"Ruski, look up. See anything familiar?"

♄

It took longer for Sergei to make sense of the oneiric vision, but once he did it stayed with him. He still believed the whole mission boiled down to what would happen once the cryobot started its storied descent into the inky ocean depths beneath them. He still believed they could find life even if their geysers' sampling showed no signs.

And to think a few decades back the only place believed to have liquid water was Earth, Sergei reasoned. Nowadays, Earth keeps sliding down in the oceanworlds rankings. Just in the Saturn system there's Titan and Enceladus, likely

---

26   Enceladus is the whitest object in the Solar System, but Dione and Rhea are not far behind. Both are whiter than freshly fallen snow, and ten and thirty Enceladus would fit inside the former and the latter. And both seemed to be soaking in oceans with as much or more liquid water as on Earth, splashing and churning beneath their thick shells. Dione's water ocean may have been liquid throughout most of its history, as old as the Solar System's, adding the vital element of time for life to evolve and differentiate.

Dione and Rhea. *Different possible solutions to the life equation—who knows, maybe all are inhabited.*[27]

Ø

An alarm rang in Derya's helmet while a third of the visor was occupied by a frozen image ... of water? There was also a sonar reading. *Sonar? It's not possible. Sonar is used by whales, submarines, and Waltzy Mole to detect objects through sound propagation—in water.*

"Sergei? Are you ...?"

For several seconds they remained baffled and clueless.

"Move away!" Sergei's voice rang inside Derya's helmet. "The probe is coming back!"

Derya looked down and froze, noticing the rope connecting him to the rig. Precious instants later, the adrenaline bolted his right hand forward. His perception was sharp and precise as he reached out his fingers for the carabiner. He frantically tried holding down the spring-loaded gate a few times before realizing his hand had landed on the wrong side. *I'm as helpless as a leashed dog.*

The last thing he saw was the ground under him exploding into a jet of water.

Ø

The geyser was so thick and high it darkened the night above Sergei, completely obscuring Dione's searchlight. The savage gusher was soundless in the void of space, incongruous to an earthling as lightning without thunder.

"Derya!"

---

27   And, critically, each one independently from the other—a very different story from Earth and Mars. Meteoritic transfers are not only possible between the red and our blue planet, but have occurred repeatedly, as evidenced by the 118 confirmed Martian meteorites found so far on Earth. If Mars ever had life, it could have been imported from or exported to Earth via stowaway microbes free-riding on rocks, the theory known as panspermia. Experiments with bacterial spores exposed to space on the ISS showed they could survive for long periods of time, maybe thousands of years, if buried deep enough inside rocks. Perhaps the long quest to find Martians has failed miserably because they hid where nobody cared to look for them, inside each one of us. At their closest, Earth and Mars are 34 million miles away. Saturn and Earth? Nearly 750 million miles. But there may be an even more formidable barrier, the ice shells covering each of the water oceans hiding inside the four Saturnian moons.

"Derya!"

"Derya!"

The alarms went silent. He only heard his breathing. The murderous silence pointed in one direction only.

"Derya!" His voice resonated increasingly muffled and distant inside his head.

"Derya!" he said again, now repeating it to himself. "Derya."

When it's darkest, men see the stars. But the stars had vanished under a canopy of frozen mist.

The neural command to his legs was lost somewhere in between, as if they had been severed from him.

Derya is gone.

He let his body fall back and he landed in slow motion on the ice. He felt nothing. He couldn't think. He was depleted and hollow. There were no feelings, no sensations, just numbness. He laid there, inert, for what could have been hours or years. It no longer mattered.

53 | NATURE'S SIBLING

Moments later

MOUNTAIN VIEW, CALIFORNIA

Google had opened the Moffett Airfield to the public. The public responded by flooding it. Route 101, the highway stretching from Los Angeles to California's north end, had turned into a parking lot across exits 396 and 399, using three of the four lanes in each direction.

Media and police helicopters hovered over the million-plus crowd covering both former military runways. Hangar One loomed in front and above them.

Nitha and Belinda stood on a crane's wide aerial platform five stories above the ground. Nitha's speech was drawing to a close and she was about to pass the baton to Belinda, who was experiencing all the symptoms of stage fright: cardboard-dry mouth, cold chills, arrhythmia, and trembling hands. But for all the stress, she kept getting the same answer from inside. *This is what I need to do. This is what I will do.* She looked up to the left at another crane hanging the projection equipment ten stories high to minimize the image distortion. Behind them, Nitha's face acquired Godzilla-like proportions framed using most of the hangar's inward curving wall. Ahead, thousands of reporters were in front with everyone else behind. *And that was quite literal.* Under Nitha's supervision, the concept of 'Very Important People' was dead in the water. Belinda smiled at the thought. *Nitha—meritocracy's poster child—sparing no ammunition in fighting against old boys' networks or any form of preferential treatment.* Today she had won. *VIP members want to come? You're welcome. Now mingle with everyone else.*

"—and with that, I hand the microphone to Belinda Egger." Nitha patted her shoulder and gave her an unexpected, slightly awkward kiss on the cheek. Belinda needed no microphone adjustment, they were similar in build, both slight. "I love you too, Nitha." Small gestures can go a long way. People watching, including those still suspecting government collusion, were reminded that this was a person, not an institution.

She scanned the multitude, which seemed compact to her for a million souls.

Her last long, deep breaths picked up a whiff of coastal redwood trees. The scent that perfumed the air throughout her third date with James. *In Jimmy's favorite place, Yosemite.* That promise of an innocuous, recreational hike turned into a two-day epic, including a petrifying 1,000-foot rappel down to the valley floor. Dangling from a pinkie-thick rope, she had asked herself, *Who is this man?*

Belinda blocked the crowds out and concentrated on a single person in the first row, which she conjured into a smiling James.

Her right hand dove into the pocket for her written speech but found nothing. It fumbled luckless. *It's here. I checked three times—it was safely tucked here.* But she panicked nonetheless. Her left hand plunged into the other. No longer trusting her sense of touch, she did a frantic visual confirmation. Behind Belinda, her blind scrabbling was magnified a hundred times to everyone, everywhere. Nothing. She instinctively looked at Nitha, gaping back at her. She looked down at her smiling James for some sort of salvation. The person, sensing something was awfully wrong, stared back in dread.

"I … I have … as an astrobiologist …" The insecurity echoed back derisively. She stopped. *And if I confess losing the aide-mémoire? Then what? No excuses, Dad would have said—he's staring at me right now from his TV.* She had prepared the speech for six straight hours. *The information may be jumbled and coiled, but it's all here in my head. All I need to do is find one of the ends.* More time passed. The crowd moved uncomfortably. She finally acknowledged to herself that any attempt to retrieve the practiced speech was a lost cause.

Time didn't linger, but Belinda couldn't speak until she had something—anything—to say.

She started to improvise, insecure and reticent.

"When I was little, I lived in a castle … when I was in my teens, we returned to a house … I was baffled … the overgrown indoor garden where I hid from monsters and spied on gnomes had shrunk to a miserly square with a few naked shrubs and flowers … in time, the Tooth Fairy and the Easter Bunny faded into everyday reality … in my case, what kept the magic alive was *The Lord of the Rings* and *Harry Potter*, but especially the night sky … it ran counter to everything else. When the rest was turning gray, here was this something full of the supernatural, riddled with mysteries that if deciphered sprang into one hundred new ones … when I was 9, those twinkly lights hanging from the night sky suddenly became stars. I began counting them. Once I got to 2,000. I later learned just our Milky Way galaxy has four. Hundred. Billion stars. And almost all of them surrounded by planets. Can you even picture a number like that!? It is awe-inspiring, and it is profound, and it is mysterious, and it is adventure.

Adventure like we can't even begin to fathom … the Universe never ceases to amaze. I frequently surprise myself daydreaming, nowadays mostly about Jimmy, but the cosmos is never far behind. From the large—where a single teaspoon from a neutron star weighs a Mount Everest; to the small—where atoms are mostly empty space. If we could remove that space, the same teaspoon would contain all humans alive plus all that have ever lived … so when my time came to choose a line of study at university, I knew it must be something that explored the astonishing Universe. So, I picked biochemistry. When the time came for a PhD, astrobiology picked me. Studying the small in the big … which takes us to Enceladus. But to understand what may lurk in its ocean, we first need to understand ourselves."

She stopped to lubricate her sandy mouth with water. She knew the speech was starting to meander, but she did not dare tamper with her inspiration.

"Because contrary to what you or I would like to think, we are not special. If we were made of rare elements, say polonium, einsteinium, platinum, and thorium, then we would be right to suspect we are exceptional until proved otherwise. But the six most abundant chemical elements in the Universe are hydrogen, helium, oxygen, carbon, neon, and nitrogen. Helium and neon are loners, unwilling to marry with anyone. Which leaves hydrogen, oxygen, carbon, and nitrogen. Life on Earth? Well, 99 percent is made of those exact four. Someone could argue back that we barely look at the Universe through the night's window. What truly matters is the environment. Life should assemble from the most readily available elements around it … not quite. Earth's most abundant four are oxygen, silicon, aluminum, and iron. No, that someone could retort, I meant Earth's oceans, the cradle of life. Leaving aside pure water, H_2O, there's sodium and chlorine, which combined make table salt, and then magnesium and sulfur. This is absolutely remarkable: humans are closer relatives to the Universe than to our own planet! From this we can derive two crucial consequences. First, life should be common in the Universe given how abundant its raw materials are. And second, extraterrestrial life should probably be made up of roughly the same elements. Now we have the tools to understand Enceladus' critical importance in both the search for alien life and the quest to understand the origin of life on Earth: it has life's four main chemical elements; it has liquid water; it has an energy source; it has hydrothermal vents. All the ingredients for life-as-we-know-it. And yesterday the cosmic doors finally flew open."

The multitude was perfectly still in their vigil. A tribe around a bonfire.

"Yesterday, for the first time in history, we witnessed the fingerprints of intervention in another oceanworld. Note the word 'we.' It's not false modesty.

This wasn't a prodigious intellectual leap. This is no general relativity. I am surprised—and yes, proud—that I somehow found the pattern before a computer or someone else did. But it was a matter of hours, so I can't possibly claim ownership of the discovery. And to those rightfully wondering, how convenient that James' wife was anointed the chosen one, I'll put your objections at ease. Astrobiology is a small community. So small in fact you can put all of us in a single room. Indeed, we do just that a few times each year. If you additionally consider how many of those have dedicated a significant portion of their work to organosilicon compounds, it drops to a handful. My probability now has increased to something around 20 percent, quite achievable for a woman you see …"

Clueless to whether five or thirty minutes had passed, Belinda decided to wrap it up for questions from the press and media.

"Regarding what happened yesterday, we must be careful with the language that we use. We haven't seen a microbe waving at us. We haven't found alien life … yet. We have identified a pattern that seems to violate randomness. We have an indication of a strong anomaly. It's likeliness, not certainty … having said that, the chance of this pattern happening spontaneously is, at least according to our current understanding of chemistry, extremely unlikely. Possible, yes. Probable, definitely not. Which leaves us with a bewildering number of questions and no answers. That's why Waltzy Mole is so critical. I can't stop imagining what the Mole will register as it drops to the ocean floor, and what will happen when it stares right at extraterrestrial hydrothermal vents. What will we find?"[28]

---

28   Later, during the Q&A. "Graeme Arnott from TVNZ in New Zealand. Could you explain the possibility of organosilicon life in layman terms?"

      "Great question, Graeme," said Belinda. "I think even if heady and sciency, we all need to understand what was found, because only then can we comprehend the implications of what could happen in the coming days. We have indications not of carbon-based, not silicon-based, but carbon-silicon-based life … allow me to make a digression. Science is built by standing on the shoulders of each successive giant. After four centuries that's one seriously tall construct. In the 18th century, you could become an expert in any scientific field by spending an afternoon at a library, if you could find one. Today, you need a PhD just to figure out what the important questions are. A scientist no longer has the luxury to know a little about a lot. Today one must commit to study a lot of a little … this can be treacherous and risky. You can inch your way in a subject for years or even decades before realizing it's a cul-de-sac. When I picked organosilicon or carbon-silicon as a field of study, some colleagues warned me against it. Their logic was impeccable. This was a particularly low probability corner in astrobiology. In theory, organosilicon is even more promising than carbon as the scaffolding for the chemistry of life. But in practice, there's a large roadblock and an enigma: silicon is all but ignored by life-as-we-know-it, even though it's almost one hundred times more abundant than carbon on Earth. I picked it because I concentrated on the other part of the equation. If the reward for being right is huge, it can still make good sense to pick a low probability subject. Especially as a society, maybe less so as an individual ... what happened yesterday seems to redeem carbon-silicon."

Belinda took another drink of water and continued. "What's the allure of organosilicon? It's a multidimensional answer, but I'll give you maybe the most important example ... the Book of Life, DNA, treads a high wire. It is written with four letters. Each one of those letters is a molecule formed by around fifteen atoms, of which four or five are carbon atoms that glue everything else together. If those carbon bonds had been too strong, life would never have evolved and we would still be unicellular bacteria. Why? Because evolution innovates by making very infrequent microscopic errors in DNA, which creates mutation. This is the tightrope.

"Mutation can be good, but most times it's bad. Ultraviolet radiation from the Sun penetrates the skin, the cell, the nucleus, and sometimes knocks-off or adds-in an atom from DNA. Cigarette smoke does the same in the DNA of lung cells. When this corrupts the genetic code you can get cancer, which is bad. But extremely rarely that missing or extra atom creates a slight modification that is beneficial. A variation that allows the organism to be superior to the rest. Say a longer beak in a bird that allows it to reach the pollen of an elongated and otherwise inaccessible flower ... over hundreds of millions of years and generations this has created the plant and animal kingdom cornucopia on Earth today. However, if those carbon bonds were too weak, the rate of mutation would be too fast and irremediably corrupt the genetic code within a single generation, possibly triggering extinction.

"Enter silicon. Silicon is the direct 'glue' competitor of carbon, its structural analog: it can also bind up to four other atoms and its average bond strength is roughly the same, but is tougher or weaker depending on the other chemical element, its atom counterparty. A molecule using both carbon and silicon might get the best of both worlds. In fact, we artificially synthesize precisely these for pharmaceuticals, sealants, herbicides, and television screens, among other things. We have even coaxed living organisms to chemically bond carbon and silicon together ... so what would organosilicon life look like? We are clueless, but immensely eager to hear nature speak. I know one thing though: let's prepare to be bewildered for the rest of our lives. The advances we could make in molecular structure and biochemistry would change our world's biology forever."

"Hi, Belinda. Tobias Simon from Deutsche Welle in Germany. I'm still lost as to why you decided to study organosilicon. The evidence was against you."

"Maybe it wasn't," said Belinda. "Silicon may represent 30 percent of the Earth's crust, but early in the life of our planet it married to oxygen. That bond is very strong, lasting for millions of years. You want to test that love? Most grains of sand on Earth are made of those two, as are most rocks. This view, which I endorse, says that silicon wasn't ignored by life. Silicon was forced to remain a bystander in that early world of experimental chemistry because it married too early. I call this the Original Sin, and it carries far-reaching ramifications. Finding life using something other than carbon as the fundamental Lego pieces exposes us to the possibility that maybe there's another configuration that is fundamentally better than the one used by life on Earth, which would carry deep philosophical implications. Maybe our chemical composition is not the result of the optimal global configuration but a local optimum.

"Let's say you're a settler from a kingdom in the mountains and are told to establish a new city near the largest body of water in the world. If you didn't know about the existence of oceans, you may settle, content and in peace, by the largest lake you saw ... maybe the puzzle pieces did not perfectly match but worked well enough for life on Earth to continue building from there. Then there was no turning back. It's not predestination but circumstance ... also, if Waltzy Mole confirms the existence of alien life—life created from building blocks different from carbon—then it means that life has occurred twice, independently, just in our humble Solar System. Which makes the realization that there's life everywhere inescapable. And you know the most astonishing thing about this whole story? It's true. And it's happening now!"

54 | SPΛCEBORNE

ENCELADUS

Derya regained consciousness with a reflex cough that cut into his chest like a scalpel, his awareness wholly focused on the pain on both sides of his ribcage. Trying to breathe in brief, speedy puffs quickly got him suffocated. His body took over in an uncontrollable deep breath so unbearable he blacked out.

He was revived by the clamoring coming from his helmet. Disoriented, he noticed the two beams of his head-mounted flashlights getting lost feet away in a snowstorm. Feeling weightless, his mind grappled with the situation. *No, no, no, no.* The extreme freedom of movement with nothing to interact against felt paradoxically like being in a four-point restraint: move as much as you like, there's no way to flip over. He turned his head around to a Sun shrunken down to a tenth of its size, rising above the wrinkled physiognomy of Enceladus. Seeing the moon's exaggerated curvature far below him seemed as if Derya's retinas had become fisheye lenses. A flood of horror drowned him and his right hand seized the small joystick of the backpack propulsion unit. The thrusters spun him out of control. The terror escalated until it could only go out through his mouth in the form of a shriek that displaced the broken ribs, a sting so brutal it made him pass out again.

Meanwhile, Sergei had been shouting through Derya's intercom, "—I repeat, under no circumstance fire the thrusters—we need them to bring you back down—"

Ø

Sergei the person had been trying to calm Derya down. Sergei the engineer reviewed the situation again, trying vainly to find a better solution. *Enceladus' weak force of gravity is claiming him back—but imperceptibly. If not fast enough, he'll die from suffocation—I'm sorry but no miracles: he used all of his propellant.*

"Please help me … please, my friend, help me …" Derya mumbled while sobbing. Hearing him implore was gut-wrenching. Derya was trapped inside his body, a pulp of flesh hovering thousands of feet above the surface. A guilty thought kept flashing in Sergei's head: how to make him commit a painless suicide. *But there's no easy way out. In Caird it would have been straightforward.* Without helmet, open the cabin depressurization valve just enough to lower air pressure and oxygen to the point of inducing unconsciousness, quickly followed by death. Death in a spacesuit would not be kind. Depressurization would be deep and fast with collapsing lungs, skin swelling, and boiling saliva as the last sensations before death.

Out of options, Sergei said, "Derya, listen. I need you to stop hyperventilating. You're consuming too much oxygen …" Derya's unresponsiveness forced him to say, "It may take hours for you to land."

"I can't control the vomit anymore. Please, help me, Sergei."

"Calm down and listen to me," Sergei said in the best way he knew how. "If you throw up, one of two things will happen. If there's not enough puke, it will float inside the helmet, clog the air supply, and you'll slowly asphyxiate. If it's enough, you'll drown in your own vomit. Both are grisly ways of dying." He heard dog panting at the other end, but no answer. "Starting now, you don't think anymore. It has already been done for you. Follow exactly what I say, do exactly what I say. Understood?"

Sergei heard a murmur.

"I need to visually locate you. For this, you are going to look in every direction until you find the surface … do it now."

Sergei spotted the airborne lights high up, merged into a single dot by the distance. He extrapolated the fall line. It looked fairly certain the landing would be within the Baghdad canyon, which simplified things. But he worried that he might fall into one of the long, abysmal crevasses spitting water up. If so, he could do nothing but watch his partner being swallowed by Enceladus.

"I've spotted you, my friend. Your fall line is secured," Sergei lied. He spaced the next comment. *In this context it will come out brutally merciless and insensitive, but there's no point in being impractical.* "Derya, are you attached to the Mole … or can you see it anywhere?"

"You … uncompassionate … piece of …" Derya began weeping. "No … lost," he said in an extinguishing voice. After a few seconds, having regained some fortitude and hope, he asked, "What now?"

"What goes up must come down. We wait for gravity to do its work."

There was a long pause before Derya asked, "What?"

"I was saying that—"

"THAT'S IT?"

Sergei heard a new, calm breathing over the intercom. His visor showed Derya's heart rate was back to normal. *Loves fainting, this one.*

With no Mole going anywhere, the chances of finding life had dropped to zero—*unless I sample the artificial jet.*

Whereas Enceladus' naturally occurring geysers shot already frozen water that had seeped through thin cracks for miles, the borehole was a straw sucking straight from the source.

Water was coming in liquid form, but he noticed the borehole was becoming clogged and would soon be choked. *Hey up there, don't move,* thought Sergei sardonically.

Sergei went to Caird to get insulated containers for sampling. *For science's sake, I better keep the water liquid at all costs—even disrespecting The Flying Deutschmann over my head.*

55 | THE RINGS OF SΛTURN

Two days later, September 15 2030. Main Mission day 12

APPROACHING SATURN

Shackleton was falling toward Saturn, a few hours from completing its first orbit around the gas giant.

Yi remained immobile above Bacchus' Observation Window. Derya's near-death experience and long road ahead to recovery put him in a sad place, so he opened his eyes and was instantly hypnotized.

His entire field of view had been taken hostage by Saturn. Continent-sized cyclones, three clockwise and four counter-clockwise, churned before him a few Earths away from each other. The cloud tops outside their rim moved quietly, but everything within the wild cauldrons swayed and whirled like a thing possessed. The disturbed atmosphere of Saturn is the deepest of the Solar System. The rotating cloud belts of Jupiter reach 2,000 miles below the cloud top, in Saturn they double or triple that depth. *Almost one hundred times Earth's*, thought Yi, his body shivering in response. At this distance, his eyes could already single out cloud decks towering fifty miles above the rest of the planet's cloud tops, betrayed by their long shadows. Without absolute conviction in orbital mechanics, anyone would have sworn Shackleton was aimed straight at them. He was a believer, but vertigo began to overcome him anyway.[29]

---

29 He closed his eyes and forced himself to think about something else. He distracted himself with Saturn's hydrogen and helium atmospheric composition. *We should take some of that helium back to Earth.* The second most abundant element in the Universe and there's scarcely any left back home. *Its fault for being a loner.* Helium is inert, and it barely reacts with other elements. It is so light, lighter than air, that it escapes the atmosphere into space unless secured inside canisters or natural pockets underground. Hydrogen is even lighter, but it reacts with a huge number of other elements to form molecules such as water. Helium is chaste as hydrogen is promiscuous.

∅

James concentrated on the rings a few hundred miles below or above the space-ship—'up' and 'down' mean nothing in space—to counteract the yearning to be back with Emma and Belinda. He was in the other Observation Window, one story 'above' in the flight deck. It was his shift, although in about an hour both Sophia and Yi would join him, and they would all don their spacesuits and stay on deck for the rounding of the planet, hardly a few thousand miles above its cloud tops. It was just protocol, as no maneuver was necessary. Shackleton was steered by the invisible hands of orbital mechanics.

A while before, the background of stars was interrupted by the F Ring, a 300-mile-wide solitary highway of two gray lanes separated by a white line that Shackleton cut through in seconds. It was the outermost edge of the visible rings, a halo twenty-two Earths in diameter from one side of the giant planet to the other. Then it was a few minutes crossing the 2,000-mile-wide gap between the unsung F Ring and the superstardom of the A Ring, a vacuum cleaning achieved by the gravitational influence of tuber-shaped Prometheus—a giant in the world of potatoes yet a pigmy among Saturn's moons at scarcely eighty-five miles in length and hardly 140 Everests in mass using mountain currency—the feat of a single cowboy herding 1,000 cattle. Now he looked at the hypnotic A Ring: what from afar looked homogeneous, continuous, and monotonous turned into a succession of smaller rings of 1,000 colors and widths, the ultimate intricate oriental rug. *Awe-inspiring and magnificent as they are, they go far beyond looks*, thought James. The rings were a miniature model for the dense, bright disk of gas and dust surrounding the early Sun, the raw material that clumping together gave birth to the planets. *But its teachings scale to rotating disks of a far, far grander scale: spiral galaxies such as our own Milky Way.*

The crew had asked to fly tens instead of hundreds of miles over the rings. Scientists cheered. Mission Control tempered expectations. The rings are unfathomably thin at four stories tall, but among the zillions of ice chunks forming them there are outliers. And at the spaceship's speed, an ice cube the size of James' fist would be enough to nuke Shackleton to shreds.

He looked up at the orb spanning the sky. The rings cast dramatic shadows over the behemoth as the Sun cut through their translucence.

Ø

Sophia couldn't care less about Saturn or its rings. *Yesterday's news as far as I'm concerned*, she thought. She was locked in her cabin, wanting no distractions to intrude her reveries. *It's as if I time-machined to an 18th-century English spring, when trees still arched by the weight of their fruits kissed the floor. Any one of them a breakthrough discovery or invention waiting to rock humanity—I am living the greatest story ever told: when humans reached for the stars and discovered life beyond Earth. The Universe will never be the same again.* She stared at the low-resolution images, trying to squeeze out further wisdom. But pixels were pixels. *This is probably how emerging markets feel when they sell sugar cane and buy back Skittles.* Earth, infinitely further from Enceladus than Shackleton was, had a few hours per day of communication window with Caird, whereas Shackleton and Caird would continue to be incommunicado for days—even though Sophia could visually locate the wrong side of Enceladus at this very moment. Caird sent the information about the two discovered specimens to Earth, and Earth relayed the information to Shackleton: the tyranny of radio waves traveling in straight lines.

In lieu of hard data, she mentally rehearsed her nearing first encounter with the two life forms. *Only a week before we meet.* Derya had the honor of naming the little fellows. *And after his nearly fatal accident, almost deservingly so.* One became *Albus Darya* and the other *Noctem Darya. Shameless egotistical self-reference—unfortunately the binomial nomenclature works.* In Latin, *Albus* meant white or clear, *Noctem* meant night or darkness. And in Persian, *Darya* meant ocean. The first microscopic alien was the size of a bacterium, the second the size of a red blood cell. Now she needed to exercise patience before she could get her hands on those Petri dishes. *I'll be the first to observe vistas of a parallel Mother Nature under the microscope ... and then get a three-year head start to decipher the critter's chemistry and structural blocks ... and with the DNA sequencer and other goodies in my lab, maybe even decode their genetic book ... I'll be the first to*—a cloud tarnished the deep blue yonder. All of that depended on Sergei and Derya being able to keep the water in a liquid state at all times until they rendezvoused with Shackleton. Frozen water would rip apart the internal structures from the first forms of extraterrestrial life ever observed. *Something so atrocious as to be unthinkable. Except it's not—Derya, I will learn to love you like a brother if only you don't screw this one up. Sergei, I won't lie, you're substantially more problematic.*

56 | UNSCRIPTED OUTINGS

Hours later

ENCELADUS

The rings under Derya's eyes rivaled the dark purple circling his thorax. Seven broken ribs and compression fractures in his spine guaranteed an unforgettable night, every night. *Sergei's not doing bad himself,* thought Derya. His nocturnal hissing efficiently spread the misery around and Sergei's military propensity about being aware and alert at all times precluded earplugs' salvation.

On Earth, the healing would take a month or two. *In space, we shall see.* He should have died during the lingering hours of hovering. *Yet here I am.* No major blood vessels ruptured, and no punctured lungs, liver, or kidneys probably helped as well. But he was still highly vulnerable to suffering, and Sergei was forcing him to explore new harmonies of pain. Both donned their spacesuits between snorts and spits from Derya. *For the benefit of just one. Bloody sadistic brute.* Having missed the first rendezvous window, Sergei was about to leave for the second off-script reconnaissance of the Baghdad valley. And he intended to pull off two or three more before it was time to leave in five days. It was an unnecessary, irresponsible risk but Sergei saw it as an invaluable opportunity for serendipity to occur. *And more importantly, he did not ask for my consent.*

"What if you don't come back?" said Derya, his last unconvincing attempt to dissuade Sergei.

"You mean, what if I die? We've discussed this already. Nothing happens. You're not religious, so you're exempt from farewell prayers; and Caird is programmed to intercept Shackleton autonomously."

"We changed history," said Derya, pointing to the box containing the two microscopic alien life forms. "Don't screw it up."

Sergei helped Derya put on and fasten the helmet. Not the most caressing of hands—the locking it in place caused Derya to sputter an entire Hail Mary. Yet, like a well-trained fakir from Varanasi, there was edification and rapture behind Derya's screaming pain. *The end is nigh, with one of the most significant discoveries in the history of our species right under my arm. Let's call it one of the most stunning insights ever uncovered about our Universe—now it's about transferring from this matchbox to the birdcage of Shackleton, then quickly packing the bags and getting the hell out of Saturn.*

♇

Three hours later, Caird was beyond sight, hidden behind the horizon. In quite a literal way, Sergei was the loneliest human being, primate, mammal, animal, or terrestrial being all the way to that first unicellular organism, the ancestor to all life on Earth billions of years ago. He was adrift within a monumental heap of seracs and blocks of ice towering hundreds of feet above him and sinking to unknown depths below. The ice surrounding him breathed and moved as he climbed through a narrow passage that looked like a cascade of melted wax from one hundred candles in a forgotten Russian Orthodox monastery. An obelisk-shaped ice block had crumbled in slow motion, soundless before his eyes. He had been drawn into a crevassed cemetery, slinking to collect his body. And yet he felt euphoric, intoxicated by the most powerful epiphany of his life.

Like any good Russian, his engineering background did nothing to dispel an upbringing that was suffused with the supernatural, beginning at birth when his mother—like all Russian mothers—kept him away from prying eyes for the first two days of his life. A childhood hearing and sometimes even spotting the furtive hairy Domovoi inhabiting their house, and the rare glimpsing of the Baba Yaga hut standing on its chicken legs, deep in the Siberian forest of his youth. Luck and fate, misunderstood as superstition in the West. It was no coincidence the greatest science fiction movie of all times, Andrei Tarkovsky's *Solaris*, about the fate of the crew of a research station orbiting a mysterious sentient planet, was made by a Russian. Some things were not meant to be understood.

This time he had ventured further than any other spacewalk. His life support system had six hours and forty-seven minutes left, plus half an hour of emergency supply. He would need to turn back in ninety minutes.

Sergei was immersed in thoughts of times past, but the tearing agony was no longer there. It had first happened yesterday on his initial foray into the narrowing Baghdad canyon north of Caird. The further he had walked, the stronger it got. But nothing had ever felt this intense before. The memories were extraordinarily vivid and multi-sensorial. He could see Iman's face with a level of detail he had thought gone for good: the dark, silky skin, the deep, thoughtful eyes, the tilt of her Roman nose, the sensual mouth. He heard her exotic, accented Russian. His nostrils got drunk on her skin's perfume. And for the first time since … he killed her … the accident, she was smiling at him.

Ø

Years of patient waiting had turned into days of anxious anticipation. Derya was desperate to be back in their home-away-from-home. With the mission completed, the prospect of heading back to Earth agitated his mind at all times. He missed people. *Random ones will be fine*, he thought. *And lots of weather: the sound of rain tapping the roof, of wind rocking the trees. Being outside. The simple things in life. The important things in life.* Instead, here they were: two men for two weeks in a capsule with the internal space of an SUV. It was at these moments when it helped him to consider 1965's Gemini 7, when Jim Lovell and Frank Borman lived for fourteen straight days orbiting Earth in a space the size of the front seats of a Volkswagen Beetle.

He remembered to check on the little children residing inside the Petri dish. Derya moved the sealed container under the microscope, and as soon as he rested his eye on the ocular his body experienced goosebumps. Something had changed, a lot. The computer quantified the hunch: *Albus Darya* and *Noctem Darya* had multiplied many times during the last day. He promptly sent the data to Earth with the headline "I believe there are grounds to get drunk today." *No need to be an expert to understand the significance. The results speak not about what's in the Petri dish, but about what's not. It means there's a violent Darwinian ecosystem down there keeping them contained … it means the two life forms are at or near the bottom of the food pyramid … it means there's bigger, perhaps much bigger, beings concealed in the dark waters of Enceladus.*

57 | SΔTURN

ORBITING SATURN

Sophia had grown uneasy watching the immensity of Saturn through the flight deck's Observation Window. Even at Shackleton's height, 1,700 miles over its cloud tops—seven times higher than the ISS orbited the Earth— the horizon line looked uncompromisingly straight. The circularity of the planet was only given away by the infinity of the curving rings overhead.

They were still on the dark side, but silvery sunlight mirrored by the rings elucidated the turbulent rivers of clouds below in dim bleached gray. Something curious kept happening to her. The scale of Saturn's upper atmosphere currents and eddies and fuzzy canyons—some larger than her home planet—inevitably tricked the brain into discarding facts and embracing visual cues: the spaceship could only really be cruising a couple of miles above the clouds.

But what turned her stomach were the irregular lightning bursts beneath them, revealing the planet's innards and exposing the vertical structures of the huge swirling masses of gas. At those moments, the deceiving heavenly pastoral illusion of the dayside revealed its true bottomless depth.

James agreed to rotate the ship so the Observation Window looked away from the orb into the starry sky. The thrusters gradually turned them with a force comparable to a person moving a school bus by tapping it. *The wonder of weightlessness*, she thought.

∅

"—then why do you expect our bodies to need re-acclimatizing? We've been under partial gravity at night, we have no meaningful bone loss ..." said Yi.

"Boy, I don't know," said James. "I'm simply extrapolating from coming back to Earth after my stint on the ISS. Muscles are 3D, so using them does not guarantee they won't be rusty in certain positions—"

"Sorry to interrupt," said Sophia, doing mid-air somersaults above James and Yi, both in their seats at the flight deck. "Q for Yi. What should be the brightest thing in the sky from here? Jupiter, no?"

"By far," said Yi.

"My take," continued James, "is that the leg muscles will be atrophied for walking under Earth's gravity, which means we'll be enjoying traveling to places mostly by watching television, at least the first few—"

"How many moons does Jupiter have?" cut in Sophia.

"Seventy-nine total, but unlike Saturn only four have any meaningful size," said Yi. "Sorry, Jimmy. So, what's your take on food?"

"Disappointing news too if you were dreaming of stabbing the proverbial steak that keeps ambushing my mind. It may go down the muzzle, but only to spring back as beef pudding soaked in gastric juice. And the heartburn after! Not pretty. After six years of spartan diet, your intestinal bacteria will be xenophobic, radicalized, and diehard."

This time Yi gestured for an interruption. "You can't see Jupiter's moons from here without a scope." About to go on, James was stopped by another announced interjection. "Also, Jupiter is in the opposite direction to where you're looking—sorry, Jimmy."

Sophia halted her whistling.

"In any case," James continued, "we'll be quarantined for a month. Adjust expectations. Better to assume hospital food during that time."

Sophia had canceled her spinning and looked intently out of the window. When the reticence of being ridiculed succumbed to the fear of being right she whispered, "There's something strange about those stars ..." She held her breath, hoping to hear James laugh.

Instead, he said in a stern voice, "Sophia, come to your seat. Now."

⌀

Yi froze as he watched thousands of shiny stars coming at them. In spite or because of the panic, he connected the dots in one sweeping moment of clarity. *That Saturn explosion seen from Earth in March*, he thought. *The measles-like spots peppered across its face a week ago ... they were impact scars—And I'm looking at their common source.* The gleaming diamonds swarming the sky could only be the fragments of an icy visitor ripped apart when Saturn's tidal forces eclipsed its gravitational self-attraction. *And the thirty-degree inclination from the planet's equator betrays their origin.* Somewhere in the outer reaches of the Solar System. *It's like Jimmy's dream ... only on the wrong planet.*

"What do we do?" Sophia's alarmed voice echoed in the back of Yi's mind.

"We wait," answered James in a severe but controlled voice. "There's nothing we can do. They should fly past us."

Yi's lucidity seemed to have come at the expense of controlling his body, which felt paralyzed. His hands were clamped to the seat as if spot-welded in place. He vaguely sensed James slamming a helmet on his head, noticing the visor turning the white comet fragments into sepia and the click when it locked in place.

Debris began crossing Yi's field of vision at such speed his eyes couldn't resolve shapes, just the blur.

A thump shocked Shackleton. For a few seconds it seemed to have stopped at that, but soon his head and body were commanded to lean left by a growing centrifugal force.

His sense of time disappeared and his conscience divided reality into constituent parts. His eyes noticed the revolving, repeating shadows. Then he heard muted shouts from James. Then he was aware of his body being governed by an invisible force.

He had become a wax sculpture. *This is how Stephen Hawking must have felt. A racing brain cloistered inside a broken shell—barring a miracle, we'll be sucked into the savage abyss of Saturn, something so deep, dense, and hot that even hydrogen and helium eventually become metallic.*

Yi, impotent, watched James in awe. *If miracles exist, this one carries Jimmy's name.*

Ø

James was terrified but at this time that was the opposite of petrified. He would fight until the end. *If I need to slay destiny, I will*, he thought.

"Methane fuel tank has been compromised," declared TiTus in its anodyne voice, with a calmness that could only come from artificial intelligence. "Estimating 440 to 470 seconds before depletion."

"Locate ... the leak," James shouted. He tried to move but the centrifugal force kept sucking him back into the seat. "I need ... you to ... neutralize the—" James' inner ear told him the spinning was becoming more tolerable. *It doesn't make sense*—until he started sensing the vibrations in his spine.

The spinning was decreasing, the shaking was intensifying.

"Commander, the precise hull location cannot be identified," TiTus said.

The atmospheric friction was acting on Shackleton's delta wings to cancel the rotation. James raised his head to the Observation Window, now entirely filled with yellow and orange hues. *No, there's a thin blueish horizon line whirling around the window. There's still hope.* They were sinking diagonally.

"Height!"

"970 miles."

No longer pinned to the wall, James unlocked the seat harness. "Reverse stalling," he said, while clambering out.

"It is not advised," answered TiTus. "Without proper damage assessment, igniting the engines can lead to an uncontrolled combustion."

Translation: Shackleton explodes into a ball of fire. "You're the pilot now, TiTus. Use the thrusters to decrease pitch or we're toast. Sophia, I need you. Follow me to the cargo door."

He propelled himself with an abrupt kick in the direction of the cargo area. This time the straight glide he had repeated to perfection for years sent him slamming into one of the walls, as the spaceship was buffeted by the atmosphere.

Ø

Yi expelled a dispirited, "Shit."

Far ahead, the hazy brownish air between them and the cloud tops hundreds of miles below was being replaced not by one but two bright yellow suns setting the night alight. The biggest was developing a vast deck above, optically distorted as a mirage. He forgot about himself and witnessed the aftermath of two fiery bombs set aflame with the power of a million Hiroshimas. The expansion across Saturn's upper atmosphere was swift and two familiar mushrooms abandoned their spherical shape into small Saturns, becoming gargantuan trees, turning into scorching clouds climbing ever higher with burgeoning halos around them.

Ø

A flashing wall beacon confirmed the emergency depressurization was complete. The cargo area was now equalized to the external pressure.

Sophia finished mounting the backpack propulsion unit on James' back and he sprung forward and opened the cargo door to an exterior no longer black.

Following the emergency procedure, Sophia started preparing the Dragon.

James exited the spaceship and even though the atmosphere was still tenuous he felt the density of the air for the first time in three years. He hooked the two tethers to a handrail and moved toward the ship's rear. He knew speed was mandatory, not only for the leak but because maintaining grip with the ship would soon become impossible and the thickening air would shortly burn through his suit. His muscles noticed every tick in the escalating *g*-force.

James' mind had emptied to nothing but the path onward, actively avoiding glimpsing at the immensity before him. *Grab the handrail with your right hand. Move forward. Unclip the tether with your left. Stretch the arm and clip higher. Repeat—this is too slow.* He let go of one tether, which fell sideways and became taut, as if fastened to an invisible hook.

He identified the leak a dozen feet away, bleeding a gush of methane into Saturn's atmosphere.

His breathing was heavy and his movements unsteady. The ship was shaking hard.

"The fuel tank is almost depleted!" he heard over the intercom.

The next hurling frontwards was cut short by a yank. He looked at his harness. Having forgotten to unclip, the tight tether went back eight feet. Retracing was not a possibility, so he detached his harness from it. His hands were now the only things connecting him to Shackleton.

"TiTus, get ready to fire the engines on my command," he shouted, panting.

"Aye aye, Commander."

James got within an arm's length from the sprouting leak, a hole the size of a fist. Freeing a hand, he grabbed from his harness a mechanical seal that looked like a screwdriver. He tried inserting it inside the hull but the pressure of the escaping methane kept winning. *If only I had a tether to free both hands.* He almost lost the device in his progressively frantic jamming. The lactic acid in his arms was stiffening and weakening his grip. *Now or never.* He drove his hand into the leak with all he had and pressed the trigger.

On the hull's interior the front detonated open into a metallic umbrella that the methane's own pressure locked into place against the inside wall of the tank. The leak cut off.

"Start the engines!"

James counted on a human response lag, which TiTus didn't have. The thrust was instant as the engines blasted into full power to climb out of the atmosphere. He looked in astonishment at both his hands, freed. With human response lag his right hand lunged for his life, but the separation was already twice as long as his arms. He was no longer attached to the ship. *Emma! Belinda!*

Sophia's screams of joy were heart-wrenching. *I know something that you don't.* He powered his propulsion unit in desperation but being little more than a few aerosol cans joined together, it proved pointless.

"I'm detached! I detached from Shack!"

For a moment his plea was received with ungrateful silence.

"Shut down the engines, TiTus," yelled Sophia.

The sense of being airborne, skydiving toward Saturn's cloud tops, was disorienting, sickening, and terrifying, but he forced himself to speak back, "TiTus—don't. Do not. That's an order."

Shackleton was diverging fast, already hundreds of feet away.

James scanned around for the first time. Picture the most memorable flight you ever took, on top of puffy clouds dyed in sunset orange. Unfasten the seatbelt. Eliminate the seat. Erase the airplane.

Sophia's voice was shaky, "I'm freeing the Dragon ... I'm going in to rescue you ..."

The atmosphere was heating his spacesuit. Both his body and brain wanted to shut down, as if self-preservation was no longer capable of wrestling against the *g*-force and ghastly terror. He heard himself as if he had unfolded in two, the soul listening to the body. "NO! We have only one ... task ... saving Shack."

He blacked out shortly after.

Ø

The unmanned Dragon disengaged from Shackleton, firing its engines and diving toward James, tracking his spacesuit. He was not even a dot anymore.

Ø

Shackleton escaped the claws of gravity and exited Saturn's atmosphere, re-achieving orbit.

Sophia drifted into the flight deck, sobbing uncontrollably. Yi remained motionless in his seat, holding his head in his hands.

She saw James' vital signs on the screen. He was still alive. His heartbeat was under one hundred.

"He's unconscious." Yi's voice came out in grunts.

The Dragon was closing in fast on James. In less than two minutes the reading '1,570 feet' rekindled Sophia's hope. Her overcast eyes stared through the Observation Window, even as she knew human sight couldn't possibly resolve the two infinitesimal specks against the endless background of clouds far, far below.

'1,140 feet' … '890 feet'

"Jimmy, over … Jimmy, over. Can you see the Dragon? Over."

'560 feet' … '350 feet'

"Jimmy! Jimmy, please!"

'287 feet' … '209 feet' … '134 feet'

The heartbeat monitor on the screen jumped by twenty.

Ø

James was still alive only because his body flew the ten miles a second in an exceedingly gradual atmospheric entry angle toward Saturn. Regaining consciousness, he could perceive his limbs burning, but without pain. All his senses except his sight remained suppressed, which is why it took a while before he identified a faint, indistinct sound. Concentrating on his ears, he finally heard, "JIMMY! LOOK AROUND!"

He took over a minute to clasp the Dragon's hatch handle. Getting in was grueling. Contracting his body to enter changed his aerodynamic profile, sending him upward, downward, sideways.

Once inside, he began to feel the skin sizzling. *Burns be damned, nobody ever died from pain.*

"I'm in," he managed to utter.

"We are telecommanding the Dragon. You have fifteen seconds to strap to the seat." James was startled to hear a very formal Yi, almost aloof.

Sophia's voice was hopeful. "Jimmy! You're 240 miles from exiting the atmosphere. You'll do this!"

James felt the tug with his eyes closed, promptly falling into an involuntary drowse while the cabin re-pressurized.

Ø

An incredulous Sophia gaped at Yi. "What … happened? What's going on?"

He avoided looking back but her stare broke him at last. The mask was gone. His face became congested and, in weightlessness, tears formed around his eyelids.

Yi pressed the digital button to cut communication with the Dragon, which since Sophia had already done moments before, resumed transmission instead. "He won't make it … there was never enough fuel in the Dragon to save him."

Sophia could no longer control the shuddering. "Why? Why didn't you say so?"

"Because I can't bear," Yi broke down but tried again, "because I can't bear the thought of him knowing he's about to die."

∅

James heard. *I will never embrace my Emma, that little person I love more than life itself.*

He lost consciousness soon after. The console read 17-g, higher than the murderous acceleration of a seat ejecting from a fighter jet.

58 | INTO SATURN

A throbbing twinge stirred James awake. *Where am I?* His awareness was dulled and his memory was an impenetrable fog interrupted by two lighthouses, Emma and Belinda smiling at him. But the vision made him wary. It felt like an old postcard, real yet bygone. *Where am I?* He tried to concentrate and noticed an acute pain in his head, as if someone had squashed his brain inside the skull of a child. His eyes rested on his lap. The bright blue of his spacesuit had become a dark olive. He sniffed a pungent charred smell. Trying in vain to remove his helmet, he noticed the numbness of his hands. He had no feeling under the wrists. *WHERE AM I?* Struggling, he managed to unlock his left glove. An ebony hand came off with two fingers replaced by mostly skinless yellow bones. His mind tried to stop the swelling suspicion, sensing a terrible truth. It circumvented logic in a desperate attempt to bury reality. *I made it? I made it!* An irrational euphoria persuaded him for a moment, but it was bright outside the Dragon's windows, which wasn't unusual but outright wrong in zero gravity. *Am I ... dreaming?* He closed his eyes and noticed the subtle rocking of the capsule as well as a hissing sound outside. The reality landed on him like a mace. *The Dragon is gliding—the air is cushioning the free fall.* The capsule had somehow fallen into the gas giant at an angle that shaved speed without incinerating the vehicle on entry or subjecting him to lethal *g*-forces. The twenty miles per second had become a terminal velocity of 150 miles per hour, much like a skydiver back on Earth. The Dragon was no longer battling gravity. It was falling into it. The burns on his body were so deep they had seared his nerve endings. *That's why the pain is tolerable.* But the grief was not. Escaping from it, he took refuge in his body. *The real pain won't start for several days, when the nerve endings grow back and sense the carnage around them ... but there's no 'several days' for you,* he reminded himself. He desperately searched for another distraction. He felt the compression on his back and an intense lumbago. Out of ideas, he was forced to confront the truth. There was no fear of death, only the desolation at having lost Emma and Belinda forever.

He freed the straps of his harness and moved to one of the five windows.

What he saw was both the most beautiful sight and the saddest moment of his life.

If he hadn't known that the limitless, fathomless whiteness of magnificently detailed cumulonimbus clouds around him were the upper cloud decks of Saturn's troposphere, Heaven would have been the natural guess. His only sense of scale and distance was indirect: no clouds looked close enough to break the illusion of solid into ephemeral phantoms of vapor and gas, which could only mean everything was far away and immense. By contrasting their plunging speed—he preferred 'they' instead of 'him,' it felt less lonely—against the null change in perspective, James understood that the cloud pillar they seemed to be almost brushing against was instead distant and fabulously tall, shooting dozens of miles above them. Much like childhood memories of staring at the sky while lying on the grass, the majestic collection of soaring ridges, bottomless gorges, plateaus, and rivers of clouds around them kept shapeshifting. At moments the skyscape resembled a Japanese forest in winter, a blanket of white over cones of cotton, where any of the trees measured in Everests. At others it turned into Canyonlands National Park, full of stacks and arch formations shooting heavenward. At another an Eden of cauliflowers. And now the spray and body of a huge wave smashing against coastal spits and outcrops.

But any illusions of Heaven or Valhalla were dispelled the moment he looked down. The clouds were engaged in a chaotic dance, driven by the fastest winds in the Solar System after Neptune, many times stronger than the worst storm ever recorded on Earth. If he were to deploy the Dragon's parachutes, the vicious lateral buffeting would cancel out the fall as they got sucked into Earth-wide belts endlessly circling the giant, the spacecraft becoming a blender battering James into a fertilizer bag of vaguely human shape. He could see they were dropping toward a vast low-pressure zone where convection currents sank planets-worth of gas into Saturn's depths, a cosmic Niagara Falls.

The wound in James' soul martyred him, bleeding despair and melancholia. He spent a long time in contemplation, waiting for a grisly death. The further they sank, the worse it would get. At their speed it would take days to cover the distance to the center of Saturn. He imagined the voyage ahead. The dreamy clouds beneath were made of ammonia. After an hour cutting through them, they would arrive at a familiar water cloud layer, an agreeable ambient temperature but with a punishing level of pressure. From there things would go south. As they continued uncloaking Saturn's much-hypothesized interior, the air density would keep creeping up, slowing them down while pressure and temperature outcompeted each other. At some point the hydrogen would liquefy under the titanic pressure to become a hydrogen ocean. Friction and static electricity would create massive lightning arcs all around. Deeper down, the Sun's surface temperature would become comparatively crisp while the pressure would be thousands of times higher than the crushing depths of Earth's deepest ocean trenches. Hydrogen becomes metallic as its single electron collapses into the atom's nucleus. This new state of degenerate matter conducts electricity, creating the planet's powerful, crackling magnetic fields. After this ninth circle of Hell, the gates to Saturn's inferno would be near: the giant's core. The spacecraft's composites, however, would melt much, much higher in Saturn's elemental abyss, and prior to that the pressure would collapse the Dragon into a stamp. And yet, the thought of becoming a part of Saturn was strangely soothing to James.

He had a couple of hours as he awaited his execution. *Time to put things in order.*

James shifted to the console, determined to give meaning to his otherwise senseless death sentence. He activated the sensors' recording of temperature, pressure, and wind speed, turning the Dragon into a much-dreamed of, never-before-implemented meteorological descent probe. *My loss will be science's gain.*

He instructed the Dragon to link and begin transferring data to Shackleton.

59 | LEADERSHIP

Moments later

Yi was startled when data began streaming from the Dragon. *I thought we had lost contact for good.* He saw Sophia's eyes glittering with newfound exuberance.

"Jimmy! Jimmy, can you hear us?" Sophia screamed after activating the intercom.

"Sophia ... don't. Look at his vitals ... he's gone." James' health information was no longer displayed on the flight deck's screens.

Minutes before, TiTus had reminded them that Yi was in charge now, as third in the chain of command after James and Sergei. Shackleton's situation required immediate attention but Yi was drained of any willpower. *I need sleep.* The dreadful silence was interrupted by Sophia, staring at him. "What do we do now?"

It took time for Yi to ride through the invisible obstacle of acknowledging that James was dead. "We have already burned our ticket home. There's not enough fuel to go back to Earth ..." He restrained himself from saying more. *All luck comes to an end. We may be breathing, but we are dead.* Which, infringing upon basic human survival instinct, felt preferable to carrying the weight of James' death.

"No! No, no, no, no. I won't accept losing his life for nothing!"

"Sophia, I'm the commander now. To honor Jimmy," he stopped and inhaled a few times, trying to reign over his desolation, "the best we can do is keep orbiting Saturn ... try by all means available to rendezvous with Derya and Sergei before it's too late for them, decode as much as you can from the alien microbes ... and then organize and prioritize the terabytes of data to keep transmitting information to Earth well past our—our expiration date."

"No," she replied defiantly. "We will play the one wild card we have."

Yi looked at her, clueless. *What's she talking about?*

"Titan," she asserted.

"Don't tell me it's because of its methane seas ..." said Yi. Sophia's face remained impassive. "That's lunacy!" In other circumstances he could have laughed at such an outlandish proposal.

"That's your fighting instinct?"

"That's my rational brain thinking. We won't compromise the biggest scientific payload in history for having one shot at a … a hopelessly improbable outcome," said Yi.

"That may be true, but we can't and we won't condemn Derya and Sergei to death without them having a say—TiTus, do we have enough fuel to make it to Titan and attempt a landing?"

"That's enough!" Yi could have stopped at that but chose to give more perspective. "Think coldly for a moment. You know at what depth on Earth diamonds are made, available in quantities we can't even fathom? About one hundred miles under our feet. Yet *nobody* is making the business case to go and get them. You know why? Do you know why? Because it seems close but it's unreachable." *She won't cave,* he realized looking at her stubborn face.

"We're on board Shackleton."

"So what?" said Yi, confused.

He could almost hear the gears inside Sophia's brain turning. "Probabilities can freeze you from attempting something crazy," she said. "What were the odds of dying when Ernest Shackleton decided to cross the Antarctic Ocean on a dinghy? Nine out of ten, at best?"

"Tweety, we are as close to Titan as medieval people were from flying. You may get the illusion that it's attainable but don't be deceived. It's impossible. Stop this nonsense … that's an order."

"If you're unwilling to look for a solution, you're no longer my captain."

TiTus interrupted the conversation. "Affirmative, Sophia. Preliminary calculations show there should be enough propellant to land on Titan."

"Could we use some of that propellant to modify our trajectory and rendezvous with Caird before heading to Titan?" asked Sophia.

"Sophia," said Yi.

"That requires extensive simulation. It cannot be assessed currently," said TiTus.

"Start working on it," said Sophia. And staring at Yi she continued, "Then we figure how to land. And then we figure how to—I don't know—refuel, I guess. We do it piecemeal, one step at a time."

"I'm sorry, Sophia, but that request requires commander clearance," said TiTus.

Yi wanted to be upset. *But a captain unwilling to sail is just a misnamed longshoreman. Instead look at her, refusing to give up.* After a long pause he said, "TiTus, do whatever Sophia asks."

Past the roadblock of hesitation, Sophia did not spare an instant. Two minutes later, the SOS message rushed to Earth at light-speed.

Ø

Sunlight had greatly diminished past the seas of ammonia crystal clouds above. Having cleared that, the Dragon now cut through hazy but otherwise clean space, with the next deck of water clouds still far away beneath. The light reflecting and refracting from the canopies of clouds gave an ethereal glow punctuated by the occasional rainbow. The world of fleeting shadows from before, flared away in an instant by almighty Sun strikes, was raided by ever more confident penumbras, and all would soon be stormed and reigned over by darkness.

For the time being, the billows underneath mirrored the rolling, spiraling streams of white overhead, which in a free fall where the bottom seemed to never approach and the top never retreat, made James feel trapped inside a celestial casket with the arrow of time broken.

He kept rewatching the two videos sent for his birthday ten days before. Emma walking solemnly to the camera with a birthday cake. The 'y' frosting letter of 'Daddy' about to fall off its side. The other was from Belinda undressing for him. *"My boy, not a minute goes by without your face, your voice, your laugh. Three years have been a long time, but the next three will fly by."*

Why? He had kept asking himself. Not anymore. He chose to believe his sacrifice puzzled out the enigma of the recurrent nightmare of his past. *A comet killed me. I took humanity's spot.* It gave him a sense of closure and made the heartache ever so slightly more tolerable.

Within minutes the shaking got noticeably worse and soon after it became unbearable. *It's time.*

He repeatedly tried to record his goodbye voice message to Belinda, but every few seconds a wind gust would smack the Dragon, leaving him battered and wheezing. *She can never know the distress I'm going through. To her my death will have happened suddenly and peacefully.*

To Sophia and Yi he was already dead—James had done it to spare them from pointless suffering. But he was being forced to talk to them one final time.

As a last resort, he called Shackleton.

Ø

"Jimmy, I can't," said a distressed Sophia. "You know me. I'm not a leader. I never have and never will—"

"I brought you all here." James' voice was heavily distorted by white noise. "There's no more time, Sophia. You are the new commander. Promise me you'll do everything to get the four of you back home alive."

Sophia broke down. "I—promise."

After the short exchange she had nothing left to say. It was an awful feeling. Three close friends separated by circumstance, unable to find common ground anymore.

"I'm so sorry ... please forgive me, Jimmy ... I wish it could have been me," Yi managed between sobs.

"Jimmy ..." But Sophia's throat no longer emitted intelligible sounds.

A minute later every fiber inside her was rebelling, but she couldn't quit. James was dying as he dictated a goodbye that nobody but Belinda should have heard. She concentrated on the increasingly incomprehensible words behind a wall of static while trying to keep her grief at bay.

Yi pleaded again, "Jimmy ... please ... you can end it all ... depressurize the cabin." Suicide was the one way out of a horrible death but James was not quitting.

"—don't fail. Make this count—" were the last words they heard from Saturn.

Ø

Thousands of miles beneath them the Dragon fell erratically through an endless cloudy abyss of darks and grays, brightened momentarily by monstrous electrical storms.

James' last conscious thought was his failure to free Belinda. He meant to say she should find someone else, but there was no force capable of making him say it.

60 | THE NEWS

Minutes later

CANBERRA, AUSTRALIA

t was 5:39 AM, yet the sheep-dotted rolling hills of green surrounding the Canberra Deep Space Communication Complex were already discernible, carved sharply against the dark blue sky that was steadily being invaded by spring daylight. Those hills—shielding a bowl-shaped valley from line-of-sight electromagnetic noise from radios, telephones, and televisions—convinced NASA in 1965 to turn this immaculate countryside into one of the three facilities 120 degrees apart, the other two being in Spain and California, that handle all communication to and from every mission in outer space.

At the end of a windy road coming from Canberra, a sign hanging at the entrance gate reminded visitors to turn off cellphones and laptops to "help listen to the whispers from space." Here, amongst the six massive dish antennas stationed on site, there was also a smaller, older-looking one. At 08:18 UTC, July 20 1969, this third of the world was directly under Neil Armstrong when he took the first steps on the Moon and declared, "That's one small step for man, one giant leap for mankind." All images and sounds from that historic moment were intercepted and transmitted to a speechless world from that lone piece of metal.

Now this part of the world pointed at Saturn.

The Control Room, with its futuristic screens and floor-to-ceiling windows that looked out at the towering white bowls scattered over the rolling meadows, was staffed with five highly caffeinated technicians counting down the minutes for the first day shift. Space never sleeps.

They were alerted of the incoming data by five beeps. The behemoth 200-foot dish began rotating to lock onto the signal from Saturn. At the time of reception, after traveling a billion miles, the signal was a murmur from space billions of times weaker than the power of a mechanical wristwatch.

Immediately after the handshake between the computers and the radio signal from Saturn, the screens displayed the downlink information oscillating like heartbeats in an electrocardiogram. T-tump-t-tump-t-tump. As the sequence of zeros and ones were decoded, the bloke under the "Post Office of the Universe" sign started the customary process of validating the data. Even after nine years working there, the drowsiness of a long night, and the routine nature of the operation, the first lines of translated binary code always gave him a warm jolt of wonder. This time was different. The adrenaline surged through his body while he experienced an emotional shock. Choking up, he managed to say, "David … there's been an accident."

Ø

SAN FRANCISCO, CALIFORNIA

The 'PRIVATE' caller ID on the ringing phone could only mean Enceladus news. Belinda answered eagerly but the person at the other end remained silent. "Yes? Anyone there?" She was going to hang up when she noticed the strained breathing on the other end of the line. "Yes?"

"Please … talk to me," she said softly. The specter of her nightmares reappeared fully formed. Her body started shivering. And then, just the way he said "Belinda" was enough to make her fall to her knees. "Please no," a plea no longer directed at him.

Ø

WASHINGTON, D.C.

At the end, the President's convenience became secondary to the need for a very large room capable of remotely connecting multiple counterparts around the world. While this was a decision where no single country had jurisdiction, a formal United Nations Security Council emergency meeting would have required high-ranking officials physically present in New York, something unachievable at such short notice. The meeting was set to happen in an hour. The heads of state of China, Colombia, France, Germany, India, Japan, Morocco, Nigeria, Peru, Russia, Singapore, Sudan, Sweden, Ukraine, the United Kingdom, and the United States—as permanent and current non-permanent members—would each have veto power. The rest were invited to participate as guests. To avoid airport delays, the US President was flying from the UN Headquarters in New York City to the Pentagon in Washington, D.C. in the Marine One helicopter.

In the meantime, important American bureaucrats who should and some who shouldn't have been there were trying to hammer out the recommendation for the President. Even with direct prohibition from the White House, quite a few were taking advantage of the chaos to leak scoops to the media.

The civility of the room was hanging by a thread.

"—the Titan 'plan' requires a long sequence of events, each one of them going from hard to extremely hard; and every single one needs to resolve flawlessly for this to have a *chance* at succeeding. First, managing to rendezvous with Caird; second, entering Titan's ultra-dense atmosphere; third, sticking the landing; fourth, sticking the landing by the shore of one of the methane seas or lakes; fifth, said sea or lake needing to be of nearly pure methane instead of a mixture of ethane or nitrogen. I skipped many critical middle steps and I won't even mention what happens in the improbable case that all goes according to plan and they manage to exit Titan. Starting with the sobering fact they almost certainly won't have enough fuel to decelerate for Earth's re-entry. Multiply those probabilities, and their odds of surviving very quickly become zero. In summary, the reality of the situation does not support your optimism. I apologize for being so blunt, but these are dead men walking."

"Excuse me, who are you?" said Tom Doyle, US Senator, war veteran, retired Navy Captain, and former NASA astronaut.

"Stephen Helvey, the new Deputy Assistant Secretary of Defense for Space Policy."

"Yes, but who are you besides the fancy government title ... what have you actually done for this country besides cashing a monthly check?"

"With all due respect, Senator Doyle, I don't think there's a need to be condescending or confrontational. You may not know me, but I pride myself with a flawless and exemplary career in public service. Regarding today's subject—"

"Son, my problem with people like yourself is that in that compact bureaucratic mind of yours, somehow today's subject is the same as tomorrow's or yesterday's. To you, what we are debating is just one more paper to be rubber stamped and archived ... but you are profoundly wrong when you extrapolate your worth into those exceptional five—four stranded on Saturn. This long stopped being a private enterprise with crew from a few nations. They are the spearhead of our civilization, of our species. They are not only our heroes, they are our soul. They are our hope for a different future. A better future. This is a momentous time for humanity. We cannot abandon them ... let me remind you what the President said an hour ago: we are not in the business of finding fault, but in the business of finding hope, however slight. If they make it back, it will be through sheer will despite everything stacked against them. We should do everything within our reach, however humble, to help bring them back alive. Right now, that little something happens to be the elimination of a nonsensical legal hurdle, which they could very well ignore anyway. And besides, who around this table or indeed anywhere on this planet has the right to condemn them to die? Nobody, and most certainly not you, or me."

"Excuse me, Senator," said Helvey, "but I have a duty to represent the high-profile individuals, including some scientists, who oppose manned landing on Titan—"

"Tell me who they are, because I'll personally go and punch their yellow bellies and kick their wimpy asses. Goddamn sons of bitches."

The room erupted into chaos. Despite repeated calls for order, the clamoring got worse until the blaring, coarse shouting of an Army General prevailed, "ORDER! Stop this damn circus," and once it quieted down, he said, "Senator, your point is clear and shared by many ... however, I think it's good to hear from the minority. Continue, Hillbil."

"It's Helvey, sir. And to be perfectly frank, I wouldn't be so adamant about calling us a minority. I think you are bound to be surprised ... I want to first remind the room about planetary protection and ask each of you to forget for a moment the spiritual attachment to the mission and its crew. Article IX of the Outer Space Treaty of 1967, which the vast majority of the world has ratified, requires nations exploring celestial bodies to, and I'm quoting, 'conduct exploration of them so as to avoid their harmful contamination and also adverse changes in the environment of the Earth resulting from the introduction of extraterrestrial matter and, where necessary, shall adopt appropriate measures for this purpose.' Our own National Aeronautics and Space Administration has designated Titan as a Planetary Protection Class V Restricted Earth Return body, which concerns the protection of Earth from back contamination resulting from extraterrestrial samples, which in this case corresponds to an entire manned spaceship, which not only *could* potentially but will *actually* be carrying back indigenous extraterrestrial life forms ... in this regard it states in no uncertain terms, and I'm reading, 'the absolute prohibition of destructive impact upon return to Earth.' And as all of you know by now, in the, uh, improbable case that everything goes well and they start closing in on Earth, they will be running on fumes at a speed so great to make any rendezvous impossible, which is definitely not enough to guarantee a successful landing with any sort of safety margin. Which is to say, there's a—and I would say rather high—likelihood that they will burn up on re-entry, dispersing said extraterrestrial life into the four winds."

"Are you hearing yourself, Hilly?" asked Miriam Silberstein, Chairman of the Senate Subcommittee on Space, Science, and Competitiveness, "Your assessment may be legally accurate, but it's factually wrong. You can't possibly paint a probe return sample and Shackleton with the same brush. That's just insensitive and frankly ignorant. If they make it out of the Saturn system, they will have three years to conduct all necessary tests and actions, monitored from Earth, to make re-entry safe no matter what the outcome turns out to be ... I also find it hard to believe there's more than a few misfits opposing the landing on Titan. We Americans are naturally predisposed to exploration and adventure, going back to the Manifest Destiny of the 19th century. Just watch Hollywood movies, we love it when the good guys conquer adversity. It feels almost preordained that Shackleton finds itself stranded just like Shackleton's expedition in 1915, beyond the longest sea ever crossed. And just like then, the human spirit will prevail."

Other officials came to Helvey's defense, counter-arguing the assault. The discussion was heating up again when a lanky clerk stormed into the room. Helvey was not the only one to look at him with slight contempt, noticing the likely purchase of his ill-fitting attire from Ross Dress for Less. His scornful grin disappeared when the clerk cried out, panting, "The decision has already been made." He ruined the confusion and anticipation by blurting out, "They are calling it the first worldwide referendum ... over 1,700 million people have stampeded to Facebook ... to cast their vote ... and over 13 million are joining every minute ... to have their say about the question 'Should Shackleton be allowed to land on Titan?'" He stopped to recover his breath. His gasping was the only noise in a room filled with over seventy people.

"And?" someone finally spoke in exasperation.

"Until now, 98 percent approve," he said.

The news took seconds of complete silence to decant. The importance of the meeting deflated to little more than a class reunion.

"Besides Hillbil, who are the morons of the 2 percent?" said somebody.

"A planetary decision to a planetary challenge," said another.

"This is the twilight of politics. Us old dogs better start learning new tricks," stated yet another.

"This may be the mission's greatest legacy," declared a fourth.

61 | MURPHY'S LΛW

ENCELADUS

Derya stared at the screen in disbelief. *There is no way this is happening, for two reasons. Make it three*, he thought. *First, I'm experiencing a strong déjà vu, meaning it's all really just a bogus memory trace. Second, I'm biting my right thumb and it isn't bleeding. Third, it would be not merely unfair but extraordinarily and immensely undeserved. Fourth, it would mean we are supremely, utterly, and irrevocably fucked.* He took his finger out of his mouth. It looked like a red latex glove stolen from a porn shop. *Ach Nein.*

The SOS message was terse, clear, and unsparing:

```
***URGENT*** SHACKLETON HAS SUFFERED CATASTROPHIC
ACCIDENT. FUEL TANK COMPROMISED & NEARLY DEPLETED.
JAMES EGGER IS DEAD. SHACKLETON HEADING FOR TITAN
LANDING. RENDEZVOUS WITH CAIRD ONLY POSSIBLE
**TODAY** AT 20:41 UTC. ***ACT IMMEDIATELY***
```

Heilige scheiße.

Mission Control intentionally sent the message sparse and clinical, so there could be no possible misunderstanding and not a moment was wasted. Now, exactly 180 eternal seconds later, an emergency audio message arrived in the in-box and played automatically. It was from Nitha. Brief and to the point. Jimmy was dead. Derya's mind couldn't really assimilate the words. The extreme gravity and urgency of the situation was, however, fully absorbed. *A crisis so acute that somebody has decided attempting a refueling on Titan is somehow the most viable course of action—'viable' being insultingly hyperbolic.* And this was, comparatively, the good news.

Due to the combination of the oppressive rules of orbital mechanics and the destitute condition of Shackleton's fuel tank, the one and only close encounter with Enceladus as it headed to Titan would be more hand waving than handshake, flying by 2,000 miles away. *But that's just the beginning.* The approach was happening in—he read it again slowly as four lives depended on it—three hours and fifty-seven minutes. *Noooow ... fifty-six.* In other circumstances this would be laughable and not even worth trying, but Caird would run out of water and oxygen in a week. Missing the bus meant the final curtain. *But this is a communist collective, an astral kibbutz: if Shack cannot rendezvous with Caird and recover our good Sergei as pilot, my capital punishment gets immediately apportioned to Sophia and Yi as well. Which takes us to the elephant outside the room: not a moment will be wasted, but minutes or even hours; since, strictly complying with Murphy's Law, Sergei Dmitrievich Lazarev is still strolling beyond the horizon.* On Earth, radio waves may work indirectly by bouncing off the upper atmosphere in all directions. But in the void environment of Enceladus, the laws of physics are unbendable: communication only works in direct line of sight. *The Ruski will remain blissfully unaware until he decides to reappear.*

Derya wanted to prepare, but there was nothing to prepare without Sergei. All the sensors would be simply abandoned, and that was the extent of his getting ready. Meanwhile, every extra second decreased their chance of rendezvous.

The longest forty-nine minutes of his life by a factor of 1,000 eventually went by. "Caird over. I'm coming back."

Derya felt a perverse glee answering, "There has been an accident. Jimmy is dead and we must rendezvous with Shackleton in ... three hours and seven minutes. Otherwise, we die." Remembering Sergei may have been suicidal as of late, he added for effect, "The four of us die."

$$\varnothing$$

Sergei's sickening angst was back. His deliberate and unnecessary protocol violation had likely condemned the entire crew.

"MOVE, MOVE, MOVE!" he kept shouting at himself, his ears ringing from the clamor.

After his jetpack ran out of juice, Enceladus' negligible gravity slowed him almost to a halt. He was prairie prancing, bound by a very lax gravity. He climbed in thin air at an impossible height before coming gently down. Things improved whenever he encountered a boulder. He slowed down a few feet beforehand to then propel himself by pushing his legs against it, creating a comparatively speedy horizontal flight.

In his desperation, he thought it possible for TiTus to maneuver autonomously a perfectly planned and executed Titan entry sequence, except for the visual identification of the exact landing spot, which would need to be done by Sophia and Yi. The risk of failure would be very high, but anything below 100 percent was quickly becoming a boon.

Except Derya was not having it.

"Leave me here I said!"

"You have no seniority over me," answered Derya.

"You are compromising the entire mission."

"No. You did."

Ø

The last 1,000 feet it took Sergei to reach Caird felt immortal. Derya was living a nightmare with a werewolf closing in on him while he ran for his life up an escalator moving backward.

Ø

Finally, Caird took off from Baghdad carrying the most sensational discovery of modern times, having perhaps a 70/30 chance of losing it along with everything else.

As Caird transitioned from vertical climb to horizontal speeding over the shrouded oceanworld of Enceladus, the vantage point gave perspective to the canyon they lived inside of for the last ten days, recycled constantly by its unusual icy crust spreading. Like a conveyor belt operated by Atlas, hefty sheets of ice were forced out one end and driven back into the ground at the other, with a breathing, moving minefield of colossal shards in between.

The radio came alive with that familiar, unintentionally histrionic modulation. Yi's voice was optimistic, but the residue of distress was apparent in the pitch and pauses.

"Sophia and myself … you … you can't understand how eager we are to have the two of you back with us soon."

"Where's your commander?" asked Sergei.

"Sophia … she's not coping well. I convinced her to take a tranquilizer. She's in her cabin, aware but lethargic … Mission Control said the rendezvous depends 100 percent on Caird converging on speed and aligning in direction, so we're just bystanders really …"

"That's correct. It's good to hear from you, my friend." Coming from any other person this would have been an everyday comment, but Yi flushed at Sergei's words.

"Likewise … friend," probably sounding more awkward than needed, "and thanks to you, and Jimmy, for committing us to aerocapture when we arrived at Saturn. Without the extra propellant we would be finished."

"Hold your horses, mandarin cowboy," said Derya. "Salvation is still an optical illusion, or as the French would say, a *mirage*."

62 | BRAINSTORMING

Moments later

MISSION CONTROL @ HANGAR ONE, CALIFORNIA

The Control Room had become a throwback to the days around Shackleton's launch. As she entered, Nitha swallowed a lump in her throat. Seeing her twenty-seven Mission Specialists and the Navigation Team staring back at her, everyone as stationary as a tin soldier, could only mean one thing.

She searched around the room for the Navigation Team's chief engineer, "Kostya, we are only accepting good news today."

"Caird won't make it," said Kostya flatly. Nitha made an effort to keep her characteristic determination but became unsteady enough to rest her small frame against one of the long desks. Kostya continued, pointing to the screen wall, "You can see it on the orbital trajectory display."

"I only see Shackleton," she said.

"Yes, unfortunately. The signal we're receiving from Enceladus shows that Caird hadn't launched as of eighty-seven minutes ago. This means they can't make it. Caird won't be able to close in on Shack by a speed delta between 960 and 1,540 feet per second, depending on when they finally took off." The uneasy silence forced him to continue speaking, "They took too long. They will be a hair's distance from rendezvous ... I'm terribly sorry things turned out this way ..."

"How close?" Nitha asked.

"I was speaking in outer-space scales, so, well, the distance between, uh, call it Miami and Tokyo." As if trivia made it less cruel, he added, "At least there's no chance they'll see each other. It would be like trying to spot an airplane flying above Florida from Japan, but moving sixty times faster."

Everyone was silent and motionless except for minor head movement.

In a very physical way, Nitha breathed out her frustration and inhaled her doggedness back. "First things first—who knows of this?"

"Nobody besides us here," said Kostya confidently.

"All right. This can never leave the room." She took the time to glance at each person present. "No one else should know Sergei cost us the rendezvous. We're a team. Somebody screws up, we cover it as a group. I'll take the blame. A brief press conference stating a mathematical blunder that gave us false hope. If anyone disagrees, now's the time to say so ... good. Because besides the need for compassion—especially since ... the loss in Saturn and given it's Sergei—the disclosure of this to the crew could escalate personal tensions, derailing any plan to save them ... which takes us to the next question: how do we recover from this?"

"Everyone on my team is bringing sleeping bags and we'll work 24/7 until Shack touches down on Titan," said Kostya. "We just talked to SpaceX and working jointly we think it's possible to make the necessary adjustments to their algorithms and to code them into TiTus for an autonomous atmospheric guidance and touchdown without Sergei. There will be a lot of finger crossing but we think there's a decent—well, a probability—of making it down safe ... however, the Grasshopper's role is crucial so its team is also moving in, sleeping bags and all."

"Great. You people are awesome. Okay, what about Caird?"

This time a hush fell over the Control Room again. Nitha looked around for Luca, the head of the Caird team. He shook his head heavily.

"No, no, no! There must be a way," said Nitha.

"There's really no way to—to save Derya and Sergei. They run out of oxygen in nine days and, and even if everything goes splendidly with the refueling, they will be dead by the time Shackleton leaves Titan. It's not happening before two weeks. Plus, two to four days to reach them ..."

Nitha swept her stare across the room. "We're all engineers here. You're telling me there's no solution whatsoever? How's that even thinkable? I want each one of you, individually, to tell me it's impossible to my face. Right now."

There was an awkward tumult. Everyone seemed embarrassed and uncomfortable. This was much more than a professional defeat, even beyond their failure to Sophia, Yi, Derya, and Sergei. This was an affront to human ingenuity.

After an inordinate amount of time, when the wretchedness and tension were making the air stifling, an engineer named Andie, one of the older ones, said bashfully, "I think there's a way. We would need to run the numbers and do a bunch of simulations, because, I mean, we're really breaking Caird's propellant piggybank here, but my preliminary analysis," she accommodated her throat, "shows that we can send them ... to the rings—" She stopped after seeing a legion of rolling eyes.

"AND?" urged Nitha.

"The rings, there is, I mean, they are an almost infinite source of frozen water—"

Another engineer interrupted, "You must be shitting me, Andie. You mean they go there and start collecting chunks of ice like watermelon harvesting season?" He shut up as Nitha's glare fell upon him.

"I'm going to summarize—and correct me if I'm wrong," said Nitha. "Andie, are you saying there's enough fuel in Caird to get to the rings?"

"Yes." It was patent by the noise that not everyone bought it. Nitha looked at Kostya for Caesar's thumb up or thumb down. He had been taken by surprise, but after consulting with someone to his side he nodded.

"And that once there," Nitha continued, "they grab some ice from the rings, melt it, and electrolyze the water to break it into oxygen and hydrogen?"

"Yes," Andie replied.

"Then we have an Apollo 13 situation here," said Nitha. "People, we need to figure out how to assemble an electrolyzer from the materials on board Caird."

Having found a potential path forward, a few young engineers seemed to have flipped into brash self-assurance. "Bah, that's elementary school physics," said one.

"Most engineering today only goes up to 19th-century physics—elementary school physics, as you call it—yet that hardly makes it a slam dunk. I can think of two major challenges right off the top of my head," said Nitha. "First, making a safe electrolyzer: in that same elementary school experiment you mentioned, I learned that oxygen plus hydrogen plus spark equals explosion. No bueno. Second, in weightlessness the bubbles of hydrogen and oxygen don't naturally escape from the liquid, which could render the process unviable unless we come up with some sort of centrifugal system to simulate gravity."

There was electricity in the air and some people were boiling over with excitement. Luca and his Caird team asked for permission to leave and go work inside the Caird replica, visible a few hundred feet away from Mission Control's fishbowl.

"Back to Andie," said Nitha. "Assuming we can solve the water and oxygen problem, are you implying there will be a way for Shackleton to rendezvous with Caird on its way out of the Saturn system?"

Kostya took over. "Here's where it may get complicated."

"I think we can manage complexity," said Nitha.

"Even assuming Sophia and Yi recover Shack's methane deficit, we won't really know if it's possible to rescue Caird until Shack exits Titan and we redo the fuel budget for the remainder of the mission. My hunch is that it should be feasible ... making a few concessions."

"Define 'concessions.'"

"Say Shack is able to rescue Caird, then we're only guaranteeing they are able to reach Earth. How they manage, if it can be done at all, to enter and land here is another story entirely."

"Got it, Kostya, but that's tomorrow's problem—Andie, this is brilliant. Anybody have a competing idea?"

None was put forward.

"This is a really big decision. Anybody object to studying the viability of Andie's plan?"

Andie herself raised her hand. Everyone looked confused.

"There's no time ... this necessarily requires canceling Caird's second engine burn. Otherwise this possibility dies."

"When ... is that?" asked an alarmed Nitha.

"Very soon. We have fifteen, thirty minutes tops to call off the engine burn."

Nitha's heart sank. *What if there's another, better, solution?* she thought. This was a life or death quagmire, and the decision needed to be taken immediately, with seriously incomplete information. It was little more than intuition supported by back-of-the-envelope scribbling.

"I need a conscientious vote from all of you. If there is one vote against, we cannot proceed."

63 | W∆TERING HOLE

A day later, September 16 2030. Day 13

HEADING INTO THE RINGS OF SATURN

Enceladus shrank faster than Derya anticipated. Most details were now hidden behind the moon's pristine white shine. *But we, the citizens of Enceladus, know better,* he thought. *Goodnight Moon, good morning rings of Saturn.* The last few hours had been an emotional roller coaster, *one that only seems to go downhill—well, that's not entirely true.* There was a little upward slope when minutes after learning they wouldn't reunite with Shackleton, Derya said, "I guess this is where I start saying goodbye ..."

"How so?" asked Sergei.

"One of us gets to survive," he answered.

"We're in this together. It's both or none." *Wow. Relieving? Yes. Unexpected? You bet. Comrade Lazarev keeps pulling mystery cards out of thin air.* Yet Derya was sullen. *While it's not at all clear missing the rendezvous had much to do with Sergei, it sure as hell didn't help—but I guess you don't taunt Mike Tyson in the ring if you'll be stuck with him in the locker room later.* So, his negativity radiated to the Universe without a clear addressee.

The oppressively restricted communication window between Caird and Earth/Shackleton had burst open. The solitude changed but didn't necessarily diminish, because Derya was realizing the protective shield of the transient nature of their stay had also been blown to pieces. *Our new post may be forever. And like the pact between Faust and Mephistopheles, this contract is rather vague on details.* One thing was certain: unless they suffered an accident, in a few hours Caird would become an oddly shaped but otherwise indistinguishable addition to the nameless trillions forming the legendary rings.

Derya ran mentally through their plight, stopping at starvation. Humans can survive a couple of minutes without air and a few days without water. They would tap into an endless source of water ice, consequently melting and electrolysis would check those two items off. But nourishment was a more complicated case. *A healthy human can live forty-five to sixty-five days with no food, but as with all Freemium services, there's always a catch: only the first month is complimentary. 'Cause once the body finishes feasting on itself, having devoured all fat and then muscles, it's bad guys' prime time.* Unbearably itchy skin rashes. Fire-eating whenever there's the unavoidable swallowing. Unceasing diarrhea. Extreme irritability, which in his case seemed to have commenced early.

Ø

"This is rubbish. All a dungheap of lies," shouted Derya. "Did you see the weather forecast the Grasshopper has been piecing together since it landed? Titan's northern hemisphere is heading into a months-long storm—why are you smiling? That's where Shackleton's heading right now! Know what that means? I can think of at least four ways in which we are screwed. Shackleton descending the disturbed, turbulent atmosphere with toddlers at the wheel! A magic wand makes us survive that one; then on landing the wind topples the spaceship over! We magically survive that one too; then with a seventh of Earth's gravity imagine the size of the wind-induced waves … and we are splashing down on the shores of a methane ocean!"

"Refueling Shackleton requires loading hundreds of tons of methane. If they are not directly on top, it's like filling a swimming pool with a syringe," said Sergei.

"Precisely."

"So, what's your alternative?"

"There is no alternative. That's my whole point. We are bloody ruined. Look at us, mate. Days—no—hours ago we were seated on top of an ocean. We could have opened an oxygen refueling station had we wanted to. Now we're spending all our fuel to get to a cemetery of ice blocks."

"Cemetery?"

"You're so ingenuous. Almost childlike," said Derya. "We are gazelles going into a watering hole at the end of a dry summer. Crocodiles, lions, death in one hundred different shapes, silently awaiting. We hit one of the infinite chunks of ice rubble in the rings, we die. A single spark during electrolysis, we die. We will receive Hulk-inducing levels of radiation, courtesy of Saturn's magnetic field … and throw in for free mentally enduring two more weeks inside this cage. With you."

"You're starting to sound suicidal."

"Funny you should say that."

"I'm recovering."

"How so?"

"Take and rub some of my optimism on your face. You might even smile. We will touch the rings of Saturn. Isn't that worth dying for?"

64 | THE BLΛCK HOLE

Hours later

HEADING INTO TITAN

Sophia was trapped inside her stormy mind, her consciousness folded inward. She glided from the flight deck to Bacchus seeking a distraction—any distraction. The room was dressed as Cracow's rynek, its lively 13th-century main square on a summery evening. *Maybe this will work*, she thought, trying to be optimistic. But the illusion broke when she noticed a series of burnt out pixels in the sky above one of Saint Mary's gothic towers. She spotted more areas. *They look like termites eating up the last remains of normalcy.* It made her feel ever more distant from everything she held dear.

Escaping to her room, she stopped by the Observation Window searching for home in panic. *Thank God.* She found the blue speck in the distance and with it, some refuge. *Please, Mother Earth, help me. Embrace me. Comfort me.* Looking fixedly, she grew uneasy. *Something's not right. Where's its companion?* It was the second time she had this impression in less than a day, and the first time had turned their lives upside down. *And where's the Sun?* The realization that she was looking at Neptune, at the opposite direction to Earth, and at the infinity beyond the Solar System threw her back into a nightmarish landscape of desperation. The pulses and reverberations of despair were like the sound of night creatures, always there if you paid enough attention. The memory of Jimmy was a barbed nail, gashing her temples.

There's a hole right under my toes, inviting surrender. Her body was exhausted and her mind felt like it had been hit by a speeding train. Yi's tranquilizer pills were looking at her seductively. *But it's deceit. If I surrender, the hole will become a vortex with no escape.*

I'm the commander—yes, the commander of a ship with a single sailor—if I give up our fate is sealed—and if you don't, the result will be the same. Why fight it? 'Don't fail, make this count' flashed through her mind. *But he's dead—no, not his memory—he's dead. He isn't looking at you down from a high place. He just stopped existing.*

She forced herself to fly toward James' hatch. It unlocked with a clean clack. She entered his cabin feeling like a burglar. *You haven't even had the decency to reach out to Belinda—I can't! Not yet—Belinda! Your friend.* She knew what she had come for, the book, but couldn't avoid glancing around. And then she saw something totally unexpected Velcroed to the side of James' bed. And she also knew exactly what it was and what it meant. Belinda had once shown her a picture of a smiley 8-year-old James in baggy white jeans, lime green shirt, and his dad's oversized chainsaw helmet, failing to imitate the Buzz Lightyear action figure he held in his hand staring back at him hands-on-hips.

Sophia glided to his bed and grabbed the toy. She pictured the young James spending the entire summer running around outside or gobbling lunch, always in the company of Buzz. *You're a war veteran.* The enamel around the sound buttons had rubbed off, none of them worked anymore, one wing was missing, and the left leg was bandaged in a Campbell's chicken noodle soup sticker.

"What's going on, Tweety?" she said, mimicking Buzz Lightyear.

"Nothing, Buzz—it's just that I'm very scared. I have so much weight on my shoulders. And look at me! I'm tiny." Tears beaded around her eyes. "I don't know what to do—I can't fail Jimmy, but I also don't have the strength to fight. Where—how did you summon the nerve to step out of the Eagle?"

"Hold on, Tweety. You're mixing up your heroes here. I'm no Aldrin, I'm a Lightyear." She chuckled and rubbed the tears from her eyes. "I know one thing though. You came to Saturn, which can only mean the Force is already with you—and if you need proof, read that book."

Sophia got closer until the book was a foot in front of her. She had heard about it from James many times but had never seen it. *His talisman.*

The hard cover was made of black cloth with letters and an intricate Endurance drawing on silver gilt. It was worn out, particularly the corners and spine, but instead of appearing decrepit it gave the book nobility, magnified by the musty smell. *South: The Story of Shackleton's Last Expedition 1914–1917.* This recounted the same expedition but it was different from the late-50s bestseller they all had to read as per James' request. At the bottom of a first page missing the upper third it said "Published March 1 1919, First Edition." The next made explicit what she should have guessed: the account of one of the greatest struggles of man against nature, told by one Ernest Henry Shackleton. At the bottom half, the start of each word was thick and stern, but the blue ink handwriting was balanced and sparse. "To my dear friend Giles. Your struggle may seem opposite, but the rival—adversity—is one and the same. Do not surrender to the inner demons. Keep waging battle and you will soon prevail. Yours truly, E.H. Shackleton, June 1920."

As she scanned through the pages, she saw some paragraphs highlighted by Jimmy. "The temperature was not strikingly low as temperatures go down here, but the terrific winds penetrate the flimsy fabric of our fragile tents and create so much draught that it is impossible to keep warm within. At supper last night our drinking water froze over in the tin in the tent before we could drink it. It is curious how thirsty we all are."

"Huge blocks of ice, weighing many tons, were lifted into the air and tossed aside as other masses rose beneath them. We were helpless intruders in a strange world, our lives dependent upon the play of grim elementary forces that made a mock of our puny efforts." The black-and-white photos were bewitching. The last big push, Shackleton and five others aboard James Caird, crossing the most treacherous, tempestuous ocean in the world in an open boat for fifteen harrowing days. She felt the cold cutting through flesh, saw the mountainous waves chasing them down, tasted the salty water splashing on their faces, the ever-looming threat of starvation. *And yet they made it. All of them.*

Jimmy had highlighted a quote, "Loneliness is the penalty of leadership." She was the ship's commander. Direct in the line of succession of two of the most eminent explorers in history. *Seemingly impossible odds do not dictate history, only inform it.*

65 | TWILIGHT ZONE

A day later, September 17 2030. Day 14

THE RINGS OF SATURN

From their height, the A Ring resembled a behemoth vinyl record being inspected up close through a magnifying glass. Each spiral groove was colored slightly different from its siblings. Going a few hundred spirals in or out, the colors transited from dark gray to light cream, but not always incrementally. Wide areas of fair colors were interspersed with dark, and vice versa. Being the second largest and densest after the B Ring, it seemed carved out of a single piece of material.[30]

Derya's wowing had become perennial as he witnessed the mysterious balancing of gravity that harnessed and safeguarded the rings over unfathomable timescales. He could visually spot forces being triggered seemingly out of nowhere, propagating through the rings. He saw jumbo waves traversing huge sections of the A Ring and splashing at its edge into vertical walls taller than mountaintops on Earth. He saw shepherd moons hurling particles thousands of miles in front and behind their wake. He saw particles clumped together into thick islands dozens of miles across, suddenly blasting apart. He saw clouds of dust kicked up in impacts between space debris and the rings. From all this it was natural to infer the ruthlessness of the rings against dissent—a chunk of ice altering the order being quickly smacked by others until its random motion

---

30   *But acting assuming that would be fatal*, thought Derya. Already in 1859, James Clerk Maxwell—responsible for unifying electricity, magnetism, and light, widely considered to be the third greatest physicist of all time—had used his formidable powers to deduce and demonstrate that Saturn's rings could not remain stable if made of unbroken solid or liquid. *Meaning they're made of countless particles, each independently orbiting the giant.* The particles are 99.9 percent pure water ice and the rest are the impurities that explain the wide color gamut of the rings. The particles range from the size of tiny marbles to the size of mountains, but the overwhelming majority sits between half an inch and four inches. *And yet, the particle density is such that they behave as a fluid.*

dissipates back into submission. *Theirs is a Roman legion constantly in motion and incessantly under attack.*

Orbiting Saturn cheats its gravitational attraction by speeding around it. The closer to the giant, the stronger the gravity and the faster one must rotate.[31] *If Caird was heading straight to Saturn, a collision with an outlier ring particle would be like a head-on car crash at 1,000 times the speed limit.*

But Caird was floating 200 miles above the ring plane, moving from the outside toward the outer edge of the A Ring. Instead of cutting straight through the rings, the spaceship was converging into a circular orbit around the giant planet, approaching the speed and direction of the rings below. This didn't neutralize the risk, which is why they were descending into the rings in steps, scrutinizing before committing to the next drop. And it was why they wouldn't station for their night amid the A Ring but in the twenty-six-mile-wide Keeler Gap within.

Shackleton wouldn't approach Caird and the rings of Saturn for over a week—*if ever*—so Derya had plenty of time for contemplation. *Yesterday's urgency is today's wait.*[32]

Ø

Derya glanced at Sergei. Even he appeared to be moved by the wonder and strangeness before them. The A Ring rim border seemed cut by a scalpel, delineated against the blackness beyond. *Keeping the outward creep in check is a work of precision and love, done by the action at a distance of a confederation*

---

31 The inner edge of the D Ring and the outer edge of the A Ring, the closest and furthest of the main rings, travel around Saturn at 14.7 and 10.1 miles per second respectively.

32 Five hours later, having dropped to thirteen miles above the ring plane and closing in on the outer edge of the A Ring, any preconceptions about coming near to the moon Atlas flew out of the window. *Bye-bye Sergei's landing delusions,* thought Derya. The sight was unforgettable even by Saturnian standards. Discovered in 1980 in a corner of one of Voyager 1's images, the closest Cassini ever got in its thirteen years exploring the Saturn system was an Earth away, managing a few high-resolution pictures and no video footage. Until today.

Atlas was some 120 miles ahead of Caird, floating in space while almost grazing the ring's border. *If it wasn't twenty-five miles too big, you could have confused it with a flying saucer prop from a 1950s B-movie set.* Gazing at it, it was evident to Derya that the baptism by astronomers was sheer poetic license: the moon's chaotic orbit stumbling around the dark did not agree with holding the rings on its shoulders like its namesake, the Greek god Atlas, held the sky above the Earth.

of moons, including Atlas, Prometheus, Pandora, Janus, Epimetheus, and Mimas. Derya wasn't stunned by that anymore, though, but what he saw a few miles inside. *The rings are marvels of balance between their immense width and their paper-thin height. Just not here*, thought Derya. The otherwise perfectly flat rings abruptly turned into a coastal ridge of dead vertical, fluffy peaks looming as high as ten Eiffel Towers stacked on top of each other. Walls of icy rubble casting long, slithering shadows over the endlessness of the ring plains below. Caird went past just a few miles above them. When they did, Derya experienced an absurd but very real fear of heights. *This makes the Wall in* Game of Thrones *look like a track and field hurdle. And a small one at that.*

∅

Some forty minutes later, Caird was suspended 2,000 feet above the ring plane. Derya saw nightfall racing toward them in a windshield wiper motion across the rings. The rays of light hid behind Saturn, yet this was a darkness much different from that on Earth. The ring glare gradually faded to night and its golden hue became the milky white of moonlight. No twilight and no black night. His eyes followed the speeding shadow slicing the great ring expanse beyond while avoiding catching sight of the huge orb towering above them all. *There can be no competition*, he thought. *This is the most magnificent sight I'll ever see.*

"This is likely the most spectacular view in the Solar System," said Sergei.

"Fools seldom differ," answered Derya. He kept trying to discern the granularity of the rings for the first time in history, but it was too dark and they were likely still too high.

Before them laid the Keeler Gap. For extra safety they would move Caird a few miles inside it, which they had confirmed through radar as well as visually to be devoid of ring particles.

"Shall we move to our new zip code until—and if ever—Shack tries to rescue us? Tomorrow is harvesting season and I need to sleep well and long before it begins," said Derya.

∅

I should go to bed now, Derya thought while watching Sergei snore. *Bed?* Caird was not only missing beds, it also butchered the going-to-sleep ritual. Brush teeth, swallow the toothpaste, close your eyes. *Sleep?* He was overdosing on pain medication and sleeping pills, yet 'a good night's sleep' was still beyond his horizon.

He stared through two opposing windows. They had already dropped to ring plane height and both ring shores were clearly visible. It was a peaceful, dreamy spectacle. *The perks of sailing the dark waters of the Acheron, separating the realm of the living from the underworld.*

Tomorrow after breakfast they would carefully move back to one of the ring shores to attempt collecting ice from the inexhaustible assortment in all shapes and sizes, to melt into water and cook into oxygen.

66 | THE HARVEST

Derya stared at the nutrition bar with contempt. "I can no longer trick this throat into passing down the soap bar, and then scrubbing its starchy excrement texture with fruit-flavored powder juice. I'm done with this breakfast, now and in general—feel free to steer Caird."

Since arriving at the rings Caird had pointed in the direction of their rotation, west to east, same as all planets in the Solar System—a relic from the spinning hot gas cloud that formed it all. Now, Sergei rotated the spaceship ninety degrees to approach the ring shore.

Derya was the first to sense the soaring shadow and his instinct fused his hand to a rail while letting a shriek loose. Sergei turned over.

The vision was a geometrical upheaval seemingly cheating the laws of physics. About to reach them, the smooth flat rings had folded into the phantasmagorical vertical waving of a planet-sized magic carpet, some of its crests miles above them, some troughs deep under the ring plane. The flapping was in slow motion, as if certain that no matter what Caird did, the impending doom was no longer avoidable.

It was *Alice's Adventures in Wonderland*, a world of absurdity resembling reality by traces of believability. Like prey hypnotized by the rhythmic rocking of a cobra, Sergei stared at the reality-bending source of all this, a giant rock cruising in the middle of the Keeler Gap yet barely using a fourth of the cleared highway, floating unhurriedly as it advanced toward them.

Derya was curled into a ball, moaning like a newborn from twitching his broken ribs. "—DO ... SOMETHING—"

♄

Sergei finally disentangled his own stupefaction. *It's Daphnis, Saturn's smallest satellite,* he reasoned. It had been on their heels since the day before. *But without a rearview mirror, we couldn't see it.*

"It appears to be getting closer but it's an optical illusion," he said. Derya's panicky, bloodshot eyes did not seem relieved, whenever they weren't squeezed shut by the pangs of abdominal cramps. "It's all good."

Daphnis, hardly five miles in diameter, managed to clear the gap from all debris. A vacuum cleaner operating on force fields. *Come to think of it, size is relative. An asteroid this size obliterated the dinosaurs 66 million years ago. Sitting it on Earth's surface would require cruising commercial airplanes to alter their course to prevent collisions.*

Ø

As they closed in on the A Ring coast, its solid-looking nature became gradually diffuse. *Yet transparent it's not*, thought Derya. The Sun glared off of the ring on one side and scarcely three stories in length later, the light escaping out the other side dropped to 1/100 and its color transmuted from whitewash to blue tinge.

When Caird got within 1,000 feet, it became clear to Derya that the poaching wouldn't be hassle-free. Individual particles jumped out of the ring thickness like a flea infestation on a dog's coat.

"If this is how the rings behave ..." said Derya. Both stared through the windows. "If we can see the catapulted stones from here, it means they're large and it means it's a battlefield down there."

As they got a few hundred feet closer, the swarming trebled. *Bees protecting the hive. And we're the lame fruit fly busybody—one kiss from a refrigerator-size particle is all it would take for us to go belly-up.*

"What now, boss?" said Derya.

"We spy."

They spent the morning analyzing the frequency, size, and jumping height of the outliers, assessing the probability of getting hit and the speed plus magnitude of the impact. The results were dreadful.

Caird drifted away from Daphnis by moving forward inside the Keeler Gap, with the hopeful or hopeless expectation that the frenetic activity was influenced by the moon. *If not, checkmate.*

Ø

It was. The ring shore eventually calmed down.

As they got closer and closer, the ring edge turned into a semi-transparent white ocean floating in outer space. The sunny side sparkled with untold diamonds, making it easy to spot the rare outlier. They soon heard the first clang against Caird's hull quickly followed by many more, but the intensity was that of a hailstorm drumming on a car. In fact, being inside the ring morphed it into a low-visibility snowstorm of fluffy snowballs.

We've just bought an extension on our termination date, thought Derya. *We are not dying in this ocean, at least not of thirst just yet.*

When three-quarters of an hour later the hatch opened, Derya leaned out but couldn't muster the presence of mind to follow Sergei, even after the other started giggling and was soon laughing contagiously, a chortle that reminded him of his niece, the innocent early-age glee of discovering the world.

The Ruski exited as a poor Santa with an empty sack and came back a rich snowman. Sergei floated back inside the capsule covered in woolly white, particles sticking all over his spacesuit.

Ø

That night they had guests over their house. Three ice blocks floating inside an improvised impermeable bag. They looked the same as any on Earth: mostly clear with minor impurities. *No major surprises here. H_2O is H_2O in this galaxy or the next*, thought Derya.

Once the melting started, they would supplement their diet with extraterrestrial water. It wasn't clear the exact mass of the harvest but assuming 300 pounds of ice and using two-thirds of that for water splitting would get them 180 pounds of oxygen. *Enough to survive for a couple more weeks. One less thing to worry about, 1,000 more to go.*

"'For once you have tasted flight you will walk the Earth with your eyes turned skywards, for there you have been and there you will long to return,'" quoted Sergei. "Leonardo da Vinci. And a century later came the great man that forged their future and made our present. How do you think Galileo would have reacted if someone had told him that one day humanity would extend its arm and touch the very thing he discovered through his telescope? We have touched the stars!"

"And starting tomorrow, we'll drink them," said Derya. *Bravo, Sergei. That was a strong deviation from an entire life dedicated to servicing the art of the monosyllable.* After weeks living secluded together in a space so small he could hear Sergei's neurons synapse, Derya had become convinced any intimate conversation with him was off-limits. *But something's going on.* Sensing the vault half open for the first time since he had known Sergei, he said, "Can I ask what's going on? I feel something happened to you. It's about Iman, isn't it?"

But Sergei didn't acknowledge the question, verbally or physically.

They had a silent dinner. Derya's contentment withered. Their kinship was his invention. A delusion.

And then he experienced a spine-chilling vision. There was no blood and guts about it. It was worse. It was the sinister silence and desolation after that last candle of hope called Shackleton had been extinguished. They would be floating much as they were now, but it would be over. Each of them the executioner of his own destiny, choosing his way to die. He thought in dread about those last hours when there would be nothing left to say. When the last strand of human interaction would have passed. When each one would await for Death to impart its judgment. Not five feet from each other, yet divided by a gaping chasm.

Ø

"Something happened on Enceladus ... can't put it into words," said Sergei in a soft, meditative voice. Derya felt a rising tide of joy. "Her presence ... it engulfed me. Iman was there, embracing me." Sergei sounded to Derya as though he was deciphering an old manuscript for the first time, hitting the right words but not quite sure of what they meant. "She forgave me. I don't deserve it and never will, but she did ... it felt like a gust of crisp mountain air after holding my breath since ... the acci ... since her death. This may be impossible in your astrophysical Universe, and there's nothing tangible to show, but it happened. I know it did."

"The Standard Model of cosmology," said Derya, "our best theory so far, says that out of the total mass-energy of our Universe barely 5 percent is ordinary matter with the remaining 95 percent comprised of dark matter and dark energy, two phenomena we haven't the faintest clue about. We don't even know what or where they are. As for the ordinary matter, weighing all visible stars and gas inside galaxies—the matter we can interact with—hardly gets us to 10 percent of the 5 percent ... then when 99.5 percent of our Universe remains not just unexplained but completely out of bounds, when we're still so far from the absolute truth, well, that was an astrophysicist's abridged way of saying, what do I know? Can I ask how you're doing? And ... were you ... suicidal?"

"I lost count of the times I prepared to commit suicide. I decided to do it as a spacewalk ..."

"Why?"

"To spare you from dealing with a corpse on board."

"Well, that's considerate … and what kept you from doing it?"

"The four of you. I didn't deserve to live, but you don't deserve to die. We depend on each other. The torture did not free me from duty … so I tried to stay afloat amidst the stormy sea of my mind. Waves of depression set out to drown me, sometimes a dozen times a day. They would viciously seize and drag me to the bottom. I survived in part by being knocked unconscious most of the day with drugs, but mostly by finally confronting the truth. It's counterintuitive: by diving into the wave like surfers do, you dodge its aftermath. But it meant facing up to what I did. It's impossible to describe …"

As Sergei's words dried up, Derya took over. "It's a prison where you're both the prisoner and the captor … it's a cathedral of shadows that veils time: a day morphing into months and weeks spanning hours … it's a traitor that poisons your memories and drains the present into a perennial sepia … it's your worst enemy, living inside the one part of your body you can't sever … it's the moment your will to live is conquered by your desperate search for relief."

Sergei looked baffled as he asked, "How do you know?"

"I know a thing or two about dark places, having nosedived deep inside one. See, before the Arcturus breakthrough I had a falling out with my own life: disowned by my family, scarcely any friends left, my career as a physicist in tatters. And one day I caught my fiancée cheating on me—in our own bed. My meltdown happened right as the university where I taught ended its academic year. I stayed in bed for weeks, comatose, unable to really sleep, barely eating, mulling over the dead end of my existence. Until one rainy day I put on some clothes, went to a pharmacy, and bought a double-edged razor blade. Coming back, my survival instinct raked my feverish head for something, anything, to justify living. Lying in bed defeated, I decided to give myself some resemblance of pleasure before my final act. I played my favorite record, the Brahms second piano concerto with Emil Gilels, Eugen Jochum, and the Berliner Philharmoniker. What came out of the speakers was rubbish. That was the final nail. I could no longer even enjoy something that used to be so dear—I thought about writing a note, but to whom? I had no one."

Derya noticed the moist redness in Sergei's eyes. "I rested the blade against the jugular but couldn't force my arm to cut. 'You're not only a wreck but a coward,' I kept provoking myself. But it was the unbearable agony of being alive that did it. I put the blade on my left arm, resting it below the elbow joint, and drove down until it touched the bone. The blood came gushing along with acute pain, but I felt I wasn't dying fast enough so I somehow grabbed it again with trembling fingers and extended the cut. I felt the electrical impulses in my arm getting short-circuited. The white sheets soon became a red halo around me. I was surprised at the blood's thickness as it coagulated. I put my head down and closed my eyes. My mind started quieting down, finally finding peace as life ran out of me. When that cunt … my former partner, Karl … opened the door I remember his muted screams but mostly my disbelief and disappointment. I had been so close, minutes away … I crawled back into recovery, relearning to walk through life."

"Why didn't you tell me this before?"

"Sophia and I were terrified of you, waiting for the rampage. I thought your soul was unreachable—that's an alternative way of saying I didn't think you had one."

"How did you manage to trick the mission's recruiters? It's as much ground for disqualification as missing all four of your limbs."

"I suffered a terrible barbwire accident a few days after learning about Shackleton," said Derya, as he showed a scar running erratically around the circumference of his left forearm.

Sergei guffawed with his big, loud register for the first time since Derya knew him, and he followed right after.

"You have some balls, man," said Sergei.

"They never produced enough testosterone for Father's liking, though … mate, I'm telling you all this because the roots of our depression are different but the solutions to fight it tend to be common. Depression hasn't made you fallible, it has reminded you of what it means to be human. It's spirit-crushing but if you survive, it can be your best teacher. It leaves no choice but to revise, rethink, and reorganize your life."

"The grief I felt when our child—my life's path had always been clear and then I found myself lost in a black forest. We tried so hard for so long, and when it finally worked and then he died—well, I blamed her. That unborn child who was becoming the center of our existence suddenly turned into an irreparable chasm branded in the soul. When she needed me most …"

"When you confess all your sins, you realize there aren't that many."

"Two capital ones is all it takes. I killed everything I loved."

"And you hit the bottom, the pit of your life. Now—now you are ready to commit to the second half. You have been forgiven and get to have a second chance. Honor your wife and son by making the best out of what you have left."

There was a new silence in Caird. A silence of communion. Simple, unassuming happiness.

Maybe it's the soothing peace preceding some form of death, like hypothermia, thought Derya. *The merciful cherubim masking the horror of death beneath hills of white flowers—so be it, Death be damned.* "I don't care about alien life anymore," he said, "I have found life where I thought there could be none … in you."

67 | TITΛNIC WINDS

Six days later, September 24 2030. Day 21

TITAN

The fuzzy pale orange ball of the past few days had become a looming Titan. Shackleton was past the point of no return: whatever happened would happen within its towering atmosphere, ten times taller than Earth's.

Seated and strapped alongside Sophia at the flight deck, Yi stared in both awe and alarm at the unfolding spectacle. Blackness became dark blue, moss green, and finally dusky yellow as smog shrouded their invisible gateway behind them. He remembered Nitha's voice message. *Characteristically optimistic and predictably bullshit-proof. Keep expectations low, in so many words.* The probability of success was unknown, but it wasn't good. Yi could already feel the mounting friction of the atmosphere against the spaceship. *If it survives entry intact, it will need to stick a landing within a sixty-foot radius. If it hits the bullseye, the sea's composition is anybody's guess. And if it deviates more than a dozen or so percentage points from pure methane ...* But whatever his rational mind told him, his heart betrayed.

The intercom went live again. Sergei's voice said, "Good luck crew ... do not give up." Shackleton and Caird would be in open mic for as long as feasible. There was a chance, even accounting for the four-second delay each way, that Sergei could prove decisive. *"Do not give up,"* a forewarning coming from one of the most undaunted humans alive. Unfortunately for them, Titan, like Venus, is a super rotator. *An appellation that soils underwear upon sole mention.* Its upper atmosphere rotates much faster than its surface.

The screen in front of them showed a globe map of Titan, with Shackleton connected through a dotted line to a triangle thousands of miles ahead, 500 miles below. That triangle was the Grasshopper, functioning as a tracking device to guide Shackleton's main computer and make the high-precision autonomous landing possible. *Likelier.*

Yi tensed his muscles as the structural tremors worsened. *The marathon has begun.* His harness was overly taut. *Too late to seek comfort.* The acceleration pressed him tighter against the seat.

"241 miles above the surface, 12,700 miles an hour," said TiTus, immune to body punishment.

For the next ninety seconds the strain became excruciating. Yi felt a steamroller squashing every cell in his body. He soon became frantic when he could no longer inhale. His chest seemed to be compressing his lungs. *There must have been a glitch on the entry gradient.* When his eyeballs went from being shoved against his eye sockets to someone jabbing fingers against them, the flash of pain made him black out.

⌀

Sophia regained consciousness and noticed her body hyperventilating. Her mind shut down but the body kept clinging to life. The pressure gluing her body to the seat eased. The screen said 134 miles of altitude and 1,140 miles per hour. *We've survived atmospheric entry!*

A familiar noise became pervasive. Outside air rushing against the hull. External sound had been reborn, finally able to find enough atoms to propagate for the first time since they left Earth.

The sprint now over, Shackleton was unceremoniously thrown inside a churning washing machine.

⌀

Shackleton had become a plunging penguin. Before, it behaved as a ballistic missile, its speed so great that any atmospheric disturbance was imperceptible. Having erased most of the speed made it prey to air perturbation. Never an airplane, its lack of proper wings precluded gliding or negotiating turbulence. The spaceship's terminal velocity on Earth, the outcome of gravity against air friction, borders 300 miles per hour. Titan's gravity is a seventh and the air is 50 percent denser than Earth's, which slashes this to around fifty miles per hour. *The good news,* thought Yi, *is we can jump out without a parachute and perhaps survive impact. The bad is what happens when our puny terminal velocity interacts with the super rotating upper atmosphere of Titan.*

The jolts became swift and savage, accelerating Yi's body forward one moment, leftward the next. *This is what Sergei meant by "do not give up."* Nothing could have prepared them for what was about to come. There was no preparation possible, physical or mental. His spatial sense disintegrated. Focusing on the screen became an ordeal. He fixed his sight long enough to read 'WIND SPEED: >250 mph.' He saw in the corner of his eye Sophia vomit on a tug so hard it traveled horizontally before splattering against the hull.

Yi was losing touch with his surroundings, his head drugged by the mercurial acceleration. He tried to concentrate on the screen and when he managed to capture a mental screenshot, the letters and numbers rotated inside his head like a runaway carousel. *No! No! No!* His mind trying to forget what it just deciphered. "ALTITUDE: 106 MILES." At their falling speed it would take three hours before they crossed the sixty-mile mark, the point where the Huygens probe detected wind speeds under 120 miles per hour during its legendary descent in 2005.

On his last moments of lucidity, Yi looked at Sophia. Even strapped tight to her seat she had become a crash test dummy, her limbs moving aimlessly around.

Ø

THE RINGS OF SATURN

Far within the rings, at a distance three times that between the Earth and the Moon, Sergei stared at the data log coming from Titan, deeply worried. The problem wasn't Shackleton's vertical but its horizontal speed. The violent westerly winds, times the low gravity, times the thick air, were drifting the spaceship over four feet east for each foot of vertical drop. The upper boundary from all simulations done on Earth was 2.3 to 1. *The Grasshopper meteorological reports are right*, he thought. *There's something brewing in Titan's atmosphere.*

Under different circumstances the straying would have been tolerable. Huygens itself was designed for touchdown on any type of land or liquid due to the impossibility of anticipating Titan's atmosphere, which kept the landing precision radius in the thousands of miles. This time the atmosphere was better understood but the wind prediction had gone seriously off. *But the mandatory landing site cannot be changed, and neither can its unforgiving sixty-foot radius high-precision touchdown.* The wind was creating a massive flight path deviation that would soon kill any hope of salvation.

"What can we do, Sergei?" begged Derya, fixated on the data meters and graphs on Caird's long, rectangular display. "We were trying to stick a landing comparable to—to Robin Hood hitting a target from across the English Channel. Now we must do it while riding on top of a unicycle."

"There's only one way out: down."

What Sergei was about to ask Shackleton had never been attempted, or possibly even imagined, in the history of spaceflight, manned or unmanned.

68 | TOUCHDOWN

Minutes later

Sophia's mind was a current drifting between mental states: bobbing in the void; trapped inside febrile nightmares; or in a low-level consciousness. In the latter, the distant clattering of the spaceship was drowned out by the sedative howl of wind, yet now an insistent tin drumming kept calling her attention from her torpor. She forced herself into a higher state of awareness and the price was immediate, searing pain. *Where am I?*

"SHACKLETON, OVER———KLETON, OVER–SHACKLE—"

Her crumbled sense of reality began putting pieces together. *Are ... are we ... falling?*

"—MINUTES BEFORE———FAIL—YOU MUST—"

Sergei. The static made it an impossible word game puzzle. *Sergei shouting ... not normal.*

She was being tempted to go back where she came from, to stumble back down the rungs of consciousness. Guilt arm wrestled against her lost will. It took a monumental effort to supersede her rogue instinct, and then to force words out of her mouth. She finally managed to answer back to Caird.

Sergei's intermittent voice came back, "———don't have time—override —TiTus——"

She barely understood each word and couldn't possibly connect them into a coherent sequence. About to give up, James' last words flared in her mind, 'Don't fail. Make this count,' with an adrenaline rush right behind them.

⌀

Two days before, Shackleton had received a tiny file that a large team had been working on since the accident. It carried a set of differential equations packaged into a repurposed algorithm derived from SpaceX's nearly flawless high-precision autonomous rocket-landing track record. Four lives and the most important discovery in history depended on mathematics that fit on one side of a sheet of paper.

Shackleton had a simple-to-describe, wickedly-hard-to-execute challenge: how to get to the landing target without running out of fuel. The spaceship was being tossed around by the atmosphere, constantly altering its position and speed, therefore continuously changing the problem's solution. The Grasshopper worked as a beacon to calculate the vertical position and velocity with respect to the ground.[33]

Ø

Override!? She partially understood the instructions but they seemed stolen from a Dr. Seuss story: jingly and nonsensical.

"—OVERR——LANDING ALGORITHM——DRIFTING——— FIRE DOWNWARD"

Sergei's instruction required breaching the preset limits of the autonomous atmospheric guidance algorithm. Burning fuel to accelerate downward was outside its parameters because it had never made sense before. Except now it did. Shackleton would miss the target unless she, the commander, verbally instructed TiTus to follow Sergei's orders.

The ship's shaking was dragging her back to unconsciousness. She kept trying and failing to give an intelligible order for system overrule but her body, the lateral yanking, and dwindling awareness made her mouth slur as if drugged by excess Margaritas and dental anesthesia.

She yelled the words in a last attempt as she slipped into a black hole.

Far off in the remote distance of her shrinking cognizance, she felt an abrupt thrust stronger than all the others.

Ø

Two hours later, Sophia opened her eyes, trying to focus past the internal earthquake and nauseating migraine—which could only trigger painful gags and abdominal cramps after already having scattered all her stomach contents around the flight deck. *We made it. We made it? We made it! Past an Ironman triathlon followed by a thrashing from a mob of hooligans.* The wind was steady and smooth.

---

33   This created a three-dimensional geometric shape in which mathematical tools first developed in the 1920s by the father of game theory, John von Neumann, were applied to find ultra-high-speed convex optimization to recalculate trajectory-to-target.

She strained to turn in Yi's direction. He seemed to be having a mild seizure. Sophia tried to speak but nothing came out. She stared at the displays and saw that Yi's vitals looked normal.

"ALTITUDE: thirty-nine miles," announced TiTus. "Touchdown in 145 to 147 minutes."

She noticed the mild gravity pushing down her seat. *Shack's falling upright.* She then raised her eyes to the Observation Window and her jaw dropped at the stupefying view before them. An extraordinarily Earth-like, sunset-orange mackerel sky of rather poor visibility, a common smoggy sight to a native Angelino like Sophia. She leaned forward, trying to see below. A herd of wooly cumulus clouds floated a dozen miles beneath them. Her eyes were drawn to a glittering patch in between. *The methane seas of Titan!* They were falling into the only other surface liquid bodies in the Solar System. And then searching for the light source of all this, she saw something to the side of a miniaturized Sun: the hardly noticeable outline of a colossal orb sitting on top of the horizon. Saturn looked like a solar eclipse—as if the Moon's dark silhouette was obscuring the Sun, leaving only a blazing corona around—gashed right through the middle by a flaming slit twice as wide as the planet, the head-on rings of Saturn.

⌀

THE RINGS OF SATURN

"I think we should tell them," said Derya, after quickly considering the pros and cons. "While they sure have enough on their plate, Shack's instruments have been recording all this time and the infrared camera log could give us clues about how quick the storm's moving north."

The Grasshopper weather forecast had been anticipating a months-long storm at the north pole, where the vast majority of the seas and lakes of Titan were concentrated. The massive storm was a regular event documented since the 2010s at the height of the Cassini mission. It incubates in the moon's desert-dry equatorial regions, where moisture eventually funnels it to the poles.

Since Shackleton fell past the atmospheric section of ultra-high winds, the steady fall allowed its antenna to be pointed at the rings and Caird unencumbered. Both crews had spoken and said a preliminary goodbye in case the connection dropped before they talked for the last time. Derya then analyzed the partial weather data arriving from Titan and realized the storm brewing in the equator seemed to be moving out.

"I'm reticent to stress them if we don't strictly need to, but do what you think is right," Sergei said.

Derya spent a few more minutes deciding. "Shackleton, over," he said. But Shackleton was no longer in direct line of sight, having fallen under Titan's horizon and thereby cutting any communication with Caird until and if they ever managed to escape its surface.

I can warn Mission Control. They can relay the message back to Shack—Titan is a huge moon, though, Derya told himself. *There are thousands of miles of safety margin between whatever happens in the equator and its north pole, no? Sergei is probably right.*

∅

TITAN

Yi was now functional enough to communicate in short, sparse phrases. He wished to have been more expressive in his goodbye to Sergei and Derya.

With over an hour before touchdown, he decided to inspect the infrared and radar video feeds obtained in the past few hours side-by-side at high speed. First came the Shangri-La region, the immense plain of dark material where Huygens landed in 2005. Next was the Australia-size Belet region, home to the most spectacular sand dunes in the Solar System. He saw the endless rippling piles of sand rising 1,000 feet over the surrounding landscape, carved and sculpted by ancient winds, belittling their Saharan counterparts. The dunes were contained from the south by a tall, jagged mountain range extending many hundreds of miles. Yi wasn't expecting goosebumps, but a massive cloud stood where the Senkyo region was supposed to be. Kraken Mare, their destination, was a long way directly north. As when spotting the alpha male among lions, he instantly knew he was looking at the megastorm.

I wish we could have consulted with Derya, he thought. *Cocky, but something of a meteorological expert. Drop 'meteorological.'* Derya knew an inordinate amount about an absurd number of subjects. *A walking talking encyclopedia.* The amount of data the two spaceships had traded was a hundredfold what Shackleton could share with Earth, precluding a solid weather prediction from back home.

It was impossible for Yi to guess the time it would take before hell broke loose over the north pole. It could be a day, a week, a month. *Worrying doesn't empty tomorrow of its troubles. Whatever it is, it is.*

Titan is tidally locked: the same hemisphere is always oriented toward Saturn. That makes a Titan day equal to an orbit around the ringed planet at sixteen Earth days long. Shackleton was falling toward the huge body of liquid known as Kraken Mare in the north polar region facing away from the planet. Nightfall would arrive there in three Earth days and linger for another eight. *Plenty of time for refueling*, Sophia thought. *Assuming Shack splashes in the right chemical soup. If we don't ... 'goodbye dear life' will be certain although we have enough supplies to survive for years.* 'We' being Sophia and Yi. The countdown for Derya and Sergei was measured in weeks, on a shoestring. In this scenario it could sound preposterous to imagine a flourishing career as an alien life hunter, but consistent with Nitha's suggestion to keep expectations low, that's what she was doing. It tempered her anxiety. *If there's life on Titan and we can find it, there's enough equipment on board to make some of the grand scientific breakthroughs I won't be making with Enceladus' little fellows.* She got greedy. *If we ace the landing and the sea mix is compatible, the refueling should still allow for some highly conservative, ultra-responsible scouting. Don't get me wrong, I mean just a few humble thousand feet around Shack. Look at it this way, not doing it would be an inconceivable crime. And no, I'm not being hyperbolic. Have something more important to do? Oh yeah? You go ahead and polish your toenails. Anyway, I think we should start by sampling Kraken Mare; then, depending on—*

Yi screamed in Mandarin. *Never a good sign.* "Yi?"

"Look out the window," he said in barely repressed ecstasy.

She did and saw seven miles under them the chaotic drainage network of narrow channels, steep-sided rivers, and wide deltas feeding Kraken Mare, the largest sea on Titan's surface, named in 2008 after the Kraken, the fearsome sea monster from Viking mythology. *Aptly named, at least on account of the rough, Norway-esque coastal topography and proliferation of fjords and archipelagos.*

"Very impressive," she said. Yi stared at her, disappointed. She continued, "Beautiful and ... sooo similar to Earth. No? Okay. Big? Photogenic, maybe? Deep?"

"Look at that cape where the tall coastal range sinks abruptly into the sea, there, on the right-hand side," he said, his voice singing in excitement.

"It seems to be capped by thick, low clouds."

"Yes! No! Tweety, you're watching the plumes spawned by a spewing ... volcano. An ice volcano erupting with slushy lava not of molten rock but water.

You can sort of see its cone and crater, camouflaged by its snowcap. Water snow, isn't that insane?"

"Like—like the type people ski on?"

"Yes! But that's nothing," Yi was yelling by now and even Sophia forgot her extreme fatigue for a little while. "We've finally discovered the long-predicted but never-proven communicating vessel between Titan's exterior and its subsurface salty water ocean. Forget Enceladus! Titan has as of this very moment become a supersized Enceladus in the quest for life, 1,250 times more massive and with a subsurface ocean many times larger than all of Earth's oceans combined!"

Ø

MISSION CONTROL @ HANGAR ONE, CALIFORNIA

Like lighting a firecracker, there was a noticeable delay between the moment when Sophia's exhausted voice popped across the room and everyone burst into applause and hugs. Nitha's own embraces felt like round twelve hugging in a boxing match. Everyone had run themselves into the ground over the last few days. *They made it through the tumble dryer*, she thought. *Next stop, landing.* Mission Control was piecemealing the problem. *Nobody can ever steal this triumph from us—but it's made inconsequential if we fail. And we have zero room for error: every domino is within toppling distance from the rest.* For starters, the landing location was circumstantial, not engineered. The instant the decision to attempt touchdown was made, it was circumscribed to an area barely 0.002 percent of Titan's surface. *Meaning the area within reach for the Grasshopper,* which wasn't only the essential beacon to guide the landing but had also visually inspected the proposed touchdown spots over the last two days. Before the accident the quadcopter had been scouting the mountains near Kraken Mare. If Mission Control had not managed to move it to the coast in the days prior, there would have been no chance of success. And after exhausting its twelve-mile range it took three days to recharge its batteries, which gave a meager strip of coast to choose from. Within that, they had selected the flatter, most consolidated terrain.

Nitha wished to jump in her car and cruise along Highway 101. It never failed to clear her mind. Driving struck her as the quintessential opposite to what they were going through, an obvious path forward requiring nothing beyond reflex decision-making. But that was a luxury beyond reach, so she settled on the women's restroom outside Mission Control. She splashed her face and stared in the mirror. *I've seen better hairstyles.* There were bags under her eyes, dark enough to contrast with her olive skin. They weren't just from overwork and lack of sleep, but the dragging physical pain of James' loss. She hadn't had time to mourn, which was perhaps better for her mental health. Going back to Mission Control, she glanced outside beyond the hangar's giant clamshell doors. The sunlight strained her eyes and it took some time before she could resolve the runway in front and the distant Diablo Range mountains in the background. *Last time I left the hangar ... it's been a week already? No, four nights.* The coming challenges kept bouncing around her mind. *Shack's free fall is only that of a speeding bicycle.* Even so, if it didn't land upright it was over. If it did land upright, Titan's low gravity and dense air make any standing object prone to toppling over by gusts of wind. *And its dimensions, tall and skinny, are particularly vulnerable.* Sophia and Yi would need to immediately attach the spaceship to the ground with improvised cables. *And then we should all get into the habit of praying no freak weather hits during refueling, which given the dimensions of the fuel tank versus the beggarly gauge of the improvised hose will take anything from twelve to sixteen hours.*

When she opened the door to Mission Control, the smell of old pizza and sour milk assaulted her. *Nitha Sharma, Fostering Great Work Environments Since 2026 ®.* She half meant it. *Assuming the landing is spot on, we gain access to the methane lottery.* This was a gamble so uncertain that it wasn't even possible to speculate on the odds. Not only were the overall chemical composition and physical properties of the lakes and seas unknown, they presumably varied from one to the next, possibly even from one shore to another.

The physics of Titan's hydrocarbon cycle, analogous to Earth's water cycle, strongly suggested seas, lakes, and rivers mostly made of methane and ethane.[34] *But that doesn't cut it. A campfire is an easygoing, broad-minded, indulged combustion. It eats almost anything. Plastic. Clothing. Gin. Shoes. The goat of the burning kingdom. Superior performance, high-precision rocket engines are more like pandas: exceedingly finicky.* If Sophia and Yi found a liquid blend deviating just 15 percent from pure methane, engine combustion would suffer. A handful

---

34 The simplest carbon and hydrogen molecule is methane, CH_4. Next is ethane, C_2H_6. Then propane C_3H_8. And butane C_4H_{10}. Further up the hydrocarbon ladder, C_5H_{12} to C_8H_{18} makes gasoline; C_9H_{20} to $C_{16}H_{34}$ diesel, kerosene, and jet fuel; over sixteen carbon atoms makes anything from lubricating oil on the low end to asphalt on the upper end. Same two elements, dramatically differing properties and performance.

of percentage points above that and it would fail. And there could be contaminants like nitrogen or argon. *What happens then is like tossing a can full of coins into the air.*

ø

TITAN

A loud, unsettling beep marked the last 1,000 feet. Shackleton was coming down fast. *Much too fast*, thought Yi. *Remember, autonomous landing is not about leisure but extreme fuel efficiency. Throttling down would be fuel-costly and potentially fatal. Large rocket engines are very bad and inefficient at hovering.*

Beep 800 feet.

Instead, the algorithm will make Shack hit zero velocity at exactly zero altitude. Or so we hope.

Beep 700 feet.

If we reach zero too low, Shack will crash and tip over—this thing is moving way too fast.

Beep 600 feet.

If we reach zero too high, it will crash as well. With his eyes focused on a screen showing a camera view pointed at the ground, it seemed to Yi the surface was much closer than 600 feet. *Something has gone wrong.*

Beep 500 feet.

We'll crash! Maybe the landing legs will absorb the load and prevent it from tipping over.

Beep 400 feet.

He tensed his muscles, expecting the hard landing at any moment.

Beep 300 feet.

The ground kept getting closer but touchdown kept getting delayed. Then he saw the shadow.

Beep 200 feet.

He was seeing Shackleton's shadow on the ground, and they were coming in at the wrong angle. *We're not going to make it!*

Beep one hundred feet.

Yi shut his eyes, anticipating the impact. He felt a sudden lateral acceleration as the spaceship self-corrected by pivoting sideways, and opened his eyes just as the legs' outline disappeared under Shackleton's shadow. Instants later, the rocket kissed the ground, and right after a cracking noise boomed from outside the spacecraft. The upright, stationary rocket slanted a few degrees.

"What was that? Sure as hell wasn't splashing," said Sophia.

"Whatever it is, we've made it this far," said Yi in a frail voice, despite his elation.

Fight-or-flight hormones depleted right after shutdown and he experienced an exhaustion like he'd never felt before. Within minutes both had sunk into a stupor. Yi regained consciousness at some indeterminate time later, but the urgency to mobilize wasn't strong enough. He convinced himself they needed to be well rested. *Besides, until we do the methane test, it's probability and not fact. If the news is bad, I'd rather wait to keep the hope alive,* he thought, promptly falling back into a deep sleep.

69 | Δ |ULES VERNE WORLD

A day later, September 25 2030. Day 22

Yi awoke with a bad hangover, a mind still impaired, and a terrible hunger. A bay of placid waters resembling the scales of goldfish greeted him past the Observation Window. The sky was a hazy orange with the brightness of an early twilight. It was as if he wore glasses with a penchant for reds and yellows. The Earth's messages urging attention cut the surveying short. Glancing at the screens on top of their seats, he realized seven hours had passed since landing. Sophia was asleep.

"Captain, Tweety. Come on. Nap time's over. Every minute counts," he said. She didn't speak or open her eyes but did start moving.

It took him a few minutes to gather strength, unbuckle, and step out of his seat. He experienced the startling gravity of Titan, one-seventh of Earth's. Walking was awkward, replaced by hopping.

By the time they read and listened to the messages from Earth, answered back, and fed and suited themselves, another two hours had gone by.

Getting out of Shackleton was comparatively a breeze. The airlock between the two airtight doors no longer required depressurization because the outside was no longer a vacuum. *The atmosphere above us weighs 1.6 times that of sea level on Earth*, he thought in wonder. If the average surface temperature wasn't -290 degrees Fahrenheit and the air had some oxygen to make it breathable, he could have walked around in his underwear. *Indeed, an Everest climber with his breathing mask and in his expedition down suit would survive for as long as his oxygen bottle allows him—assuming he didn't stay still.*

The outside door opened to the world of Titan. *Uncanny. This could very well be the Pacific coast of the Atacama Desert in Chile.* An infant Sun stood timid and low on the horizon. *The land of the setting Sun.* The soupy cloud torrents that they survived high up in the skies were shrouded by murky air, while the first dozen miles above the surface were clear except for thin clouds slithering north in a hurry, which broke the spell for Yi. *I have seen the future. It's nearing from the south and isn't pretty. No time to waste.*

A vertical ladder had mechanically unfolded from the door and ran seventy feet to the ground. He skipped clipping himself to the rail. Falling from up there would sprain an ankle at worst. He descended and landed on the ground by the side of one of the ship's three massive landing legs. He waited for Sophia, inspecting the landing location in the meantime.

"We landed on a slab of ice," said a surprised Yi, while kneeling down and scraping off ice crystals from the surface.

The ice strip, about 150 yards across, extended for miles in both directions, with land on one side and sea on the other. *The material isn't surprising but the location is.* Over 95% of Titan is thought to be composed of water ice and rock.

They walked around the ship to assess its tilt. Yi 'walked' by a mixture of striding and hopping, perfecting his technique with each step. The 14 percent of Earth's gravity, similar to the Moon, felt totally different from the videos of Apollo astronauts. The air, instead of the vacuum of space, turned the experience into something similar to walking at the bottom of a swimming pool. Shackleton was a few degrees from dead vertical. One leg had pierced through the ice and sank to the bottom, past the hydrocarbon liquid.

"Bad for stability, yes. But it left the sea exposed. Now we just need to submerge the hose and start refueling," said Sophia.

"Let me take a liquid sample to figure out whether we're grounded here for life," said Yi.

"The leaning of the ship has left us really exposed to the wind. We need to anchor Shack with cables right away."

Yi was okay with that. *I don't mind it at all.* Delaying the moment of truth, as long as they were doing something useful, was fine by him. Surely Sophia agreed, but he wouldn't ask. He didn't want to sound hopeful. Yi was terrified with the result because he had started to believe they might make it back to Earth after all.

They spent close to three hours anchoring cables from mid-hull to the icy ground. They used the bolts that were intended for a potential Enceladus emergency rescue by the Dragon, now lost for good. Each bolt carried an explosive charge that drove it into rock-hard ice. *A far cry from any peace of mind, but certainly an improvement.*

Right after finishing, instead of fishing for the liquid sample, Yi began inspecting the ice breach around the ship's leg. His heart was pounding. "It's not water ice, but some hydrocarbon ice mixed with nitrogen bubbles," he told Sophia. "Water ice is less dense than liquid water, that's why it floats back on Earth. But it's denser than liquid methane so it would sink here. Did you know that methane freezes at a higher temperature than its liquid state? So, it also sinks in liquid methane, that's where the nitrogen bubbles come in handy ..."

"I think ..."

"Yeah ..." He inhaled deeply and stretched down his right arm while holding the trunk-wide landing leg with his left, dipping the test tube in the crack around Shackleton's leg.

They both stared at it, scarcely the size of a finger, while squatting. *That fluid inside holds the key to salvation ... or else.* Giving the moment its proper importance, Yi looked at Sophia. She nodded hesitantly. He inserted it in the slot of the spectrometer, itself the size of his palm. The principle is simple: flashing a light through the fluid and splitting it at the other end into its color spectrum. Different atoms and molecules have different colors. After a short delay, a small screen flashed displaying the results.

Yi's head got dizzy and he sat down, crushed. Sophia grabbed the device to see for herself and soon sat as well, devastated. There was nothing to say. This was fundamental physics. *There must be something wrong—No! Don't you get it? There's no ground for subjective interpretation.* The reading on the screen was 4 percent ethane, 27 percent butane, and 69 percent methane. *We needed over 80 percent methane. That's it. This is our new home, and somewhere in its backyard is our tomb.*

"Let's sample a few more times," said Yi in an empty voice. Sophia nodded back.

⌀

Back on board, Sophia kept racking her brain for a solution. *We humans are inherent optimists*, she thought. *Give us an impossible bet in anything but name, with a one-in-one-hundred-million chance of winning, and we swarm to buy lottery tickets.* But she was internalizing the vast difference between abysmal odds and knowing you've failed. *We will load the fuel tank anyway and try to start the engines. Maybe miracles do exist ...*

Dinner in Bacchus had the inevitability of the Last Supper.

When Yi stood up to leave, Sophia asked, "Is there any chance we're misinterpreting the results?" Yi shook his head languidly. "What if we sampled incorrectly, somehow?" she insisted. He stood there as if waiting for more suggestions.

Out of nowhere an idea sparked in her head. The four readings had deviated a few percentage points from one another. She flipped from angst to agitation. "Yi. What if … what if—we must go down!"

"What? Why?" said Yi, already carried away by unfounded optimism.

"We skimmed! Don't you see? What if there's a butane film on top?"

Sure enough, some forty minutes later, a belated refueling started.

∅

No time to waste doesn't mean no wasted time, thought Yi. Their biological batteries were replenished but the spacesuits' life support systems needed another 170 minutes.

While waiting they heard the uplifting and moving hurrahs from Mission Control over the intercom, stripped of any science, engineering, or mathematics, but full of raw, infectious humanity. Nitha had great news: the propellant calculations, assuming full recovery of the lost fuel, allowed a rendezvous with Caird at the rings of Saturn before continuing home.

Their side of Titan was a few hours from losing line of sight with Earth, which would make Shackleton incommunicado for a full week or until they exited Titan's atmosphere. As a farewell, Nitha's recorded voice made a heartfelt appeal "to get the hell out of there as soon as humanly possible."[35]

---

35 Two hours before heading out, Sophia the commander was taken over by Sophia the biologist, as she gave Yi a crash course on the speculation of life on Titan.

* * *

Back to the basics of life on Earth. At a biological level, what do animals do? First, ingest organic material and inhale oxygen; later, at a cellular level, the organic material reacts with oxygen, giving us the necessary energy to survive. As waste product, we breathe out CO_2. That's about it. Animal metabolism in a nutshell.

Plants? Ingest our CO_2 and consume sunlight; photosynthesis gives them energy. As waste product, they breathe out oxygen.

That fresh, intoxicating mountain air is pure waste product from algae and plants. Life is a circle: one organism's waste is another's food.

Titan, instead, seems to be the land of the (freezing) free lunch. Methane is broken down by sunlight high in its atmosphere, that's what creates its thick ochre haze. Food is made in the sky and falls back down, manna from heaven. If you are an organism on Titan, or given that Sophia and Yi are spoiling the equation, from Titan, it should be an easy, worry-free life.

What would they eat? Probably something from which they can get as much energy as possible with the smallest possible effort. For instance, acetylene plus molecular hydrogen.

Combine the two, $C_2H_2+3H_2$, and get a nice energy kick and fart two methane molecules, $2CH_4$, as waste product.

As opposed to on Earth, no need to humiliate anyone into inhaling your fumes for lunch. Instead, methane in gas form goes up to be executed by the Sun firing squad, photochemistry. The cycle then restarts. A simpler circle of life.

And here comes the crux of the story: life on Earth changed our planet by producing lots of oxygen in the atmosphere. If life on Titan was widespread, it would reveal its presence by an anomalous depletion of acetylene and hydrogen at the surface, both on land and in the sea.

This was the prediction astrobiologist Chris McKay made in a paper in 2005, published unintentionally on January 13, a day prior to Huygens historic landing on Titan.

Nothing happened until 2010 when two independent studies were published. The first posing the mysterious disappearance of hydrogen near Titan's surface. The second showing unexplained low levels of acetylene on the moon's surface.

* * *

"And?" asked Yi, burning with curiosity.

"And what?" replied Sophia.

"And what happened?"

"Nothing happened."

"But both were perfectly consistent with the hypothesis ..."

"Chris McKay, who was my boss at NASA's Ames Research Center, cautioned there could be other explanations; maybe some unidentified chemical process in action, or maybe flaws in our current models of material flow."

"I don't buy that."

"If this was a claim about anything but this, maybe ... maybe you could have publicized it as the leading hypothesis. But we are talking about the most important enigma in biology. The problem is syllogistic logic: 'shit in, shit out.' No data, no results ... after Huygens stopped transmitting an hour after landing there wasn't any additional information the Cassini mission could extract about Titan. You can't do any of this data capture remotely, the precision required is too high ... humanity would need to wait decades before something lands again on Titan ..."

"Why didn't you tell me this before?"

"Now we need to scoop up some soil and scoop out some goo from the seabed and run the Gas Chromatography Mass Spectrometer on board ... if there's alien life, it should show up in one or both," Sophia couldn't contain her excitement and was delighted at Yi's search-for-Titanian-life infatuation. "What I'm saying is that we don't need to see life to find life."

She marveled at how easily fortunes flip. *Just a few hours ago ...*

The lecture continued.

* * *

Finding life on Enceladus hadn't eclipsed the implications of finding it on Titan. The scientific community is still full of water chauvinists: all the large-scale ongoing investigations of potential exoplanet candidates for life focus on the Goldilocks zone of orbits around a star, where it isn't too hot for water oceans to boil nor too cold for them to freeze. Finding life on Titan's surface would increase the chances of finding life across the galaxy by orders of magnitude. It's much easier to find a world with liquid methane than one with liquid water. It would also mushroom the limits of biochemistry: impossible-to-imagine strangeness, exotic life forms indifferent to liquid water, dependent instead on the truly alien liquid methane environment.

Life has no intrinsic timescale it should follow. Life on Earth has for the most part an hourly or daily metabolism—animals such as humans eat several times a day. Yet life forms living at very low temperatures in Antarctica or the Arctic have much slower metabolisms. And those temperatures are tropical compared to Titan. A single life form could exist for thousands or millions of years, its processes so lethargic it may be impossible to detect.

Titan's atmosphere is thought to mimic early Earth 3.5 billion years ago, before the oxygen build-up era. It is a planet-scale laboratory to study chemical reactions that may have led to life on Earth or that could be occurring on exoplanets around other stars.

And this may be the most tantalizing prospect of Titanian life: finding a universal pathway toward the ingredients of life. Astronomers and the new generation of telescopes coming online could start searching for atmospheric chemistry that betrays the existence of life in other stars, tens or even hundreds of light-years away from us.

70 | HUNTING LIFE

An hour later

t was time to suit up. They walked down Shackleton's central ladder from Bacchus to the cargo area, instead of gliding through as they had done for years. They found themselves quickly adapting to the mild, newfound gravity.

Right before donning their helmets, Sophia restated each of their tasks.

"Yi, you go sample the sea. Remember, at least six independent samples, fifty feet or more from one another. Three scraping the seabed, three from the liquid mass ... I will go for the land samples. Then we switch."

"Again, why switch?"

She grinned. "You've already made yourself a reputation around Titan ... no, really, it would be imprudent, inexcusable not to do so." And as Yi raised his helmet, she finished, "We are to be back on board no later than four hours and ... seventeen minutes from now."

"I still can't see why. We have eight hours of life support in the spacesuits."

"We are not risking getting out of here."

"The refueling will be finished in," he looked at the clock on the wall, "eleven hours—I'm just saying, you're welcome to relax the requirement at any time."

"Searching for life is secondary to saving our lives. I'm pretty sure Derya and Sergei would agree if they could ... Yi, are we on the same page here?"

He nodded passingly but she didn't budge.

"Yes, Commander. Understood," Yi said.

They stormed out for against-the-clock scientific scouting.

Ø

The outside door opened to reveal Titan for the third time, unfolding a landscape of strangeness and majesty. Eight hours had gone by since his first glimpse yet the meek Sun had barely moved a step or two, still within pricking distance from a steep spire-crowned mountain outlined against the saffron orange horizon. Yi gazed at the sky. The clouds racing away from the south had thickened. He felt goosebumps on his arms and the hairs at his nape bristle.

Once back on the ice, they walked in line toward the solid ground. This was mostly rocky, a grooved dark irregular surface with intricate veining. There were light-colored pebbled patches and others of dirty, grainy water ice. Yi stopped to absorb the surroundings. Half a mile of mainly flat coast quickly gave way to a forty-degree slope scattered with long tongues of debris, which itself gave way to a towering face with a summit plateau thousands of feet above the shore, dripping in golden, glinting streaks of either ice or liquid that looked like honey oozing out of a comb. Shackleton had landed at the edge of a horseshoe bay about three miles long, bounded on both sides by the mountain arms, tall stone ridges falling abruptly for hundreds of feet into the sea. Yi guessed that the only way to climb out of their geographic imprisonment by foot would be through the few ravines clinging to the incline.

Something boomed like the snapping of grown trees, startling them. Yi swept his sight across the terrain—half expecting an alien on a downslope moving toward them—and thought he saw far away rocks crumble. They echoed for an unusually long time. *It's the high air density*, he reasoned. *The amplified sound waves travel much farther than on Earth.*

Sophia passed Yi and continued walking toward a boulder from whose top they would plan the scouting.

That's what's unsettling me. It seems like a world made by aliens to imitate Earth, but designed by studying a single postcard. So extraordinarily similar yet so clearly foreign.[36]

✸

Sophia spotted the one distinctively alien thing a few dozen yards away.

They approached the Grasshopper. *Oh my! My champion, my knight.* No

---

36   "Tweety—Commander, so you don't think we're contaminating Titan by being here?" Yi asked more to break the silence than anything, "It is what it is, but I wonder."

    "No chance. If there's Titanian life, 'they' can't hurt us and we can't hurt them. There's a transparent but impenetrable wall between the two. It's called temperature. See, even the hardiest of Earthly microbes completely stop their metabolic activity and reproduction capacity at -14 degrees Fahrenheit. Look at the upper-right corner of your visor. It's -288 degrees. 'They' on the other hand would presumably be made of liquid methane or ethane, so the instant the temperature jumps a few dozen degrees they puff out of existence, vaporized … now that you say it, though, if you somehow fell inside that volcano you showed me and splashed right into the subsurface water ocean somewhere far under our feet, then yes. But I promise there'll be no *Journey to the Center of the Earth* during this visit."

peep or flashing, it looked as inert as the pebbles around it. *Not the shiniest that armor of yours, my lord.* About three feet in diameter, it looked like a futuristic unmanned drone on the front cover of a 1940s science fiction magazine, a boxy gray quadcopter with two propellers per arm and an ungainly dish antenna. But what it didn't get in looks it got in performance: it was the only nuclear-powered drone in the Solar System. A thermoelectric generator converted the heat from decaying plutonium-238 into electricity. Nothing was wasted in the Grasshopper, the excess heat kept it at a balmy internal temperature of seventy-seven degrees Fahrenheit. And barring a disabling malfunction it would remain operational for years, covering thousands of miles of terrain. Carrying an onboard laboratory and meteorological station, it would examine the surface up close and, in time, characterize Titan's complex atmosphere, climate, and methane cycle. Perhaps even infer the existence of life indirectly. *Unless an extraterrestrial gazelle gallops in front of its cameras.* The engineers at Mission Control had pushed it to the brink in the days prior to launch and now it recharged its batteries for the next flight, unrushed.

"May you have a long, prosperous life," Yi kneeled to pat it. "What were the odds we would ever see it again, or more even, that it would save us? Zero. Yet here we stand."

They arrived by the base of the boulder, which seemed to have dislodged eons before from the wall towering above the bay. Its flat top had been bridged to the ground by a dark porous hydrocarbon snow, making for an easy climb. It gave a good perspective of the place.

The waters within the bay were quiet but the rolling sea beyond wasn't, in a way Sophia couldn't quite make sense of. She strained her eyes. Aside from an island shoreline suggested in the far distance within shrouds of haze, the reddish ocean ruled most of the horizon. It didn't seem to ripple yet its surface rolled and flexed. *From here it resembles a Buddhist monk's robe.*

"They look like a procession of slow-moving camel humps," said Yi.

Same as having stared vainly at a Magic Eye illusion, Yi's cue allowed Sophia to see differently. "Are ... are those ...?"

"Titanic waves."

"That just can't be," she said enthralled, while looking at the giant, bell-shaped waves plodding right past the bay.

"There's this American novelist from the 19th century named Mark Twain—"

"Every American knows Twain, Yi."

"Anyway, he said the only difference between reality and fiction is that fiction needs to be credible. See those rock columns standing in the sea? There, beyond the ridge that closes off the bay from the right-hand side?" Sophia nodded. "See how some waves submerge them? And they are probably a good fifty feet tall."

The brief she studied as they closed in on the moon mentioned waves on Titan can be about seven times taller and three times slower than on Earth. As common-sense-breaching and mind-altering as the view was, it complied.

"Something's not right," said Yi. "They are ... moving south? It doesn't make sense. Look up."

She did. Dense clouds, which she hadn't noticed until now, flowed north at a rapid clip. If the waves weren't wind-induced, what was pulling them? While waiting for Yi to have a revelation, Sophia heard the wind's humming for the first time. It was irregular and shy, as the mountain behind and bay in front were sheltering them from wind and waves.

"It can only be the Throat. We're less than thirty miles from it in a straight line," Yi said.

The brief also explained Kraken Mare was a giant sea split in two by the Throat of Kraken, a narrow channel dividing north from south. At eleven miles wide, it was almost identical to the Strait of Gibraltar dividing the Mediterranean from the Atlantic. With one fundamental difference: tides, the rise and fall of sea levels.

On Earth, they are caused by the Moon's gravitational pull. On Titan, they are caused by Saturn. Titan's tides are hundreds of times stronger than Earth's, flowing north and reversing south through the Throat each day.

"Until today," Yi sounded bewildered, "nobody knew how strong the currents were. We don't either. But I can tell you that when the strong winds are hauling giant waves that the tides force to retreat backward ... well, that's incredible power." Shackleton had landed on a bay that was part of the very peninsula that thirty miles away became the Throat's western wall. "If we ever colonize Titan," Yi continued, "we just identified a virtually unlimited source of 24/7 hydroelectric power."

For the next five minutes, they surveyed the area and selected sampling spots.

"Unless something changes, we meet right here in sixty minutes and swap roles," Sophia said.

In each one's visor, a timer started the countdown.

Sophia headed up, Yi set off for the coast.

71 | THE KRΛKEN

Minutes later

Gingerly walking over thinning ice then crawling the last few feet, Yi got to the edge and stuck his chest out over the liquid. He gazed down. It had an orange-hued translucence, allowing his eyes to follow the seabed for maybe one hundred feet.

He splashed his gloved palm against the liquid, which displaced more or less perfectly around the contour of his hand, followed by countless drops jumping out unimpeded and falling back down like rain. *Amazing. The viscosity is half that of liquid water, at most,* he thought. *Liquid water loves round, smooth shapes. But this ...* It brought memories of oil sputtering as his mother dropped fresh pork chops into the frying pan. Low density and low viscosity explained why stirring his hand felt closer to flapping it energetically in the air than moving it in water. *The friction drag is barely a fourth. This is outrageously fun!*

Tidal power shrank to irrelevance as he envisioned the scale of Titan's fuel reserves. *Just here, Kraken Mare,* he thought while running his hand through the liquid, *has tens of times all the known oil and natural gas reserves on our planet.* For an unapologetic environmentalist like Yi, here was yet another measure of how upside-down this world was: *if there isn't indigenous life, warming up the atmosphere will not only be acceptable but advisable if we ever want to live here. And why wouldn't we? Except for the temperature, this is hands down better than Mars. And this needn't be a remote outpost, but one of our civilization's strongholds.* Here, fossil fuel gluttony and greed become virtues. *If wars are ever fought to control resources around here, they will be for the missing portion of combustion: oxygen.* Not oil but water wars, to get rid of the hydrogen and keep the oxygen.

Yi extended his arm and scraped the sea bottom. In a minute he was done with the first sampling and continued crawling along the edge until he found another shallow bottom. *Second sample is in the bag.* He kept moving until he saw an odd shape buried in the seabed. He tried reaching but it was deeper here. The bottom seemed about waist-deep. *Spacesuits are, by definition, waterproof.* He sat over the edge and carefully let himself slide into the liquid.

It all happened in an instant. *Shit.* His feet managed to touch the bottom but before he could even stand, his whole body was sucked out to sea. The pull from the current was so strong he briefly thought a creature was dragging him away from the shoreline. *Shit, shit, shit.* He frenetically tried to swim back but quickly realizing it was pointless, attempted to dive back to the surface instead. But the low liquid density made it impossible. He couldn't make himself buoyant and couldn't fling enough thin fluid to propel himself upward. He saw the liquid surface recede as he kept being sucked under.

The adrenaline didn't allow self-pity and instead he kept going back to Sophia. *I need to tell her.* He tried radio communication over and over but, same as in water, it didn't work when submerged. *I need to find a way to tell Sophia. If I don't, she'll search relentlessly and put the escape from Titan in jeopardy.* He may have accidentally killed the entire crew through his stupidity. *True idiots never learn.* Swindled by sea currents for the second time in his life. He realized his terrible error was thinking the tide was strictly directional, from north to south. *But when water is poured from a jug, it gets pulled from all directions, even if the final route is straight down.*

Ø

Both surface and bottom had disappeared from Yi's view. It was pitch-black, which made him think he was deep. How deep? Over its 127 Titan flybys the Cassini mission was able to survey the second largest sea, Ligeia Mare, much better than Kraken Mare. Its radar detected the seafloor up to 560 feet below the liquid surface, yet in many places it was too deep to measure.

He no longer screamed in terror. *I'm the only one who can hear myself and I never liked my voice anyway.* He wouldn't drown, he would die submerged once the spacesuit's life support system failed or ran out of juice. *I'm floating in a strange liquid, in a strange place, pulled by a strange unseen force.*

Ø

You better not be messing around, Yi Meng, she told herself when, in fact, she implored he was.

"Yi, over." Sophia couldn't repress the thought any longer. *Something very wrong has happened.*

She scanned the landscape, panic-stricken, one more time. Everything looked unperturbed, indifferent to her plight.

"Yi, over." Her voice was now pleading and desperate.

Calm down. He can't have vanished. Maybe you're dreaming. She searched for cues. The soft resting, almost floating, of her butt on a rock reinforced the hope. *I think I'm in a dream.* She felt better because she was no longer certain of the disaster. But a fleeting thought of James is all it took for her sandcastle to crumble.

Sophia abandoned the sampling equipment and raced to Shackleton in a frenzy. Once her feet touched the snow, she veered left and went to the locations they had singled out. After 200 yards she stopped, gasping for breath. *Please help me. God, I'm lost. I need your help. Please guide me.*

The Grasshopper. She dashed back to Shackleton, desperation seizing her by the throat. Climbing the ladder, her limbs shook so badly it was hard to grab the next rung and even harder to keep her palms closed around it.

She was committing a grave spacewalk sin by crying, but gravity assisted by causing the tears to run down her face.

Once inside, she kept dodging a looming meltdown by cramming information into her mind. *How do I wake up the Grasshopper?*

72 | STRANGER IN A STRANGE LAND

An hour later

Yi regained consciousness. He was still submerged but a dark yellow glow now flickered above him. As the minutes went by, he saw the seabed once more, covered in jumbled ice blocks, rising to the right. Soon after he saw a fast-approaching underwater upslope in front, stroked it, and stopped moving.

What's this? Some sort of sludge? he thought. Yi tried moving his arms but they hardly budged. His chest was glued too. *It's like tar.* It was worse than being fastened to a giant Velcro pad. It stuck like gum, the stubborn strands of ooze unwilling to let go. After a long, taxing fight, he managed to crawl up the slope and out of the sea onto oily but solid ground. His visor was splattered. He tried cleaning it with his gloved hand but made it worse. He then glanced at his spacesuit: practically no bright blue spots left outside of a muddy brown.

He noticed a deafening roar, like a flushing toilet and a waterfall in unison, and looked around. The giant waves had smoothed out to ripples, yet the furrows and grooves in the sea surface revealed torrential movement forward. *The waters must be very deep.* He had been caught by an embankment. *The tar probably saved me.* There was a tall rock face stretching for dozens of miles on the distant opposite seashore. Turning his head, he saw a soaring, smooth rock wall above him running straight in both directions, seemingly identical to the one on the facing coast. *This is a flooded, U-shaped canyon funneling masses of … wait, it's the Throat of Kraken. I better be on the right shore.*

He changed the display on his visor. *I was dragged for almost an hour.* He then attempted communication with Shackleton. *I just need a few radio waves to bounce off the thick atmosphere and hit Shack's dish antenna.* No luck. He kept trying while visually searching for a way out of the canyon. The sky flowed northward, the clouds thickened and darkened. Yi identified a steep promontory that branched high up into two ridges. One of them seemed to top off the wall. *Exposed but perhaps doable.* From that point he may be able to cut across the mountains and eventually drop off into the bay where Shackleton was stationed.

With no time to spare, he started hiking.

Ø

He stopped to recover after ascending hundreds of feet uninterruptedly. *Keep up this pace and we'll live to fight another day.*

Turning toward the fall line, he found the source of the roaring. The narrowest part of the Throat was a mile or two ahead, where the wall he was climbing turned dead vertical. *This has been the Panama Channel of the Kraken for tens, maybe hundreds of millions of years.* If the enormous forces at play weren't clear from the extreme rock erosion, he counted five giant whirlpools guarding the strait. He guessed any of them would have gulped down the container ship that rescued him off the coast of Taiwan.

The sudden, unmistakable radio crackling was never more welcome.

After the bare essentials, Sophia cut to the central issue: the Grasshopper had been airborne and was now heading toward him, its batteries still at one-third capacity. It would map the stretch between him and Shackleton and get close enough to Yi for a wireless downlink of that data so he could plot his way back.

He knew Sophia all too well not to hear the troubled undercurrent behind the cheerful tone. "We said no bullshit. Tell me what's happening?"

Sophia sounded unsure, "Downdraft. Shack is starting to sway."

"Reloading?"

"We're at 69 percent."

I'm not the critical path to escaping Titan. Not yet, anyway. He tried to sound serene, matter-of-factly, "I'll be back within three hours. Or I won't."

Ø

He climbed the last few dozen steps of a saddle that put him over the canyon. The Throat was 1,000 feet below yet it looked even more imposing than before. It resembled an immense hourglass, its neck directly under him and each of its two bulbs, the upper and lower Kraken, hijacking both northern and southern horizons. *It's not only an allegorical clock. It quite literally measures the passing of Titanic time, in scales actually comprehensible to us humans.* The sea flows south through the Throat for eight Earth-days and then north for another eight Earth-days, completing a full orbit around Saturn.

The display on Yi's visor showed the Grasshopper barely making headway toward him, as if ricocheting against an invisible wall. He changed the display mode and a low-resolution topography map sent via radio from Shackleton revealed the hurdle. It was trying to climb over the highest feature between him and the spaceship. His eyes gazed around for the least improbable path ahead of him. It roughly kept his current altitude by following the contour of a mountain curving south before continuing northeast, where he needed to go. The heavily serrated summit ridge, several hundred feet above his tentative route, was being battered by violent winds from the south, apparent by the drifting snow. Near what he guessed was the end of his traverse, a sharp crest was the only seemingly possible mountain pass to cross over to the other side. The crest was being pummeled, with clouds of snow clinging to it like smoke from a stack. It was the highest point of the route and he immediately knew it was the Grasshopper's obstacle. *The drone and me are looking at the same gap from opposite sides.* Assuming he could negotiate the crossing of that section he should be able to glimpse salvation, the bay and Shackleton somewhere below. *Going down will be much faster, by just jumping forward and letting gravity do the rest.*

Before restarting out, Yi checked his spacesuit. He had slid many times in the loose, grainy rock climbing up and the fabric around the knees already showed severe damage. *I need you to hold out only a few more hours.* How many? Depending on his metabolic rate, he had between 4.5 and 6 hours left before running out of oxygen. *More than I anticipated, and with worsening weather certainly beyond what Sophia and Shack can afford to wait—a pair of wings would have made this a breeze.* On Titan, where terrestrial rules are swept aside, the story of Icarus would have had a happy ending and a different moral. Since Yi's 140 pounds on Earth became twenty pounds on Titan, the denser air makes the power requirements of flying minimal. Strapping on a pair of wings—or even better, a hang glider and flippers—would have put an end to his predicament. *Had the Grasshopper been slightly bigger I could have been an acceptable payload. Wait a moment. Maybe—*

∅

Around ten minutes later, any hope of *deus ex machina* was crushed when the Grasshopper, attempting forward movement but hardly able to hover through the relentless punishment from the developing storm, was abruptly hurled down and slammed against the rocks.

Not all was wrong in this world though. Yi had moved materially faster than expected as he now stood before the apex of the route. Turning his head to where he came from, he gained vertical perspective on his two close calls. He was on top of a wide, featureless ice slab slanted toward the fall line, which he had clambered on to and had been scrambling across for some time. Beyond its edge came a vertical drop of about 700 feet, with dark crevasses awaiting at the bottom. *The same ones that swallowed the Grasshopper.* The fierce white winds he had seen from afar had disappeared. *Good news welcome.* Yi estimated about forty yards before the natural bridge he was standing on tipped over into the next gorge, Shackleton Bay. For the last hour he had been naming hitherto uncharted terrain, which instantly made it more familiar and less hostile.

With hardly forty yards to salvation he resumed moving ahead, intentional and watchful of each step. This was no time to worry about Shack rocking on the verge of disaster. *Which Tweety's optimistic voice only makes more obvious.* As he gained ground, the view of the other side grew. A few more steps and he saw the end of the odyssey, ahead and below: Shackleton little more than an upstanding grain of rice. *Grasshopper, your ultimate sacrifice was worth it.* But three footsteps later made it clear that this was not over: a blast of wind hurled his leg sideways. His last step had moved him past the corner where the rock wall that had protected him for hours gave way to southern exposure.

He retreated to safety behind the wall and for minutes remained undecided. He had seen another plausible path but it meant backtracking a good half-hour, without any promises. At the same time, testing the wind by extending his arm forward proved it to be savage, treacherous, almost vindictive. He eventually stuck his head out too. His high vantage point exposed a sweeping vista to the south. The entire skyline had been seized by a dark cloud with three distinct layers. The bottom was almost black in a torrential downpour while the top was a gargantuan tsunami, the crest of the wave full of claws that reminded Yi of *The Great Wave off Kanagawa* woodblock print by Katsushika Hokusai. *Impossible to say how far, hopefully still hours because it looks like the Apocalypse descending upon us.* This sealed his verdict: it was either onward or downward.

He gathered strength and banished every thought from his mind. His body was now the one in control. *Just thirty leaps to safety.* He felt the slippery ground through his boots. There would be nothing to hold on to with his hands. He waited for the wind to abate and when it did, he sprang forward. After a few leaps, a wind gust threw him down. He jumped back up but a new squall sent him flat again. He tried to crawl but an overpowering gale began sliding him. He noticed the edge of the precipice inching toward him. In a desperate move he sprung up and raced ahead, body inclined against the gale. The air resistance pressed against him but he used it to his advantage. He dived ahead and managed to cross to the other side, only to arrive and find no features to grab hold of.

He realized the absurdity of the situation. *I can't maintain my position.* The merciless wind slid him toward the void, and after a pointless battle trying to grab something, anything, dropped him into the precipice.

He was falling on his back. The acceleration minimal, the fall gentle.

"I'm falling." Yi heard his own voice devoid of anxiety, not for lack of emotions but out of disbelief.

Some twenty seconds later, the fall was slow enough to see himself disappear inside a crevasse.

∅

He opened his eyes amidst darkness, panting in pain. *The worse the condition, the louder the pain speaks.* He scanned his body. *Nothing's missing.* The pain was horrible. *Broken joints? Feet, okay. Ankles, okay. Knees, okay. Hips, okay—I should be able to walk out of here—Hands, okay. Elbows, okay. Wait ...* His right arm bent backward well past its shoulder's range of motion and was looking very wrong.

The golden-brown sky did not seem far, but the V-shaped icy walls in which he was wedged made it unattainable. *How to get out*—but before anything else he had to answer a despairing Sophia.

∅

Sophia was not taking it well.

After a long pleading both ways, Yi cajoled her into programming a rule into TiTus. That way she wouldn't kill him. A computer would. Whenever the swaying, shaking spaceship moved twelve degrees past vertical, TiTus would trigger the countdown and Shackleton would launch autonomously soon after, with or without Yi. Methane loading was 89 percent, enough to escape the Saturn system and let the Sun's gravitational influence claim it back.

Sophia knew the fall had killed him even if he wasn't quite dead, yet Yi's voice over the intercom sounded serene and thankful, which wrenched her soul. "I won't be able to claim my life insurance, but maybe I get to be called a hero instead."

She mustered a tragic smile while two transparent streams connected her eyes to her lips.

"Did you bring your Titan samples on board?" His voice suddenly picked up.

"Yes," she lied. That comforted him.

"I need to go now," Yi finally said. "Knowing you was one of the greatest pleasures of my life. You ... you are that sibling I looked up to but never had."

Between sobs Sophia tried to say something, but he had turned his radio off.

73 | TITAN'S FAREWELL

An hour later

Yi came out into the open again.

He had spotted a sliver of twilight to his left soon after falling inside the crevasse but decided not to tell Sophia. It would have given the illusion of possibility while snowballing the chance of disaster.

The sky was murky and overcast, an inverted stormy ocean rocking in heavy swell with strokes of surf riding fluid mountains. It was also raining, but the mammoth storm hadn't arrived yet. He could hear it approaching, though. Colossal thunders cracking open the inner ear. Big, pear-shaped methane drops floated down from the sky at the speed of snowflakes, splashing on and plodding down his visor. The shadows had become piercingly sharp, as if the contrast had been dialed up inside his retinas.

He was trudging through eternal ice fields, stabbed each step by throbbing pain, when he heard it. Shackleton's engines roaring with a fury that left no doubt they were flying out of Titan. On his count of seven their sound had been buried under the storm's howling, yet he knew Sophia and Shackleton had left forever.

A wave of peace overwhelmed him. *We did it.*

⌀

Had he sat down, the cold would have soon tempted him into a painless, timeless sleep. Instead, he had continued ahead and a long wide beach greeted him under the cliff he now stood on. He still had two hours before asphyxiating, according to the visor, but he already felt the effects of hypoxia.

A shrine of five round stones on top of one another was before him. Under it the letters "Jamesburg" were carved in the ground.

Uncanny, he thought. *What's the chance two stones spontaneously arrange themselves one over the other? Three stones? Four? Five? Six? At some point the probability of self-arranging becomes effectively zero. Am I … seeing evidence of intelligent Titanian life?*

He lost his train of thought. Bemused, it took a few seconds before he could focus again. He saw the five round stones anew. *Imagine the day there's an Earth colony here: sky covered in airships, sea ships approaching and leaving its port. And if we ever master nuclear fusion, we could heat a giant settlement, maybe even the entire moon, by harvesting helium-3 from Saturn's atmosphere. And every element of the periodic table exists in incalculable quantities, easily accessible among the moons of Saturn. If I had a say as the first pioneer, I would have proposed baptizing—*

He noticed the letters in the ground and was first startled and then embarrassed. The cognitive slide had started. *I'll never be whole again, and in two hours I'll be no more. I'm ready to go. I … I only wish I could have wandered more.*

Yi stared into the distance. He thought he could see a large, fast-folding curtain shape against the twilight sky. *Like those hypnotic bird cloud formations shifting in seemingly impossible synchronicity back on Earth.* He couldn't be sure. He no longer trusted his mind.

I now know the greatest cost of exploration: incurable longing. Longing for having uncovered some of the great mysteries encircling and staring at him. Longing to return to Earth, to be re-embraced by nature's leafy arms, to have rejoined humanity. Longing for falling in love again. *But for the next hour my mind travels faster than the speed of light.* He went back to his 8-year-old self, rubbing hands over a wood cooking stove while admiring through a fogged-up window the snowy, triple-peak mountain looming over their Inner Mongolian village, daydreaming of once reaching its summit and being able to see as far as Beijing and Moscow and America. *I've reached the summit of my own metaphorical mountain, Titan. And I've seen the Universe and its unfathomable immensity. And I've come further than it was thought possible to travel. Now at the end of my life, I can look back and ask, was it worth it?*

As further evidence of the breathtaking, heartbreaking, otherworldly beauty and weirdness around him, the Kraken had developed an unbroken rainbow spanning the sky, with a perfect reflection in its surface, completing a full ring of reds, yellows, greens, and blues.

∅

Awareness became sparser as ever more regions of his mind capitulated to the perpetual veil of darkness. His memory was fracturing into tangled fragments without chronology and too small to be coherent, yet he remembered himself many years back, hopelessly lost in an endless ocean. Now he was by another ocean. *But I'm no longer lost. I have finally found my destiny.* The turmoil in his soul had been replaced by peace. He only wished to have spoken with Sergei one last time. His last conscious thought was for him. *Before you quit, try. Before you die, live.*

74 | SΛTURN'S FΛREWELL

Three days later, September 28 2030. Day 25

THE RINGS OF SATURN

Shackleton hovered half a mile above the Keeler Gap.

Sophia floated above the Observation Window, which looked down at the slowly approaching Caird.

She remained oblivious to one of the most magnificent views in the Solar System. And as much as she tried to look forward to the rendezvous and their reunion, her spirit flickered between an empty shell devoid of emotions and one bleeding them as a branding iron of sorrow smoldered within.

⌀

Both seem so relieved, thought Sophia, while having dinner at Bacchus the next day. *And look at them, it's as if they can anticipate each other like those old couples killing days sitting out on the porch. They went out as opponents and came back as brothers. What did I miss?*

She was appalled at Derya's appearance. Not only had he lost a fourth of his former weight, but the compression fractures in his spine had left him hunchbacked. Sergei, on the other hand, had put on some weight.

⌀

That night, after each of them had time to read and ponder the dossier sent by Mission Control and ten or so hours before the engine burn that would propel them out of the Saturn system, the moment to make the fateful decision regarding the energy budget had arrived.

"Closing in on Earth solves nothing," Sergei was saying. "I've told you already, our problem is speed. We'll be moving at twenty miles per second, almost three times the fastest Earth re-entry ever attempted, even by unmanned vehicles. We *have* to shave speed. Take my word for it, you can't really assimilate what a re-entry is until you've done one."

"But there's a way around that. I say we go for the stone-skipping maneuver and hope for the best," said Derya, while his eyes ping-ponged between Sophia and Sergei, hoping one of them would budge. "For Christ's sake, people. Jupiter? Really?"

"I am with Sergei," said Sophia. "At that speed nothing man-made can intercept us. We'll have the largest audience in history but besides the prayers and moral support, we will be completely on our own. And it's a pretty stark menu: we continue falling into the Sun, or we burn trying to enter Earth's atmosphere, or we pull off a landing."

The discussion boiled down to oxygen. Shackleton's engines used methane as fuel and oxygen as oxidizer, in the exact ratio of one pound to 3.6 pounds. The visit to Titan gave access to unlimited methane, but it cost them non-replenishable oxygen. By the time James sealed the leak, methane had dropped to 23 percent from what it was right before the accident, while oxygen remained unaffected at 100 percent. After escaping Titan, the budget stood at 69 percent on both methane and oxygen. Enough to approach Earth but not enough to decelerate to an acceptable speed to initiate re-entry. This left two options, both dealing with the challenge of slowing down as close as possible to five miles per second, the routine speed for Earth atmospheric re-entries.

Derya's pick was a ballistic lob, researched for the Apollo program but finally archived due to its complexity. It had never been tried before. The spaceship enters Earth's upper atmosphere, decelerates at the cost of heating up, then skims back into space to cool down. Repeat again. And again. The number of 'agains' to erase over ten miles per second is high, and without a fuel buffer each one has the risk of entering at too steep an angle, in which case it can't escape back to space and burns in atmospheric hell, or too shallow, in which case it bounces too far into space and skips Earth for good.

Sergei and Sophia's alternative was opportunistic. Saturn orbits around the Sun every twenty-nine Earth years. Jupiter, at less than half the distance to our star, takes twelve. They were currently not only on the same side of the Sun, but Jupiter was at a relatively close distance from the direct trajectory between Saturn and Earth. By modifying Shackleton's path, they could intercept Jupiter. Then, by sailing close to the giant and going against its rotation, the spaceship would achieve a reverse gravitational slingshot, decelerating a couple of miles per second depending on how close to Jupiter they were willing to tread. The penalty was delaying the return by eight to nine weeks and being exposed to

Jupiter's magnetic field, by far the strongest in the Solar System after the sun-spots on the Sun's surface.

"You two seem to have grown fond of the gas giants. I have not," said Derya. "Do you even know how much radiation we would be exposed to?"

"There are ways around that," said Sophia.

"Oh yeah? A couple of Band-Aids to reattach a severed leg? You would also stretch out our return by months."

"We always had a food and oxygen buffer. Now it's 40 percent larger," said Sergei.

Derya knew they were answering out of respect. The decision had already been made.

⌀

MISSION CONTROL @ HANGAR ONE, CALIFORNIA

It was past midnight. The fishbowl was deserted except for two, and the entire hangar was for once silent. Even the vitals of the crew, displayed on one of the large screens, showed them to be sleeping.

Nitha sat on a chair, leaning forward and rocking anxiously like a teenager in detention. *The good news is that they picked Jupiter. The bad news is that they picked Jupiter. I never thought it would be this hard.*

"I'm going now, boss. You go to sleep soon, okay?" said Nico, one of the mission specialists.

"Yes ... Nico," she said, lost in thought.

He walked out but then stopped, turning. "What's going on, Nitha?" After a few seconds of silence, he continued, "I know you've—we've lost a lot. The recent events have been terrible ... but they've also been miraculous. And the future looks bright. We'll do everything from this room. They don't need to do anything during the reverse slingshot around Jupiter."

"Yes they do, Nico. They need to survive."

75 | HYPERION

Four days later, October 2 2030. Day 29

LEAVING THE SATURN SYSTEM

Sophia and Sergei's eyeballs were locked on Bacchus' Observation Window while Derya's were glued to his telescope's eyepiece.

It had started as a tribute to James, who back on Earth did not convince enough people to put the moon among the secondary mission objectives. Somebody at Mission Control had realized that after re-routing to recover Caird, a minor course correction allowed for a close encounter with Hyperion right as Shackleton escaped the Saturn System.

The three were bewitched by the floating potato. With no point of reference in the darkness of space, it could well have been the size of a fist—the apparent size from their vantage point—instead of its 220 miles in length.

Hyperion was full of secrets. It was the largest body known with such a highly irregular shape. Gravity should have enforced a more spherical form. It was saturated with deep, sharp-edged craters that made it look like both a sea sponge and a honeycomb, including one that covered half of one of its sides. Scanning its surface, it was indisputable there needed to be a lot of empty space inside, a porous interior. It was also a requirement to justify why such a colossal impact didn't shatter it to pieces and, instead, hard-pressed a crater seventy-five miles long and a Mariana Trench in depth.

It was also the biggest body known to have chaotic rotation, which made it impossible to predict which side would be simultaneously facing Shackleton and the Sun, requirements for tonight's single-chance scouting.

⌀

With the moon face set, Derya at last identified what appeared to be a moving shadow inside a potential cave. He set it as the primary target for pointing the instruments. TiTus set the parameters for the radar and laser altimeter.

"Hell, may as well go all in," said Derya. "TiTus, increase laser pulses per second beyond the manufacturer's threshold. We need the highest topographical spatial resolution we can possibly get."

"Done, Derya. Commander, closest approach in 196 seconds. Instrumentation ready for data capture," said TiTus. In an unexpected gesture, Sergei, the heir apparent, had declined the commander rank in favor of Sophia.

Ø

Six, five, four, three, two, one. It all happened within seconds. No fireworks, no special sound effects. The instruments looked as quiet and passive as they did before. Did they bungle it?

Ø

Derya's face relaxed into a grin. He began manipulating his tablet and replaced the iconic Earth landscape around the curved fuselage wall with a strip of ground from Hyperion superposed with layers and filters. He made a close-up of a surface feature and rotated it. A two-dimensional hole became a three-dimensional zucchini.

"You're looking at a cave almost three miles deep, apparently a few hundred yards in width, with a mouth eighty-seven feet in diameter," said Derya. "Carved in ultra-strong water ice, with walls miles thick. Just this one cavern is thousands of times the volume of Shackleton. A space habitat only missing a door really … and if we found one, it's probably full of them. A veritable Swiss cheese. We could connect them from the inside and turn it into a giant colony of hundreds of thousands of people. An ungainly, potato-shaped spaceship with the surface area of Great Britain, waiting patiently for billions of years for its occupants to arrive."

"We could bring nuclear reactors and house them in caves isolated from living things by hundreds of yards of pure ice, which at these temperatures is stronger than steel," said Sergei.

"Yes! With the heat we melt water," said Derya. "With the electricity we split water into hydrogen and oxygen. We pump oxygen and pressurize the cave system to one atmosphere, sea level on Earth. With hydrogen and oxygen, we have unlimited rocket propellant. And as we map the maze of caves and tunnels and get progressively deeper into Hyperion, we find its rocky core, where we mine iron and other metals to expand into new colonies on other moons. We plant forests inside—"

"And the view!" Sophia joined in excitedly.

"Best in the Solar System," said Sergei, infected with the merry spirit.

"This is the essence of human space exploration. Serendipity," said Sophia. "It wasn't among the mission objectives because no one, not even Jimmy, saw this coming. Whatever happens, I think we can safely claim to have taken more than a few timid steps in making humanity a spacefaring civilization. We made this count, Jimmy."

Ø

The sharp snipping sound of illegally clipped toenails in Bacchus pleased Derya. *In the same guilty-but-gratifying way of daring a vile one out at dinner and triumphantly blaming it on Yi,* he thought, grinning. But it was late and knowing the chance of getting caught was negligible detracted a bit from the experience. As he proceeded with the filing part of the ritual, he fancied life after their return. *Politics is definitely calling my name. It should please Father—I mean, if that doesn't sway him, nothing ever will.* And then yesterday's wholly unexpected email from Karl. *Whichever way you read it, it's a love letter.* He had reread it enough times to quote it from memory. *Why not? I say we give him another chance. People do change. I changed.* At the sight of his reflection on the Observation Window, the nail file jerked out of his fingers. He was repulsed. *Maybe drop politics and become Notre-Dame's bell-ringer instead.* By the time he searched for the nail file it was, predictably, gone. *That's why everything has Velcro, you fool.*

Derya wasn't sleepy. The Observation Window displayed the Milky Way's thick disc sprayed from side to side and dots of light sprinkled everywhere else. Saturn had been banished from it for good. He felt the urge to look at it one last time and asked TiTus to show recorded footage. The wall screen filled with the giant orb. After a few minutes he noticed a barely discernable succession of chickenpox smudges on its surface, scattered across like a bandoleer. *Explosions smearing the cloud tops.* He searched around the screen for the date and felt a ripple of goosebumps before he fully absorbed the information: September 15, a few hours before James' accident.

Without warning, a dam brimming with repressed emotions gave in abruptly and completely, releasing an unstoppable flood. As he wept, he felt an almost physical sadness gradually wash away, and by the end of that night the only thing left was gratitude for his two friends.

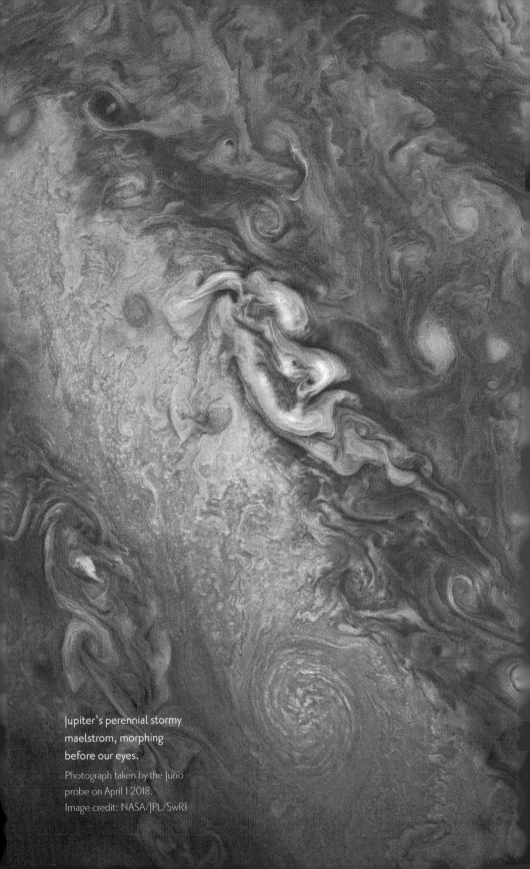

Jupiter's perennial stormy
maelstrom, morphing
before our eyes.

Photograph taken by the Juno
probe on April 1 2018.
Image credit: NASA/JPL/SwRI

PART 5
THE ROAD BACK

76 | DECODING ΔLIENS

July 16 2031. Return Day 291; 2.1 Years to Earth

HANNOVER, GERMANY

Messegelände Hannover, one of the world's largest convention centers, was teeming with a very specific crowd: scientists. The masses were predominantly young with no prevalence of lab coats, rimmed glasses, or eggheads. It could have been a rock concert, and in many ways it was, at least for the keynote speaker.

The assembly of over 100,000 attendees made it the most wide-ranging, cross-disciplinary scientific conference ever, smashing the previous record three times over. The usual walls that grow and harden around different fields had crumbled under an irrepressible force exerted from billions of miles away, by microscopic entities occupying a space smaller than a hundredth of a pinhead.

Chemistry, biology, and medicine were particularly well represented as the overall sentiment was that some of the most important breakthroughs of the coming decades in each of those fields would spawn from the extraterrestrial biological cargo on board Shackleton.

Everyone walking these grounds already knew the two people, one on and the other one off our planet, who would soon be collecting Nobel and Breakthrough Prizes. One of them would present in less than an hour. There was no need to look at the fairground map to figure out where the keynote presentation would take place. Everyone headed to the same location.

Ø

The vast majority of attendees were outside the protection of the pavilion in the open-air space under an unforgiving summer Sun clocking ninety-four degrees in the shade. Yet nobody seemed to mind. There was change in the air and everyone could feel it.

Belinda walked onstage with her left hand in her pocket, holding onto the speech tightly. The arena burst into applause and the cheering lasted for over a minute. Trying to disguise her self-consciousness, she focused on the one person not standing, an old man with a cane seated in the third row. He clapped, watching her with a caring, compassionate smile. It was one of those rare moments when two perfect strangers could communicate with no need for words. *He knows how it feels to lose the person you love.* It reminded her of Leonard: in their phone conversation the month prior, he had told her between sobs masked as coughs from his emphysema, "a son should never die before his ..." *He said 'elders' but he meant 'father.'*

⌀

"—and in our scientific quest for the truth, the first question we must answer is 'What.' What am I seeing under the microscope? Then we must solve the 'How.' How does that chromosome transfer instructions to the proteins? But the really essential, all-encompassing question is 'Why.' Why does the book of life use four letters instead of two, or twenty-six? Through my personal loss, through the long healing process ahead, I have come to realize the 'Why' can also help to make sense of Jimmy's death." She stopped out of necessity yet remained stoic and composed.

"Soon after we started dating, Jimmy confided that he thought he had been born 200 years too late. To him, a life without adventure was a life without meaning. One of his climbing heroes, Reinhold Messner, once said 'without the possibility of death, true adventure is not possible.' He told me this because it was fair play, a full disclosure of sorts. I needed to know what I was getting myself into. Maybe his call was to go where no man had gone before ... to reopen the frontier. To launch a new golden era of exploration. To nudge those free spirits craving adventure to fulfill their destiny and drive us all forward. It turns out my Jimmy is—was—a continuation of a long and distinguished breed of pioneers.

"One of his predecessors was a woman by the name of Marie Skłodowska, better known as Marie Curie, who also gave her life for something worthwhile. Decades conducting trailblazing research on radioactivity irredeemably damaged her DNA. Even today her notebook is so radioactive it's kept in a lead box. She was the first person of a grand total of four to win two Nobel Prizes, and the only person to ever win a Nobel Prize in two different sciences, physics and chemistry. Then the answer to the 'Why' ... a 'Why' I need to learn to live with ... is that individual sacrifice may be needed for society to progress, to expand our horizons, to improve our well-being, to better ourselves. You ... we ... are richer because of their sacrifice."

As seconds of applause went by, the out-of-sync clapping forged into a single, sharp, thunderous ovation that rebelled against its ephemeral nature.

"What I'm about to tell you, we owe to them ... these are very preliminary results that haven't yet scratched the surface. Sophia and I have seen maybe a hundredth of a percent of what awaits us, a revolution in life sciences that will likely know no boundaries. You won't hear any real answers today, mostly more questions. Yet we're starting to tackle the really essential, sweeping one. The 'Why.'

"For hundreds of years of scientific inquiry, the answer to one of the most fundamental questions has remained off-limits: why does all life on Earth descend from a single ancestor? We believed that the first spark, the one that switched life on, was extraordinarily improbable. We now know, however, that extraordinarily improbable does not mean extraordinarily rare, because of two ingredients: time and repetition. An example is the several million chemical reactions per second occurring in each one of our cells. Given enough time, on the order of millions of years, chemistry will flourish into stunning complexity. We can assert this because it's a fact that life has begun, independently, at least twice in our dear but humble Solar System.

"Today we can also tackle another sweeping question. Was that first chemical structure that crossed the threshold of inanimate matter the best solution to the life equation? The two, possibly independent, strains of life found on Enceladus categorically say 'no.' The universe of chemical possibilities is huge. For instance, the number of possible proteins one hundred amino acids long built from combinations of the twenty amino acids naturally produced by our body, is larger than the number of atoms in the Universe. Life on Earth or Enceladus did not have the time to try all possible sequences before appointing the best. Rather than a quest for ultimate perfection, the creation and evolution of life is a haphazard result of trial and error that picks whatever works first. Many features of today's biology are not optimizations or improvisations for the modern world but vestiges from ancient times that were too costly to replace ... and the implications of all this are, as we will see, far-reaching."

She stopped and took a sip of sparkling water from a plastic bottle, enlarged 1,000 times on the screen behind her; the bubbles fizzing and popping turned into symbolic harbingers of what was coming.

"Why does the genetic code, the book of all life on Earth, use four letters? By inference, the answer seems to be 'just because.' The two Enceladus life forms took vastly different roads from our own and from each other when it came to the information challenge. The genetic code from the carbon-silicon microbe is extremely efficient, using the minimum viable alphabet size: two letters, just as computers do with their zeros and ones. The carbon-based life, however, which should have been our natural choice as test subject, uses nine or possibly ten letters.

"This shaped our research. Sophia asked me to devote all of our time to the lesser-known carbon-silicon so we could dig deeper and extract as much information as possible before re-entry ... in case something goes wrong. And so we left the familiarity of the carbon world in exchange for the simplicity of carbon-silicon's genetic language. So far it seems to have been the right decision.

"When our civilization decoded the human genome in the year 2000, the ensuing celebration commemorated one of the most impressive achievements in the history of science as well as the beginning of a new era where death and diseases would be conquered. That enthusiasm proved premature. The sobering reality is that there isn't just a single gene out of our 19,000 that's devoted to intelligence, or longevity, or eyesight. Instead it is the combination of many, which makes the problem exceptionally hard, even seemingly impossible at times. Because we do have the answer to everything in front of our very eyes, but each answer is a sentence of unknown length, fragmented in an unknown number of volumes, in unknown locations around the library of DNA.

"An analogy Yi Meng would have liked is that our genetic code is a Beethoven manuscript. A masterpiece no doubt, but a tortuous and chaotic one full of blots, smudges, notes struck out and rewritten, whole pages of illegible code, cul-de-sacs, and booby traps. Instead, the carbon-silicon genetic code appears to have been composed by Mozart. It seems dictated flawlessly from the heavens to the paper. The vast majority of its genetic code looks functional. It's simple to read."

Ø

"But enough prelude. Even with our limited equipment and severely limited man-hours on Sophia's end—after all, she's the one that must carry out all the experiments—we can assert that once the treasure trove arrives on Earth, many of us gathered here will be working, in one way or another, on or around the Enceladus alien life forms for the rest of our professional lives.

"I'm about to present a few findings today. The first one has to do with our understanding, almost since the discovery of the double helix structure of DNA by Watson and Crick in 1953, that all living beings become increasingly imperfect with time as the continuous cell divisions accumulate corruptions from the original genetic code. Because even though most cells in our body are replaced by new ones every few months, this recycling happens to cells that are themselves ever more corrupted, so the penalty is increasing disease proclivity and eventually one of those diseases causes death to the entire organism, what we call death from old age.

"With Sophia we have learned to control both the speed of cell division and the core temperature of the cell within the carbon-silicon life form, two key molecular triggers of aging. We need not guess at the implications because we are already seeing the results.

"The experiment is straightforward. The organism has an average lifespan of about twenty-three days. We remove a single cell at birth and at the middle of its life we reinsert it with an accelerated biological clock for its division. The cell descendants soon displace the old cells of the entire life form. The result ... we have a population of four organisms more than fifty days old, and looking as good as new—"

A collective wow cut her off.

"For the carbon-silicon life forms we think we are on the verge of achieving what in practical terms becomes biological immortality."

The world had changed again and everybody present heard it first.

The commotion was a sight to behold. Stock prices of biotech companies around the world were already swelling upward in wild speculation.

77 | THE VEILED SL∆YER

June 3 2032. Return Day 614; 1.2 Years to Earth

APPROACHING JUPITER

The one known as Marduk to Babylonians, Zeus to Greeks, Odin to Vikings, and Erentüz to Turks and Mongols stood dead center in front of the Observation Window. Even from this distance, forty times that of the Moon as seen from the Earth, it was already bigger. *Don't get overly cocksure—humility is a virtue, you know—but I'm starting to see why the Romans called you God of the Sky in addition to King of the Gods*, thought Derya. *They were also prone to poetic embroidery, so keep it cool.* The planet's brief ten-hour day meant its kaleidoscopic clockwise and counter-clockwise cloud belts whirled in front of patient eyes. *Like circling drapes of your celestial toga.*

Never a superstitious man, over the last few weeks Derya had nonetheless—as countless before him—anthropomorphized and personified the giant. *Your crown and aura may be invisible, but not to me.* Jupiter's massive liquid metal core creates a magnetic field 20,000 times stronger than Earth's, making it the most severe radiation environment outside of the Sun, by a wide margin. Even a cheap amateur radio kit tuned to the right frequency back on Earth encounters Jupiter's crackling radiation shrieks. It had been weeks since he last heard the spooky drifting tone of white noise, oscillating from screeching to roaring, like synthesizer chords in a horror movie soundtrack. *I acknowledge it's a social construct, but hearing* The Exorcist *was a welcome mat a few shades too dark for my liking, Jup.*

His mind could picture what his eyes could not: a hair-raising, flooding, electric-blue magnetic field discharged from the north pole and regained by the south pole via a giant perpetual closed loop in the shape of a torus, or doughnut, surrounding the planet. *There's no way to bypass that one. We'll take the full dose, ranging from bad to awful.* But there was another much smaller doughnut of slightly larger diameter than Jupiter surrounding it at the orbit of the innermost of its Galilean moons, Io. The really ghastly one:

Io's plasma torus. *If crossing the large one is running through a water curtain, crossing the smaller one is diving to the bottom of the sea.* And yet the Maneuver & Trajectory Team on Earth, the ones threading the Shackleton needle around Jupiter, could only avoid plunging but not skimming the smaller torus.

The challenge was multifold. They were about to risk their lives in order to achieve a reverse gravitational slingshot, an invisible pull where the gas giant would steal speed from Shackleton. However, the further they were from the planet and the steeper their angle with respect to its equator, the less speed they could shave. Additionally, all planets in the Solar System are coplanar—on the same plane. Their orbits around the Sun are so flat they could be drawn on sheets of tracing paper and simply placed on top of each other. The conceptual problem is a sphere surrounded by a doughnut with a wider inner hole. The ideal trajectory to minimize radiation exposure is approaching the sphere by entering right under the doughnut and exiting over it. But such a steep angle would equate to both jumping off the plane and rendering the slingshot ineffective. Therefore, Shackleton would briefly enter the smaller torus both on the way in and on the way out.

Their closest encounter with Jupiter would happen in eight days.

There was little to be done to prevent the hazardous ultrafast charged particles from damaging the ship's electronics, besides turning off every system not absolutely essential for the sporadic but critical nudges by the ship's thrusters to fine tune its trajectory and keep the crew alive.

As for the crew, there was more or less one thing that could be done to protect Sophia, Derya, and Sergei from certain death: wrapping themselves in water. Here the simplest solution was also one of the best. Water is dense. It packs a lot of atoms in a small area. A radiation shield blocks particles by interacting with them. The thicker the shield, the higher the probability a given particle hits a hydrogen or oxygen atom, losing part or all of its energy. Because there would be untold high-energy electrons and ions slamming against them, and because this is the realm of quantum mechanics, there was no clear measure of how radiation poisoning would play out. But without water protection the calculations showed a person falling into a coma ten minutes after entering the torus. *Even with water protection there will be contamination,* thought Derya, while looking unimpressed at the igloo. *Even in the best of cases our life expectancy will be shortened.*

The igloo was a roundish cage made of the rubberized fabric of inflatable boats filled with water between its outer and inner walls. It had been designed as an emergency shelter in case of an improbable solar flare. *Very improbable, because it looks like shit.*[37]

---

37 **A day later**

"Scored. 0-0-1," exclaimed Sergei. After minutes with their eyes closed, he was the first to experience a small explosion of light inside his eyeballs as a cosmic particle hit his optical nerve.

Tonight, all worries were put aside to celebrate James and Yi. Shortly after leaving Saturn they instituted a day per quarter dedicated to remembering their friends through their own pursuits. This time it was about astronomy while listening to Debussy, Gershwin, and Scriabin.

Sophia, Derya, and Sergei floated by the flight deck's Observation Window, right by Derya's telescope.

"Yi ... that childlike curiosity he had, remember? He used to get so enraptured whenever I retold the story," said Derya. "Formidable storytelling skills helped, no doubt," he added.

The occurrence was well documented and began happening as soon as astronauts and cosmonauts ventured outside Earth's atmospheric cocoon in the mid-1960s. The chance of it happening on Earth's surface was extremely improbable as the atmosphere acts as an exceedingly effective shield and filter.

"The particle that just hit Sergei's retina may have originated during the Big Bang," continued Derya, "traveling unimpeded without encountering a single atom for 13.7 billion years, crossing endless galaxies until it suddenly finished its journey by vanishing against your optical nerve. Here's where things get even more interesting because of general relativity. For the Universe, 13.7 billion years have evidently elapsed. But for the particle? Not quite. Elementary particles such as photons have no age because time does not apply to them. Let's assume a clock traveled *almost* along the ray of light, arriving at your optical nerve a second later. It would have measured only 1,600 years! And had it arrived a millionth of a second later, twenty-six years, time almost frozen. And if we violated the laws of physics and traveled alongside, no time would have passed. Time traveling is not only legal but real and pervasive across the Universe. The only requirement is to be moving near the speed of light or being close to a monstrous gravity well, such as a black hole. I say cheers to you, Yi Meng."

* * *

They recreated another of Yi's staples: locating the blue speck amid a sea of night and then reciting from memory what Carl Sagan, that scientist and poet who painted words with stardust, said of the famous Pale Blue Dot photograph, taken by Voyager 1 from beyond the orbit of Pluto on February 14 1990 as it turned its cameras one final time, across the great expanse of space, to look back at the Solar System.

"Look again at that dot. That's here. That's home. That's us. On it, everyone you love, everyone you know, everyone you ever heard of, every human who ever was, lived out their lives. The aggregate of all our joys and sufferings, thousands of confident religions, ideologies, and economic doctrines, every hunter and forager, every hero and coward, every creator and destroyer of civilizations, every king and peasant, every young couple in love, every hopeful child, every mother and father, every inventor and explorer, every teacher of morals, every corrupt politician, every superstar, every supreme leader, every saint and sinner in the history of our species, lived there—on a mote of dust suspended in a sunbeam.

"The Earth is a very small stage in a vast cosmic arena. Think of the endless cruelties visited by the inhabitants of one corner of this pixel on the scarcely distinguishable inhabitants of some other corner of the dot. How frequent their misunderstandings, how eager they are to kill one another, how fervent their hatreds. Think of the rivers of blood spilled by all those generals and emperors so that, in glory and triumph, they could become the momentary masters of a fraction of a dot.

"Our posturings, our imagined self-importance, the delusion that we have some privileged position in the Universe are challenged by this point of pale light. Our planet is a lonely speck in the great enveloping cosmic darkness. In our obscurity—in all this vastness—there is no hint that help will come from elsewhere to save us from ourselves.

"It has been said that astronomy is a humbling and character-building experience. There is perhaps no better demonstration of the folly of human conceits than this distant image of our tiny world. To me, it underscores our responsibility to deal more kindly and compassionately with one another and to preserve and cherish that Pale Blue Dot, the only home we've ever known."

"Such a perspective shift," said Sophia. "I wish we could snatch and capture it inside a bottle. Not the outer beauty but its deeper meaning, and then give a sip to every human being on the planet."

"There's this famous quote by Alexander von Humboldt," said Derya. "'The most dangerous worldviews are the worldviews of those who have never viewed the world.' If the 8 billion of us could be sitting here, looking back at our home, I think it would achieve the communism that two other compatriots, Karl Marx and Friedrich Engels, authored and theorized and you, the Russians, experimented with and practiced. The self would dissolve within the collective. From here the simplicity of things is so ... transparent. I wonder who I will be once we're back."

* * *

The telescope emitted four long beeps.

Derya looked triumphant. "Gazing at the Earth was the appetizer. *This* is the main course. We're replicating the Hubble Deep Field, one of the three most important space pictures of all time. If 1968's Earthrise stirred the environmental movement and the Pale Blue Dot reminded us of our fleeting existence as a species, this one ballooned the immensity and weirdness of the cosmos. See, the trick is worthy of Houdini or Copperfield except there's no illusion, only magic. You take a soda straw, look through it at a spot in the Big Dipper completely devoid of stars—an area less than 1 percent that of the Moon—and keep staring at it for ten more days. That's what the Hubble telescope did in 1995, and that's what the Terzi telescope finished doing just now. TiTus, run the ten days of footage in two minutes, s'il vous plaît."

"Any particular reason you switched to French, Derya?" asked TiTus. "You have never done that before."

Derya rolled his eyes at Sophia and Sergei. "We better have made some major artificial intelligence inroads over the last five years 'cause this makes me pretty ambivalent about technological progress. All looks and no brains."

"Derya!" said Sophia, embarrassed at the abuse.

TiTus waited in vain for clarification and after three seconds dimmed the ambient lights and turned on the screen over the cockpit. A black display gradually became a cluttered, multicolored Kandinsky of roughly circular shapes, as the scant photons traveling across intergalactic space for millions to hundreds of millions to billions of years slowly collected over the previous ten days in the back of the telescope's primary mirror, which now traveled again from the screen to their eyeballs at the speed of light, becoming a signal imprinted on their brains.

"Each one of those thousand blobs is a galaxy, each one housing billions upon billions of stars. The 3,000 galaxies that appeared seemingly out of thin air changed physics forever ... and yet the Hubble Deep Field almost didn't happen. Nobody knew a priori what to expect. Who would dare throwing away ten days of the most sought-after instrument in science, with reams-long waiting lists of astronomers, on looking at an utterly empty patch of the sky? Well, Robert Williams, the Hubble director at the time, did."

"I really wish Yi was here," said Sophia, almost to herself.

"Before Edwin Hubble, one of the greats in astronomy, our galaxy was our Universe. He was the first to identify that the nebulas that kept sprouting in the ever more powerful telescopes weren't clouds of gas but galaxies beyond our Milky Way. Our Universe was suddenly vastly bigger. He didn't stop there. In the 1920s, he discovered the Universe was not static but expanding, which meant it had been born somewhere in the very ancient past, what decades later would become the Big Bang theory. Over the following decades, calculations showed the expansion of the Universe from that original explosion should be slowing down due to gravity. The Hubble Deep Field showed unequivocally the opposite. Implausible as it sounded, the Universe is inexplicably *accelerating* its expansion. Decades hence, it remains one of the greatest mysteries in science. Whoever cracks it will join the likes of Newton and Einstein. And while we wait for an explanation, we have inferred that the Universe is composed of three things: ordinary matter, dark matter, and dark energy—$E=mc^2$ reminds us energy and matter are one and the same.

"Ordinary matter is what we can see, everything from galaxies to atoms. Dark matter is a hypothetical type of matter that has never been directly observed, but whose existence would explain a number of otherwise perplexing astronomical observations, particularly a gravitational pull much larger than that explained by ordinary matter. The other black horse, dark energy, is a hypothetical type of energy that has never been directly observed, and which we have charged as the unknown force driving the accelerating expansion of the Universe. The current consensus model exposes our abysmal ignorance: dark energy represents 68 percent of the total mass-energy of the Universe, dark matter 27 percent, and ordinary matter 5 percent. Therefore, 95 percent of the Universe is not only unexplained, but thoroughly imperceptible to us."

"Now I really wish Yi was here," said Sergei.

"What if that 95 percent is how much Heaven and Hell weigh?" said Sophia.

"Look back at Earth, right there," said Derya. "Convince me that an Almighty created the whole Universe not solely for our planet, not solely for humans among a million other species, but exclusively for Christians, or Hindus, or Muslims? I think espousing that is awfully disrespectful to the rest of the Universe. We—Sergei and I—have found two strains of life on Enceladus. Life has started independently, just in our trifling Solar System—our own backyard—three times! A third-rate moon has created life two times, putting Earth to shame, and you tell me 'God' was only thinking about us? How outrageous, how insulting is that? The implications of our discovery means there's life everywhere ... and I bet the Universe is teeming with intelligent life as well. Probably right now there's an intelligent life form gazing in our direction from the Andromeda galaxy. How seriously do you think he, it, they would take your claim? Or the parody of God sending His son to us so we could kill him? And while we're at it, He better be printing Jesuses by the billions to shuffle them around the Universe."

"The Laws of Nature may not require a Designer but they do not forbid one—or indeed many," said Sergei. "What if God is in fact subject to the constraints of this Universe like the rest of us? If so, to be all-seeing and extend tentacles across the Universe, It or They would need a stunning amount of everything. Maybe that's where all the missing energy and matter is ..."

"Now that's a fascinating claim," said Derya. "Because what you call God would be indistinguishable from an ancient alien civilization that had billions of years to evolve."

"Yes!" jumped in Sophia, clearly excited. "Cropping and manicuring primitive sentient beings like us around the Universe. Tossing an intentional stone at Earth to unseat the dinosaurs so that mammals could have a chance. Nudging archaic humans into mastering fire. Watching us with fascination evolve, make mistakes, amend our ways ... caring, lovingly. Our forefathers in all but bloodline."

"Look at Andromeda," said Derya. "Our giant galactic neighbor would look six times bigger than our Moon if we could easily spot it from Earth, except so few photons manage to traverse the enormous distance and then Earth's atmosphere that it can only be seen by the naked eye on a moonless night." Here, in the unending night of outer space, its majestic oval shape and spiral arms were perfectly discernible against the void. "It's a shame," continued Derya. "If it shined like the Moon does, I think its immensity in the sky would have tempered our arrogance, our chauvinism, and our persistent geocentric stubbornness. But anyway, what I wanted to say is that it's 2.5 million light-years away. At our extraordinary speed, twice as fast as our closest competitor, Apollo 10, it would take us ... er, help me out here, TiTus."

"Assuming constant speed, about 34 billion years to arrive," said TiTus.

"Almost three times the current age of the Universe!" said Derya. "So, unless wormholes are real and big and stable enough to allow sizable things to pass back and forth, we are trapped in our galaxy."

"It's hundreds of billions of stars spread across 150,000 light-years. We are having trouble moving around one star. I say there's no particular hurry in finding those wormholes," said Sophia.

"What I mean is that biological organisms are bulky, spoiled, fallible, and fragile. Say in the distant future our civilization builds a Noah's Ark for a million people and then travels successfully through interstellar space for 1,000 years. Yet a ten-minute hiccup in the oxygen supply system is all it takes to kill every single human on board. Look at us. We need all this support machinery and regeneration systems to keep us alive, forcing a huge spacecraft that in turn forces fuel restrictions so severe we move at barely twenty miles per second—this compared to the speed of light's already shamefully slow 186,000 miles per second—and even so we feel like we're living inside a sarcophagus. Worse yet, sharing it ... no. Human 2.0 will not be made of carbon. They will be made of silicon. Not Enceladus' biological silicon. I mean Silicon Valley silicon. I mean uploading the consciousness of a living person into a computer. In case you haven't noticed, artificial intelligence is overrated. Much better to have human intuition and powers of deduction coupled with superhuman processing and mnemonic power. Sometime in the future we'll be able to simulate through software and hardware the neuronal wiring of the human brain. Then we'll get rid of our bodies and upload ourselves into the cloud. That means achieving immortality but also shrinking spaceships to finger-sized vessels carrying hundreds, maybe millions of people. Then and only then are we ready to expand across our galaxy and beyond."

"Which brings us full circle to the Designer," said Sophia. "The God, plural or singular. If It or They are a hyper-developed ancient alien civilization, then it's indeed intelligent design itself, imparting intelligent design around the Universe. Biological species that once upon a time evolved from gunk much like ourselves on a habitable world, until they upgraded themselves into second-generation, sentient computer programs that expanded across the Universe ... if so, most of life in the cosmos may not be carbon-based, but silicon-based. Silicon Valley silicon."

"We wanted to honor Yi the Curious and Jimmy the Adventurer. I say mission accomplished," said Derya.

78 | REVERSE SLINGSHOT

JUPITER

"Lamb, naturally. Roasting outside on a stick over firewood embers, for never less than four hours, turned every once in a while," said a day-dreaming Derya. "Dripping fat, which upon contact with the embers assaults my nostrils. Eating in quantities that guarantee an unbearable heartburn later—but later doesn't matter; it's all about the now."

Sophia's head was so near that Derya's breath caressed her clammy left cheek. The three had been inside the igloo, barely able to move without elbowing one another, for eight protracted hours. The closest approach to Jupiter was coming in four hours and thirty-seven minutes, yet no one had nor would exit their shelter until Shackleton abandoned the worst of the radiation belts in seventeen hours.

As they waited for Sergei to start talking, her ears picked up on the unsettling stillness around them. *If Shack was a person she would be in an induced coma,* Sophia thought. *For the first time since launch even the fans' whirring is on holiday.*

"Come on, Serezha, quid pro quo," she said, while watching Sergei's handsome reddened face not two feet away, upper lip and temples beaded by the muggy air. *A polar bear stranded in the Amazon rainforest.*

Their last skirmish against tension and tedium consisted of imagining a favorite activity for when they landed back on Earth, one of the few pastimes endless repetition didn't blunt.

"Let me give it a try," said Derya. "Dropped off in a Siberian winter with a hunting knife, a wool mat, and flint and steel. Or three matches. You pick."

A worthy guess.

"Perhaps later. Go to the zoo really, as long as it's after hours," said Sergei.

"Now you have my attention," said Derya. "Fearing the onset of arthritis from signing autographs?"

"Not really, I was famous way before you, but for half a decade we've had the social interactions of cavemen. Once back you'll feel like you have Asperger's."

While Sophia hunted around her mind for anything to keep chipping minutes away from the hours, the sirens went off. The sensors around the ship were triggered by exceedingly high radiation levels. The crew did not need a reminder, but Earth's decision not to disable them was to avoid modifying the large, single block software code controlling the alarm network on board Shackleton. As the return home became less hope and more fact, everyone was becoming overly cautious. *The Angel of Death descending upon us.*

She wished the din had the familiar wailing of an ambulance. Instead, it had a petrifying nine-second ramp up to a deafening scream that released into a long descent in tone and volume before picking up again, like a World War II air raid siren. Her primal fear was reaching deep down and clenching her soul.

"Best snooze alarm ever," said Derya.

Thanks for trying to lighten the mood.

"Earth didn't want to specify the thresholds," he continued, "so I checked the code myself. The trigger is the radiation level at Hiroshima's ground zero minutes after the explosion."

I take that back.

∅

Silence had settled for hours and Jupiter's closest approach was behind them.

Deep inside you know we'll survive, Derya kept telling himself. *What we've overcome makes any impending obstacle doable.* But then he pictured the radiation belts enveloping them, particles subjugated into the fourth fundamental state of matter—plasma—and flung at super high speeds into perpetual loops. *They call them chorus waves, the ant-sized version of which are responsible for the northern lights on Earth, because when converted to sound they become the demented chirping chorus of terrorized birds.*

"—no, I'm saying the *very* first time you ever kissed someone," said Sophia.

"And I just told you, it was Iman," said Sergei.

"But you were, like, 27 ..." said Sophia.

"A virgin at 27!?" asked an incredulous Derya.

"I didn't say a virgin. I said my first kiss," answered Sergei.

Really? You can bayonet with no prelude? In my eyes you've grown an inch taller. "If you say so," said Derya.

"How's that possible?" asked Sophia, enthralled. "Not the virgin part, the kiss bit."

"I'm digging deep into my trove of secrets here. This only Iman knew, so I expect some form of reciprocity ... the most popular boy title meant I wasn't supposed to care, but I did. To me that first kiss needed to be magical, with someone special. Like Disney. Like *Sleeping Beauty*. It didn't happen at 15 and each new year the stakes got higher. What if I was bad at it? What if I didn't feel anything? What would that mean? So, then it was 18 years, 21, 24, and finally 27." He let out a sad smile to himself. "It was well worth the wait."

Look, she's eating him with her eyes, Derya thought. *And he turns out to be a vulnerable orchid disguised as an invincible android. How cute. Meanwhile, Maleficent—also goes by the name Jupiter—is piercing Shack with trillions of high-energy particles each and every microsecond, with many killer ions, electrons, photons, and neutrons bombarding our bodies fast and hard, some finding cell nuclei along the way—incubating cancers, nurturing cataracts, damaging the central nervous system, wiping out bone marrow stem cells, destroying blood cells, devastating neurons.*

"TiTus, status please," said Sophia. Derya realized the regular reports from TiTus had ceased and it had been an abnormally long silence from the computer.

"Commander—Commander—Commander—Commander—"

"TiTus, what is your status?" repeated Sophia in a clear yet urgent voice.

This time there was no answer. They looked at each other.

Scheiße.

"TiTus. Full ship report."

"TiTus. Full ship report. Now."

Scheiße.

"You think ... maybe there's a problem with the voice activation controls?" a hopeful Sophia asked while looking at Derya.

"Tweety, its brain has fried," said Derya categorically. *We knew the risks.*

Some of the zillion magnetic particles slamming Shackleton were bound to fly against its electronics and knock atoms off the chip or electrons out of position in the circuitry. *And TiTus had no radiation vault ...*

Had they known about the reverse slingshot, the electronic parts would have been made larger, a jump into the past. Transistors, the fundamental building blocks of electronics, were currently made of two atoms. Three decades before in Moore's law, circa 2000–2001, would have required 650 atoms for that same transistor. And hence the paradox. Losing one atom in an old transistor would mean no perceptible functionality loss, whereas it obliterates the functionality in a modern one. *For once in history, older computer tech is superior to the cutting edge.*

The clueless hush was slain by Sergei, "I'm going to the flight deck. Need to shut down TiTus and check if manual course correction is needed."

Derya gazed at the blue eyes in awe, glancing back briefly.

Words were superfluous. Venturing out may cost Sergei his life now or years later, but not going could doom them all.

The frying of electronics will get worse before it gets better and a full shutdown decreases the risk of damaging more circuitry and transistors. Hopefully TiTus is crippled and not dead because it is indispensable for a successful re-entry to Earth.

In less than a minute Sergei's body disappeared from view as he closed the tiny igloo entrance behind him.

⌀

The cargo area was pitch-black except for a line of red dots disappearing up the passageway like a runway at midnight. Sergei glided toward it in a silence so complete he heard the ratcheting inside his mouth as he swallowed.

He deftly grabbed a rung and launched himself forward to the flight deck four levels ahead. Feeling as if someone was pulling on his hair, the longest it had ever been, he placed his hand on top of his head and sensed the static. *I'm the coal mine canary*, he thought.

"TiTus, commence mainframe shutdown," he shouted, expecting and receiving no answer.

As he crossed the sleeping quarters level in his interminable glide to the cockpit, his mind fixated on what he had recently read about Hiroshima survivors with acute radiation syndrome. *People being brought to the hospitals with no injuries developed crippling vomiting and diarrhea within hours. As days went by their hair fell out by the handful and sores and bluish spots erupted all over their skin. Many soon began bleeding from the mouth, nose, and ears. Doctors gave them vitamin A injections and the results were horrible: flesh started rotting around the hole made by the needle. Every single patient died after enduring days to weeks of excruciating pain. Autopsies showed their organs had been cooked from the inside out—time will soon tell if I get radiation poisoning.* He was anxious but level-headed.

Once on the flight deck, he kept his sight intentionally low while his hands positioned him mostly from memory back into his seat, yet as he dashed his eyes from the floor to the main screen, he couldn't entirely prevent his retinas from soaking in the psychedelic shapes and colors of Jupiter.

"Ничего себе."

In the minutes that followed, as he checked the ship's trajectory, the corner of his eyes kept trying to seduce him toward the Observation Window.

"Sophia, Derya, over," he finally called over the intercom. "Good news. No additional course corrections needed. We're heading back home having shaved over ten miles per second." *And carrying a giant question mark: with TiTus gone or crippled, how are we going to re-enter and land?*

Sergei manually shut down the mainframe.

I've earned the right. He faced the Observation Window and abandoned himself to the cloudscape before him.

There was no perspective whatsoever, the entire window had been seized by what at a glance could have been Van Gogh's *The Starry Night*: rivers of turbid cobalt flowing into emerald seas, zinc-yellow maelstroms farrowing a dozen whorls and eddies, white parasitic tendrils swarming across ultramarine night skies. The mesmerizing stockpile of fluid shapes and swirling colors seemed obedient to a single rule of no straight lines.

Sergei found an abstract way of grasping perspective. They were 26,000 miles away from Jupiter's cloud top chromatic maze. At that distance, our Moon would have had an apparent size in the sky of half a fist on a fully extended arm. Instead, seemingly everything in all directions belonged to the gas giant. Each second resounded in his mind like a pendulum clock marking twelve yet he leered, hunting for clues that denied the possibility he was dreaming an oil painting on canvas. He found three almost concurrently.

He perceived the curvature, although it felt as if they had been sucked inside a giant balloon and he was looking at its internal wall. *I knew 1,300 Earths fit inside Jupiter, but knowing is not the same as understanding.* He also discerned movement betraying the seething cauldron of colored billows before him. And he saw the shadow, no bigger than a ping pong ball, of one of its moons etched against Jupiter's cloud tops.

Thereupon he propelled himself out of his chair and flew for cover back to the igloo.

Ø

The moon in question was Io.

A few days later, once out of the danger zone, they took turns spying on it through Derya's telescope.

Whereas Saturn's court favors an exotic diversity of sixty-two moons,

Jupiter's sacrificed quantity in favor of four sisters—Io, Europa, Ganymede, and Callisto[38]—the very moons which convinced Galileo in 1610 that the geocentric model that had reigned for fifteen centuries was dying before his eyes.

Europa, and perhaps Ganymede and Callisto, have global seas under their icy surfaces. But that's their only evocation of serenity, as the four orbit the harshest part of the radiation belts. Io, the innermost of the moons, is also subject to the mutant gravitational pull of the giant plus its three siblings, and it has the scars to show for it. By far the most volcanic place ever observed, it produces the closest real-life depiction of a medieval Hell.

Sergei had settled his eye over the telescope's oculus and it seemed to him as if he was peeking through a keyhole into Dante's Inferno: the abscesses running rampant across Io's sulfurous skin were volcanoes, some blasting the moon's guts hundreds of miles into space before settling back down into rivers and seas of molten lava criss-crossing its surface. A moon barely larger than ours capable of crushing terrestrial fact and legend: with a mountain, Boösaule Montes, twice as high as Everest with a sheer southeast face ten miles tall, three times taller than any on Earth; meanwhile, Tolkien's Mount Doom would sit in the mid to low ranks among the hundreds of volcanoes of Io.

"You're sure this is the ping pong shadow I saw over Jupiter's cloud tops?" asked Sergei to Derya.

"Yes, 100 percent."

"And you're saying this orange thing is …" Sergei was looking at an umbrella shape distorting the otherwise perfectly circular moon outline.

"An erupting volcano," said Derya. "The comparatively low gravity creates sprawling radiuses of lava fallout that look like the water curtains of fire sprinklers. That one's shower is covering an area the size of Alaska."

Ø

Two months later, Derya was watching *Dances with Wolves* in bed when a twinge in his stomach made him screech. In moments the stabbing pain clutched his whole abdomen. He had been disregarding the increasingly periodic cramping that developed a few weeks after leaving Jupiter, but the pain had never reached this level before. *Shhhhhhhhhhhhhhhit. This … is … inhuman. Fuuuuuuuuckkk,* he thought deliriously. Every nerve in his chest seemed to be

---

38   There are are 79 known moons in Jupiter, however, the other 75 comprise barely 0.003% of the total moon mass.

sounding the horn and a congestion of electric signals flooded his cortex. *Faint. Please black out. For God's sake make this stop!* The spasms jerked his body from one side to the other. For an instant his eyes opened and he saw a face in the mirror so contorted as to be unrecognizable. Without losing consciousness he abandoned the Solar System and burned inside the core of a hypergiant star. The mindless suffering was atemporal—perhaps endless or perhaps fleeting— unimaginable and unrelenting. At some point it eased and at some point later it stopped. He lay in bed, physically and mentally spent. When he tried to stand, he began coughing. He used his towel to muffle the noise, set on not alerting Sophia or Sergei. *This … must remain between you and me … our dirty little secret.* After a particularly strong bout of coughing he noticed his yellow towel peppered with red spots. "No. NO. NO!"

79 | SOLΔR STORM

ophia watched Derya from a dozen feet away, wishing she could bear some of his burden. His head pointed to a small Earth past Bacchus' Observation Window. She could see the reflection of his face, sad exhausted eyes lost in rumination.

Nobody could have known, she thought. The three were the guinea pigs from which medicine on Earth was learning from. Radiation and altitude sickness were similar in that it was so far impossible to determine who would be affected. Some people seem to be much more vulnerable than others. *His one susceptibility was a weakened body and immune system after the Enceladus accident …* She felt fatigued most of the time but that was a nonspecific symptom that could hardly be connected with mild radiation sickness. *And then there's Sergei.* Derya said it best on an audio interview with Russia-1 television: "Here's an Übermensch if ever there was one. A physique carved by Michelangelo and a psyche stolen from the pantheon of Greek intellectuals. Nietzsche, Wagner, and Hitler would have been in turn mystified and horrified after realizing he's as Slavic as Mother Russia herself. *A verbose way of saying he looks great.*

"What a bully this destiny thing. I mean, why not, right? Let's throw these Shack people another unsporting hurdle and see if they can survive it," said Derya. "I get it. My dashing looks confound and I agree my disability license plate was not displayed prominently enough. But still, come on."

"You have no cure," said Sophia caringly.

"Shite, you're probably right," he said to his mortified friend with a tired smile. His hair was as long as when Sophia met him for the first time, but it now looked as if someone had evenly plucked four out of every five strands and the jet-black sheen had become a lank ash. His eyeballs had bled for months and his sight had deteriorated to the point where his neck rocking forward and backward and a perpetual squinting replaced the focusing of his corneas. He hid most of the sores under long sleeves and pants but his lips always carried one or two.

"Want the secret to a long life?" came Sergei's voice from the flight deck where he spent most of his time training. "Worry only about the things over which you have control, be carefree about the rest." He had been rehearsing to pilot Shackleton and then Caird through the hours-long deceleration, re-entry, and touchdown for weeks. TiTus was still functional but had proven unreliable. It was having regular buffer underruns requiring partial or full resets, and if any of those were required during re-entry, it was R.I.P. to all and sundry. Sergei was universally acknowledged as the best possible human candidate to pilot through the full maneuver leading to landing, yet for almost two decades SpaceX and, soon after, everyone else relegated humans to the passenger seat for a reason. Two really: fuel consumption and safety. Humans are simply not fast enough to adjust trajectory in real time, so instead of moving along the optimal deceleration, or later descent path, the vehicle is constantly overshooting, drifting around the elusive target. That's propellant intensive. On the safety side, asking someone to maintain full concentration for hours and to be unerring and faultless during all that time is, well, inhuman and foolhardy. But as things stood, they either gave up now or played the hand they were dealt.

"You know the drill. Everything that can go—" Derya's voice halted. Sophia was about to fill the awkward silence when he continued, "Everything-that-can-go-wrong-will-go-wrong." He sometimes spoke blinking-fast to dodge the memory lapses.

His wondrous intelligence is untouched. But the memory lapses were becoming painful to witness. *He knows he's becoming impaired and he knows you know.* He wasn't the most affected mind, however. That went to the severely handicapped TiTus. *Earth's terra firma was virtually obstacle free. Not anymore.*

"Wait, anything I should fret about? More solar storm omens?" asked Sophia.

"Perhaps," said Sergei.

"Serezha, don't play mystery man with your commander," she said. "What's the latest?"

Active Region 7790 was at that moment the largest group of sunspots on the Sun's surface. The biggest of them, about eleven Earths wide by fourteen tall, was on a rampage. Two days ago, it had released the most powerful solar storm[39] since 2017, an X13. The press nicknamed it the Firing Squad.

---

39 Fortunately for life on Earth, our Sun is a yellow dwarf. This makes it a stable star. Considering it's a giant fusion nuclear reactor 1.3 million Earths in volume, this is important. It also helps to be middle-aged: 4.6 billion years old is well past unpredictable adolescence yet still billions of years away from becoming erratic. But it still has a temper and sometimes it does get violent.

Besides the permanent, steady stream of light and solar particles bathing its planets, the Sun is always developing spots across its surface. These last from days to months. Occasionally

"The Sun's rotation will point Active Region 7790 straight at Earth, that's also us, in four days," said Sergei. "This morning—third X-class storm in a week. NOAA Space Weather Prediction Center released a statement, which some are interpreting as a hint that this could be the big one."

"Great. Just great. And we get to be the innocent, compulsory-bystanders-that-get-killed-by-any-bullet-that-goes-astray-or-ricochets," said Derya.

The previous night, Derya had explained to Sophia that compared to the naked body of Shackleton, planets are suited in body armor. *And yet, when the Earth is once again in the way of one of the big ones, our civilization won't ever forget it.* Even though neither Earth nor the people on it will be directly in danger. Earth's molten iron core creates a magnetic bubble many times larger than itself—the magnetosphere—that acts as a bow shield deflecting the vast majority of Sun particles. The few remaining are absorbed by the thick atmosphere. *And still when it happens the devastation will be unimaginable.*

On July 23 2012, a solar superstorm with the power of 1859's Carrington Event, an X45—the mother of all superstorms—missed Earth by nine days.

Right before noon on September 1 1859, English amateur astronomer Richard Carrington detected a giant solar storm from his private observatory just outside London. Some eighteen hours later, people as far away as the Caribbean saw stunning northern lights above them while telegraph lines were knocked out amid fires and telegraph operators across Europe and North America were electrocuted.

In the technology-dependent society of today, the consequences won't be as pastoral. Electricity blackouts around the world, with electricity grids shutting down for weeks in the best of cases, and years in the worst. The global communication network jumping decades backward as scores of satellites are

---

in and around these, when the Sun's magnetic fields get twisted and tangled, solar flares—enormous explosions of energy—burst out into space, sending light in nearly all wavelengths, from radio waves to X-rays and gamma rays. Solar flares are sometimes followed by coronal mass ejections, huge clouds of superheated plasma and high-energy particles slung out of the Sun, racing through space at millions of miles per hour.

The vast majority of these solar storms are not strong enough to pose major risks to the inner planets: Mercury, Venus, Earth, and Mars. But for the rest, the Sun acts as a giant revolver rotating on its axis every twenty-five days. The inner planets are forced to play Russian roulette. It sounds worse than it is as planets are miniscule and very far between, plus this revolver has thousands of empty cylinders and an unknown but small number of bullets, sometimes in unnerving succession. Any solar storm above X1 is a bullet, doubling in power with each digit increment.

permanently disabled. A GPS network wipeout. Untold numbers of dead people from cold during winter seasons. Trillions of dollars in losses. *And humans won't be the only animals to suffer.* Sperm whales have been known to strand in large numbers when their navigation, which uses geomagnetic fields, is disrupted by solar storms hitting the planet.

The auroras will be unforgettable though.

80 | GΔIΔ

August 15 2033. D-Day, Earth's Re-entry

ATSIMO-ANDREFANA, MADAGASCAR

The only movement around the village was a cart pulled by a gray, bony zebu, raising a lingering ochre dust that tinged the late evening sky into a dirty carrot orange. On it rode two shirtless boys, coming down the dirt road toward the red adobe huts. One of them jumped out and came running to join the community of seventy or so people gathered around the millennial baobab with its hefty naked trunk and scrawny branches of sparse leaves high up. From it hung a couple of sheets tied to each other and anchored to the ground, which along with a borrowed image projector from a church in Morondava, a knee-tall speaker, and the village's grumbling diesel generator, allowed them to join the rest of humanity, impatiently awaiting Sophia Jong, Derya Terzi, and Sergei Dmitrievich Lazarev.

Most had been watching the French news channel, which was filling the airwaves with second-hand accounts to kill time before the main event, since the early afternoon. But minutes earlier, the official worldwide broadcast had finally begun. For now, the sound feed was Shackleton's Mission Control bustle and buzz punctuated by Nitha Sharma's recognizable voice without Malagasy subtitles—it hardly seemed to matter. The image feed was coming from Gran Telescopio Canarias on the island of La Palma in the Canaries, the best location to track the spaceship for another seven minutes. It showed a bright dot moving against a coal-black background with fixed twinkling lights. Even the 7-year-old sitting cross-legged in front of the improvised screen was intensely absorbed. Even the 7-year-old knew the dot was Shackleton, less than an hour from starting the deceleration and atmospheric re-entry marathon.

Perhaps we would need to go past early civilizations, tens of thousands of years back to hunter–gatherer times, to find an instant when most of humanity shared the same thought, maybe as they heard the howls of predators behind the trees just beyond the bonfire.

"We are still here, Mr. President," the sudden audio replacement for the unmistakable Sophia ignited shouting and arm shaking from the crowd. The prior video was supplanted moments later by an onboard camera showing the three space travelers strapped to their seats.

"I know how useless I am right now but is there anything, *anything* I can do to help?" asked the President of the United States.

"Mr. President, you can pray for us if you are into that sort of thing," answered the commander.

Some villagers seemed to have received the message before it was even uttered.

No one needed a reminder that the crew was on their own. With Sophia, Sergei, and Derya on a live camera and open mic—which due to their proximity to Earth had essentially no time lag—anyone, meaning everyone, was forced to make a conscientious decision: knowing of their demise was very different from seeing and hearing them burn alive.

🜨

LOW EARTH ORBIT

Captain Qiang, along with the rest of the crew on board the Tianhe-3 space station, peered in silence through the circular window at the planet beneath them enveloped in darkness. The only glow was the onion-thin blue line becoming an incandescent white as the Sun emerged from behind the horizon. He had been watching attentively in the approximate direction for minutes, hearing over the speakers the three inside Shackleton like the billions below.

"There!" said someone.

A fiery dot had appeared from above and passed in front of them at a ludicrous speed. To Qiang it looked like a bright cannonball curving downward, about to dive into the atmosphere. His mood wasn't festive. The optimism from below didn't translate well up here.

The crew did a military salute as the shining mote of Shackleton, hundreds of miles away, flashed past them. *Much too fast*, he thought. He wished Tianhe-3 went unnoticed. *Speed in space is imperceptible until a point of reference is identified.* The Chinese space station was orbiting at 4.8 miles per second; Shackleton thirteen miles per second. Unless they started decelerating against the atmosphere within the next few minutes, they would miss Earth and continue falling into the Sun.

Godspeed, Sergei Lazarev, Derya Terzi, Sophia Jong. Everything to do with space is calculated 1,000 times and prepared one hundred, so that the one execution is unfailingly flawless. The dot fading against the rising Sun did not abide by the same rules.

Their only chance of survival was to shave speed before a full re-entry via an unproven, untried ballistic lob: trade speed in exchange for heating up by entering the atmosphere, skim back into space to cool down, repeat. Everybody who has tried skipping flat stones across the surface of a lake knows how hard and precise the maneuver must be. The entry corridor angle was paramount. Lower than 4.7 degrees and the spaceship bounces off into space and misses Earth. Steeper than 7.2 degrees and the ship crosses into the thicker part of the atmosphere too fast, turning into a blazing fireball right before disintegrating. And instead of only once, they would need to nail the operation many times in a row. *Not by an automated computer re-entry but by the manual piloting of Sergei Lazarev. Can't bear the thought of it.*

☉

TOKYO, JAPAN

The thousands of anime, electronics, and video game billboards covering every building structure that made the Akihabara shopping district famous had been turned off for the first time since World War II. The rainbow of colors had migrated from the vertical to the horizontal, where a multitude carrying umbrellas and lit candles—blanketing every square foot of street and sidewalk—faced the wide, tall scaffolding on which a giant provisional screen hung in front of the Akihabara railway station.

The voices of the crew reverberated across the open space with the paradoxical intimacy of a pulsing heart.

"One small step for man ... I'm sorry, Sergei must have intentionally shuffled my cue cards," said Derya's voice. "What I wanted to say is that no matter what happens during the next few hours, it has been my greatest honor to have met and lived with you two ... I have never felt this close to anyone before."

All the world saw and heard the protracted hugging, a moment sensed more than understood. History being written no matter what the outcome.

Unexpectedly, Sophia addressed not her crew but the entire world, "To each one of you down there—down here, I want to ask a favor ... life is a fight.

Sometimes you win, sometimes you lose. I've had the chance to confront my mortality and that of the people I love … my fear of death does not overpower my conviction that, whatever happens today, we should never think this mission was in vain. It was not … and to Derya and Sergei, you are not my crew, you are my family, my blood. We have lived, eaten, slept, and fought together through unimaginable circumstances and impossible odds. The best and the worst moments of my life I spent with you. This adventure has made me more alive than anything I ever did before. If the price turns out to be death, I'm ready."

✺

LOW EARTH ORBIT

Strapped to the middle seat, Sophia couldn't believe her eyes: after three hours and five atmospheric dips, Sergei had blacked out from exhaustion. It was a fitful slumber, as if his conscience was trying to stir him, face beaten and covered in sweat. *I wish we had the luxury to let him sleep for twenty more minutes*, she thought. She turned to Derya. On their first episode of extreme deceleration he screamed in pain as his crooked back compressed against the seat. Later he grunted. And during the last and worst he stopped breathing. *His body is giving up.* His eyes were closed and his face constricted. *He's resting or asleep.*

The cockpit display showed their speed, over eight miles per second. Sophia searched among the digital rows for the remaining propellant. Enough for two more deceleration dives. *But with Serezha's fatigue the risk of decelerating further on board Shack may be even higher than the risk of pushing Caird into a re-entry at a speed beyond its specs.* There was no clear-cut protocol for her life-or-death decision. She went for the latter.

Shackleton would re-enter Earth's atmosphere in a quarter of an hour. *Not a second to waste.*

✺

In the cargo area, Sergei was inside Caird strapping Derya to one of the two seats on board.

"Hey, bear," said Derya, forcing out a mumble. "You know during the Apollo program … the condoms?"

379

"Yes," said Sergei, coming to his friend's aid. "The spacesuit's urine collection. Looked like a catheter with a condom-type sheath."

"You know they had different sizes … Small, Medium, and Large?"

Where is he going with this? thought Sergei. "Yes, you told me. There were so many spilling accidents they relabeled them Large, Gigantic, and Humongous. Leaks vanished."

"Right. No one should measure … how much of a man you are … by the content of your pants …"

"… but by the content of your character," finished Sergei.

"Nowadays … diapers. Much better for self-esteem … mine's very full right now."

"What's going on, brother?" Sergei said in a conspiratorial voice.

"From brother to brother … I'm terrified, Serezha. I don't want to die."

"And you won't," he managed to say in a casual voice.

Sergei saw Sophia slide inside Caird, protecting a small box containing six years of history-defining discoveries summarized in two Petri dishes and three hard disk drives.

There were two seats and three people inside Caird.

"I really think—"

"No, Commander," Sergei cut her off. "This is not musical chairs."

"My body is lighter and—"

"No, Tweety—Commander. The decision was agreed a week ago and it's final."

The mission never considered an emergency that could require tossing Shackleton before Earth's re-entry. It was too much outside the scope of what was reasonable. And even so, each of the Dragons allowed the mounting of up to five seats. Caird had two and the other carried three. *But then again, the mission never considered it would lose one of them the way it did …*

Sergei helped to fasten Sophia into her seat.

He glanced at the improvised webbing attached to the floor fast enough for Sophia not to notice. *The beating will be brutal—but at least it will keep the 220-pound mass of flesh, me, from free-floating inside Caird.* The contraption would secure him to the capsule's floor. *Or that's the plan at least.* This wasn't to prevent a collision with the other two passengers but to avoid shifting the vehicle's center of mass. Because once Caird entered the atmosphere, the steering needed to save the capsule from burning would be that of a surfer riding a mammoth wave: minimal, precise, with no margin for error. *As for the moment of impact … it will be a car crash without a seatbelt.*

"See you two in a minute," Sergei said, as he climbed out of Caird.

The override of the safety procedure meant Shackleton's hatch was already open to space. Within seconds Sergei disengaged Caird from the mechanical arm—*too safe, meaning too slow, for this emergency separation.* Using his right hand to push against it, he slowly drove the five tons of hardware with minor bumping past the cargo door.

The familiarity of the South Pacific Ocean, which he had flown over thousands of times before, did not detract from it being the most ravishing and anticipated sight of his life. *I'm home. Well, almost.* The soft yellow reflection of the Sun on the ocean while the whole planet reeled under him, or the flat clouds of all shapes and sizes that formed their own shadow on the waters below, made it look like ice fragments expelled from Antarctica. He was no longer a cosmonaut but a 23-year-old Russian Federation Air Force lieutenant feeling the vertigo before jumping out as paratrooper for the first time.

The reverie was cut short when Sergei felt Shackleton's quivering as it started to interact with the still ultra-thin atmosphere. *Damn! We should have separated already.*

Sergei clung to Caird's hull, his sole connection to life, and using his legs propelled the capsule and himself away from Shackleton.

As he accessed the capsule's inside, he heard Sophia scream. He turned to see Shackleton rushing toward them.

◐

KOLKATA, INDIA

There was no practical reason for most of the 68,000 people crowding the Eden Gardens cricket stadium to be there. For the majority, the single screen at the opposite end of the grandstand looked smaller than a smartphone display and at an angle. But as with thousands of other stadiums around the world, people had flocked to it in search of community.

A clang shut off Caird's live transmission.

The entire stadium gasped.

Seconds later the broadcast resumed, replacing Caird's fisheye view of the three passengers with a confused frenzy at Mission Control.

After two harrowing minutes, one controller shouted to Nitha Sharma, "FLIGHT, I have Caird on the line!"

The atmosphere had thumped the two spaceships against one another. All critical systems seemed normal except for Caird's long-range antenna. For the moment, Caird and Mission Control were communicating by relay through Shackleton.

The stadium screen showed Nitha rushing over to CAPCOM's desk and murmuring, "And what happens when Shack disintegrates?" while the world eavesdropped.

Given Caird's circumstances and speed, its re-entry trajectory was unplanned and impossible to predict. The only way for the rest of the world to know where they would touch down was via radio. Without it the capsule would become the proverbial needle in the giant South Pacific Ocean haystack.

After minutes of riveting brainstorming in front of the world—in the form of shouting and verbal sparring between mission specialists—CAPCOM summarized the situation, "Their signal reach is that of a cellphone, maybe fifty miles in open sky if we're lucky. If all airplanes tune to the S Band in the 2.52 to 2.67 GHz frequency, well, we could create a synthetic worldwide telecom web. And then if an airplane intercepts their communication, we can use it as a triangulation device to figure out their approximate landing area ..."

"That's an awful lot of ifs," said Nitha.

❂

UPPER ATMOSPHERE

"What do you see, Tweety?" Sergei asked, flat against the floor and bundled in webbing between the two seats.

Sophia strained her neck to see through one window. "Blue. Unvarying blue except for some cloud ribbons—wait, I see a thin strip of white at the very end ..."

"Antarctica," he said. *This is not great*, he thought. *This is very far from great.* They were at about seventy-five miles of altitude, still well above the Karman line, the arbitrarily defined edge of space. Their vantage point covered hundreds of miles in all directions and yet everything Sophia was seeing was liquid or frozen water. *Cut off from the world and falling into the ocean all but guarantees being lost, drifting forever. If Yi was here, the absurdity of the situation would not have escaped him.* Another thing troubling him was the thump against

Shackleton. *It was slow—yes but what's worse? Being hit by one hundred tennis balls at 160 mph or a train at 3 mph? It was slow but Shack's twenty times heavier than Caird. If the ablative shield suffered damage, we're toast.*

As it began diving into the atmosphere at 8.2 miles per second, Caird shattered the record for the fastest re-entry speed ever achieved by a man-made object. Within seconds the scant air molecules thickened and the capsule started vibrating. The gentleness degenerated faster than Sergei expected into a spinning earthquake. He couldn't see Sophia's face but her limbs shuddered as if undergoing electric shock. Meanwhile, Shackleton—entering the atmosphere out of position—was probably breaking up. *So long, Shack, you get to be buried in the sky—*

"Is this normal!?" shouted Sophia.

Before he could answer, giant sledgehammers started raining down on Caird from all directions. The *g*-forces became brutal and the makeshift webbing keeping him in place felt like piano wire as his body strained against it. The wrenching in multiple directions was pummeling their bodies, accelerating their bones faster than their flesh. *Like watching a punch to a boxer's face in slow motion.* He grew distressed thinking about Derya. *His heart and internal organs are being battered by his own ribcage.*

The tumbling lessened as the air drag stabilized the capsule, but the *g*-force surged well past the worst he had ever experienced, his vision blurred, and he quickly forgot about Derya as his body entered survival mode. Their speed was such that the air slamming into Caird bounced backward and collided with more air, heating it to 4,000 degrees Fahrenheit, 40 percent of the Sun's surface temperature, breaking apart the chemical bonds in air molecules and creating an electrically charged plasma surrounding the vehicle. The sparks flashing past the windows soon became a torrent of fire turning them opaque and then completely black. Sergei smelled smoke. *Something has gone awfully wrong.*

And then the crushing compression gradually eased, the drogue parachute eventually deployed, and deceleration gave way to gravity.

At four miles high the three main parachutes unfurled, whipping and spinning Caird. The jumping up and down stabilized and the capsule soon hung tautly. The canopies had slowed down the descent to thirteen miles per hour. Six minutes until touchdown.

Sergei's head spun and a crippling lumbago settled in. "Is he still breathing?" he slurred. He noticed the burned layers covering the windows had partially peeled off, allowing blinding daylight inside.

Seconds went by before Sophia replied, "Yes."

The silence of exhaustion settled over Caird—Sergei could hear the breeze outside—but there was no time to waste. He counted to fifteen twice before mustering his strength.

"Tweety, what are you seeing outside the window?" And after a few quiet seconds passed, "Tweety! I need you back here. Focus. There's no time."

"Ocean … we won't land, we'll splash."

We won't splash. We'll drown. The abnormal burning smell could mean Caird's buoyancy was compromised. "Look out the other windows. Same?"

"No! White in two of the five. Antarctica?"

"I think so—I need you to activate the radio distress signal. Do it now."

✦

37,000 FEET OVER MARIE BYRD LAND, ANTARCTICA

The aircrew and 200-plus passengers were on the edge of their seats in anticipation for what was happening somewhere above their heads. It had been an easy flight. Besides a few minutes of turbulence, the airliner had been gliding on a feathery cushion of air. That day they also got the infrequent bonus of an unbeatable view: wind and weather had pushed the flight path deep south, over the edge of West Antarctica.

They were flying over the nearly unknown Marie Byrd Land in West Antarctica, to the east of the Ross Ice Shelf. Because of its remoteness—even by Antarctic standards—it remained the largest unclaimed territory on Earth, bigger than France, Germany, and Spain combined. The transition from the interior to the coastline was abrupt: the magnificent white uniformity developed three deep stretch marks and was soon after severed into the blue ocean, where seven years prior stood a piece of ice the size of Portugal.

"—ayday, Mayday, Mayday. This is Caird falling down some———Antarc—"

The first officer gaped at the captain in disbelief, who hadn't yet processed what was happening.

His voice didn't carry the expected composure when he answered. "This is Qantas Flight 27 from Sydney to Santiago …" he stopped, barely able to continue, "welcome home, Caird."

For the couple of minutes before the connection with Caird dropped, they served as relay between Sophia on board Caird and Nitha in Mission Control.

Both captain and first officer alternated between staring at the cockpit speakers and at each other while the soundbites doubled through their headphones with the slightly delayed worldwide transmission.

After reconfirming Caird's coordinates for the third time a triumphant Nitha said, "From earthling to earthling, this exact instant is the absolute zenith of my life."

When it was over, the captain opened the intercom to the cabin to announce, "Good evening, passengers. This is your captain speaking … yes, that airplane was us."

◊

MARIE BYRD LAND, ANTARCTICA

A miniscule ellipsis floating down against the cloudless sky became three red canopies ferrying a small, cone-shaped capsule.

"—and now what do you see!?" Sergei shouted.

Sophia saw the ice shelf in two of the windows and a frigid ocean populated by icebergs in the other three as Caird disappeared under the white, 300-foot-tall cliffs. She prepared for the splash by clenching her teeth to prevent biting off her tongue. *Sergei,* was the only thought that crossed her mind while a jarring rear-end collision took her breath away, followed by four hard bounces as the five tons of metal and flesh came to a full stop. *Not water?* She saw the canopies drape gracefully to the ground.

There were no sounds on board.

"Sergei! Derya!" she cried in terror. *If Serezha didn't break his back, it's a miracle—and Derya's is made of splintered porcelain as it is.*

Sergei answered right away. She turned her head to a motionless Derya, who tried replying to Sophia's calls, but only wheezes would come out. Too debilitated to move, she looked through the windows: the ocean extended limitlessly a mile or so from the stable pack ice on which they had landed, while the ice cliffs towered above them 1,000 feet in the other direction.

◊

Sergei managed to kneel despite that old acquaintance, gravity. Helping himself up with both hands, he stood up by Derya's side and carefully removed his friend's helmet. Derya tried to say something and Sergei neared his ear.

"It's cold outside, brother," Sergei replied. "The rescue team should be here in five to eight hours."

◑

Sergei opened the hatch and struggled out into the daylight. The forgotten cornucopia of smells, pungent seaweed above all, made him lightheaded. *The sweetest smell I've ever experienced,* he thought. He dropped to his knees and dug his hands into a patch of snow that he took to his mouth and rubbed on his face. There was so much light around he kept his eyes almost shut and yet they still hurt. He didn't mind one bit. *Never forget this moment.*

He turned over to look at Caird, scorched but still in one piece.

Extricating Derya out of the capsule took Sergei and Sophia a long time.

He had worsened dramatically. They rested him on the ice over pieces of fabric they had ripped out of Caird as insulation, and against their better judgment agreed to his increasingly delirious plea to take off his spacesuit. His body was an emaciated rag doll. Even in the cold evening his body was overheating. Once he fell asleep, they covered him in blankets and rested his head on Sophia's legs. For the coming hours he drifted in and out of consciousness, inching toward the dark alley, the eternal void.

◑

Derya woke up abruptly and screamed, "I can't see! I'm blind! Help me, please help me, Sophia!"

An overcome Sophia stared down at a pair of eyes with a terrified, unfocused gaze that made her and the world around them transparent.

Exhausted, Derya's head fell back into Sophia's lap and he soon slid back into a fitful slumber. She caressed his forehead, which seemed to appease him.

Perhaps fifteen minutes had gone by when his lost eyes sprung open wide once more. "I'm going to die," he said, with a serenity that made it all the more tragic. But the fear soon clenched back, "I don't want to go! Serezha, grab me. Keep me here. Don't let it take me!"

He only calmed down once he saw blurry shapes coming to their rescue.

"I'm going to sleep now," he finally said, peacefully.

Sophia kissed his forehead while Sergei made a superhuman effort not to break down in front of him, "See you soon my friend."

He faded away forever.

Sophia and Sergei weren't alone: seven curious emperor penguins had left the colony she had identified earlier. They waddled past the canopies, halting and then walking a little more, uttering calls that sounded like a dirge.

Sergei grabbed Sophia's hand. She stood up. A long embrace placated the sobbing and became, unpredictably, a kiss.

Honoring the undaunted
from the past that built
promise into our future.

EPILOGUE

81 | NEW FRONTIERS

38 years later, October 2071

WASHINGTON, D.C.

It's a crisp autumn morning as father and son walk past the entrance of Arlington National Cemetery.

"—it's one of my staples whenever family visits, hon," they overhear a middle-aged woman telling a pair of tourists, "must, must see are the Kennedy graves, the Shackleton Memorial, the Tomb of the Unknown Soldier, and Arlington House."

"That sounds about right, Billy," says the father. "We nail those four and then run back to the hotel to pick up Mom."

Leaves from lime green to walnut brown decorate the avenue of oaks, maples, and elms—the darkest are also starting to color the ground—their soft tremor blending with the peaceful silence of the tens of thousands of white headstones.

❂

"Dad, did you know there are twenty-eight astronauts buried here in Arlington?" says Billy while looking at a garland of white roses resting over the sober grave of John F. Kennedy.

"I did not know that," answers his father while turning around to contemplate the view of the Lincoln Memorial and Washington Monument beyond the Arlington Memorial Bridge.

"Did you at least know one of them is Buzz Aldrin, the second man to set foot on the Moon?"

"Got me there too, junior."

Billy shakes his head disapprovingly.

He then looks up, searching for Earth's natural satellite, and finds it northwest. The hand of humankind is conspicuous even in daylight and even in its first quarter phase: a succession of minute black rectangles stretching across its lower third like a broken line on a roadway. In eight years, giant solar developments will encircle the Moon, allowing 24/7 solar power to Artemis, its first and so far only city.

Sophia and Sergei were instrumental in convincing billions to finance the city's development through individual contributions instead of government funds, which made Artemis a sovereign state—and the one with the strongest territorial claims over vast swathes of the Moon. For two decades, while her husband favored the privacy of their dacha northeast of Saint Petersburg for raising their kids, Sophia embarked on an extraordinarily successful career as a biochemist. Yet in 2057 the couple left Earth as Mars settlers, where Sophia became—predictably—the planet's first Prime Minister. Seven years later, while leading an expedition into a deep Martian lava tube, Sergei disappeared. At his funeral, Sophia said, "We both went to Saturn, but only one of us truly returned to Earth. We left our cradle again and only then, on Mars, Serezha finally found home."

Only nineteen more years, Billy daydreams. *By the time I'm 30 years old, I'll have my PhD in Electrical Engineering from Harvard, I'll be a retired NASA astronaut, I'll have spent a few years working for SpaceX, and I'll teach at Stanford. Two years later, I'll meet my future wife—we'll really love each other more than life itself. And at 35 I will depart to, uh, Neptune! And then nothing bad happens and we just live there on its moon Triton with our daughter for ever and ever.*

❋

"Dad! See, I told you!" Billy shouts indignantly. He had overheard every other visitor talk excitedly about it, but his father kept saying it would be too much of a coincidence.

"What are we talking about here?" his father asks absent-mindedly.

"Belinda, Dad! Belinda is here visiting Jimmy's memorial!"

At least his father is now patently interested. Billy runs toward an elderly woman on a mobility scooter.

"Excuse me, ma'am. Can you tell me where you saw her?" Billy asks urgently.

"Saw …?" she answers.

"Dame Belinda Egger," Billy says incredulously, as if the lady had forgotten her own name.

"Of course, I'm sorry. Got confused—anyway, yes, just follow the crowds."

❊

"It's definitely her."

"Shh! Emily, don't," the man whispers to the woman, "let's leave them alone, okay? Not here, not now."

Belinda and her family are strolling some thirty yards in front of the couple.

"I'm a doctor, darling, and she's Belinda Egger. Belinda Egger, get it?" the woman says in an intentionally high pitch for Belinda to overhear. "Six people have received two Nobel Prizes in the history of, like, the Universe. And of those, only three have received two in different sciences: Marie Curie, Sophia Jong, and Belinda Egger. I say we women are kicking some ass, don't you?"

"I'm a nurse, sugar," says the man. "Chemistry prize in 2038 and Medicine eleven years later. But I *really* don't think it's cool to—"

The woman was already striding uphill toward Belinda.

❊

As they near the Shackleton Memorial, Belinda puts on dark glasses and a wide-brimmed straw hat. Arm in arm with Emma, she sees her three grandchildren dart ahead and coalesce into the crowd.

They pass an Eagle Scout addressing his twenty-three-strong troop, "—so that's the thing: no one will ever know which one it is. Remember how when Yi's mom died, he inherited her wooden carved Buddha? We know he took both on board Shack and we also know, from Sophia's memoir, that Jimmy was wearing one as a pendant a few days before the accident. And then as they were leaving the Saturn system she found one in the cargo bay—which by the way I saw two years ago in the Shanghai Science and Technology Museum during the 37th World Scout Jamboree. A-*maaay*-zing, as in karaborrah-karaborrah-sis-boom-bah!—so, its twin is either on Titan's surface or inside Saturn—"

The memorial had been unveiled on the fifth-year anniversary of the mission's return to Earth: a single piece of white Carrara marble chiseled into three human-sized deities—Saturn, one of his Titan brothers, and his son Jupiter—supporting a twenty-foot-tall Shackleton. *Magnificent and a tad over the top,* Belinda thinks. It looks like what would result from commissioning the *Raising the Flag on Iwo Jima* photograph from an ancient Roman sculptor. And interred right under its pedestal are a few tons of Shackleton's remains that had washed onto beaches far around the Pacific.

Belinda and Emma make their way between pilgrims representing most continents to a spot overlooking the Potomac River and Washington, D.C.

"Right there in that boxy white building, Grandma?"

"Not the most flattering description for the place where Lincoln's buried and Dr. King delivered the 'I Have a Dream' speech," says Emma.

"Yes, Oliver. On its steps," Belinda answers.

"And where Nana fell in love with Grandpa," Poppy, her youngest granddaughter, declares. "And where did *he* fall in love with you, Nana?" she follows, already anticipating and savoring the answer.

"If we were to believe what he told anyone who cared to ask, well, that happened the moment he saw me—a few hours before I did, anyway," says Belinda.

"I believe that, Nana," Poppy says with a reverence that could only come from exhaustive repetition.

While her family basks under a balmy Sun revisiting well-trodden conversations, Belinda sneaks out and dodges the scattered bouquets, smiling at a child resting a vase of flowers on the ground.

Was it worth it? Belinda rests her ear against the cold, stone pedestal. She feels a far away reverberation coming from inside but, as with every other time, it comes without answer. *Was it worth it?* Anyone would agree the world is a better place because of it. The sacrifice of a precious few for the very many. "It was in the destiny of our species," some have even said. *And perhaps one day I will accept that too—you are and always will be my prince, the one and only man I ever truly loved.*

Trying to restrain the tears, she follows with her right index finger, from memory, the contours of the engraved letters. It says,

THE REASONABLE MAN ADAPTS HIMSELF TO THE WORLD; THE UNREASONABLE ONE PERSISTS IN TRYING TO ADAPT THE WORLD TO HIMSELF. THEREFORE ALL PROGRESS DEPENDS ON THE UNREASONABLE MAN.

—GEORGE BERNARD SHAW

APPENDIX

Appendix

IS THIS POSSIBLE?

Is a manned mission to Saturn, as portrayed in this novel, plausible in the near future?

This section will argue that if SpaceX develops a spaceship with similar specifications to those made public by Elon Musk in 2017,[1] the answer from a technological point of view—ignoring the psychological aspects relating to the crew—seems to be yes.

The biggest technical challenge for such a mission would undoubtedly be this: how to take a 75[2]-ton[3] payload to Saturn and return back to Earth, within a reasonable time frame.

Orbital mechanics marries ballistics (the field of throwing objects) and celestial mechanics (the field dealing with the motion of astronomical bodies) to the science and art of taking a spacecraft from point A to point B. For the purposes of this discussion, it boils down to a trade-off between minimizing propellant[4] or minimizing time.

For the entire history of space exploration including today, minimizing time has been a luxury beyond our reach. Not just that, but the need to minimize propellant has usually been extreme. This is best exemplified by the Cassini mission, which orbited the Saturn system from 2004 to 2017: it took the largest rocket available at the time to launch scarcely 6 tons of payload to Saturn, and it only arrived—after a 7-year journey—because of the extra velocity gained from a series of flybys around Venus, Earth, and Jupiter.

---

1   Elon, if you are reading this, I unsuccessfully tried reaching out through 28 different channels to learn the latest specs of Super Heavy/Starship. I thought my network was pretty strong. I'm less confident now.

2   This number is arbitrary but appears conservative for a 5-person crew on a ~7-year outer space mission. According to Mitchell R. Sharpe's classic 1969 book *Living in Space: The Astronaut and His Environment*, the metabolic daily needs of an astronaut of average size are 0.84 kg of oxygen, 0.62 kg of food, and 3.52 kg of water. Considering current oxygen recovery (75%) and water recycling (93%) technology on board the International Space Station, the requirements decrease to 0.21 kg of oxygen, 0.62 kg of food, and 0.25 kg of water. Therefore, a 5-person crew, 8-year supply of oxygen, food, and water amounts to 16 tons. Let's assume a 10-ton Environmental Control and Life Support System (ECLSS). Let's also consider the two Dragon spacecraft as cargo mentioned in the novel (each 4.2 tons dry mass + 5 tons of propellant, equipment, and consumables). Adding all this up leaves a healthy buffer of 30 tons for to-be-determined payload.

3   While the novel was written using the Imperial System to make a rather challenging book more accessible, this chapter uses the language of science: the Metric System.

4   Given there's no oxygen for fuel to react against in space, a spacecraft must bring both fuel and oxidizer, hence "propellant."

Without a radical new approach to rockets and spacecraft, manned exploration of the Solar System will remain safely within the confines of science fiction until the end of time.

Enter SpaceX's Super Heavy/Starship architecture.

Super Heavy, the launch vehicle that will hoist Starship into orbit around the Earth, will be the largest rocket ever made. But that's not revolutionary enough. The greatest innovation will be the ability to refill Starship in orbit. According to SpaceX,[5] Starship with a full tank would allow the following curve:

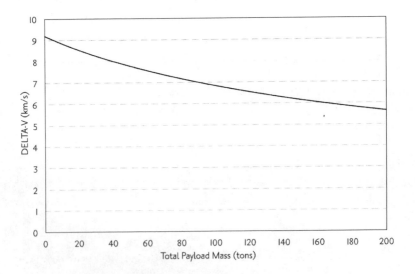

This would, clichés be damned, change everything.

How? By opening the entire Solar System to spacecraft carrying large payloads, including those of the human variety.

Why? By having a lot of propellant or delta-*v*, a term that allows for direct comparisons between the range of a vehicle and the propellant cost to reach the multiple destinations around the Solar System—this is rocket science after all.

---

5   Elon Musk's September 27 2017 presentation at the International Astronautical Congress (IAC).

Moving around outer space by minimizing propellant

If we are following the illustrious tradition of minimizing propellant to go from Earth to elsewhere, the Hohmann transfer orbit is generally the cheapest way of getting there. The Hohmann propellant cost to get from Earth's orbit to orbiting any of the planets is shown below:

Destination	Hohmann Transfer Orbit delta-v (km/s)
Mercury	12.5
Venus	4.0
Mars	4.3
Jupiter	6.6
Saturn	7.8
Uranus	8.8
Neptune	9.0
Pluto*	9.2
Infinity**	8.8

* Yes, I listed Pluto as a planet. The decade-long scientific debate is far from settled.
** This means escaping the influence of the Sun, allowing an object to permanently leave the Solar System.

Plotting the above values onto the previous SpaceX's Starship curve puts things in perspective:

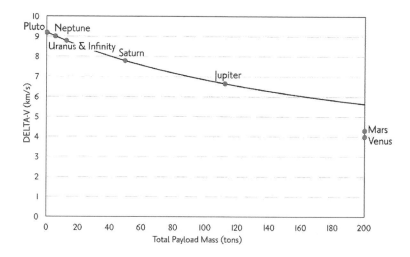

399

The implications are hard to overstate. A few examples:

- **Mars and Venus.** Starship would be able to take a stupefying 200 tons of payload to the inner planets' orbits,[6] with fuel to spare.
- **Saturn.** The Cassini mission would have been able to send nearly 50 tons of payload, almost 10 times[7] more than it did—without any need for flybys to accelerate the probe in order to reach Saturn.
- **Leaving the Solar System.** 10 tons of payload. For contrast, Voyager 1 and Voyager 2—both already in interstellar space—had a launch mass of barely 0.8 tons each and still needed to use both Jupiter and Saturn to catapult themselves to infinity.

SpaceX's Super Heavy/Starship architecture would turn what's preposterous nowadays to not just technically possible, but also economically feasible.

However, this is still not good enough for a roundtrip mission to Saturn—getting there and coming back to Earth—a rather desirable requirement for a manned spaceship.

A roundtrip mission requires an extra layer in the Super Heavy/Starship architecture: in addition to a conventional launch of Starship into orbit, another launch of a Super Heavy with little or no payload to take it all the way into orbit (instead of bringing it back from the upper atmosphere to the surface after hoisting a Starship). Fully refill them. Join them together. Ignite Super Heavy and once it's running low on fuel,[8] disengage Starship to in turn burn its own engines and thrust itself toward Saturn. This would mean an upper displacement[9] of the previous curve:

---

6   Landing is an altogether different challenge, requiring—among many other things—extra propellant.

7   At launch, the Cassini probe weighed 5.7 tons, of which 3.1 tons was fuel. From the remaining 2.6 tons, barely 0.3 tons were the actual scientific instruments making the observations and taking the measurements, each of which had extreme weight restrictions during the design and assembly phases. It's impossible to fathom the additional discoveries that could have been made with essentially no weight limits for the science payload—in what's already widely considered one of the most successful science missions in history.

8   This would leave Super Heavy in a highly eccentric orbit, similar to a geosynchronous transfer orbit, which could allow the Super Heavy to be landed back on Earth.

9   This calculation is entirely speculative given that no specifications have been publicly shared by SpaceX regarding the latest iterations of Super Heavy. The Tsiolkovsky rocket equation is used with the following parameters: a specific impulse of 380 for the Raptor engines, a final total mass of 1,185 tons, and an initial total mass of 2,500 tons.

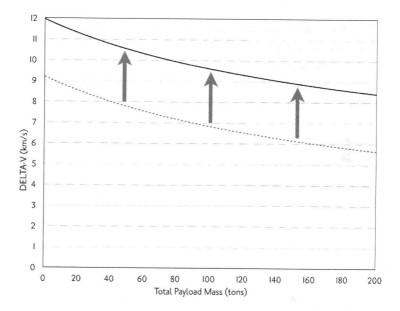

This permits not just a roundtrip to Saturn but also allows the design of a shorter mission duration at the cost of extra propellant. Which takes us to,

Moving around outer space by minimizing time

Focusing the discussion on Saturn, let's analyze the following roundtrip mission:

Step 1. The spaceship departs from Earth's orbit toward Saturn,
Step 2. The spaceship is captured into Saturn's orbit and stays there for 112 days,
Step 3. The spaceship escapes Saturn's influence and falls toward the Sun, converging with Earth.

NASA Ames Research Center's computations are used to plot the shortest duration roundtrip trajectory for every year between 2020 and 2035, capping the maximum delta-v to 10 km/s in order to allow Starship to carry 75 tons of payload:

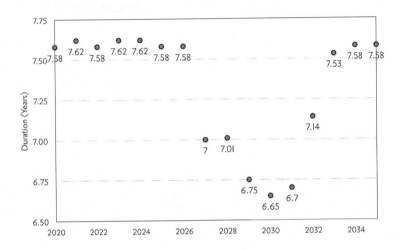

Let's zoom in on the shortest roundtrip, a 2030 departure with a total length of 6.65 years:

Saturn Round-trip Rendezvous Mission		
	Date	Delta-v (km/s)
Earth departure	July 30 2030	7.59
	3.46-year transfer	
Saturn arrival	January 14 2034	0.92***
	112-day stay	
Saturn departure	May 6 2034	1.44
	2.89-year transfer	
Earth re-entry	March 27 2037	
Total mission	6.65 years	9.95 km/s

*** This could theoretically be an almost propellant-free maneuver via aerocapture, as depicted in the novel.

We now have, in essence, the very mission narrated in *Oceanworlds*—only three years later.

But what about the folks on board?

While there are a number of physiological challenges for the human body that would need to be addressed,[10] the biggest hurdle for a long-duration manned mission will likely be psychological.

There are extensive studies about the psychosocial issues that affect astronauts in space, from studies performed in space-analogue experiments on Earth (space simulation chambers, submarines, permanent stations in Antarctica, etc.), to studies conducted in space, notably on board Russia's Mir (1986–2001) and the International Space Station (2000–present).[11]

However, nobody knows the mental toll of being surrounded by the deadly vacuum of space, in a severely restricted environment, with a small group of people, past the point where Earth becomes yet another dot in the cosmos—perhaps it could prove too much pressure for the mind to endure. And we simply won't know until a heroic few undertake, as President John F. Kennedy dared humanity in 1962, "the most hazardous, dangerous, and greatest adventure on which man has ever embarked."

---

10   One of the many is sustenance. Nutritionists at NASA have not yet developed food with more than a few years of shelf life—mostly because there hasn't yet been a need.

11   One could even make the case that extreme cases of solitary confinement—for those inmates that manage to survive the ordeal physically and mentally unbroken—would share similarities with such a mission in terms of both physical space available and time spent in isolation.

Δ SHORT HISTORY OF
SPΔCE EXPLORΔTION

The librarian came out into the splendor of daylight. The cool, damp air inside the large building was replaced by the scorching heat under the oppressive Shamash, the Sun-god. The drumbeats from the festival engulfing the city and culminating in tomorrow's sacrifices under the Temple of Marduk sabotaged his tranquility. The brutality of what would happen there may appease the crowds but it troubled his mind. Yet the insulting smell of rotting fruits and feces from the crowded bazaar a thousand steps away reminded him of their fortune. He looked down with pride and wonder at the main avenue, filled with thousands of pilgrims from across the kingdom.

He marveled at the unlikely set of circumstances that turned this land into the shining city, the exuberant oasis amid the arid plains. The measure of the empire's achievement would always be the geographical invasion and cultural absorption of the greatest civilization that ever lived, its towering pyramids the mirage of an era of prosperity and technical prowess the world would likely never see again, fading behind the haze of time. Even at his age, the librarian hadn't surrendered the childhood dream of one day standing before the magnificence of Giza towering over the Nile. It depended on scholars like him to keep the legacy alive in the grand library behind him. Now that the inevitability of the city's great future was secured, it was their responsibility to extend the reach in all directions, to house all human knowledge in one hallowed, central place.

It was the fateful year of 612 BC. As night fell, a messenger struggled past the massive walls and fainted from exhaustion in front of the king. Something terrible was coming from beyond the horizon. Nineveh—famed in the Tanakh and Old Testament, the greatest city in the world and capital of the Assyrian Empire—was about to be sacked by a coalition of its former subjects: Babylonians, Persians, Cimmerians, Medes, and Scythians. Nergal, the god of war, glowed red above the city.

Some historians believe the mythic Hanging Gardens of Babylon—the only one of the Seven Wonders of the Ancient World whose location or existence has never been confirmed—may have been here, destroyed by the great fire that ensued. What is fact is the ravaging by flames of another marvel, the Royal Library of Ashurbanipal and its 40,000 clay tablets, the largest and most important repository of knowledge up to that time.

The city's fall meant the spectacular renaissance of Babylon, whose former glory days as the largest city on the planet had happened a millennium prior, around the 18th century BC.

When in 331 BC Alexander the Great and his colossal army crossed the Tigris, the ruins of Nineveh had been unoccupied for centuries. Persian and Armenian traditions say Alexander felt an eerie sense of foreboding as he closed in on the monumental ruins. He dismounted his horse Bucephalus and 47,000 troops watched him enter the ghostly rubble alone. The penumbra couldn't conceal the majesty of the inside, nor the scattered clay tablets. Tutored by Aristotle himself until the age of sixteen, barely nine years before, the sight of pillaging and desecration deeply moved him and inspired one of his most important legacies. It would be protected for posterity by the greatest empire that ever lived, a single territory stemming from Greece to India. A monument to human intellect in the Egyptian city he had founded a few months prior. The Great Library of Alexandria, where many of the famous thinkers of the ancient world studied, remained unsurpassed for almost two millennia. By the time the printing press was invented circa 1439 AD, the whole of Europe had a few thousand books, a mere tenth of the Great Library.

Nineveh remained forgotten until the decisive Battle of Nineveh in 627 AD, where the Byzantine Empire defeated the Persian Empire. This proved ephemeral as the Arab Caliphate soon conquered the entire region and kept it for another millennium.

The reconstruction of most of the genesis and early history of astronomy and astrology—until recently one and the same—stems from just two broken clay tablets, known by the first two words in their text: the Mul Apin. Unearthed by one Sir Austen Henry Layard in 1847 from the remnants of the Royal Library of Ashurbanipal, many of the Mul Apin contents come all the way from the Sumerians, who invented writing and cities around 3000 BC.

The olden people's reverence and obsession with the sky may be perplexing for us contemporaries. Seem impractical. Anything but. The canvas above directly affected their daily life. The Sun's transit defined the notion of day. The Moon's rotation over its four phases defined a month. Winter and summer solstice, spring and fall equinoxes defined a year. Sirius, the sky's brightest star, rising above the eastern horizon just before sunrise marked the flooding of the Nile. As nomadic tribes embraced agriculture, the sky became their guide for planting and harvesting. It hastened the growth of our civilization and its expansion. It told when the easterlies would blow or which season had no trade winds. The three dots of Orion defined the cardinal points and thus guided travelers and sailors. No one ventured across vast oceans without being able to chart their courses against the heavens. Countless stars pinned to the firmament could only provoke our knack for patterns, finding shapes in randomness, hence the twelve zodiacal constellations, or five bright wandering stars that danced across the sky, later known as planets. With this prism, it's hard not to think that deciphering the skies could help predict the future or determine one's life course. How could they not see prophecy in a solar eclipse or an unannounced comet traversing the heavens and vanishing as weeks went by?

Had it not been for that momentous day when something caught the attention of a 25-year-old Alexander—just a week before the most important battle of his life and one of the most decisive in history, heavily outnumbered by Darius III and the Persian Empire—the Mul Apin would stand as the only surviving wisdom from the great civilizations of Mesopotamia, the rest forever lost to the sands of time. Instead, their celestial erudition was adopted almost verbatim by the Greeks, then inherited by the Romans. Thus, Marduk became Zeus and then Jupiter, king of the gods. Ninib became Kronos and then Saturn, Jupiter's progenitor.

About 150 AD in Alexandria—by then a Roman province—as Western civilization was plunging toward the Dark Ages, a Greek-born astronomer called Ptolemy produced the *Almagest*, one of the most influential scientific texts of all time. The mathematical and astronomical treatise on the motion of stars and planets summarized all thinking up to then, becoming indisputable orthodoxy for the next fourteen centuries in both European and Islamic worlds.

January 10 1610. Galileo Galilei breathed three deep breaths, the latest attempt to bridle a racing pulse conspiring against him, and looked again through the eyepiece of his latest and most powerful cannocchiale telescope. Change was in the air. Ever since Copernicus' 1543 seminal *On the Revolutions of the Celestial Spheres*, intellectuals across Europe had been trying to assimilate to the baffling notion that the cosmos didn't revolve around the Earth. But this revision of the Universe did not sit well with the most powerful institution on the continent, the Catholic Church. Just ten years prior, the Inquisition had burned Giordano Bruno at the stake, the Dominican friar espousing the Copernican model, who had the temerity to propose that stars were distant suns surrounded by their own planets and that the Universe was infinite. Discovery dramatically sped up in June of 1609, when Galileo heard of a device being patented in the Netherlands capable of seeing things far away as if they were nearby. That's all it took. In a month he had built his own with 3x magnification as a flood of breakthroughs were igniting all around Europe. But tonight, something else was happening. His new telescope had 20x magnification, and what his strained eye was seeing would change history. The thrill of discovery was dizzying, as was the sense of exposure. His renown among scholarly circles in Europe stemmed from his famous experiments on gravity two decades past. But this—this would forever change society, religion, and philosophy. For all of history, planets had been wandering stars, brighter but otherwise indistinguishable from the ones in the background. But three days ago, as he pointed humanity's most advanced device at Jupiter, he saw for the first time its sheer immensity, along with "three fixed stars, totally invisible by their smallness" by its side. Now, one of them had disappeared and the others had shifted. He closed his eyes and set his thoughts aside, but they came screaming back. The third moon was behind the planet. This demolished Ptolemaic astronomy, whose main principle was that all heavenly bodies should circle the Earth. After six decades, the Copernican evolution had been triggered with the force of a supernova. The scientific revolution that ensued would know no boundaries.

In Galileo's mind, his triumph of ingenuity had one dark spot that troubled the great man until his death in 1642. Saturn. The first time he saw it through a telescope in 1610, his excitement was such that he dashed a letter off to his friend, the famous German astronomer Johannes Kepler: "I have observed the highest triple bodied planet system." The news got to the Austrian emperor Rudolf II, who requested commentary from Galileo. He explained that Saturn wasn't a single planet but three touching each other. Today, any pair of binoculars can achieve Galileo's visual feat, with Saturn looking like a small non-circular dot. The conundrum presented itself two years later when the side planets vanished and then reappeared in 1616. The axial tilt of Saturn means twice every Saturnian year—or once every fifteen Earth years—the rings disappear from view as they angle directly edge-on to us. Thus, the obsession with the otherworldly behemoth was born and would never abate.

Nowadays, a $50 telescope easily goes past the 30x magnification required to see the ring system around Saturn as well as to spot its largest moon, Titan. But it took until 1655 for another polymath, Christiaan Huygens, to solve the mystery that plagued the genius of Galileo.

By 1684, Giovanni Domenico Cassini had discovered four other moons and the division that separates the main rings. But Saturn's enormous distance from Earth—more than twice that of the far away Jupiter—meant that besides a few sparse discoveries, the gas giant was shrouded in almost complete mystery all the way to 1979.

The Exploration of the Outer Solar System

In a way, NASA's formation on July 29 1958 echoes the birth of the US Constitution: as Thomas Jefferson in Paris wrote to John Adams in London, the group of people crafting it "really is an assembly of demigods." As a result, NASA's long-term plan was brilliant, far-reaching, bold, and in hindsight, clairvoyant. The exploration of the Solar System would be done by (at the time, theoretical) robots in a three-phased approach: i. reconnaissance missions to pass by every planet from the mid-60s to the mid-80s; ii. an orbiters and landers era, which we are currently in; and iii. a sample-return-to-Earth future.

In 1964—while the Apollo program to put a man on the Moon was in full swing—a 30-year-old NASA aerospace engineer named Gary Flandro discovered a jaw-dropping free lunch. Every 175 years, the alignment of Jupiter, Saturn, Uranus, and Neptune enables a single spacecraft to visit them all. The once-in-many-lifetimes Grand Tour, as it came to be called, gained enormous traction, but the unknowns were nerve-racking, such as the risk of crossing the asteroid belt or the untested, essential technique of using one planet's gravity to slingshot the spacecraft to the next. Also, the speed gain of the slingshot increases the closer the vehicle is to the planet, which for Saturn meant flying between the rings and its atmosphere—yet no one knew if this empty-looking region was a safe opening. The solution? Sending cheap trailblazers, twin robotic probes Pioneer 10 and 11, as cannon fodder.

Pioneer 11 flew by the Saturn system during September 1979 unharmed, paving the way for the Grand Tour. It took the first close-ups of the giant, low-resolution photographs that even today retain the haunting mystery of that first encounter. Its humble payload achieved important science, including confirmation that the two gas giants—Jupiter and Saturn, 1,300 and 800 times bigger than Earth—hold 92 percent of our Solar System's planetary mass.

The Grand Tour launched in 1977 in the form of science-packed twins Voyager 1 and 2. Budget constraints forced a triage between visiting Titan and Pluto. Saturn's largest moon, bigger than Mercury, won. Pluto would need to wait until 2015 for its flyby. Voyager 1 would pass by Jupiter, Saturn, and Titan. Nine months later, Voyager 2 would cover Jupiter, Saturn, Uranus, and Neptune. Both missions were exceedingly challenging. NASA deemed the enigmatic Titan so crucial that if something were to happen to Voyager 1, Voyager 2 would alter its trajectory, sacrificing the ice giants for a Titan flyby.

Voyager 1 encountered the Saturnian system in November 12 1980. By 6:00 AM that day it flew over Titan. The only moon in the Solar System with a thick atmosphere, its ultra-dense yellow haze prevented any visual observation of its surface. Yet the atmospheric composition, temperature, and pressure hinted at the sensational speculation that liquids could exist on its surface. By 10:00 PM it whizzed by Tethys, a moon stained with blood-red streaks and traversed by a gorge twice as deep and four times as long as Colorado's Grand Canyon. Midnight marked the closest approach to Saturn, and instruments measured sustained winds in the upper clouds of over 1,000 miles per hour, five times stronger than the worst hurricanes on Earth.

By 2:00 AM the next day it was Mimas' turn, a moon scarred by an enormous crater that makes it *Star Wars'* Death Star's doppelgänger. Eight minutes later came Enceladus, made of pure water ice, making it the most reflective and one of the coldest objects in the Solar System. By 6:00 AM it was Rhea, Saturn's second largest moon. And by 5:00 PM it was the sponge-like, potato-shaped Hyperion, the largest irregularly shaped body ever observed. Mission complete. Almost two decades and millions of man-hours gambled with no room for error in under thirty-six hours.

The flawless performance meant a new lease of life for the spacecraft. After all, its plutonium-238 energy source still had decades of power remaining. NASA extended the mission. In 2004, six years after overtaking Pioneer 10 as the most distant man-made object from us and the Sun, Voyager 1 started crossing the termination shock, the bubble-like interface where the high-energy solar wind particles pushing outward from the Sun clash against the tide of high-energy interstellar cosmic particles pushing inward. In 2012, it officially exited the Solar System and entered interstellar space. By the mid- to late-2020s we will finally lose contact.

On August 26 1981, Voyager 2 followed its two predecessors into the Saturn system. Two days prior it flew over the furthest large moon orbiting the gas giant, oddball walnut-shaped Iapetus, called the yin-yang of the Solar System due to its two contrasting hemispheres, one bright as snow and the other dark as freshly poured asphalt, the latter crossed by an equatorial mountain ridge more than twelve miles tall, twice as high as Everest. By 3:00 AM it flew by Saturn, analyzing the intricate structure of the rings and the preposterous contrast between their huge width, 280,000 kilometers or twenty-two Earths wide, and unbelievably narrow height, averaging just ten meters tall, smaller than the human tower world record. Half an hour later was UFO-shaped Atlas' turn. By 4:00 AM it went past the cratered Epimetheus and Janus, locked in an endless relay race that causes them to exchange orbits every four years. It ended the Saturnian tour a week later by flying past Phoebe, a very dark moon orbiting in the opposite direction of most others, now identified as a primordial object captured by Saturn from the early Solar System. Even the small sample from Saturn's extensive moon catalog displayed nature's mesmerizing creativity. The probe went on to become the first and only human object ever to pay a quick visit to Uranus and Neptune.

The Voyagers will continue traveling into forever. Messages in bottles drifting in the cosmic ocean long after the Earth has been engulfed by a Sun turned into a giant red predator. Every 225 million years they will complete an orbit around the Milky Way's center. And if one of them ever runs into an alien civilization, it will have something inside to share: the Golden Record—a time capsule and a phonograph containing pictures and sounds from children of the Universe by then long forgotten. The last remnant of our existence, Chuck Berry's "Johnny B. Goode" singing while knocking on eternity's door.

Far from waning our curiosity, the Voyagers and Pioneer 10's flybys revealed that the giant winged planet and its entourage of moons could guard the answer to one of the most consequential enigmas of our time: Where Do We Come From?

The Saturn system is a laboratory. Sharing the chemistry of the Sun, a bigger ball of gas would have had enough gravity for the enormous heat and pressure in its core to ignite nuclear fusion. Saturn is thus a failed star. And the largest collection of moons of any planet functions as a miniature Solar System. Studying it would help understand the origin and formation of our Solar System. Titan revealed itself as a primeval Earth frozen in time, full of rich, carbon-based compounds. Analyzing it could illuminate the development of complex chemistry and help decipher the origin of life.

The Cassini Mission

Planning for the next mission began in 1982. By necessity it would be the most ambitious and expensive robotic expedition ever. All three previous flybys were, well, flybys. No more first, fleeting impressions. This would be a deep dive into Saturn's psyche, a long-term character study of the colossus and its minions.

Titan was key mission objective, and to better understand the giant moon, landing was the only choice. In an unprecedented collaboration, NASA would build and operate the orbiter, a thirty-passenger school bus named Cassini, while the European Space Agency would be in charge of Huygens, a meter-long probe that would travel attached to Cassini, destined to parachute into Titan's atmosphere.

It would take almost two decades of preparation before setting off for destination Saturn. It proved to be one of the greatest voyages of discovery in the history of science.

The sharpest eyes yet to peer at the Saturn system from up close, Cassini began uncovering new natural satellites a month before arrival. By the end of its journey the headcount of intriguing and phenomenally diverse moons in the Saturnian wonderland reached sixty-two.

July 1 2004. Cassini soared above the rings, crossed the ring plane just outside Saturn's F ring, turned itself, and with zero margin of error fired its engines to decelerate. At seventy minutes from Earth at light-speed, real-time remote maneuvering was impossible, making an autonomous orbit insertion mandatory. At 3:54 AM it made history by completing its capture by the giant's gravity, which bent the probe's path and sent it flying in the opposite direction. For the next thirteen years, Cassini completed 292 elongated orbits that toured the entire Saturn system, swinging back to the gas giant each time before accelerating and being thrown out again every couple of weeks.

January 13 2005. It was time for one of the most awaited moments in space exploration. Huygens broke through Titan's massive 600-kilometer atmosphere, ten times taller than Earth's, deployed parachutes, and fell for two and a half hours into a Jules Verne fantasy world. The video feed transmitted from Huygens to Cassini, then relayed to Earth, shows extraordinarily Earth-like meteorology and geology: clouds, dunes, mountain ranges, flat plains, a surface sculpted by winds and rain with deep, serpentine canyons and rivers flowing to what appear to be mist-shrouded coastlines and islands. Cameras measured a yellowy surface illumination level similar to Earth's sunset. It touched down and continued frenetically sending precious data before the mothership disappeared beyond the horizon. That was Huygens' last contact with Cassini. Titan had become the most exciting location in the Solar System.

February 16 2005. Competition was coming from the unlikeliest of candidates. Cassini's magnetometer detected something abnormal about Enceladus, a small, icy moon 500 kilometers in diameter, equivalent to an area twice that of Germany. Its south polar region has a balloon-shaped bulge that bends Saturn's powerful magnetic field.

July 15 2005. In a pivotal flyby, Cassini returned to the south pole, encountering young terrain strangely devoid of impact craters and crisscrossed by four deep, 130-kilometer-long tectonic fractures: the Tiger Stripes. It unintentionally solved the riddle while presenting one hundred others with a baffling, unexpected discovery: a cloud of water vapor and ice particles.

July 21 2006. Titan's breakthrough. Cassini's radar found not just lakes but entire seas, complete with tributaries. Not of water but of liquid methane and ethane. The discovery turned Titan into the only other place in the Solar System with stable surface liquid bodies—excluding the scorching lava lakes of Jupiter's moon Io.

March 12 2008. An ultra-low flyby allowed Cassini to sample Enceladus' plume, finding a brew of organic molecules: the building blocks of life as we know it.

June 21 2011. Confirmation of a warm global salty sea, bigger than the Pacific Ocean, beneath Enceladus' icy crust. More than one hundred individual geysers spew high-speed jets of water that collectively feed the plume, towering 1,500 kilometers above the south pole.

April 12 2017. NASA announced a showstopper: hydrothermal activity deep down at the Enceladus seafloor. The unassuming moon instantly turned into the best candidate for alien life anywhere.

By now Cassini was running on fumes. With the little propellant left, NASA designed a series of twenty-two daring dives between Saturn's cloud tops and the innermost ring: the Grand Finale. A close-up of the giant's atmosphere, and the most recognized feature in any world, the ethereal rings.

Both Saturn and Earth have fast-flowing 'wind rivers' known as jet streams. Back on Earth, eastbound flights over the Atlantic Ocean usually ride them, allowing for faster travel than westbound flights. Jet streams on Earth average 180 kilometers per hour; on Saturn they can reach ten times that speed. On Earth their width is a few hundred kilometers; Saturn's equatorial jet stream's width is five times the size of our entire planet.

Cassini saw a mammoth storm called the Great White Spot that develops roughly every Saturnian year, equivalent to thirty Earth years. The storm dredged fabulous amounts of water ice from the planet's depths, depositing it atop the clouds. For a moment, it was larger than Jupiter's Great Red Spot, with the biggest whirlpool ever witnessed, churning around the planet for twelve weeks until it encountered its own tail and sputtered out.

Over the course of a month Cassini saw two giant storms on a collision course, each the size of the Earth, clashing and merging into an even larger one. Saturn is blanketed with electrical thunderstorms, some the size of the United States, with lightning bolts a thousand times stronger than those on Earth, suddenly emerging and lasting for weeks or even months at a time.

It is known that storms on the gas giants can last months, years, or even centuries. Both of Saturn's poles share enormous stationary hurricanes that appear to be raging uninterruptedly. The south pole's is half the size of Earth. At the north pole, a colossal swirling eye wall the width of India surrounds its angry center. Cassini also studied one of the strangest climate phenomena ever witnessed, the north pole's stunningly symmetrical hexagon-shaped jet stream, twice as big as our planet, with a shimmering aurora on top. The seemingly artificial shape provoked wild speculation until scientists reproduced it in the lab. In the gas giant, the paranormal quickly becomes commonplace.

The rings of Saturn are the magnificent remnants of a comet or asteroid that ventured too close and was savagely torn apart by the colossus' gravity. Like fractals showing never-ending complexity at every scale, what seem like two giant disks from afar on closer inspection become seven major subdivisions, which themselves become a kaleidoscopic psychedelia of endless minor rings. They are formed by trillions of chunks of water ice, ranging in size from tiny, dust-sized icy grains to blocks as big as mountains. Theirs is a high-wire act, a harmony of exquisite balance between their sheer, delicate magnitude and Saturn's unsparing gravity.

And then September 15 2017 came and Cassini plunged into the gas giant in a death dive, a shooting star across Saturn's sky. The end of the intrepid probe's quest marks an inflection point in the exploration of the Solar System: the completion of half a century of cataloging every self-respecting stone or snowball around the Sun. The mapping age of human space exploration is over. Now starts the biological search to attempt answering what may be the most fundamental question ever posed: Are We Alone in the Universe?

The Search for Extraterrestrial Life

Our once-held belief that the Solar System is a dry, barren desert with a single shining beacon of hope called Earth was replaced, following Cassini, by one soaked with water. Scientists looking for extraterrestrial life have long stuck to a golden rule: 'follow the water.' And before Enceladus, the Goldilocks zone—where it wasn't too hot for oceans to boil nor too cold for them to freeze—barely covered the orbits of Earth and Mars. The small moon proved that sunlight is not the only way to heat a celestial body. In very particular conditions, gravity can do it as well. Had Enceladus' orbit around Saturn been perfectly circular, it would have been a spherical ice cube through and through. But the constantly changing distance from the massive body shrinks and expands the moon's waist, creating friction and heat in its interior. Using what Enceladus has taught us, we now know that at least two other Saturn satellites, Titan and Enceladus' big sister Dione, harbor oceans of water under their cold, icy surface. So do Jupiter's big moons Europa and Ganymede. Even Pluto, four times farther from the Sun than Saturn, may hide liquid water underneath.

Compare this with the continuous disappointment of Mars. We fell in love with the Red Planet in part by it being our immediate neighbor, but mostly because it promised so much. In the early days, the optimism of finding life was intoxicating on a planet covered with telltale signs of a wet past. Things deflated with Mariner 4's 1964 Mars flyby, which not only failed to spot Martians, but also showed a cratered, bone-dry, and dead world. Today, after six decades, tens of billions of dollars, thousands of people dedicating decades of their lives, and almost fifty missions to Mars, no permanent liquid water has ever been observed, nor one single molecule from past or present life. A reverberating technological triumph on the one hand and a resounding biological setback on the other.

Antennaed green men nowhere in sight? Back to basics. A minimalistic approach to life. It began in 1977 when a group of marine researchers discovered the much-theorized hydrothermal vents deep down under the sea back on Earth. Superheated gushers nourishing a rich ecosystem of life. Had we finally found the primordial soup? The place in the ancient oceans where life originated?

Some context is in order.

For centuries we thought Hell existed in Earth's center. That turned out to be quite right. Our globe's radius is almost 6,500 kilometers. The first half is the core, consisting of a solid heavy metal sphere surrounded by molten iron. It's about 6,000 degrees Celsius, the Sun's surface temperature. The motion of molten liquid iron creates Earth's powerful magnetic field that, far beyond giving us the compass, shields the atmosphere and protects living things from both solar wind and cosmic rays' harmful radiation. Our neighbor, Mars, once had an agreeable temperature and an ocean covering a quarter of its surface, but something turned off its magnetic field. Today's Mars' desolate freezing wasteland is the consequence of losing 90 percent of its atmosphere to the solar wind.

The second half of Earth's radius is composed of the mantle, a hot rock layer behaving like a viscous fluid. Scientists recently discovered deep-in-the-mantle water reservoirs many times larger than all surface oceans combined. Thanks for that. If they were up above, only a few mountaintops would pierce the waterline.

But our interest is on Earth's skin—the crust, barely five to fifty kilometers thick—standing above all else. It is hard yet brittle like eggshell, cracked into several segments called tectonic plates. The plates float over the mantle that moves them agonizingly slowly. Over eons, this shuffling broke up Pangaea, the supercontinent that existed 175 million years ago. The movement is infinitesimal yet permanent: the Atlantic Ocean grows at roughly the same pace as your nails, and that makes it twelve meters wider than when Columbus crossed it; Everest keeps getting taller by around one centimeter per year.

The boundaries between tectonic plates do two things. Collide and slide past one another, forming mountain ranges like the Himalayas, as well as volcanoes, earthquakes, and tsunamis like the Ring of Fire around the Pacific Ocean. Or they move apart, creating faults, cracks, and new islands as these two-way conveyor belts allow lava seepage from deep down in the mantle that later solidifies and renews the Earth's skin.

Enter hydrothermal vents. Back in 1977, those marine geologists found the smoking gun on the East Pacific Rise, an underwater, mid-oceanic ridge where the plates, especially near Easter Island, are diverging at the fastest rate in the world. Here, where the guts of the Earth are exposed, superheated water comes in contact with near-freezing seawater—black or white smokers depending on the feeding minerals from below. The minerals precipitate forming tall stacks of chimneys with cathedral-like structures, essentially small underwater volcanoes such as Lost City, a hydrothermal field in the Atlantis Massif a kilometer below the Atlantic Ocean.

The spotted sites quickly multiplied and all proved to be oases for life, ultra-rich ecosystems in perpetual night with fantastically strange deep-water creatures: giant tube worms, nightmarish luminescent pelican eels, meter-long spider crabs, jumbo snails. But the magnifying glass is over the base of that food chain, bacteria and archaea—unicellular microorganisms that in total absence of sunlight mimic the activities of their cousins far above, deriving their energy from chemical reactions instead of photosynthesis.

In April 2017, researchers shattered the record for the earliest forms of life by reporting fossilized bacteria from an ancient hydrothermal vent in Hudson Bay, Canada, that may have lived as early as 4.28 billion years ago. That's barely 100 million years after oceans formed on Earth. This crowns the accumulating body of evidence that points to the proverbial primordial soup at the root of our tree of life having developed around a hydrothermal vent. As unlikely as coincidences go, on that same month NASA's Jet Propulsion Laboratory announced Cassini's discovery of hydrothermal activity in Enceladus' subsurface ocean.

The excitement about Enceladus is not just understandable, it is inescapable. Life as we know it requires four primary ingredients: liquid water; a source of energy for metabolism; the right chemical ingredients; and time for the concoction to ferment. Enceladus has them all, in spades. We stumbled upon the Holy Grail in our search for alien life: the key to potentially answering whether we are the only ones.

If Enceladus broke all the conventions about where life as we know it can develop, Titan is the prime candidate for life as we don't know it.

It's a fact. Life on Earth requires liquid water. At the microscopic level, 75–85 percent of the cell volume in every living organism is liquid water; 60 percent of a human adult's body weight is liquid water. Therefore, liquid water is a prerequisite for life elsewhere in the cosmos.

Not so fast. We fall into the trap of thinking from an Earth-centric point of view. From general principles the assertion is broader: life anywhere probably requires a liquid solvent. The definition of life is deceivingly simple yet it took decades to hone in on 'something that can both reproduce and evolve.'

And in order for life to reproduce and evolve we must have a medium where atoms interact frequently and promiscuously to form chains of atoms, and those molecules must in turn interact frequently and promiscuously to form increasingly complex structures.

A solid doesn't cut it. It packs atoms and molecules tightly together—good. But it locks them in place, allowing only rare collisions and interactions—bad. A gas doesn't cut it either. Atoms and molecules are freer than in liquids but because the gas density is less than a thousandth of liquids', there's a much lower chance for collisions and interactions. The Universe is ancient at 13.8 billion years old. Yet life on Earth took at best 100 million years to occur. So, it is also simply too young for life to have occurred in the snail-paced chemistry action world of gas, or worse, sloth-lingering world of solids.

A liquid allows high concentrations of atoms and molecules and doesn't put tight restrictions on their motions. Therefore, it allows complex chemical processes, as molecules interact and form new types of compounds. Liquid water (H_2O) has the advantage of being formed by hydrogen and oxygen, the first and third most abundant chemical elements in the Universe. Disadvantage? It's only liquid between zero- and 100-degrees Celsius. Methane (CH_4) is formed by the first and fourth most abundant chemical elements in the Universe, so no slouch either. The methane oceans of Titan are at -180 degrees Celsius. Perhaps the reason Earth doesn't have methane-based life is because our planet has never been that cold. Methane boils at temperatures above -160 degrees Celsius, no wonder it is known to us as natural gas.

A golden age in the search for extraterrestrial life is about to commence. As Einstein once said, "Scientists investigate that which already is; engineers create that which has never been." Soon, the engineering marvels about to be unveiled by SpaceX and Blue Origin will help trigger the first large-scale, systematic search for alien life around the cosmos: in our backyard, by flinging manned and unmanned spacecraft armed to the teeth with detection tools to every corner of our Solar System; or in the vast expanse before us, by the launch of previously unthinkable space telescopes that will be able to search for atmospheric markers betraying life in planets tens or even hundreds of light-years away.

Warning, exhilarating times ahead.

DRAMATIC LICENSE

Here's a non-exhaustive list of areas where the story deviates from reality. As you read them, perhaps it will become apparent why I decided to keep them in the novel:

1. Chapter 36. Here is Linda Spilker and Leigh Fletcher on impact scars on Saturn, *"There are many variables that go into the visibility of the impact scars on giant planets, but chief amongst them are the momentum (i.e. mass, velocity) and the angle of impact. If the momentum were identical to Comet Shoemaker-Levy 9, then the angle is what matters, because the bolides super-heat their entry columns, causing the forced ejection of material back out of the atmosphere, which then crashes back down in concentric rings around the entry point. The debris itself is actually chemically altered Jovian or Saturnian air. A straight-on collision would create a near-circular bruise but it'd be deeper, whereas an oblique collision would be shallower and create a more elongated scar. It's true that Saturn's hazes are thicker than Jupiter's, but our models for Jupiter had the impact debris very high up, above the surrounding hazes, so my first instinct is that things would look similar on both planets. One other thought—if the impactor were a dry, volatile-depleted asteroid, then it might be able to reach below Jupiter's water clouds (and hence the debris would include a lot of oxidized species), but not Saturn's because they're deeper (and hence the debris would include a lot of reduced species). Bottom line: it would produce a visible scar. One idea around being able to see a visible scar on Saturn might be if the impact is in the winter hemisphere, covered by ring shadows. The shadows might 'hide' the impact but would also make it harder to see from Earth."*

2. Chapters 45, 67–73. Here is Alexander Hayes' perspective on various Titan issues,

    a. The Titan geography described in the novel is violent and jagged. However: *"When I think of Titan's landscape, I envision a rough water-ice terrain that has been blanketed by a billion or so years of organic material falling out of the sky. The water-ice mountaintops peak out of a rather smooth organic layer a few hundred meters thick. In fact, ~60% of the surface is covered by relatively featureless smooth plains; equatorial dune fields cover ~17%; the poles (60-90 N/S) cover 13%; the lakes/seas themselves cover ~1.4%; and everything else (mostly mountains/hummocks) covers the remaining ~10%."*

b. Regarding waves on Titan: "*While waves are ~7 times larger on Titan as compared to Earth for the same wind speed, wind speeds on Titan's surface are very low (1 m/s is a big gust on Titan) … I don't think Titan would produce large waves except in the rare cases of a freak storm.*"

c. Regarding high-altitude winds: "*The drag force you feel due to wind at a given altitude is proportional to pressure. Since pressure is exponential with altitude, it means that the stronger winds at higher altitudes exert far less drag than winds of that magnitude would near the surface. To be completely honest, my intuition is that a spacecraft or probe on a non-powered descent (i.e. parachute) would have a pretty smooth and boring ride after they have shed the insertion velocity.*" In other words, I have committed the Andy Weir sin.

d. Regarding a storm moving from Titan's equator to the poles: "*There is still a lot we do not know about Titan's climate and meteorology. A converging story, however, is that the equator and mid-latitudes are characterized by infrequent but heavy rain storms (Cassini witnessed one in 2011). The poles, on the other hand, are characterized by lighter, more frequent rainfall. In fact, some models have the poles continually 'misting' during certain seasons (not sure if these will hold up to scrutiny in the coming years). Regardless, the large storms that we see at the equator do not themselves make it up to the poles.*"

e. Regarding tides and directional flows of water in the Titan seas: "*The static tides exerted by Saturn on Titan are much stronger than the static tides exerted by Earth on the moon (and vise-versa). This is what gives Titan its tri-axial ellipsoid shape. The dynamic tides, however, are actually less. Titan is a slow rotator and tidally locked. In addition, Cassini found that Titan tends to deform with the tides instead of act like a rigid solid body (it has a high Love number). This is one of the ways we confirmed the presence of the internal ocean. So, as a result, the tidal amplitude on the seas is more like a few tens of centimeters than it is a few tens of meters.*"

3. Chapter 78. In the year 2032, Jupiter will be at the opposite end of the Solar System as seen from Saturn, making a reverse slingshot non-viable—the 2019–2022 window would be the right time, when the planet is between Saturn and Earth.

ΛCKNOWLEDGMENTS

As with any large, prolonged project, there are plenty of fingerprints all over this novel. I am, however, particularly indebted to:

Marie, my one and only, for everything—especially the half a decade when the person by your side was many times a billion miles from home.

My friends Nichole Pitzen and Arnau Porto, for their shrewd comments. Nichole, you are accountable for turning Hes into Shes.

Eduardo Bendek and Marcello Gori, two prime engineers from JPL, for their technical review, enthusiasm, and commitment to making science mainstream again.

Linda Spilker, none other than Cassini's Project Scientist, for her outstanding contributions to humankind and—closer to home—her contributions to this book.

Alexander Hayes, Professor of Astronomy at Cornell and leading expert on Titan, for his extensive notes and brilliant, invaluable insights.

Quora and Wikipedia, for the free enlightenment.

The Atacama Desert's skies, under which I lived for two years as a child, which stabbed me in the eyes with haunting, indelible vistas of the cosmos.

Finally, all mistakes and omissions are exclusively mine. A few times, to benefit the plot or for dramatic purpose, I deliberately ignored certain comments or facts.

ABOUT THE AUTHOR

J.P. Landau is a pseudonym.

The man behind it likes to think he's still in his early 30s, but that would only be possible if he had been Kerouac typing up *On the Road*. Instead, *Oceanworlds* took north of four years to complete. He does look and feel younger than he did in his mid-20s, when he worked in the cash-rich, soul-crushing world of investment finance. He cleansed for three years at Stanford, and afterward co-founded an energy storage company.

ABOUT THE BOOK

And then, at the beginning of 2015, he read an article about Enceladus that simultaneously triggered a sense of childlike wonder and a feeling of outrage. He thought of himself as a fairly educated person, so why hadn't he heard about its water ocean before? The bigger question became, how does the general public become informed about these things which—if studied and explored—could have monumental implications for each one of us? What could he do? It was too late to become an astronaut (or failing that, a scientist), so his first reaction was 'nothing.' Yet after a few weeks it dawned on him: "Tell an irresistible human story about space exploration." Make it into a book that is read by millions, and then turn that into a movie that is watched by billions.[12] This aspires to be that book.

I am one of those rare millennials that was never bit by the social media bug. You want to reach me, write to **jpl@jplandau.com**

Lastly, if you had a strong emotional reaction to the book—either because you hated or loved it—please leave a review in Amazon or Goodreads.

---

12   By some accounts, *Avatar*, James Cameron's 2009 sci-fi movie, has been watched by roughly a fourth of the world population. That's a stupefying reach. The space community needs an *Avatar*-like success to stir humanity into action.

Made in the USA
Middletown, DE
15 December 2023